Praise for *The Poet King*

"A book of old, wild magic—nothing is what it seems."
—Seth Dickinson, author of *The Monster Baru Cormorant*

"A fitting end to a gorgeous experiment in art, world-building, and character, growing in strength from book to book."
—*Kirkus Reviews* (starred review)

"Opulent, ambitious fantasy . . . Myer's intricately braided plot strands culminate in a clash of supernatural Otherworld powers. Those new to the series will have no trouble connecting with the well-drawn protagonists. . . . Readers will be blown away by the lush, lyrical prose and epic scale of this novel."
—*Publishers Weekly*

"Myer's lush prose and imagery amplify a layered plot filled with magic, prophecy, and power."
—*Library Journal*

"This riveting series conclusion is hard to set down and will leave readers hoping that Myer returns to this fantastic fantasy setting someday."
—*Booklist*

Praise for *Fire Dance*

"[Myer's] world opens like a flower, revealing fresh landscapes both beautiful and dreadful. . . . Worth waiting for."
—*Kirkus Reviews* (starred review)

"Gorgeous."
—*The Washington Post*

Tor Books by Ilana C. Myer

Last Song Before Night
Fire Dance
The Poet King

THE
POET KING

ILANA C. MYER

TOR

A Tom Doherty Associates Book
New York

THE POET KING

Copyright © 2020 by Ilana C. Myer

All rights reserved.

Map by Jennifer Hanover

A Tor Book
Published by Tom Doherty Associates
120 Broadway
New York, NY 10271

www.tor-forge.com

Tor® is a registered trademark of Macmillan Publishing Group, LLC.

The Library of Congress has cataloged the hardcover edition as follows:

Names: Myer, Ilana C., author. | Hanover, Jennifer, illustrator.
Title: The poet king / Ilana C. Myer ; map by Jennifer Hanover.
Description: First edition. | New York : Tor, 2020. | Series: The harp and ring
  sequence; 3 | "A Tom Doherty Associates book."
Identifiers: LCCN 2019050510 (print) | ISBN 9780765378347 (hardcover) |
  ISBN 9781466861053 (ebook)
Subjects: GSAFD: Fantasy fiction.
Classification: LCC PS3613.Y463 P64 2020 | DDC 813'.6—dc23
LC record available at https://lccn.loc.gov/2019050510

ISBN 978-0-7653-7835-4 (trade paperback)

Our books may be purchased in bulk for promotional, educational, or business use. Please contact your local bookseller or the Macmillan Corporate and Premium Sales Department at 1-800-221-7945, extension 5442, or by email at MacmillanSpecialMarkets@macmillan.com.

First Edition: March 2020
First Trade Paperback Edition: March 2021

Printed in the United States of America

0 9 8 7 6 5 4 3 2 1

For Yaakov, my chevalier.
We walked this road together.

NORTHERN MARCHE

■ ALMYRIA

Iberra River

KAHISHI

MARAVA DESERT

MAJDARA

Gadlan River

■ MARABAG

SERGOVANA

IRTAN

ARSHISH

JEDDA PASS

MEROZ

TANZIN

ISLANDS
OF
PYLLANKARIA

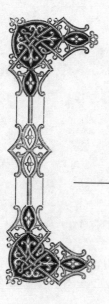

PART I

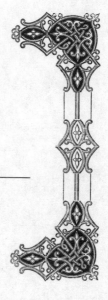

CHAPTER
1

RIANNA stood at a window overlooking the city lit gold in sunrise. A new day. Red slate roofs and cypress trees were a view she had seen all her life, but not from this height. This was the Tamryllin palace, with its towers. Blackbirds made a whooping spiral, winging around the towers and down, toward the rooftops of the city. She could hear the bells of the Eldest Sanctuary welcoming the sun.

She heard him come in, come up behind her. When she turned, she was struck—as ever—by how handsome he was. How noble he appeared with that strong jaw, the red-gold forelock with a slight curl that fell, appealingly, from the peak at the center of his forehead. He was a picture of nobility—in ways the nobility themselves rarely were.

Elissan Diar smiled a little, to see her. For him it was a rare expression; the man who had conquered Tamryllin and seized its throne showed a stern countenance to most.

By now she had often seen his smile turned to her.

"What are you thinking?" he asked.

"A good morning to you, too," was her sharp reply, and he laughed.

A part of her was immediately ashamed. Rianna knew she had been disingenuous in her sharpness.

She'd known he would like it.

"What has you gazing out so pensively?" he said, and joined her at the window. She was seated on a cushioned bench. He took a place at its other end. Despite his powerful frame, there was yet a distance between them. A proper distance, one might say.

She thought she read the question behind his question. He'd wonder whether she was thinking of her husband. "I was remembering my girlhood," she said. "Of the view from my father's house. And how . . . I was happy there."

"We never forget where we are from," he said. "Nor the places where we were happy." He spoke with a soft clarity, as if visited by memories of his own. "I'd fain see you happy once more, lady. It would become you even more than melancholy already becomes you." He smiled again. "I doubt there is any mood which does not suit your face. I would consider it a gift if I might see them all."

Rianna let a silence fall. She heard the faint, busy chatter of the blackbirds. The bells had ceased. Finally she said, "You have seen much in your travels, is that not true?"

He picked up on her meaning. It unnerved her, a bit, that he often did. "I have seen queens adorned with gems and cloth of gold," he said. "Beauty to make a man weep. Yet none to match Lady Rianna, in her plain grey dress."

She waited. She was interested to see if he would say what most men would have said by now. The obvious thing. *Your husband is a fool.* But this was the man who had conquered Tamryllin by means of enchantment. Who had moreover succeeded in winning over the people of Tamryllin in a short time. Rather than executing the royal family, he'd had them exiled—a gesture of magnanimity. He'd pointed to the destruction in Majdara, the chaos of civil war on the border, as a reason for new leadership.

For Kahishi was at war. The Court Poet somehow in the midst of it. All the more reason for the capital to surrender to Elissan Diar and his Chosen. Tamryllin's palace guard had been overcome by magical attacks. Rumor had it that warriors had suddenly appeared in every corridor, overpowering the guards within moments.

Once he assumed control, Elissan Diar attended first to stifling dissent, while at the same time put in action a plan to win the hearts of the people. He lowered taxes, including that which was most reviled— the tax on olive oil. This perfectly coincided with trade tariffs rising as a result of the border wars. Thus Elissan showed himself a man with the people's interests in mind. It helped that King Harald had been unpopular and weak; that the Court Poet, the true power behind the throne, was in Kahishi.

A man who had accomplished all this, in so short a time, would know better than to speak of Ned. He would not be so crude. He would rely upon her to remember in every bone what her partner in love and life had done: that Ned had had, if the rumors were true, a passionate liaison with the queen of Kahishi, Rihab Bet-Sorr—said to be lovely beyond description. He'd done that, and then helped her escape the palace, and had run off with her.

He'd done that.

Elissan did not need to remind Rianna of any of this. She was yet married to Ned Alterra, which made her one of the nobility. It meant she had become, in this new way of things, a lady-in-waiting to Elissan's daughter, Sendara.

"Plainness suits a married woman, and mother," said Rianna, looking down at her lap. "I am done with frippery."

He laughed. "Oh, my lady," he said. "With every word you please me more."

"I must see to my lady Sendara," she said, rising. With his back to the window, Elissan was edged in sunlight. "If my lord will excuse me."

"Wait," he said.

She stopped.

"Please, Rianna. Call me by my name. Do that for me."

She nodded, a curt gesture, and departed.

SENDARA'S hair was a curtain of red-gold to her waist. The task of brushing it out fell to Rianna, most mornings. The girl looked nervous. She kept smoothing her skirts, fidgeting with the cross-ties on her sleeves, which were the fashion. Rianna could read her well enough. Once, she had been that girl: desired by all, cherished by her father. Though not precisely that girl—there was a chilly self-centeredness to Elissan's daughter that repelled Rianna, despite that she knew she ought to have compassion. The girl had lost weight; it gave her a ravaged, hungry look beyond her years. All at court knew that Sendara was consumed by her feelings for her father's closest advisor, Etherell Lyr.

While he, though displaying the requisite devotions as her intended, was oddly distant. A distance that intensified Sendara's craving. That may have edged her voice when she hissed, "Watch it, fool—you're hurting me," as Rianna worked at a knot in her hair.

Etherell had not been to see Sendara Diar more than briefly for at least two weeks. She kept eyeing herself in the glass. The dress she had chosen was red, cut low. Once Sendara asked, as she turned this way and that before the glass, "Do I look pretty?" Struggling to look defiant, even though Etherell Lyr was not there to witness it, and these women who waited on her were, as far as Sendara was concerned, no better than servants.

Rianna spoke the truth, though without warmth. "You are beautiful."

There were other things she could have said. About men, and about power. Elissan Diar was to be crowned King of Eivar. Preparations for the coronation were under way. As the king's daughter, Sendara was a desired commodity beyond her beauty. Etherell might love her; he might also, more plausibly, have other motives. But Rianna was not here to say those things, and besides—she didn't think the girl would receive them well. There was a row of severed heads on pikes by the palace gates. It would not be wise to anger Elissan Diar's daughter. Or be heard to speak poorly of Etherell Lyr, who was in high favor with the king. Elissan may be intrigued by Rianna now, but she knew how expendable was women's beauty. She combed the hair in silence.

OFTEN her thoughts went to the day the city fell. Though that had not been the outcome, exactly—the coup had left Tamryllin outwardly the same. At least, to begin. She'd known, when she heard who had taken the city, what it could mean. There would be changes, significant ones. It was important to appear loyal. It was important to come to grips on her own with these events, before someone else could dictate the terms. She knew this even before the executions began.

At the time she'd been living with her father, and her old nurse, who helped care for Dariana, her two-year-old daughter, who every day looked more like Ned.

Rianna had borne her daughter shortly after her wedding. By the age of nineteen she was a mother. As Dariana Alterra strengthened, seemed fit to survive, Rianna came to accept that her life would never again belong entirely to her. Even though she had not made the decision to give it up.

It had happened fast.

Rianna had felt foreboding when Ned went with the Court Poet to Kahishi. Fearing for his safety. She'd never have imagined how events would unfold. She'd trusted him. That was Ned, to her—the one she could trust. But then had come that day in the spring when she learned he had vanished . . . and the reason.

So she lived with her father. She went through her days wondering how to go on, knowing—for her daughter—that she must. The rage building in her was familiar, from a time before her marriage, but the agony . . . was not. Was new. This was not her first experience of betrayal, but it was the deepest cut.

She'd killed the first man to betray her. Had slit his gullet and gut with her own knife, and though it sickened her to recall it now, she was not sorry.

This was different, however. It was Ned. The safe harbor throughout her life. Now there was no harbor, no safety. She was unmoored. Worse—abandoned.

It was midsummer, glaring heat on the streets and redolent of honeysuckle in the shade, when word came that the palace of Tamryllin was taken. By Seers, it was said. Then amended—no, by one Seer and a force of poets. Some were only students. The enchantments were back, and finally it was clear what this meant for Eivar. A power long confined to Academy Isle had asserted dominance in the capital.

Rianna had wasted no time. She'd convinced her father to take Dariana and her nurse to his estate in the south. They'd put about a story: that the child suffered from illness, needed the soothing warmth of the southlands. Rianna would stay behind.

Rianna's father had aged visibly since his imprisonment and torture by the prior Court Poet. The news of Ned's betrayal had already shaken him. And now there was this. He seemed to age further on the spot when Rianna informed him of her decision. The dangers he had thought she'd escaped—sheltered in a courtly marriage and motherhood—threatened again.

"Why?" he had pleaded. "Why won't you come with me?"

A reasonable thing to ask.

RIANNA sat at the window so she could look out on a city still aflame with autumn colors. Around her the ladies-in-waiting chattered. Each embroidered a panel for Sendara's coronation gown. The piece Rianna worked was a sleeve, to be trimmed in a pattern of thread-of-gold. The cloth was velvet, forest green. It was painstaking work. Sometimes she liked that it allowed her mind to roam free; other times, thought it would be a kinder fate to leap from the high window. She missed her father's library.

The women often tried to boost their lady's spirits with gossip. Today the story of a maid who'd been sent away after making too much of her dalliance with a lord's son—a man with a wife and children—seemed to make Sendara forget her troubles. There was pitying laughter. All agreed that the poor girl had brought it on herself, imagining such a man could have feelings for her. Rianna bit her lip against distaste. Once in a while she made an effort to smile, or even put in a comment. She knew these women had an eye on one another. If Rianna seemed to put on airs or be "above herself," they could make trouble for her.

Once she might have stored up her observations for later, to relay to Ned; now there was no one to confide in, in her cell of a room. Each night was silence.

Elissan Diar would know that, of course. How she spent her nights. There were eyes and ears throughout the palace—Rianna knew about that from Ned, who had once controlled them. She knew of the hidden tunnels, the spyholes. The Tamryllin palace was not for keeping secrets.

The date of the coronation was set for winter, on solstice day. Most foreign dignitaries sent their regrets, anticipating impassable roads, but perhaps Elissan Diar had planned it that way. The ceremony was primarily for the people of Eivar, Rianna guessed; a cementing of Elissan's legitimacy here. Lords with sizable holdings would swear fealty. It would be as if King Harald and his line had never existed.

Rianna did not think the coronation date could be a coincidence.

The winter solstice was a time of dual significance. For one, it marked the birth of Thalion, the sun god. Of the Three, he was the god who stood for justice, light, knowledge—among other things. Although Elissan was at least fifty years of age he appeared younger and gleamed with vital health. A golden god come to Tamryllin, to lead its people and ensure peace.

There was also an ancient tradition of the longest night. Rianna wished Lin were around to ask. All she knew was that for poets, it was important. Now with the enchantments returned, there was more it would mean. And Elissan had to know it. Often she wondered if, at his councils with the Chosen, he revealed his plans.

No secrets would escape the stone lips of those strange, bewitched boys.

Without Lin to ask, there was little Rianna knew. Only that at the solstice Elissan Diar would be crowned king, and Tamryllin would rejoice throughout the long night.

Lin. It was strange to think of her. She'd meant many things to Rianna through the years. No one knew where she was now. Rianna remembered the other woman as first her mentor, then friend; and then, finally, the Court Poet who had commanded Ned's loyalty. That last year before Lin Amaristoth and Ned traveled to Kahishi, Rianna had scarcely known her friend. They'd seen each other rarely, and then often when Rianna had a squalling infant to wrangle. And each of these times Lin had been cordial, kind, yet it was impossible to forget who she was: Court Poet and highest advisor to the king. As time went on Rianna began to notice a shadow in Lin's eyes, an expression that crossed her face now and again that reminded her, disquietingly, of Rayen. So over time Rianna had stopped visiting; and now she barely knew the Court Poet who had whisked her husband into a political maelstrom no one understood. All they knew in Tamryllin was that some magic had penetrated to Kahishi and instigated civil war. And that Ned Alterra had aided Queen Rihab in treason and disappeared. Likely he was with her at this moment. That luminous queen who had brought a king, and now an entire country, to their knees.

Rianna tried to build a wall in her mind against such thoughts. To focus on the work at hand. Which at the moment was a panel for a coronation gown, thread-of-gold and green.

NED used to talk to her about his work for the Court Poet. When she sat at the long dining table for the evening meal, with residents of the palace and lords assembled, Rianna knew whom to watch. What to look for. Her glance scarcely grazed that of Lord Alterra, Ned's father, though she knew he was anxious about her and Dariana. He was grateful, too—her voluntary service to Sendara Diar had mitigated whatever pall of suspicion might have fallen on him, father to Ned Alterra. The severed heads at the palace gate were those of nobility accused of treachery. Rianna had known those men. One, Lord Derry, had been kind to her when she was small. A ruddy man with a salt-and-pepper beard, who bellowed jokes to enliven any occasion. He'd had a strong presence in the council—no doubt too strong for the liking of Elissan Diar. And jokes . . . well, as any poet knew, satire was dangerous.

She watched, from her place below, as Elissan Diar and his daughter were as suns to the spheres that orbited them at the high table. There were lords who paid fearful homage. There were, standing at attention at various parts of the dining hall, Elissan's Chosen. These boys were not even graduates of the Academy, yet held a high status at court. They had taken part in the defeat of the castle. Intermingled among them were the palace guards, known derisively on the streets of Tamryllin as Ladybirds, proven ineffectual yet again. The Chosen were the true force now.

There was something chilling about these boys. They were to a man hollow-cheeked, with deadened eyes. They evinced no interest in the palace women and girls. No interest in anything.

They seldom spoke. The most Rianna heard from them was late some nights, when she couldn't sleep—their singing. A layering of voices. Meetings held in moonlight. In those trained voices raised in song was a quality like a blade tapped on crystal. Exquisite and cold.

Though he had served among the Chosen, Etherell Lyr, advisor to the king and prince-in-waiting, looked more hale than the rest. Rianna thought he probably did not participate in their activities as he once had. Not since being elevated to his current status. Rianna also thought, when it came to Etherell Lyr, that she'd never seen anyone so opaque. She could never guess what he was thinking. It was not hard to see the reason for Sendara's infatuation. Rianna thought his beauty was like sunlit snow, too blinding. One could not see beyond it.

Also in the dining hall was Syme Oleir, the king's Fool. A young man of perhaps seventeen dressed in motley, the Fool was pale, his face oddly slack. He was often at the king's side. Sometimes he entertained with tricks, or juggling, but at all times Rianna thought him strange. He was, just now, hovering over one of the lords at table with a grin: Lord Herron, who had made extensive obeisance to Elissan and provided men-at-arms. A gruff, older man, he was about the age of Rianna's father. She could not hate him, despite thinking she should hate anyone who had so entirely capitulated.

The Fool leaned over Lord Herron's shoulder as the other man tried to eat. He jeered, "What price your loyalty? A penny? A florin? Perhaps a little dance?" And then, just as the lord seemed about to faint with terror, Syme danced away with a wild laugh. He was nimble, spinning once on each foot, by turns, until he had reached the dais. Climbing the stairs, he went to drift about the king, singing to himself, a burbling murmur. A parody of a poet's song.

Elissan paid no attention to any of this. What Syme got up to was none of his concern.

Rianna paid little attention as well. Sometimes she wondered why Elissan felt the need for entertainment from a deranged boy. She kept her eye where it mattered—the high table.

She was probably not supposed to spot the note pressed into Sendara Diar's hand by a servitor. It happened fast. Even from a distance, and in torchlight, Rianna saw the girl's cheeks redden as she hastily tucked the note away.

Details like these could be insignificant. In fact that was likely. Rianna found that much of her time doing the sort of things Ned had told her about—observing, cataloguing information—often led nowhere. It was part of the work. It was only in panning through worthless stones, he'd told her, that one might on occasion discover gold.

In a palace there was one thing more precious than gold and jewels, and that was information.

When the meal was done, those at the high table were first to leave.

Elissan Diar passed Rianna's seat, though it was not in his way. He said, "You belong at the high table. With me."

He'd murmured in her ear, feather-soft. No one heard. Rianna kept her head down. But she felt the stares. And something more. Ned had been gone a long time.

LATER that night, Rianna brushed out Sendara's hair again. The girl did not complain this time. She held still, slender in her lace nightdress, as Rianna divided her hair into plaits. It was perhaps because Rianna had hair like this, though not nearly as long, that she'd been delegated this task. She knew what to do. Knew the oils to apply, when needed; how to part the tresses so they ran smooth.

It was not her job to brush down her lady's dress, laid out on a table, before it was put away. That was typically assigned to one of the other women. But tonight, Rianna had smiled sweetly and offered to take on the task herself. After Sendara retired to her bedchamber, Rianna reached into the skirt pocket and found the note. Unfolded it before returning the paper to its soft hiding place.

It was as she thought.

There was a passageway behind Sendara's rooms, as there were behind many rooms in the palace. They were cleverly concealed, but Ned had told her the signs. This passageway was hidden by a cabinet that appeared heavy but wasn't, at all. It came loose if you turned one of its handles backward, the wrong way, with a bit of force applied. Rianna had been using this tunnel for some time. She had not dared look for passageways beside Elissan Diar's chambers—not yet. She didn't know what his gifts for magic might detect. But his daughter was a different story.

The tunnel was low and cramped. Rianna had left a tinder box and wax candle at the foot of the stairs. As she climbed the stairs, shoulders hunched to avoid the ceiling that encroached, she tried to keep her breath soft.

The note had been a scrawl, one word: *Moonrise.*

As she crouched in the tunnel, Rianna wondered if her mother had ever been in here, knelt in this spot. There was no way to know—the tunnels that riddled Tamryllin Castle were innumerable. Rianna's mother, Daria Gelvan, had served as a spy for King Harald's father. A thing even her own husband had not known while she was alive.

In the end it had killed her.

The spyhole was too small to see anything through. There was only a spot of half-dark; Rianna guessed Sendara had kept a candle burning. A light no one would see under the door.

It was a long silence and once or twice Rianna thought she heard Sendara sigh. Her mind drifted. She thought of the south where her daughter and father were; where the weather would yet be mild, vineyards newly harvested. There would be autumn rains, that once she had liked to listen to by the fire, reading across from her father.

She thought of Kahishi, a place she'd never been—had once longed to see—and now hated. An hour might have passed. By the time she heard a distinct rapping, three short knocks, it was likely the moon rode high. No way to know for sure; the dark was timeless.

She heard a male grunt, heard Sendara murmur, "Let me help," then a thump. A soft laugh, definitely a man. He said, "You see what I'll do for you, my lady. Even climb in the window like some desperate swain." His voice deepened. "After all, it's been too long."

A gasp from the girl. Then, "We have to be quiet."

"Yes." A honeyed sound. "It's not like the Academy, Sendara. People here watch, and listen. I can't make a habit of visiting." He laughed again, softly. "You like that, do you? When I use my fingers. You were so ready for me."

The girl was trying not to moan. Etherell went on, a murmur, as if to gentle a horse. "You must be patient. Soon we will be married. After the coronation, once it is proper. And then it won't just be my fingers, Sendara. I'll make you mine in all the ways. Again and again until you're exhausted. And then some more. The whole castle will hear your ecstasy, and envy you."

She choked, tried to speak. Tried again. "I don't . . . want . . . them to hear me."

He laughed. "You won't care. You'll only want it to never stop."

Now there was silence, or almost a silence, but Rianna thought she heard a suppressed, frantic squeal, like a mouse. A moment, and the sound of Sendara's breathing resumed. There was just that, for a while. Then she whispered, "Why can't it be soon?"

"Your father must be crowned first. Have patience, my dear. Think how beautiful a bride you'll make in the spring."

"Are you sure . . . we are safe? What if the Court Poet returns? No one knows where she is. What if she's waiting . . . to attack?"

"Oh, you're worried about that? Poor dear." He sounded indulgent, yet something in his tone made Rianna shiver a little. "I wish you'd said so before. There is no need to worry. Your father is clever . . . I would not be at his side if he were not."

"What if the Chosen are not enough?" Sounding like a fretful child. "It is said Lin Amaristoth has great power."

"I doubt that. Alone, there is little she can do against the force your father commands. And the Chosen are not the only weapon your father has. In fact . . ." He lowered his voice. "You must promise to say nothing of this. Just know . . . he has at his disposal a magical weapon. Greater than anything anyone in this land has ever seen."

"He does? Where?"

"*Here*. Hidden in rooms far beneath us. So you see, we are well protected. But you must not tell."

RIANNA imagined herself soundless, invisible in her grey dress, as she made her way down the carpeted hallway from Sendara's rooms to her own. It was a route to which she'd grown accustomed. She knew the tapestries along these walls that depicted tales of the Three—she'd searched behind each of these for passageways. There was a painting, too, a work more recent than the tapestries. A lady in gold silks and sewn diamonds, hair in elaborate chestnut curls. This image drew Rianna's eye more than the rest. Hypnotic, when Rianna recalled how close she'd come to being that woman. The lips were curved in an alluring smile, with a touch of mischief at the corners of the lips. The dimples. Even so, Rianna thought the smile just a shade inane. To imagine oneself powerful due to fast-fading allure. There was a hard truth to it, and a stupidity—both at once.

The artist had made the woman's face and hair, the embroidery on her gown immortal. But her name was forgotten. His was not.

That painting hung near the end of the hallway. There, the turn to her room, where the carpet ended and the floor and walls were bare.

Something new was there this time, however. Three Chosen stationed at her door. She rounded the corner and froze, seeing them. Just as their heads turned toward her, with unnerving synchronicity, in a gaze as if to bind her fast. "Rianna Alterra," said one. "You must come with us."

There was nowhere to run. No choices here. The dagger concealed in her garter belt would hardly avail with three armed men. She fell in step with them. Two flanked her, one close behind. Her heart pumped fiercely but she let nothing show on her face. She recalled Lord Derry, how he'd met his end. How before his beheading he'd made a jest. "*That blade?*" he'd said, as the executioner neared him with the sword. "I can lend you one better."

There was no mirth in Rianna, no heart for mockery. But as she kept her tread measured to the pace of the men alongside—neither a slow trudge nor a scurry—she thought about dignity and the life she'd lived.

Now the paintings, the tapestries they passed, seemed to have eyes that were watching. Gods, goddesses, nobility of the past. They had seen much and would remain here long after Elissan Diar, his daughter, their golden descendants had been swept away by mortality. So it went.

The room to which they brought her was of a grand size, bright-lit. After the dimness of the hallway Rianna felt herself at a disadvantage, blinking. Coming toward her, more of his Chosen surrounding, the imposing figure of Elissan Diar.

"Rianna," he said. He was smiling.

"Why do you summon me so late?" A steely voice. Her last defense. "It is an impropriety. People will talk."

This took him aback. Which in turn surprised Rianna. She didn't think herself capable of throwing Elissan Diar off his guard. "You're right," he said, surprising her further. "I should have considered my lady's reputation. But I have news I didn't think should wait."

She felt the blood drain from her face.

"Tidings from afar." Syme Oleir, from a corner. He was standing on his head, gilded shoes pointed in the air. His face was purple. Abruptly he tumbled upright. "Tidings, tidings, turning and turning. And we, with them. Turning and turning."

"Hush, Fool," said Elissan, and turned back to Rianna. "It's not your daughter," he said. "Look, Rianna. A message for you from your husband. He is alive, in Kahishi. Or was, anyhow, at the time of writing." Now she saw. He held the paper in his hand. It was unfolded. Almost Rianna thought she could recognize, even from here, Ned's graceful hand. "I had to read it, my lady," said Elissan. "Any word from Kahishi is intelligence I cannot ignore. For that breach of privacy, please know that I am sorry." He held the paper outstretched. In a movement that seemed slow to her she reached for it. Strove to hide the dizziness that made the floor tilt and weakened her knees.

Ned.

She felt as if she watched herself from a distance. As if someone else held the note with steady hands; someone else leaned back against a couch armrest to read with greater ease.

"You need not read it here," said Elissan. He sounded kind.

"Turning and turning," Syme murmured from his corner, as he did a forlorn twirl on his pointed shoes.

She ignored them both. Her eyes swam, then cleared. She read. She took her time, allowing her eyes to linger on each line. In the room had fallen a hush. Even the Fool said nothing more.

As she finished reading, Rianna became aware of the only sound: the fireplace, a dance of warmth on an autumn night.

She strode to the hearth. Without a word or change of expression, she tossed Ned's note to the fire. Watched those graceful lines curl and blacken. Turned away again. "I am tired, my lord Diar," she said. "Thank you for conveying this news to me."

He was watching her. His eyes were blue, matching the star sapphire ring on his right hand. He said, softly, "Why destroy it?"

She held his gaze. "You know what he did."

"He denies it. He speaks of his love for you."

"The words are fine." In the low, clear voice she heard something unfamiliar; a woman much older, weary from knowledge. Which perhaps in a short span of time she had become. "If I cared for words, I'd have married a poet. Words may not mend a broken bridge. Nor heal an ailing child." She shrugged, as if to dismiss her own words as an outburst. "If you don't mind, my lord, it is late."

The Fool spoke, sing-song.

"Late the hour,
Late the day,
Late in life,
To see my love once more."

Elissan still looked at Rianna, his expression one of concern. But he only said, "My guard will escort you."

In silence those same three Chosen emerged to take her back. Rianna felt as if she walked on air as she returned the way she'd come, oblivious to the men surrounding her. Eyes sightless as her feet found the way.

Later she would think about Ned's letter. Later. For now, she had to focus on what mattered.

A magical weapon. Etherell's voice, cool and precise. Somewhere here—in the castle beneath their feet. The cellars and cold storage rooms that extended in a circuit of tunnels underground, or so she'd heard. A part of the castle she knew nothing about, where not even Ned's tales might cut a path for her. His work had been carried out aboveground, in council chambers, bedchambers, courtyards. She possessed no guide, no map for the task to come.

Her father's face before her, his stricken gaze as he implored her to flee with them. Ending in that question, *"Why?"*

Rianna Gelvan had tried to respond with gentleness despite what she was feeling. "Don't forget," she'd said to him. "I am my mother's daughter."

THE winds were furious that night. Rain drove at the shutters. One shutter needed mending, for it kept up a persistent *bang* that every now and then, when he forgot, could make his heart race. For all that he'd been undisturbed here so far, the old Seer could not be sure he was safe. Each night, the groan and creak of the cottage settling its old bones brought fresh terrors. Each tap of a long-fingered branch against the window.

The idea that they'd come for him. Those boys with their lightless eyes.

Tales from Tamryllin made their way even to this valley. The world was not what it was.

His hands shook as he fed another log to the fire. As he took out the poker to stir the logs, watched the dance of sparks. Their hiss his company.

He was not that old, in truth. It was a feeling. To be an exile was to feel cast off, spent. With nothing to show for it. Here in this remote valley where there was little arable soil, the grass punctuated with shale patches. Walls of bramble tangled up to the scree. It was not desirable land.

He had never thought to return to it.

His cottage nestled in an alder grove. Lately when he walked among the skeletal autumn trees, he felt akin to them. He, too, had been stripped bare. And now was always cold.

Bang. Bang. Bang.

He froze. It was not the shutter. There was the cry of wind, the patter of rain. And another sound. The door.

Bang. Bang. Bang.

Fatalism gripped him. If they'd found him, so be it. Living in fear was no way to live. His friend would have said so. His more courageous friend, now dead.

The Seer opened the door.

Cold spilled in with the night. Then a voice. "Cai Hendin." A woman. She lowered her hood and he saw an angular face; dark eyes. "I apologize for the hour. May I come in?"

The absurdity of her politeness as she stood in a dripping cloak, the winds pouring in, were eclipsed for him by relief. Hendin—he who had once been an Archmaster of Academy Isle—shut the door behind her. "Welcome, Seer," he said formally. "My lady. I'd feared you were dead."

She stood before him in a dark dress, her bag slung over her shoulder. She set it down, then handed him her wet cloak to spread beside the fire. She said, "You may well ask why I am here so late. Too late to save—our friend. Too late for everything."

He felt it like a blow. "No," he said. "No one knew what was coming." She was silent. He couldn't tell if she waited for him to go on, or was too overcome by her memories to speak. "I am glad you are here," he added. At once, he felt self-conscious. That she saw how he lived. She, who had been the Court Poet. In this hut in a desolate valley. An inheritance from his family, allowed him by his brother. A far cry from the Archmaster he'd been. "I have," he said hesitantly, "a little wine."

Lin Amaristoth waved away the offer. He was struck by how she carried herself. A manner of standing that made her taller. But there was something strange, he saw, as she sat in one of his plain chairs by the fire. In the firelight the backs of her hands gleamed. Strands of gold, like veins in marble. She saw him look. Flung back her sleeve so he could see how the gold veins traveled up her arm. A shimmer of all her skin. "My new . . . adornment," she said. "But that's a tale for later on." She spread her fingers towards the hearth to warm them. On her right hand, a dark gem that contained a profusion of colors.

There were tales of a gem like that—what it meant. And no Seer on record who had worn it.

He wanted to say, *What are you?*

"Cai," she said. "I want to keep you out of danger. You were dear to Valanir Ocune. He'd want you safe."

"You must think me a coward."

"No." She shrugged. "This—all that's happened to me—" She looked at her hands. "If I could do it again, I don't know what I'd do. A peaceful life . . . it is of value. He—our friend—would want that for you."

"My friends are gone," he said. Then didn't know how to go on. Leafless alders beneath a grey sky. *A peaceful life.* He thought of Academy Isle, where the sound of the sea, no matter where you were, was never far. He'd come to think of it as a backdrop to his songs. To all music. In this valley the only sounds were of birds and creatures and, just now, of the wind. Sometimes the quiet of night woke him. Other times, his dreams.

Where was peace?

The Court Poet was silent. She looked at the fire. Then back to him, her eyes hard to read. "Lost friends," she said. "We have that in common." Her smile, this time, was wistful. "I'm not here to draw you into something. I am serious about that. I only want information."

"Information."

"I must know what you saw." She leaned forward. "Everything you can tell me of Elissan Diar. Of that night. You know the one I mean."

"It is . . . important?"

He had forgotten how dark Lin Amaristoth's eyes could appear, in some lights. An inky black. Her next words nearly a hiss between her teeth. "More than anything."

HE'D been at the lakeside that night. How she knew that, or whether she only guessed, he didn't know. By then, Manaia had already changed everything. The death of Valanir. Hendin could hardly bring himself to recall the sight: the corpse twisted on the floor of the Hall of Harps had borne no resemblance to his friend. Those staring eyes. An image among the dreams that woke him.

That same night, students were killed. Dorn Arrin, and the girl Julien Imara who'd tried to save him. Some enchantment had frozen Hendin in place alongside the other Archmasters, leaving him unable to move or speak. He'd watched as both were flung to the fires. The rite of Manaia made into something obscene, or else returned to what it had once been. Even he didn't know.

Nothing could be the same for Cai Hendin after that. No longer could he regard himself as an Archmaster, a mentor to poets and keeper of lore at the Academy. Everything in this place had slipped away from him—he'd been unable even to protect his students. The children placed in his care.

He'd begun, at dawn when the enchanted fog in his brain lifted, to make ready for departure. He'd arranged it with the ferryman, signaling out to shore with a lamp from the tallest tower. Summoning a boat for the break of day.

That same night Hendin dreamed that his friend, his dear friend and mentor Seravan Myre, stood at the foot of his bed. In the dream he appeared as he had in life, without that terrible burnt mark around his eye. Unblemished, white robes a lustre in the dark. He looked down at Hendin where he lay. A face stern but kind. Though he did not speak, there was a meaning to his gaze that Hendin felt—whether by some otherworldly influence, or his own guilt.

He could not leave. If there was a chance to thwart Elissan Diar, he must try. Valanir Ocune had already given his life.

And Academy Isle was *his* home, wasn't it? He'd been Archmaster for close on twenty years. This upstart, this monster of a man had come to take it from them. It could not stand.

But in the end Hendin had not known what he could do. As one day melted into the next he pretended to have forgotten about the night of the fires, as the rest seemed to have done. He took to the library, sifting the oldest texts he could find. Seeking some hint to what was happening, to what Elissan Diar meant to do. Any historical precedent for these meetings of the Chosen. And how one might put an end to it all.

But in studying the enchantments of Eivar, there was a problem. One that surfaced repeatedly—was doubtless what had driven Valanir Ocune to consult with the Magicians of the east. In the eldest days, knowledge had been transmitted orally, one generation of poets to the next. Not set into writing. It was only later, subsequent to the spell of Davyd Dreamweaver and the loss of the enchantments, that Seers had begun to expose some things to pen and paper. What they remembered. It began as fragments. These, in turn, were extrapolated upon by future generations. Nuggets of real knowledge intermixed with random verses, tincture recipes, anecdotes about weather anomalies and crops.

It was not what one might call *disciplined*, as methods went.

At times he came upon verses that seemed to hint at enchantments; that possessed a strangeness. But the symbolism in these was so obscure as to be no help at all.

The Seers of a bygone time had wanted to keep the enchantments secret. So they had done.

Therefore when the night of Elissan Diar's ritual arrived, Hendin was no more informed than before of what was to happen. He only knew what he'd managed to overhear: That the night of the full moon would signify a great achievement. One Elissan Diar had set himself toward since the beginning.

That night when Elissan, the Archmasters who served him, and the Chosen went to the lake, Hendin followed. He kept some paces behind, hooded, under cover of hedges and trees. But Elissan did not seem to be trying to conceal his activities anymore. The procession carried lanterns, making it easy enough to follow. As if the time for secrets was over.

As if no one could stop them, so it didn't matter.

They came to a halt in a willow grove by the lake. Trees formed a half-circle. Their roof of leaves made a natural opening to the sky. Through this opening, the moon, red as a dull gem. Water lapped at the silt of the bank, at reeds painted black by night.

No one spoke. The boys took their places in a circle. Elissan and the other Archmasters at the center. Even with an Archmaster's cloak draping his shoulders, Elissan Diar was utterly unlike the other Archmasters, broad-shouldered and handsome. Beside him Etherell Lyr, a final-year student who had seemed, until now, something of an idler. Who was now nearly as much feared as Elissan Diar himself.

The boys were singing. Their melody arced unmistakably toward the

Otherworld. Hendin shivered where he hid. Saw when the boys, Elissan Diar and the rest, fell into a kind of trance.

So he also saw when a man appeared, from nowhere, in the midst of the circle. A man aflame with green, lit from within. *An Ifreet*, Elissan had said. That arrogant Seer for the first time showing fear, his face sickly by the moon and that green glow.

The newcomer, a Magician, had opened a void to another world. A chill emanated from that place. Hendin had watched as with the animal strength of cowardice, Elissan Diar grabbed High Master Lian and flung him to the void. Heard the screams of the High Master as it closed.

After, Elissan and the Magician had done battle, as the Chosen backed away to allow them space and the moon cruised behind clouds, leaving the waters of the lake like black tar.

AT the fire, Lin Amaristoth watched him. She gripped her upper arms, a bit too tightly. Outside, winds raged.

Hendin said, "This next part is hard to describe. They fought, for the most part in a manner unseen. I felt it. My mark alternated hot and cold—white hot, then like ice, then back again; and each time I felt faint. They grappled, and at first it seemed the stranger had got the better of Elissan. He injured him. A terrible wound, it seemed to me."

"Tell me about this injury."

"A sword appeared in the Magician's hand. It was fashioned of light, like the green that suffused him. Its color brought to mind a poison. He plunged it through Elissan's stomach so deep it came out the other side, out his back. Elissan screamed . . . and Kiara forgive me, I thought he was killed and was glad. So glad." He held his head in his hands. "But as Elissan fell forward, down to the blade's hilt, it brought him near his opponent. He got his hands on the Magician, even as he screamed. Set both hands to the sides of the Magician's head. To his temples. Like this, as I am doing now. And a change came over the Magician's face. He vanished." The fire was a steady mutter. "I wonder, at times, what became of him."

"He is dead." Lin spoke to the flames. "What happened next?"

"The Chosen helped Elissan back to the castle. He seemed likely to die for some days. I allowed myself to hope. I could not believe I'd come to this—that I hoped for a man's death. Especially with his daughter by his bed all that time, weeping." Hendin let out a long sigh, remembering: his own self-loathing, suspense . . . and ultimately, disappointment. "But he recovered. I believe the Chosen were instrumental in this. They were about his bed each night. Made music in the dark that disturbed my dreams. Until one morning Elissan arrived at breakfast, wincing and pale, leaning on a stick, but very much alive. That's when I knew it was over, truly over for my Academy."

For a moment she was silent. They listened to the rain pattering against the shutters. She said, "So you left."

"Yes."

"Archmaster," she said, and was now looking him full in the eye. "You will ever be thus, no matter what anyone says. Archmaster and Seer. Thank you for your courage that night. What you saw—it may be of use. He has a weakness."

He laughed, a bit shakily. "Every monster has at least one . . . as tales would have it. What do you mean to do?"

"Elissan Diar may be a monster. But that's not why I'm here." A flicker of warmth from her, though it seemed to struggle in its surfacing. "Dear Archmaster Hendin, I know the Academy has been your life . . . but it has done little to earn my loyalty." His eyes slid to the black opal on her right hand. The same shape and size as an Academy ring. The stone was dull just now, its flame retreated. "What's more," she said, "Harald was not a good king. You and I—we know this. If you want to know what I believe, Cai Hendin, it's that one king is seldom better or worse than the next. It is unwise to place such power in the hands of a man—*any* man. Harald was too weak to carry the burden. Elissan Diar is cruel. And how to guard against such men, if we cede all power to them?"

He felt too sad to be angry. It was true—the Academy had offered Lin Amaristoth nothing but resistance. Had turned against Valanir Ocune for making her Seer. And his own grievance against Elissan Diar . . . he knew that was what it was. A personal grievance, as he mourned the world he'd lost. But that mattered little for the future of a country. He saw ahead to that future—Elissan negotiating treaties, lowering some taxes, raising others. Truly, it would be the same as with any king. Except in one respect. "He has a great deal of power," he said dully. "Elissan has yoked the enchantments for his own gain."

"A Poet King," she said, nodding. "It was inevitable. Now that the enchantments are back."

"Yet you're here," he said. A sudden sharp look into her face. "Asking about his injuries. Weaknesses."

"If Elissan Diar proposed to set himself up as king, and that was all, I would go away," said Lin. "Would *stay* away. Make no mistake—he hurt me. Valanir Ocune and many, many more are dead because of him. A city destroyed, and more." She shook her head, once, as if to put something aside. "But if I were to take a battle to him for my own gain, it would be destructive. To our people. It would solve nothing. So that was my thought, at first—to remain where I could be of use. With Kahishi and its wars."

He knew only a little of those wars; what little had carried to him in the valley. He'd heard that the great palace in Majdara was destroyed. The king of Kahishi lived in exile, vied in a bitter war with the viziers. "You've been—involved?"

Her lips curled in an almost-smile. "You could say that. That is, again, another tale. But one evening a fortnight ago, King Eldakar received a pair of emissaries in his encampment. Magicians from Ramadus. They'd ridden in haste, killed numerous horses to get there—and that itself is unusual. Ramadians prize their horses. Archmaster—they were terrified. These are some of the world's most learned Magicians. A prophecy had set them journeying in all haste to the other side of the world. What they saw in their Observatory—it could not wait."

Hendin leaned forward, hands on knees. "What was it?"

She drew a breath. For the first time, he saw she was exhausted. "There is a reason Elissan Diar chose to hold his coronation at the winter solstice. A time when the Otherworld is near to us. He means to tap into something." She shook her head. "The prophecy is clouded. But even as far off as Ramadus, they are afraid."

LATER, Cai Hendin sat alone by the fire. He'd offered Lin his bed in the next room and she'd accepted, promising to be gone by morning. A curtained doorway separated the front of the cottage from the back, but even through that thin cloth, shot through with holes, there was no sound. The Court Poet had either fallen into silent sleep, or lay wakeful to the sounds of the storm that at last were dwindling.

Hendin knew he wouldn't sleep. Not after what she'd told him. It was too much to hold—too tangled a knot of feeling. One of which, to his amazement, was joy.

Tears still tracked down his cheeks. He had begun to weep when Lin told him the news, and now, still, could not make himself stop.

Julien Imara, the girl who had gone to the flames at Manaia, was alive.

He'd been so sure he'd watched her die. And Dorn Arrin . . .

"There is a possibility—I'd say, near a certainty—that if the girl survived, the boy did, too," Lin had said. She had risen to her feet. "How this must have weighed upon you. I don't know where they are now . . . if they are safe. But Julien bears the mark of Valanir Ocune upon her. He must have given it to her before he died. It gave her the power to take herself elsewhere—and you say she held fast to him, as he was thrown."

"There were no bodies, at the end," he said, eyes filling—as much from shock as from memory. "Nothing. I searched what was left of the bonfires the next morning."

"No bodies." A chill came into her voice. Or no. In the way she bent in on herself, he saw sadness. "Oh yes. That can, at times, be a sign of magic. Not always to the good. But this time . . . this time, Archmaster Hendin, it is good news."

So into the small hours, he sat at the fire and wept.

At least one thing was left. One thing that was good.

In the moments after she told him, Cai was so overcome that he almost forgot to ask what he'd meant to ask. She had gathered up her things, was a dark figure moving toward the curtained doorway, by the time he remembered.

"Lady," he said.

Looking weary, she turned. "What is it?"

"Forgive me," he said. "But you said . . . I would very much like to know . . . how you came by the gold markings. What wrought this change."

She went still. A long pause before she spoke. "I did say I'd tell you.

But now that I am facing you, speaking of it . . ." She looked away from him now, past him. Cai Hendin had the sensation that Lin Amaristoth was trying to make someone understand her, in each word she formed; but that she spoke to someone else—or wished she did. "It may not matter how it came about. What I puzzle over, more than anything, is what it means. Sometimes I think I am not entirely of this world, nor another." She smiled. "As perhaps has been true all my life."

CHAPTER
3

SHE tried to tempt me. I refused.

Words that danced back to Rianna Alterra as she sewed her lady's dress, or brushed out her hair, or watched the interplay of the evening meal. Each day the same. Too much time slipping away. Too much time left to her thoughts. These inevitably went back to Ned's letter. The first she'd heard from him since the great conflagrations in Kahishi, and here.

Ned's words came to her as she sat with Sendara and the other women in the Great Hall, off to one side, as a ceremony was in progress. Elissan Diar sat on the gilded throne. Sunlight from embrasures near the ceiling lit his hair, his face, which was beatific. Days like this were pleasing to him. A lord had arrived from the south, of a wealthy house, to pledge fealty to the new king. Antyn Rovere was of a proud line, long enriched by wines and olive oil traded overseas. Rianna had seen the vineyards of House Rovere for herself, on horseback rides with her father, in winters when they journeyed south.

The lord was strong, brown from sun, and looked to be in his prime. With him had arrived an armed retinue, a promise of what aid he could provide if called upon. Behind him, his lady arrived in a dress intended to dazzle, silver brocade. It contrasted with her raven hair.

She tried to tempt me.

What did that mean? It wasn't right that she couldn't confront him.

She couldn't demand what had come over him, to betray his oaths to Lin Amaristoth and to Eivar, if not for love.

I refused.

Ned was given to plain speech. A thing she valued. He had not explained because he knew others would read what he wrote. She knew that. Still, she simmered. Even as she believed he told the truth. She thought she did. Lies would have been more prettily packaged.

"She is not *that* pretty," murmured one of the women. Their gazes trained on Lady Rovere. Sendara Diar shrugged. Today she was adorned in cerulean silk trimmed with ermine. Breaking the flow of her long hair, a single braid that Rianna had woven with silver ribbon. About her neck, a pearl necklace, a piece that had belonged to the deposed queen. With a curl of her lip she said, "I doubt she has even been outside this land. That she has even met foreign princes, or been courted by them."

Rianna bent over her sewing. She would not say something sarcastic. So far she never had, and today would be the same. But she knew that later the young princess would be more snappish than ever when she was undressed for bed. She would continue to take out her frustrations on Rianna, on all the women, and they would continue pretending not to notice. To betray annoyance or worse, mirth, could provoke a whipping. That had already happened to one of the women. She'd been unable to work again until the stripes on her back had closed. All because she'd had the poor sense to smirk. Sendara took her honor seriously. No one with sense would provoke her.

They'd all sleep easier after that wedding, Rianna supposed. Though the idea of remaining in this castle that long, among these people, made her want to weep with a frustration of her own.

I have work here, Ned had written.

So, she supposed, was true of herself. She had work in this palace. It fell to her, since as far as she could tell, Eivar had succumbed to Elissan Diar without resistance. And it was her land. Tamryllin, her city. She wore a pendant that had belonged to her mother, an amethyst on a silver chain, tucked in the neck of her dress.

That was not all Ned had written. *I would drop it all to return to you.* All the work he was doing—whatever that was.

Of course he could not do that. Ned Alterra was of the old order in Tamryllin—the Court Poet's right-hand man. Rianna didn't know if Elissan Diar would execute him outright, but Ned could surely not afford to put himself at the man's mercy.

Lord Rovere was kneeling before the king. Elissan Diar stood over him with a drawn sword. As he touched the blade to the man's shoulders, he looked solemn, imbued with the gravity of the moment. Then Antyn Rovere rose, bowed one final time, and backed away. It was done—he'd sworn homage to the new king.

The reverent silence diffused into a stir of activity as servants entered with trestle tables and benches. Some fruits, cheeses, sweets, and wine would be brought shortly for them all to partake, to honor the new pact. The lord Rovere and his lady were seated at the center of the table, their retinue to either side.

Elissan called forth his daughter. She came to him a bit sullenly, but she had been prepared for this. He proudly introduced her as a poet and future Seer, and announced that she would sing. And so once one of the women had produced Sendara's gold harp, the girl took her place by her father's side, and began. Her voice trembled slightly on the high notes. The guests diligently took no notice, nodding smiles.

Sharing her father's light, Sendara gleamed now too: her hair, the sheen of ermine at her throat. She sang a ballad of tragic love—a predictable choice for a young girl, though at odds with the theme of the day.

As bowls of cut fruit and plates of bread and meat were brought forth, Etherell Lyr came into the Great Hall for the first time. He entered purposefully, making his way toward the king. Behind him was the Fool. It took a moment for Rianna to realize that Syme Oleir was deliberately, with a set face, walking in exaggerated imitation of Etherell's determined stride. A flurry of snickers arose from the table.

Sendara's song continued, with a plodding quality as if she forced herself to go on.

Without looking back, Etherell reached behind him and grabbed the Fool by the scruff of the neck. "You had best not do that." He flung the Fool away with force. Syme staggered, covered his face with his hands, cried, "Yes, my lord! Oh, mercy, my lord!"

Sendara brought her song to a close. She looked forlorn. Rianna could not help but pity her, though she didn't know why. There was some polite applause, but most had been distracted by the exchange with the Fool.

Etherell seemed to already have forgotten it. He was murmuring in the king's ear. There was an undercurrent of urgency. Yet the king's placid expression never wavered. At last he nodded, said something in return, and briskly clapped his hands. "Wine for our guests!" he called. "Sendara, my love—you were superb. Such a voice. She has performed in the courts of the east, you know."

Lady Rovere's show of interest was almost convincing.

Elissan was beaming at his daughter. "She will be the first girl, the first woman, to be a Seer. Yes, there was that business with Lin Amaristoth—but that was done against the will of the Academy. Lady Amaristoth's mark is disputed, possibly not even authentic. Sendara will be legitimate. A Poet Queen."

The girl appeared startled. As if she considered the idea for the first time. Rianna had never heard Elissan use that phrase . . . a Poet Queen. She wasn't sure why it rang strange to the ear, just as a Poet King had done. She thought of Darien Aldemoor, mischievous and carefree—he'd have loathed a throne. Valanir Ocune, who had worn his role of official liaison to the Crown with unease. Even Lin Amaristoth, queenly in her way, had seemed more caged by the palace than at home.

Rianna had noted all along how smoothly Elissan Diar filled the role of king. Yet he was also a Seer. For the first time, she understood that he saw himself as something more than the kings before him. Saw his bloodline, potentially, as something more.

A magical weapon.

Of course. Enchantments would be the cornerstone of Elissan's reign. Rianna had to discover more about his strategy if she was to undermine it. She had already wasted too much time on embroidery.

It was ridiculous that such a task should fall to her—what did she know of enchantments? But there was no one else.

Elissan Diar was not done speaking. With a hand outstretched to the lord he said, "It is an omen that you arrived on this day, Lord Rovere. Today is forty days to the coronation. A number of importance. The event will mark a turn in the destiny of this land. We shall become greater than ever we were."

The lord uttered some platitudes about the honor this conveyed to him. An impressive man taken on a whole, Lord Rovere faded beside the golden king. Rianna wondered if he was aware of it. A man so great in his own halls, here made small.

For the first time she noticed the Chosen, standing at attention in various parts of the room. So silent and immovable were they, it was easy to forget they were there. None were invited to sit and eat. Now that Rianna thought of it, she had never seen them eat anything. It was hard to imagine men more dedicated to one purpose. It was their fearsome reputation that had induced lords like Antyn Rovere to offer allegiance. Their silence like a threat.

Men who wanted nothing could not be bought. Perhaps not ever defeated.

Meanwhile Etherell took Sendara Diar's hand and escorted her to the table. She was staring at him, and looked back over her shoulder at him after she sat down. Clearly she expected that Etherell would sit beside her, but instead he bowed to Lord and Lady Rovere. "Regrettably, an urgent matter calls me away. But I am pledged to be married to the fair princess Sendara—she may toast this alliance in my stead." Then—also unexpected—he turned to Syme Oleir. "Come along now, Fool." And the two left without another word. The Fool followed Etherell Lyr with a bowed head, docile as a child.

The strangeness of the scene, and Elissan Diar's speech, conspired to make Rianna uneasy. She was missing something. And running out of time.

THAT evening she dispatched a note. Then she did something else. She dug into her trunk and found, near the bottom, a gown. Green silk—a good color on her. A neckline that showed the curve of her breasts. She wore her mother's amethyst pendant still. Its placement against her breastbone was like a glittering invitation. To Rianna—in some irrational part of her—it was in fact protection, reassurance.

Reassurance that she did right.

Next it was time to attend to her hair, pinned in its usual prim knot. As she began to pluck the pins and combs, strands dropped loose. They fell full and thick to the small of her back. She used first her fingers, then her hairbrush to work out the knots, until the strands were shining.

There was more to be done. She had a pot of rouge to apply to her cheeks and lips. In a glass vial was perfume for her hair, her wrists, between her breasts. A bergamot scent, notes complex and secret.

By the time the servant returned, Rianna sat waiting on the edge of her bed. When she was bid to follow, she rose. She could feel the man's stare and held her head high. Until now, she had gone through all the days clad in grey or brown, hair pinned up. No rouge or scents. Most would have forgotten golden-haired Rianna Gelvan, desired at every ball. She had married, had a child, and vanished from public life.

She'd expected to return eventually—to that whirl of parties and politics. But not like this.

Along the way was the familiar portrait of the lady. The servant's lantern illuminated it as they passed. Rianna met the painted eyes of the woman, luxuriantly lashed, limpid brown. In them, despite the woman's smile, Rianna thought she read a sadness. Something she had not seen before. And then they had passed, gone on down the hall. Through a rose granite arch, up some stairs, a turn. Another. Rianna looked down at her hands. She had forgotten to remove the ring Ned Alterra had slid on her finger the day they were married.

She doubted Elissan Diar was the sort to mind.

The servant withdrew as the door opened. The king stood with his back to her, at the fireplace. She had never been in his most private rooms. He was alone. In the next room, she knew, would be his bed.

She stepped farther inside. The servant had shut the door. Despite the sound, Elissan didn't turn.

Was this a game to him? She felt cold.

"I've been thinking," he said finally.

Rianna waited. For a time he did not say more. She had a chance to take in this room. The great satin couches would serve as well as any bed. Or the pale, deep fur rug beside the fire. So many places he might choose. Once he was done with the preliminaries.

She did not know what she felt at the thought. If she felt anything.

Elissan turned to face her. He wore a velvet robe, black and silver-trimmed. But trousers beneath, blood-colored and loose. His face was flushed—whether from the fire or something else, she did not know.

The sight of her seemed to alter him in some indefinable way. "Come," he said. "Sit with me."

He sat on a couch and gestured to the place beside him. Feeling stiff, Rianna sat. She tried to relax into her role. "What were you thinking?" she asked. A light, teasing tone. One in keeping with the message she had sent earlier.

You once said that every day I please you more, she'd written carefully in black ink. *What if I were to make it true?*

He smiled suddenly. He looked boyish. "You are so beautiful," he said. He took her hand. "In green, you might be a creature of the Otherworld. The ones said to drive men mad."

She smiled back, dipped her head to look at him through her lashes. "That can be arranged."

He threw back his head to laugh, loud and delighted. Settled deeper into the soft cushions. "You're marvelous," he said. "And now you're here. And you know what I think of you, of course. I've made no secret of my desire for you, Rianna. Ever since I saw you, sombre and grey-clad at my daughter's side. Keeping your own counsel."

"You are . . . kind." She did not know what else to say.

He looked at her with an earnestness that was new to her. It did not diminish his leonine looks, but made him appear vulnerable. At her mercy. As if she could hurt him if she chose.

Rianna felt as if she observed, from a great distance, a map: one that told her she had been here before. But this time was different. This time, she went to the wolf's jaws deliberately. She was neither virginal nor a fool.

She had killed that self, that stupefyingly innocent Rianna Gelvan, many times in her dreams. A reach for power that would never come. A desire that *she* could be the one to kill that girl, denying anyone else the pleasure.

In dreams, she found, one refused to accept what in bland waking hours were the facts.

Elissan Diar had settled himself on the couch so he faced her. Despite his vulnerability, he looked confident. And now, contemplative. "I've been thinking about my life . . . all the years," he said. "You were right to suggest—ever so delicately!—what you did, about my past.

I have known many women. All my life, everywhere I traveled. They came to me willingly, easily. Some of the most celebrated beauties in the world. I have no complaints." He grinned. Then he took her hand. His was manicured and smooth. "But lately I've come to wonder if something has been lacking in me. In my life. I've never known any woman beyond the bedchamber. Not even Sendara's mother. I entertained the idea of marrying her—I admit, because her family is rich—but they rejected me. They would not have a common-born poet marry their daughter. They paid me to be gone. Years later, I had my revenge. I stole the child. My child by rights, who deserved a destiny of her own. Not to be a pawn in some nobles' game." He laughed, this time self-consciously. "And here I'm already telling you my sins." Studying her, he let go her hand. "You look at me with such seriousness, Rianna. As if you take in every word. Passing judgment."

"I'm not given to judgments," she said. "I have sins of my own."

"I'm not sure that's true," he said, smiling. "About judgments, I mean. What you think of all of us, of this court, only the gods can know. And flattered as I am that you are here, perfumed and dressed so fetchingly, some questions linger. Could you be seeking clemency for your husband? An assurance he may return?"

For this, at least, she'd been prepared. "No," she said calmly. She took a risk. She slid her hand, the one that was free, to his leg. Up his thigh. Halted just before the groin. Her gaze held his all the while. "If he returns," she said, "I want you to kill him."

He must have been very aware of that hand—if she knew anything about men, she knew that—but gave no sign of it. "You hate him that much?"

"A man who betrays me should die," she said. "Do you not agree?"

His lips parted. Then: "What people say of you is true."

She said nothing. So people talked, then, about the death of Rayen Amaristoth. His mauled body found in the woods. Of course they did.

"I don't know if I believe you," he said. "I only know that I want you. As any man would want you. I will dream of you tonight." Gently, he took her hand from his leg. He raised it to his lips. For a moment closed his eyes. Then said, "My servant will see you out. Thank you for visiting. There is more to you than I can yet see, Rianna Alterra. I want to know you, beyond . . . the usual distractions. I want that pleasure. I've known every other kind, and while one never grows tired of it . . . I find at this time in my life, I want more."

Rianna found herself standing, being led to the door. She was confused and relieved and suddenly afraid. He wanted to know her. That was the last thing she could afford. But the face she turned to him was a mask worthy of Daria Gelvan herself. Her mother had died young, yet nonetheless, Rianna felt herself molded by that vanished hand.

Just before the door, he caught her hand in both of his. The blue of his eyes intense. In that instant she could well believe he would dream of her.

He said, "Return to me soon."

BACK in her room, Rianna changed into her grey dress. The hour was near midnight. All was quiet. In the past months, in the enemy's camp, Rianna had grown alert to the sounds around her. For a time, she listened. She did not hear the giggle of a maid or lady, pulled toward some assignation. Nor the voices of the Chosen, in some distant chamber or hall, aloft in song.

She was alone with the night and this place.

She tied her hair back with a ribbon. Taking her candle from the bedside table, she went back into the hall. The events of the night made a turmoil in her. Mostly she felt desperate. And useless. Nothing was working. She'd been certain that tonight she would be in the king's bed—or thereabouts—and on her way to solving the puzzle set for her by Etherell Lyr. To learning more about the magical weapon.

There wasn't time for the king's obdurate game.

As she crept down the stairs to the main floor, Rianna pondered her own sense of urgency. To rush things would be unwise. But to wait on events . . . that, she *knew* was wrong.

She knew little else. This dark on the stairs, as she descended, seemed a mimicry of her ignorance. Or as poets liked, a metaphor. Darien Aldemoor had used many in the songs he wrote for her. Metaphors to describe her hair, her eyes—even her skin, which at the time had made her blush.

That all seemed long ago.

When she came to the door she sought, she edged it open gingerly.

Only a faint creak. This door led to the cellar. She surmised that somewhere past the cellar, perhaps farther down, were the rooms Etherell had described. How far they extended, she had no idea.

The stairs were dank, though a light breeze wafted intermittently from below. That seemed odd. Where could such a breeze be coming from?

She felt her way with care. These stairs were in use throughout the day, as servants went to the cellar to retrieve the oil and wine kept in jars below. They'd be reasonably well-maintained.

At the first landing her candle picked out a glimmer on the floor. She squinted. It looked like gold. Rianna knelt and found a large ring, wide in span as a man's hand. It was light in her palm. Not a diadem— it was too flimsy. Perhaps wood, coated in gold paint.

She flicked the ring back and forth in the light as she considered. A memory: Syme the Fool, juggling beside the fire of the dining hall. A bright cascade of rings that caught the light.

The appearance of gold.

The Fool had been on these stairs.

Etherell Lyr and the Fool had been together today. Was this where they had gone, after their brief appearance in the Great Hall? But what would they be doing here? She recalled the way Etherell had whispered in the king's ear. It had looked strange, especially before guests. It must have been something that couldn't wait.

She straightened, shaking her head. The next moment drew a ragged breath of alarm. A man stood on the stair above her. Blocking the way out. If she turned and fled down to the cellar, she'd be cornered.

She drew her knife. "Stay back."

The man's hands went up, spread out to either side. They were empty. A voice, deep and amused. "My lady. You haven't changed."

Rianna lifted her candle to the level of the man's shoulders. Dark, shaggy hair was what she noticed first. Shadows cut the outline of distinctive cheekbones. *"You."*

"I'm afraid so," said Marlen Humbreleigh. "Would you mind putting that down?"

"How do I know this is not some trap?"

He laughed quietly. "If there is one, we're in it already—both of us," he said. "Rianna, I tell you true. Lin Amaristoth paid me a visit. Asked if I was willing to make myself useful, one last time."

"IT is the strangest thing." Elissan Diar, a glass of wine in hand. He sat at the fire. Across from him, Etherell Lyr. Sendara and her ladies on a couch nearby, embroidering the princess's coronation gown. About them in various parts of the Great Hall ranged the Chosen, still and silent. They had taken the midday meal. Outside it was raining, one of those steady autumn rains that seemed to put the world at peace.

Etherell was studying his wine at eye level, as if intrigued by its color. He did not speak. He allowed the king to go on.

"Yes, very strange," said the king, sounding thoughtful. "They say Lord Aeghar of Hambley, in the north, was murdered in his own halls. You know of Aeghar, don't you? Repulsive fellow. Used to torture animals for entertainment. Someone decided to do the same to him. Crept into his bedchamber at night, tied him to the bed, stuffed cloth in his mouth so he couldn't scream. Silk, as irony would have it. And then . . . well, word is they found him . . . everywhere in that room."

Several of the women gasped.

Etherell Lyr sipped his wine. "An odd tale." Then he smiled. "Though perhaps better suited for late at night by the fire, not in plain day. There's naught to gain from scaring the ladies now."

Some giggles at this. Sendara looked cross. Rianna allowed herself a lifted eyebrow.

"I'm surprised," said the king, "that I heard nothing of this from you, Etherell. Weren't you up that way, a fortnight past? Hunting, didn't you say?"

"I was indeed," Etherell said comfortably. "Quite lost in the pleasures of pursuit. Otherwise no doubt I'd have heard . . . such a dreadful story." Now he looked direct at his lord, his eyes bright.

"I see," said Elissan. "Did you catch your quarry, then?"

"I did."

"And you are—satisfied?"

For the first time, Etherell showed emotion—he looked surprised. "I was," he said. "I am. My focus has now—entirely returned to me. And to your service."

"Then I'm pleased," said Elissan, and drank.

Rianna looked down, resumed her sewing. She had given a shudder, but did not think anyone saw.

Then it came: a rapping at the front doors. A burst of cool air as the Chosen opened one of the doors to a man who said, "Thank heaven your guards let me in. I have come a long way."

Rianna knew the voice. And then in the Great Hall, cloak dripping and his hair plastered to his head, stood Marlen Humbreleigh. He shook droplets from himself like a wet wolf.

Elissan Diar looked annoyed. "Now is not the hour we receive. What did you tell the guards, that they allowed you entry?"

"Only the truth," said Marlen, and dropped to one knee before the hearth. "That I am Marlen Humbreleigh—the traitor, the Snake. Here to offer my sword in service to his excellency." He lifted his head, dared a smile. "And thereby, perhaps, make amends."

THEY had talked about it the night before, sitting on the servants' stairs. Marlen had decided that knocking about invisibly as he'd done, though amusing, was not profitable in the long run. "It's marvelous, the things I've witnessed," he said. "Did you know that one of the kitchen maids has two lovers—a gardener, and a manservant—and neither knows about the other? But unfortunately that's not the sort of information that will get me far. I need to be near Elissan Diar. As much in his confidence as can be."

"I'm already working on that," said Rianna, irritated. "And probably better placed for it than the traitor snake."

Marlen grinned at this. "Not at all. You'd be surprised. Everyone is a little intrigued by evil. Especially if they know it won't bite. No one here has reason to think I'd turn traitor again. My interests clearly lie with the Poet King—not with the Court Poet in exile."

"You say that and then expect me to trust you."

"It's not always in our nature to follow our interests," said Marlen. "Or . . . I should say, being honest . . . at times our interests run counter to reason. From a reasonable point of view, I should offer my services to Elissan Diar. It is a new chance for me. Yet Rianna—you don't know this, and I don't expect you'll believe it—I am sick at heart." No hint of mirth to him now. "I destroyed the lives of good men. By rights I should be dead. By doing this, I might believe there is still some purpose for my life. Even if I can't ever make amends, not really." He grinned. "So you see. I am being selfish, when you get right down to it. And you—you, who Darien loved—" His voice faltered. "I will aid you as best I can. It is the only way I might imagine myself less perverse. Do you see?"

She cleared her throat. For a moment she had been near tears, his words returning her to a pain near-forgotten. "I am sorry I doubted you."

"But you must," he said. "You can't afford to trust one such as me."

"All right," she said. "Bear in mind, then, what happens to men who betray me."

Marlen sighed. "Ned always was a lucky sod."

HE was so aggravating, Rianna was thinking the next day, as she watched Marlen settle luxuriously in a chair beside the fire. He was wrapped in a fur blanket and looked utterly content. He had been led away to change into dry clothes; now he was back, a glass of wine in his hand. Etherell Lyr eyed him with a veiled expression, something between alertness and amusement. But now she had reason to think there was much that Etherell concealed. Perhaps he suspected in Marlen Humbreleigh something of himself.

Rianna did not think much could frighten her anymore, beyond threats to her daughter. But when the king had recounted that story, of a man mutilated in his bed, she had been watching Etherell. She still felt unsettled when she recalled the look that had wandered, briefly, across the young man's face.

It was not in truth that Marlen was being aggravating, Rianna had to concede. More, she thought, that he was able to settle in so quickly and be treated as an honored guest. Rianna had to sew and dance attendance on the princess. Her one advantage was that—for now—the king looked approvingly on her face and figure. She felt disgusted with her position and envious of Marlen. But knew it was not his fault.

The women were more than a bit interested in this new addition to the court. Not only was he handsome and famously skilled at arms, but there was the mystery of his traitorous past. So they murmured to each other as they worked—the things they'd heard, the tales they could scarce believe. Marlen Humbreleigh had been involved in dark magic. More—he was said to be partnered with a demon woman. Where was that woman now, they wondered. Had he banished her to hell— perhaps repented before the gods for his misdeeds?

When she thought no one was watching, Rianna rolled her eyes.

The mystery was only accentuated by Marlen's refusal to accept the harp that was offered when he first returned to the fire, lordly in his dry clothes. With the air of an obliging host, Elissan Diar asked for a song. "It is rare," the king said, "for the lords who swear fealty to me to be skilled at music." He was being magnanimous here—Marlen was a younger son, disinherited since his disgrace. Unlike Lord Rovere, he brought nothing with the oath of loyalty but his sword.

The king motioned to the gold harp on the mantelpiece. It was a great honor he offered—for Marlen to play the king's own instrument.

"Truly, there is nothing I'd refuse your excellency," said Marlen. "But I beg you not to ask this of me. As penance for my treachery against poets, I've renounced the harp. Traded it forever for the sword."

A shrewd move, Rianna thought, and wondered if that would oc- cur to Elissan Diar as well. Music led—these days—to enchantments, which held dangers. These were clear everywhere one looked, in the dead eyes of the Chosen.

Whatever he might have intuited, Elissan Diar said, "I would not see a man's oath forsworn. And I hear that few in Eivar can best you at the sword, Marlen Humbreleigh."

The women's attention was now fully focused. Life in this castle was dull for them, with the young men at a chill remove. In a typical court there would have been gaiety, flirtation; this one saw precious little of either. And now here was a handsome newcomer who would not be partaking in the enchantments that had unmanned the rest. Rianna thought, wryly, that Marlen had better bolt his door at night.

He issued a humble half-bow from his chair. "I am eager to prove myself," he said. "By any means necessary."

Any means.

That night on the stairs he had told her why he was here. Why Lin Amaristoth had sent him. "There's been a prophecy," said Marlen. "I don't know whether I put much store in such things, but our Court Poet does. Ramadian Magicians foresee a dark fate—even for themselves—unless we stop it."

"Stop what?"

Marlen looked grim. "Coronation day."

HER head rested near his as they sat together on a couch. His hand had found hers, early on, and captured it. As they read a book together, the king did not let go.

It had been Elissan's idea, to read a book together in the closeness of his chamber as rain fell outside. They took turns reading passages to one another—his turn, now. He read in tones that brought to life the verse. They were alone. It occurred to Rianna that she could kill him with the knife strapped to her thigh. Which would lead to her own execution. So it seemed she preferred to live. It was, she thought as Elissan's fingers caressed her palm, an interesting context for finding out she wanted life. There was no fanfare, no burst of realization; just quiet certainty as a man recited poetry to her, stirred her blood with the touch—admittedly, the skilled touch—of a hand.

She had once imagined herself experienced with men. When the fact of her liaison with Rayen Amaristoth made her feel ravaged, knowledgeable beyond her years. That night, its aftermath—these had left Rianna feeling as if she'd lived a hundred lives. She had come to her wedding feeling that way—ready to close a chapter that seemed bitter and long. Certainly if anyone had told her she was still innocent, only beginning her journey, she would have laughed. Or been deeply offended, as only the very naïve can be offended when confronted with the facts.

Now she saw that while the time with Rayen had changed her— diverted the path of her life when she was a girl—it counted little against the accumulation of years. She'd been insulated from the world since her marriage, stifled since the birth of her daughter. There was more, she knew, to what she'd shared with Ned, but he was gone and it was hard to keep from resenting him. He was gone.

All this, as they read the tale of Asterian, the poet who had journeyed to the Underworld to retrieve his dead paramour, Stylleia. A tale well-worn, but this version was recent, in verse that sang to Rianna's ears. Or that might have been the smooth voice, the expert cadence of Elissan Diar. She wondered what Darien had thought of the story. There had been something of Asterian in him, after all—a poet who ventured into dark, not fully comprehending what he undertook. Or the cost.

Though if you thought about it, was that not true of most heroes? Rianna closed her eyes a moment and leaned her head against the back of the couch. He had begun on the inside of her wrist.

"What are your thoughts, Rianna?" Elissan asked suddenly, as if unaware of her responses. As if all they did, right now, was sit and read companionably, as grey light from the clouded sky filtered through the windowpanes and storm winds sighed.

Asterian was by this time in the Underworld, at its outer edge, before crossing the black river that surrounded the Isle of Souls. He encountered a creature, neither of flesh nor of the dead, who posed him a riddle. There were differing opinions of the creature—in this version, it was a gryphon. But black, with fervid red eyes and a voice like millstones. A creature of the Underworld.

If the poet answered the riddle correctly, he would gain entry to the inner sanctum of the dead. Its repository of souls. But if he guessed wrong, Asterian would be reduced to ash down to his soul, to churn on the winds of the Underworld in ceaseless torment or oblivion.

Everyone knew how the story went. That with his knowledge of the world's fashioning—the lore of poets—Asterian guessed the answer to the riddle. He would pass the portal of that bleak gate, the first living being to do so. Beneath the earth and beyond life a poet might conquer, where even a great warrior might have failed.

And yet. "It is strange, I think," she said. "In this moment of the tale, we feel his triumph. He endures so much to reach Stylleia. Has earned this happiness, one would think. Yet at the end, after all he has sacrificed—he can't help himself. He looks back, and loses her. All he has fought for, lost in an instant."

"It is terrible, in this version," said Elissan. "They are, by that time, joining hands. He looks back to see her face. After all his tribulations, and believing her lost, he is so hungry for that—to see her again. And it's the last of her he ever sees."

"In this life," said Rianna.

"True," said Elissan. His fingers threaded with hers. "They may have found each other again in the lands beyond. But from what is said . . . I doubt that is the same, or anything like. This blaze of life—we only experience it the one time."

Rianna smiled. Now she could withdraw her hand, casually, and smooth the hair back from her face. In expressing a sentiment so transparent—however neatly phrased—he had freed her. Besides, she wanted to see what he would do, if denied. A curiosity she could not explain.

It turned out not to be complex. He reached for her, a single hungry motion like a cat with its prey, and began to kiss her. Rianna only resisted for a moment. She was aware of the silence of the room, the quiet rain. But more aware of the way she responded, curving toward and against him. She buried her hands in his hair and began to tug it mercilessly, as if to inflict pain.

He pulled away after a moment and laughed. "You like violence, don't you?"

Her eyes were wide. She did not know how to answer. Was not even sure she knew.

He reached for her again and they kissed for a time. Her hands still buried through his gold mane to his scalp.

When they separated again he said, "That is perhaps enough for now. I will not fail so quickly in my experiment."

Without thinking, Rianna grabbed him hard at the groin. "Is that what I am," she sneered. "An experiment?"

But he was unfazed by this. He laughed down at her. "Perhaps," he said. "Or a future queen."

THEIR predetermined meeting place was by a fountain in the gardens; the time, an hour after sunset. Rianna and Marlen had planned to meet there as often as they could, at the appointed hour, so they might speak privately. Marlen happened to know, from his time in service to Nickon Gerrard, that this fountain was positioned out of sight of the palace. It was concealed by a wall of hedges on one side; on another, by a row of cypress trees.

By day the autumn trees were splendid. These faded as darkness grew, were further obscured by the mists that rose after rain.

Rianna had drawn up the hood of her cloak. Against the chill, and in case they were seen. She was not supposed to be on good terms with Marlen Humbreleigh, let alone meeting with him in private. In the moments they had faced each other in the dining hall that evening, she was cold to him. She had every reason to hate him, after all. Not everyone would remember that the drama that had played out between fox, hound, and snake had involved Rianna Gelvan. But it was certainly no secret.

She had cut out from a side door to be less conspicuous. At the time she went out, a flaring remainder of sunset still lingered. That vanished quickly, night pouncing with a suddenness she did not expect. The year was getting on towards winter.

The gardens of Tamryllin's palace were varied yet orderly, divided into sections by way of hedges and trees. In spring and summer, these hedges enclosed swaths of flowers. Red and white rose trees might share one space, the white planted in a spiral amid the red; and one section made a home for daffodils of yellow and white, standing in concentric circles around a spreading oak. The Sun Garden, it was called. Around this oak was a charming circular bench of imported teak where courtiers might play cards, embroider, read to one another, and sing.

No one here now, in the cold and dark. And many who had frequented this spot were gone, to exile or beheading.

The gardens this time of year held an expectant silence. As if one could sense the life that awaited beneath the earth. The green in every tree.

She took a narrow path between hedges. On her way she got lost. Marlen had given her instructions, but she had never been to this fountain. And the mist distorted her sense of direction. She took a wrong turning and ended up in a clearing with two fruit trees. So she thought they were, though they were bare. Beneath these—she caught her breath.

Peacocks roamed this garden—she had seen them herself: the males with their jeweled wings, females dull and pallid alongside. This one, she had not seen before. It was white, but in no way dull. In the emerging dusk the bird shone, its furled tail a plume of frosted silver. The crest on its head like a tiara of ice. She met the bird's eyes; they were black, long-lashed, and in that moment seemed to her endless.

After one glance the bird turned away, head erect, and drifted into the shadow of neighboring spruce trees. A departing wink from silver eyes at the uttermost edge of the furled tail, and it was gone. She stood alone in a clearing where resided two bare fruit trees and a wrought-iron bench. Rianna shook herself, feeling as if she had been freed from some spell, and went on.

Marlen was there when she arrived. The fountain, a delectation of white marble nymphs, was silent. At the start of the cold season, the fountains of the garden were shut off. Dead leaves pocked the water.

"I have it," she said.

"Good," he said. "And you—"

"I'm all right." From her cloak she brought out a silk drawstring bag. "I hope this is enough."

"I was told it need be only a few hairs." He opened the bag. "Yes. This will serve. And you are sure—forgive me, but you are sure they are his?"

"Yes."

It was a quiet evening. She heard him draw breath. "Very well," he said. "That's a start."

"Yes. What is next will be harder."

The first night she and Marlen had talked, she had learned more of his purpose in Tamryllin. By the end he had told her: Elissan Diar had been wounded by magic. By magic, then, he might be destroyed. So went the reasoning of Lin Amaristoth, who had sent Marlen on this mission. And Rianna had been roped into it since she was here, and willing. And well-positioned with regard to the king.

"A long slash runs up his abdomen," Marlen had told her that night. "Long, and deep. From an enchanted sword. Elissan used enchantments to heal himself, but it remains a weakness. Lin does not know yet how to exploit it. With the right materials, she might learn."

Rianna had narrowed her eyes at this. "Materials?"

"Some strands of Elissan Diar's hair, to begin."

That would not be simple, but Rianna knew she would find some way. The other ingredient Lin required would be more complicated—more dangerous—to obtain. That next night in the garden, standing with Marlen before the fountain, her thoughts were racing. It had been easier to purloin the hairs than she'd expected. But it paled before what was required next.

"I am not sure how we are to do it." Marlen spoke quietly. Though it would be hard for someone to spy on them here, it was not impossible. Mist swirled around and about, and the concealment of hedges went both ways. "We must make a plan."

"Oh, truly?" Rianna laughed. "I had thought to simply march up to him with my knife and cut into a vein. It is tempting."

"I'm sure it is," said Marlen. "And it would get you killed. No one is asking that of you—least of all Lin. No, we must think of something. Give me some time to get to know him . . . his habits. Our time runs short, but surely I have a few days."

"For a king's blood," she said, with a faint grin, "a few days' planning is acceptable."

Those were the two things Lin needed to probe Elissan Diar's vulnerability. Some hairs from his lustrous head. His blood. *A king's blood.* Her own words redounded to her. It was strange to think of this man, with whom she had grappled intimately, as king. There was no connection between that august title and the things he had said to her, and done, when they were alone.

Except when he spoke of making her queen.

After Rianna and the king had kissed—after she had secured the hairs in her pocket—he had escorted her to the dining hall for the evening meal. Everyone saw them enter the hall together. Not with joined hands, that would have been too much. But surely the heightened color in both their faces told its own story. Rianna was acutely aware of all the eyes on her. No one dared say anything then, but in private they would. The talk would start. It could not harm the king, but for Rianna—the potential consequences were different.

Word had a way of traveling fast. Especially when it was salacious, and concerned the king.

Now Marlen said, "I am sure Ned would understand. Why you must do . . . as you're doing."

For some reason this angered her. "I don't care. I don't care what he thinks."

"I'm sorry," he said, and sounded as if he meant it.

Her mind went back to that scene in the dining hall. The awkwardness as she'd made her way to take her place with the women, feeling their eyes. Distantly she'd heard Syme the Fool singing, thankfully not something lewd. His instincts, perhaps, not attuned to such things. There was something childlike about him.

That recollection made her say, "There is one more thing we must do together, Marlen. This weakness of the king—it is important. But I've discovered something else. That night we met, I was in search of something. A magical weapon Elissan is said to possess. I have reason to think it is somewhere beneath the palace."

"The tunnels," he said. Realization dawned in his eyes. "That's why you were down there last night. Picking up on a jester's track. Oh yes—I saw the trinket you found on the stairs. But how did you hear of this?"

Quickly she told him of the conversation she had overheard between Etherell and Sendara.

He looked thoughtful. "For Elissan to feel secure on the basis of this . . . *thing* he conceals . . . it must be powerful. We have to find it." A long sigh, and he ran a hand through his hair. "That's two tasks, now. You drive a man hard, Rianna Alterra."

She shrugged. "I will investigate further, with or without your help. Oh stop making faces. I know you will help."

"You take everything so seriously, lady," he said. "It's bad for one's digestion."

"Speaking of being driven hard," she said, "you haven't mentioned Marilla. What does she think of your being here?"

"She wants to kill me. Of course." His tone light. "So there are two things set to challenge us—a wound, and a weapon. A neat parallel. Perhaps I'll write another song someday, after all."

She smiled in the shadow of her hood. For herself, whether or not he could see it. She had not shared the thought that had begun to recur: if they failed to stop Elissan Diar and the day of coronation came, her duty was clear. No one else was positioned as near the king as she.

It would not be the first time she had cut a man's throat.

Rianna thought of her daughter's face, and of Ned, and of her father. This palace had taken her away from all she knew.

Asterian returned from the Underworld with his task unfulfilled. And that, forever after, had become his story. A celebrated poet, yet all that was remembered of him was that failure. He had failed in perhaps the most vital of life's missions—in love.

"We live a song, as ever we have," she told Marlen. Words that brought to mind Darien, the Path, all the turns and turns that had led her here. "Whether you come to write it is of no concern to me."

SHE felt as if their eyes were on her, as each woman bent to her work. They sat in Sendara Diar's chambers. Each of her ladies-in-waiting set to constructing a fragment of the princess's coronation dress. Rianna worked on the skirts now, stitching together two long panels of green velvet.

No one knew exactly what had passed between Rianna and Elissan Diar, but since the previous evening in the dining hall most believed they knew enough. So Rianna thought, at any rate, by observing the way the women exchanged glances with one another; in the set of one's lips, or the tone another might take when addressing her.

Six women waited attendance on Sendara Diar. Four were young—Rianna the only one who was married. It was likely the three young women had thought to find a match here at the castle, among the lords and statesmen at court. They could not have known what sort of court it would be.

The other two women were old enough to be Sendara's mother; and may have hoped, when they'd first arrived, that she might confide in them. After all, every girl needed a mother. That hope, if it had existed for either of the women, was soon eclipsed; Sendara disdained them all. What they knew of her inner life—her fears, her moods—they knew from watching. And then were careful not to let that knowledge show, lest insults follow, or punishment.

Sometimes Rianna wondered why Sendara Diar had women attending to her when she seemed—at least at times—to loathe them. There was the possibility that beneath her contempt was something else: a lonely girl, thrust in a position fraught with complexities, in thrall to a man who treated her much as a court musician did his lute: to be played at intervals, and put away.

Rianna had the sense that in the past, Sendara Diar and her father had been inseparable. Sendara occasionally spoke of the work she had done for him, reading old manuscripts and making notes. Such was how their life had been in courts the world over. It was only now that things had changed. Elissan Diar was focused on consolidating power. Their tasks together had ended, leaving Sendara in this room, with these panels of velvet and little but dreaming to sustain her.

Her magnificent gold harp—Rianna knew its value from her time with Darien Aldemoor—only came out on formal occasions. The pile of books beside it—more objects of value—had been allowed to gather dust.

Rianna's ears picked up a new conversation. Until then, what had been under discussion was something to do with fashions and fabrics and she didn't care, but now she had heard mention of one phrase she had long not thought to hear.

"Listen. It's to do with the Silver Branch." It was one of the young ladies-in-waiting, a pretty redhead named Marisse.

"You shouldn't be listening to anything Syme says," said another of the women, disparagingly. "He's not right in the head."

"No," Marisse agreed. "But I'm not listening to *him*. He heard it from the king's valet and babbled it out in some doggerel verse. And then the king told him to be quiet, but not before I had heard."

"Heard what?" Rianna had spoken more sharply than perhaps she ought. She was annoyed that she had missed this.

Marisse drew herself up, though not before casting a cold eye at the king's harlot. For a moment, her disgust with the person who had asked the question warred with her eagerness to answer it. But only a moment, before she said, "The words were something like:

> *Time turns, spring to fall,*
> *Ensnaring what was deathless.*
> *The deathless dies, life awakens*
> *On the Branch from beyond time."*

Rianna thought Marisse must have a good memory—it sounded like a full verse to her, quoted correctly. And into the room it brought a chill, though that might have been her imagination. Her own associations with the Branch and the Otherworld dredged to the surface of her mind. That journey, years ago. The revelation of her mother's life. Darien's death. *The Branch from beyond time.*

Sendara Diar was nonplussed. "What does that mean?"

Marisse looked pleased to have provoked a reaction of interest from the princess. "Well, leave it to Syme to make it into something odd and confused. I had to get the valet to tell me. It's just this:

One day the Seers at the Academy found that the Silver Branch was bare. Its flowers had wilted and fallen to the floor of the Hall of Harps." As she spoke, she warmed to the tale. "From silver they had turned brown, then turned to dust. As you can imagine, the Archmasters panicked. The Branch had not changed since Edrien Letrell first brought it from the Path."

"Bare," said Sendara, looking stricken. "But what is the meaning, then, of 'life awakens'?"

"There is more," said Marisse, looking smug as a child with sweets. "The Seers left the Branch on its pedestal—they didn't dare touch it. They took to their council chamber to discuss what had happened. It's said Archmaster Kerwin was quite angry, though as you can imagine, at no one in particular. Who could he blame? My guess is, he feared what the king would do when he heard. That he might blame the Seers for negligence.

"Then one night a student tasked with cleaning the Hall of Harps went inside and saw a marvel. The Branch was no longer bare. In place of flowers had emerged plump fruits—apples, it's said. And not silver. They are rosy like red gold, or copper. The first time the Silver Branch has changed in many an age, and it happens now."

Sendara blinked a moment, her lapis-blue eyes blank and exquisite as that of a doll. Then she drew herself up. "The meaning is clear, isn't it?" Her tone was haughty. "At last the Poet King has come. To make things right again."

Rianna did not dare to speak. Her thoughts like a cat chasing a ball. *Time turns. The deathless dies.*

She thought of the prophecy that had driven Lin Amaristoth back to Eivar. *Time, ensnaring what was deathless.*

Verses that came from mad Syme Oleir. There was more to *him* than he showed. If she could only discern what it was.

"Perhaps you'd like to share your thoughts, Rianna Alterra?" Sendara again, sounding contemptuous. "Or are you too busy dreaming of your dalliance with my father?"

Shock could catch you like a punch to the chest at times. This was one such occasion for Rianna. She hoped it didn't show. She went very still. Now the women openly watched her. After the veiled glances and comments, Rianna had not expected a frontal attack. She allowed herself time to collect her thoughts. Then said, "I was thinking of what changes to the Silver Branch might mean. For all of us."

She hoped that would settle it. But Sendara was not to be put off. Her eyes were hard. "You know he sees you as a diversion, don't you?" she said. "He has courted the most beautiful women in the world. None more so than my mother."

Rianna risked matching her stare for stare. "I do not in any way seek to replace your mother, my lady." *Gods help the poor woman.*

Sendara pursed her lips. "I don't trust you," she said. "He shouldn't, either."

"As you say, my lady," said Rianna, "it is likely I am nothing to him. A diversion. And therefore," she added decisively, "not something that should be of concern to you."

Deliberately, Rianna went back to her sewing. She felt the stares, but pretended not to. Her gaze was fixed on her work. She didn't know what Sendara did, but after a silence, one of the women tactfully started up a new conversation. Rianna was grateful then for the arts of women, for which she had been feeling little appreciation. It was clear she would have to be on her guard more than ever. She had the father's goodwill, but not the daughter's. And the daughter might turn the father if she set herself to it.

SHE had a chance to speak with Elissan Diar later that day. He had just met with representatives of the guilds and was in a good mood, perhaps after having successfully asserted dominance. He tended to enjoy that. He had drunk wine with them, his face ruddy in the afternoon light. He had agreed to receive her in his chambers but they sat formally, in carven chairs. Rianna did not know what had caused the change; she feared Sendara had already said something.

She hated that she was examining his decisions with regard to her, down to the choice of where they sat. It gave her insight into what it would be like to be a king's mistress. When a man held your fate in his hands, you learned him by heart, better than he would ever know himself. An inventory of his habits, moods, and preferences, composed with a single aim—survival.

Rianna hoped she showed no sign of concern as she sat upright. She had declined to drink; he had his wine. For a time she listened as he spoke of the events of the morning. Her guess had been right: he had strong-armed the guilds regarding a tax. It didn't interest her and she didn't follow it closely. Mostly, she watched his face.

"You are happy today," she observed, when it seemed he had done in the telling.

He looked thoughtful a moment. Then smiled. "It hadn't occurred to me, but—you are likely right. The business of governing, even down to its minute details, can be exhilarating. I always knew it would be."

"You were born for it," she said. Feeling in that moment as if she spoke the truth.

He looked gratified. And something else beneath that. When he glanced away a moment, took a sip of his wine, it was as if he were gathering himself. When he met her eyes again, he said, "The way you looked at me, just now. I did not expect it."

She reflected, with acidity and alarm, that her task would be overall easier if he were repellent and stupid.

"Sendara spoke to me today," she said. She had weighed her options and decided directness was best.

"Oh?"

"She is not pleased. By our . . . association. I believe she fears I will replace her mother. I tried to assure her, but . . . I thought you ought to know."

It was a gamble. She counted on his being drawn to her sufficiently to forgive this lapse—his daughter's disapproval.

Surprisingly, he laughed. "She will get used to you," he said, with indulgence that Rianna was not sure was intended for Sendara or for herself. "Sendara is still maturing. In time, my hope is that she will look to you as an example. If you will just be kind to her—please—I believe she will come to learn from you. Your poise and strength. Intelligence, she already has. But strength . . . I fear I have not allowed her to be tested. And seeing you—seeing what you are—I am beginning to think that was a failing. Much as I want the world for her."

Seeing what you are. It could make her choke. She could imagine, in that moment, giving in to him. Truly giving in. She was exhausted, and he saw her. It seemed he did. He knew she had suffered.

She grasped for what was safe. It also happened to be something that was bothering her. "You told me you want Sendara to have a destiny. Yet her ambition has slipped away. Her books gather dust."

"She is distracted by the wish to marry," he said. "She will return to her studies again, in time."

"But is it right to delay those studies? To marry so young?"

He shrugged. "She is still a woman."

Now Rianna thought she could kill him easily.

She said, "What do you think happened to the Silver Branch? Caused it to change?" A question fired, direct as an arrow.

He raised his eyebrows. "I am surprised you heard about that."

"Women hear a lot of things."

It was at that moment that the door to an adjoining room opened. Syme Oleir came in. Rianna wondered what he'd been doing in there, and what he had heard.

Syme blundered up to them with his shambling walk. His face was pale beneath tangled hair. His long, pointed shoes ridiculous. He stopped before the king's chair. "I have seen the white queen. Ice and snow, frost and rime."

"You are a fool, Syme," said Elissan, and shook his head, perhaps at himself for stating the obvious. "I told you to stay in the other room."

"She has come to visit," said the Fool. "Haven't you seen her?"

Elissan seemed to pause as the Fool's words sank in. His face went slack. He looked as if he were listening for something. A distant music.

Then said, at last, "I believe I have, Syme. In dreams of late. Do you mean to say she's here?"

"I saw her," said Syme. He held his blue wool hat in his hands, that he wrung as though it were wet. "She is gone. For now."

Rianna felt compelled to speak. "She? Who is *she*?"

"Syme is—he has a way of knowing things. Sometimes it is the broken mind that is receptive. Truth seeps in its cracks." Elissan still looked shaken. "I know what he speaks of because she has come to me. When I sleep. I see a magnificent woman in white. Glistering like the frost, as the Fool describes. Eyes like blue crystals. She looks at me, and smiles. As if she knows."

"Knows?"

Elissan looked at her with eyes she did not recognize. "Who I am," he said. "The first Poet King in living memory. That her world, the Otherworld, and our own will be wed when I am crowned. A joyous thing."

Faced with this strangeness, Rianna reached for the simplest defense. A joke. "I had thought you'd dream of me," she said.

He looked suddenly threatening. He seized her hand, hard. She wanted to tell him that it hurt, but the intensity of his gaze stopped her.

"You are real, and here. And strong," he said. "You must ground me in this world."

THAT evening in the Great Hall was different. Marlen's presence might have had something to do with it; the young ladies-in-waiting gathered around him. They had taken their sewing and moved their chairs to where he sat. He told some story of his travels, a journey he and Darien Aldemoor had taken together. "He was better-looking than I am," said Marlen, throwing his glance at all the women. "You'd have liked him." The tale he launched into concerned a sour-faced merchant and a challenge to sing a song that could make him laugh. The man had heard Darien and Marlen were a pair of comic songsters and assayed them to prove it for a purse of silver. Naturally it ended in triumph for the young poets, though not before they had run through their entire repertoire; after all, the story would have lacked drama if it did not proceed through the predetermined paces of high confidence, followed by desperation, then near-despair. At the last, their success hinged on an unlikely improvisation that involved—for some reason—a donkey, a leaky pail, and a spinning wheel. Rianna wondered how much of it was true.

Of course it ended, as such tales usually did, with the seduction of the merchant's daughter by one of the two men; Marlen didn't specify which, as if that part made no difference.

"I thank the gods I did not marry a poet," said Rianna from her corner.

"That is unkind, surely," said Elissan Diar, genially. He was in good humor. He and Etherell Lyr were engaged in a game of *tabla*.

"*Your* husband is not exactly exemplary, is he?" said Sendara. "To say nothing of yourself."

"Hold your tongue, child," said Elissan Diar, before Rianna could think of a reply. She had made the jest, in part, to provoke his interest. She had not accounted for his daughter.

Sendara jumped up, throwing down her needlework. Before anyone could say any more to her, she had stalked from the room. Rianna, feeling somehow culpable, rose to go after her.

"No . . . stay," said Elissan, in a tone of command. "She must learn not to speak so to you. Come here, Rianna. Join us. Etherell's conversation is dull tonight."

"I am not nearly so pretty, is more to the point," said Etherell with a grin.

She drew up her chair beside Elissan Diar. He took her hand. "Look at that board. Look what this wretch thinks is a good game."

"Does he dare win against the king?" said Rianna with mock concern.

"Surely," said Etherell Lyr. "He beats me because he is the better at it. I haven't spent nearly as much time in taverns as my lord the king."

"It's true," said Elissan. He motioned to a servant. "Bring Lady Alterra a glass of this. I'll see that you drink it, too. I want to see color in your lips."

The women surrounding Marlen had gathered more closely, as if his presence was a balm for them. One had dared to rest a hand on his shoulder.

The hothouse atmosphere of the castle might have been amusing under other circumstances, what with Marlen Humbreleigh contending with the advances of several attractive women at once.

Rianna sitting with her hand joined to that of the man who had beheaded innocents of Tamryllin and exiled her husband . . . that, she supposed, would not have been amusing at any time.

From an attentive bower of silks and scent Marlen called, "My lord Lyr. I hear you are skilled at the hunt."

"I am not bad," said Etherell, languid in his chair. "It might be more accurate to say that in some situations, I enjoy it."

"How about a wager, then?" said Marlen. "Something to liven the day to day. I'll wager that in three days I can take down more game than you."

Now Elissan Diar broke in. "And where is all this hunting to take place, my lord?"

"Don't you have grounds here?" said Marlen, all innocence. Rianna narrowed her eyes. Of course Marlen knew the answer to that. He knew this castle better than most.

"None here. There is a royal residence in the woods," said Elissan. "A day's journey south."

"Have you hunted there yet, my liege?"

"I have not," said the king. He had retained his appearance of good humor, but looked thoughtful. "This is not a bad idea, Marlen Humbreleigh. The time is right. Once the frost strikes, the roads will be impassable."

"Can you do that?" said Rianna. "Go off on a journey on so little notice?"

He squeezed her hand. "Rianna, I am king. That is the least of what I can do."

"WHAT'S your game?" Rianna demanded of Marlen, later that night in their garden spot. "I know you have one. You need to include me in these plans. As it is, I only caught on at the last moment."

"And did splendidly," he said. He pitched his voice soft and meek. "*Can you do that?*"

She punched his arm. "Shut up."

"Once you said *that*, he had to prove he's king. Especially to you. What have you done to the man, Rianna Gelvan?"

"Don't change the subject. What's your game?"

He sighed. "Nothing so complicated. I thought a change of scene, an . . . isolation of the king from his usual surroundings . . . might make it easier to obtain what we need. There's no reason to tell you more. I don't want you involved."

"That's idiotic," she said. "I'm close to him. You need me."

"You're close to him," Marlen said. "Exactly. You're the first they'd suspect."

THE next day was one of preparations. Rianna was commanded to pack her things. Until then, she had not considered that she might have been excluded from the journey. Elissan Diar had decided to leave most of the court behind. There would be only his most intimate circle.

But Rianna had known all along that she would not be excluded. Whisking her off like this—it was, if not the main appeal of the expedition for the king, certainly among its attractions. She tried not to think about the possible implications of that as she packed clothes in a small trunk. They would be away only a few days. There was too much work to be done for more. Elissan Diar was not the sort of king to shirk his duties . . . a trait that under different circumstances she might have admired.

Sitting back on her heels with folded clothes clasped to her chest as she bent over the open trunk, Rianna recalled the previous night. How after it had been decided that they were to go away, the king's mood had elevated, become expansive. He had been of a pleasant mien before, but with the sudden decision to embark on a royal hunt became almost giddy. She thought she saw him strive to contain it as best he could. He had continued drinking, bantering with the men, but she saw the change.

This was a man who reveled in being king. Who imagined himself born to it. This she already knew. She observed that even in the hall where they sat and bantered, the primary décor was tapestries that depicted a hunt. Lords and ladies ahorse in fine apparel, swords or falcons borne aloft. One of the noblest of royal traditions. And now Elissan Diar would, for the first time since his ascension to the throne, be a part of it. He was on the cusp of history, about to be enfolded in a bright narrative that would someday be immortalized in art and song. She watched his flushed face and thought surely some variation of this was what passed through his mind.

Rianna also anticipated where his exuberance might lead, despite his resolutions about their "experiment." She had excused herself early, pleading sudden tiredness. To his credit, Elissan did not look disappointed—only concerned. "You must rest," he said immediately. "And let me know if the slightest thing is wrong—I will send for the physician."

Rianna had, of course, not gone to sleep at all. She had slipped out to the garden to meet with Marlen, who was exasperating as ever. He thought to exclude her from his plans. As if that were his prerogative. It was reminiscent of the way men had treated her throughout her life.

Only Ned Alterra had grown into the understanding, with time, that there was nothing crueler than attempting to shield her from her own life. That she had been used, tampered with, because of protections—not in spite of them.

Rianna had been the one to kill Rayen Amaristoth while Ned held him fast. He could have protected her, delivered the fatal wound himself. But he didn't.

Kneeling on the floor of her room, Rianna drew in her breath. But she didn't weep. She hadn't done that even when news of his treachery had come. She raised herself to her feet, beat her skirts with closed fists to shake out the dust.

Out of the corner of her eye, as Rianna approached her dressing table, she glimpsed a flash of silver. But when she turned she saw only the familiar small room, its spare furnishings and narrow bed.

THEIR departure the next day had the feel of a prank, as if they were children giving their tutor the slip. The plan was to depart the city unnoticed. Sendara Diar, Rianna, and the Fool would ride in an un-marked carriage. The men would attire themselves simply. Elissan didn't want to draw attention.

The two women were packed into the carriage, hoods drawn up. It was daybreak, still dark, and cold. It would be milder in the south, despite that it was only a day's journey. In another life, Rianna and her father had made that journey from Tamryllin in autumn each year, to the estate where he grew olives and kept a vineyard.

For years Master Gelvan had taken pride in the modest output of his estate. Under the original eastern name of his ancestors, Gel-vana, he bottled oil and wine and sold it in the outlying villages. The name was a point of honor. Galicians in times past could never have hoped to own a vineyard, turning the blood of centuries' torment into wine.

As she followed the princess to the carriage, Rianna stole a glance at the men. They stood alongside their horses, talking. From their ges-tures, it looked like the conversation had something to do with stir-rups. Marlen appeared at ease. He was among his own. More than she would ever be with such men.

Etherell Lyr appeared at ease, yet there was something on edge about him. She wondered if Marlen needed to be warned about Etherell, or if he knew. Surely men trained in violence—which accounted for all men of rank—could sense that among themselves. Not hostility, ex-actly, but its potential.

Once inside the carriage, Rianna braced for a different kind of hos-tility. She'd be expected accompany Sendara Diar with no other women to diffuse the tension. She felt momentary resentment toward Elissan for not foreseeing how uncomfortable that would be.

She is still a woman, he'd said. From his point of view, the two women could resolve the matter among themselves. Their concerns a world of domestic tedium unto itself.

Sendara sat in the carriage with her needlework in a drawstring bag beside her. She was staring out the window, even though they had not begun to move. Nothing to see from here but the castle courtyard and a dreary sky.

When the Fool entered the carriage—or was pushed into it—he

looked flustered. Rianna tugged firmly at his cloak so he would sit beside her, and not Sendara. *It will be a long ride,* she thought.

The Fool was silent. His cheeks were sunken, eyes glazed. Without his usual prattle or penchant for odd dances, he looked what he was—a boy. Rumor was he had been an ordinary student at the Academy before he became one of the Chosen. That involvement with magic had made him insane.

Seeing his young, tired face in the early morning, Rianna felt a stab of self-reproach. She had failed to see Syme for what he was. Like the rest of this court—these people she despised—she had looked upon him as a thing, a creature of the king; the poor, crazed Fool.

The mind that is broken is receptive, Elissan had said. At the time, Rianna had thought nothing of it. Removed from the presence of the golden king, she saw how callous it was.

Distance could make things clear. It was useful that way, and cruel.

Rianna watched from the window as the carriage began to roll through the city streets. Day had begun to lighten the sky. She had not been out of the castle grounds in so long. They had departed through the back way, not out into the square where they would have been spotted. Rianna put her head out the window, to take in—as well as she could—a view of the brightening sky. She loved the smell of wet leaves from the trees that lined the streets. She even loved the rank odors of the city, gutter filth and sweat, that peppered her nose as they rolled past.

"Will you ride with the hunt?" she asked Sendara, turning from the window. Some way of making conversation. She wanted Sendara to know they could put bad feeling aside, if the girl was willing.

"No." Sendara sounded sullen. But at least she'd answered.

"I don't plan to, either," said Rianna, hands in her lap. "The men will have their pastime. And we will eat."

Sendara said suddenly, "I didn't want to come." Sounding near to tears. "Oh stop looking at me."

Rianna obediently averted her eyes. She thought of what she might say, but as was often the case with Sendara, decided it was not worth the risk. The girl hadn't touched her breakfast, had been staring at the back of her intended until she was urged into the carriage. He had not bid her a good morning, nor even seemed to know she was there.

It seemed wise to avoid a silence. "We do as men bid," said Rianna. "We go where they have us go. It is no easy thing to be a woman, Sendara Diar. Not even a princess."

"You wouldn't know."

"I was never a princess," Rianna acceded. "It's true. But when I was not much older than you, I was sought after. Most would have thought there was no one luckier in the world. I had my pick of men. It took me a while to understand it was the only choice I had."

Sendara looked stricken. Then her face hardened. "Perhaps that was true of you," she said. "And if that's so, I am sorry for you. But I have more choice than that. I will be a Seer. The first woman to become one."

"There is one other," said Rianna mildly. "You could do worse than be like her."

"Does my father know of your admiration for a traitor?"

Rianna shrugged. "You might tell him," she said. "But since he was not king when Lin Amaristoth was Court Poet, I can't see how she betrayed his rule."

Suddenly Syme spoke. Though it was more a mutter, to himself. "The white queen."

There it was again. Rianna was sharp. "What do you mean? Syme. Who is she?"

The Fool curled in on himself, as if she'd attacked. Began to sway this way and that, and sing softly to himself. "*She comes, she comes, she comes.*"

"I can't stand him," Sendara said. "I don't know why my father must have a Fool."

"It is one of the accoutrements of kings," said Rianna absently. Her mind was racing. She spoke to cover for that, as well as to steady herself. "Like your ladies-in-waiting, or this hunt, or the ornamental birds of the garden."

"Those are shut away now." Sendara's lips tightened. "Just as I am. Ever since we came to Tamryllin, I am shut away. Like an ornamental bird."

Rianna stared a moment. Of course, it was true. The birds of the garden were kept indoors in the colder months. Something she ought to have remembered.

The Fool rocked and crooned as the carriage rolled, out of the city and into fields, hills, and soon the vineyards of the south.

CHAPTER
6

IT was raining when they arrived at the hunting lodge—a cold, driving torrent that stirred a green scent from the woods. The king himself handed the women out of the carriage. He was soaked but happy. The rain had caught them only at the end of the day's ride; the rest of the time had seen bracing winds, through lands that perhaps it had begun to occur to him, more and more, were in his power. The wheat and barley fields, the green hills, the vineyards. All of it.

Now they were ensconced in forest. Though the residence was large, its blue-shuttered windows tall on the upper levels, it was not a palace. It could almost be a home.

Rianna shivered as she stood under the eaves for shelter. There was something about being here, away in this quiet, private place. Only one person she could trust, and even he . . . she had to remember what he was, too.

Marlen was avoiding looking at her. He and Etherell were talking companionably, as they must have done for much of the ride.

By the time the royal party went inside to be welcomed by the household staff, their clothes were sopping. The first order of business, then, was for the servants to heat water for baths. For the first time, Rianna found herself waited upon as if she were a person of importance. A girl of twelve or thirteen with a shy smile introduced herself as Alle, the ladies' maid, and showed them upstairs. Rianna's chamber here was larger than in Tamryllin, with great windows. Water so drenched their panes that she saw nothing more than a blur of green.

Aside from rain, all was quiet in a way that was unfamiliar. Rianna was accustomed to noise. The sounds of the city, the bustle of the palace, the bells . . . these together made a continuous hum that had barely registered.

Their absence did. Silence pressed in on the windowpanes.

DINNER that evening was at a small oval table in a wood-paneled room. Instead of a vast dining hall filled with courtiers and attendants, it was the six of them. All tired from the day's ride. But they were also scented, their hair wet, in the wake of baths that had soothed their muscles from the journey. As they ate the soup and bread that served as prelude to courses of goose and venison, they heard thunder. The rain had become a storm.

"Let us hope for good weather tomorrow," said Elissan Diar. "Else we'll grow fat and lazy with good food and wine, and no exertion to balance them."

"Surely that is the luxury due a king," said Etherell, ending with a contented yawn. The wet, darkened strands of hair on his forehead made him look boyish. He sat beside Sendara, whose hair Rianna had braided in two plaits after her bath.

Elissan Diar looked stern. "Not this king."

After dinner they took to the sitting room. There were various cushioned chairs, couches, and rugs. Rianna took a large chair near the fire, curled up in it, and rested her head on its cushioned back. She felt so lethargic she could nearly forget that she was on enemy ground. She stared into the fire. Her husband and child seeming farther away than ever. A dream she'd had, if not for the purple stretch marks on her belly.

"I'm tired," she murmured.

"So are we all, it seems," said Elissan Diar with a note of amusement.

Rianna sat upright. She saw where Elissan indicated: Sendara, her cup of tea not touched, asleep in her chair. With her head flung back and lips parted, she looked even younger than her years, and helpless.

Etherell lay on a rug at her feet, his hands behind his head. "I might carry my lady to bed." But he made no move, one bent leg flung over the other.

"I think not," said Rianna, and with an effort drew herself to a standing position. Much as Sendara might have preferred it, she would not allow that impropriety on her watch. Not from him. She went to Sendara and shook her arm. The girl stirred and mumbled in protest. Rianna stood firm. "Come on," she said, and maneuvered the girl's arm over her shoulder. "Let's go," she urged Sendara, who continued to protest. She wasn't tired, she said. She wanted to stay.

At Rianna's prodding, the girl set one foot in front of the other until they reached the stairs, then made their painstaking way up. Once in the dark of Sendara's bedroom, Rianna helped her undress, then covered her up to the chin in her bed.

When Rianna returned downstairs, Elissan Diar stood at the fireplace with a glass of wine in his hand. He raised it in her direction. "Thank you," he said, with what seemed genuine gratitude.

She gave a little bow, half-mocking, and took her place by the fire again. But in the time since she'd gone, the mood of the room had changed. Etherell still sprawled on his back on the carpet. Marlen had taken a chair near Rianna's by the fire. All was outwardly the same; but the lassitude, the sense of unreality Rianna felt earlier had lifted. What she felt now was an air of expectation.

A peal of thunder sounded. Dark windows seared white by lightning.

Into the ensuing silence, which seemed deeper than before, Marlen's voice insinuated itself like a spool of velvet. "It's too early for sleep," he said. "What if we were to play a game?"

Elissan Diar's eyes showed a spark of interest. "What do you propose, Humbreleigh?"

From beneath her eyelashes Rianna watched them.

"I weary of games of chance," said Marlen. "And those of skill are one-to-one. What if we played something that could include all of us—even this lout." He nudged Etherell Lyr's side with his toe. The younger man grunted in protest.

Marlen's eyes were merry, features a fine study by firelight. "It is something we used to play in the Academy—my friends and I. There is no winning or losing. Just this: We each relate an anecdote of our lives . . . some small thing. And then it is up to the others to guess if it's true."

"Surely not," Etherell groaned from the floor. "I'd thought by one's third year that game was given up."

"Not at all," said Marlen. "It grows better with age."

"How is that?"

Marlen was winding a bit of string between his fingers. His hands rarely still. "Because with the years, we gather secrets."

"We'll need wine for this," said Elissan. He looked intrigued. Rianna realized with a start that he was looking at her. "Let us all fill our glasses, and begin. Marlen, first turn is yours. Show how it's done."

Elissan was handing a glass to her. Rianna took it and swiftly drank. Then knew it for a mistake. The effect, after the exertions of the day, was near immediate. She rested her head again on the back of the chair. It was good wine, reminiscent of summers in her childhood home. A time that seemed more real than anything or anyone in this room.

Marlen stood, letting the firelight fall on him as if he were about to perform a song. But instead said only one line. "My childhood was a happy one."

Elissan Diar laughed, dispelling whatever pathos the line might have otherwise evoked. "I knew your father. False."

Marlen smiled. "Very good." He raised his glass in acknowledgment and drank. "Ah," he said, as if the wine had a new, accompanying flavor. He flung his arms wide. "That's how it's done."

Etherell sat up. His hair was tousled from its friction with the rug, his eyes dreamy as if he were half asleep. "What's to stop us from lying?"

"Nothing." Marlen's look was of private amusement. "Let's see how you do. You're next."

Etherell pouted. He'd had a good deal of wine with dinner, in addition to the glass he had drained just now. "All right, here's mine," he said. "I earned top marks on my Academy exams."

"Boring!" Marlen pronounced.

"That matters not," said Etherell Lyr with a heavy-lidded grin. "True, or false?"

"True," said Marlen. "You are the sort to want to please the Masters."

"False," said Rianna. "You haven't touched a harp since I've known you. You care nothing for music."

Etherell shot her a sharp glance. "The lady has it. Though it could have been more kindly phrased!"

She curved her shoulders delicately. "I've had wine."

"Then next must be you," said Elissan Diar, settling himself on the rug at her feet. His eyes so intent she felt them like a caress. She shifted uncomfortably. There was a haze in her mind, which worried her. Inwardly she cursed Marlen. She didn't know what he was driving at. She didn't like this game.

"I worked once in a kitchen," she said at last. For a moment thinking herself very clever, to come up with something to stymie them. And then regretted it. Only Ned knew the particulars of that time in her life. And even he did not know everything.

"False," said Elissan Diar immediately. Rising, he took one of her hands and turned it in his own. "These hands have never known such work."

Marlen was silent. He was watching her. She wasn't sure what she read in his face, whether it was compassion or remorse.

Etherell Lyr's voice intruded, laughing. "*True* is my guess," he said. "And it is a tale I would give much to hear. Go on, dear," he added in tones reminscent of seduction. Then laughed again.

Rianna closed her eyes, feeling found out. Thunder pealed again, the rain pounded at the windows.

"It's true?" Elissan was incredulous. "Rianna. Is it?" He had let go of her hand.

She met his eyes. "Lord Lyr is correct."

His face became stone. She wondered why. Whether it was disgust that she had done such work, or worse—that now he suspected she was not what she appeared. That she had experienced drudgery—perhaps even degradation, which was said to enter one's soul. And that, in turn, might get him to think about what else she was hiding.

Damn you, Marlen, she thought. And cursed herself, too, for indulgence in the wine that had loosened her tongue.

"Let's go on," Marlen said. "My king. It is your turn."

Elissan looked away from Rianna. Drew a breath as if to regain himself. "Very well." A small smile played on his lips. "I am certain Sendara is my only child."

Etherell Lyr gave a shout of mirth. "False," he cried, and the king bowed his head in mock submission.

"I *know* of no others," Elissan Diar said. "But there have been . . . shall we say, opportunities."

"In that you are surely not alone," said Marlen, and the men clinked glasses, all smiles, toasting their mutual virility and fond memories. Recalling the hot nightmare of her child's birth, Rianna stirred in her chair. Her life had hung in the balance in that time and for days after, days of fever and delirium. For a time, to escape the pain, she had wanted to die.

The rush of blood to her head was, more than wine, from a sudden disgust with all of them.

"I'll go next," she said.

"It's not your turn," Marlen began, but Elissan Diar interjected. "It is the lady's prerogative."

She rose, a bit unsteadily. The memory of childbirth had been followed upon by others. Ghosts of her life rapping at her door. She stood tall and with a sweeping glance took in the room. The men gazed back at her. Marlen looked disinterested, but wound the string tight around his fingers until they were white. Etherell Lyr reclined now on his side, aglow with beauty and at ease. And then there was the king. All she knew—this she knew for certain—was that he both hungered for and dreaded what she would say.

When she did speak, it was lightly. "I had a chance to kill a man. I showed him mercy."

There was a silence. The rain fell more gently now. Tomorrow, perhaps, would be good weather for hunting.

The silence stretched. Rianna laughed a little. "Will no one guess?"

"I shall," said Etherell Lyr. "False, is my guess. You showed no mercy." He flashed his teeth. He looked wolfish and delighted. "We are kin, you and me. I ought to have seen it all along."

She looked away.

"I have one," said Marlen Humbreleigh. He sounded subdued. Whatever he had sought to unleash tonight, it was probably not this. "I have in my past many sins. I made atonement."

"No," said Rianna, before anyone else could speak. "For such things we can never atone." There was an ache behind her eyes, a weight heavier than tears. "I'm going to bed," she said.

As she made her way up the stairs, a candle in hand, she heard the storm tear at the trees with renewed force. The winds a great sighing gale. Her room was dark. She sat on the edge of the bed and looked at her hands. Thought of the things she had said. It had not just been the wine. *For such things we can never atone.*

She did not really believe it; but also, she did.

Something had entered her heart that day in the woods years ago; something cold like the blade she'd used. Not even Ned could melt it. Not even a daughter. All along she concealed it; flourished, for a time, in love. She probably could have lived the rest of her life that way, with the coldness no more than an occasional flash in the dark, brought on by a certain song, a turn of the wind. But with those she loved stripped from her life it had surfaced; was all she could see.

When the knock came, she was not surprised. Still it felt dreamlike in that moment to stand, to go to the door. In this quiet house wrapped in woods far from everything, the most ordinary acts felt strange.

"So?" she said when Elissan Diar had shut himself in the room. "What is it?" She had never spoken so to him. Never sounded so harsh to herself.

"I had no idea," he said. She looked up. There was a vertical crease between his eyes that was unfamiliar. He put a hand to her breastbone. "There. That is your heart. You can't convince me you don't have one. The more you try, the more I see what I had not seen. Not until to-night."

She backed away a step. "And what is that?"

"Your sadness."

She shook her head.

"That is the missing piece to you," he said. "Or else the key. And I have not been touched so deeply by anything in all my life."

"Please," she said, pointlessly. She needed to go on hating him. To hate everything about him, with all her soul, or else she would fail at the end.

He understood her differently. He led her to the bed, with his fingers snuffed the candle. "I would know you in darkness now," he said. "My dear, my love."

GREYNESS touched her eyes when she awoke; it was barely dawn. It was quiet in the room. No rain, no winds. A perfect stillness.

Stillness within, too; she felt nothing. Even when she turned onto her side and saw that Elissan was gone.

This has happened before. Quick malignance of a thought. She shrugged to cast it aside. She was committed to a lack of thought, a lack of feeling. She walked naked to the washstand and soaking the cloth, began to apply it to her skin. Later, when Alle came to attend her she would bathe, so that the course he'd taken down the length of her would be washed away. Perhaps it was that easy.

Or, not quite. Secreted in her trunk was a glass bottle. She'd had it for a long time. One drop on her tongue, if it was only the next morning, and whatever seed he may have planted would be expelled. Would die.

Thinking of such practicalities—washing herself, averting a pregnancy—kept her focus. But as she sat on the bed, wrapped in her robe, the perfect stillness of her mind began to fray. Fragments of memory prodded at her defenses.

She'd had no defenses last night. That was the terrible thing. Immobilized in her sadness, she had been pliant, entirely passive. Even the inevitable responses to him had seemed to come from elsewhere, from someone else.

And now he was gone. Perhaps her passiveness had been a disappointment. With word and glance, in the past few days, she had promised more. No doubt she'd descend the stairs to find him distant, or taking an interest in one of the prettier maids. He'd put that sort of behavior on hold for her; after last night, would know his mistake.

Last night she had revealed she was broken, and a king could have what he chose. He would want someone whole.

The herbs were bitter on her tongue. A taste so awful she thought it must be a punishment, for the crime of being an unnatural woman who did not want a child. For the act of love a woman must pay. One way or another.

Soon she vomited in the chamber pot, loud and long until she felt the last ounce of strength wrung from her. That seemed right. She hoped it meant the herb was working. Afterward she washed her mouth with a peppermint rinse. There were ways, despite everything, to make herself clean again.

She was collecting herself, readying for a bath, when the door opened. She turned to hiss at whoever disturbed her privacy and saw it was Elissan Diar, standing in the doorway with a high color and shining eyes. Knowing she was in every way the opposite—drained and colorless—Rianna could only stare.

His exhilaration flagged when he saw her. "I'm sorry," he said. "I should have knocked. I just . . . I ran all the way back here. I couldn't contain myself."

He was fully dressed and had clearly been outside, his clothes dew-dampened.

"We must get you dry clothes," she said automatically, and he started to laugh. He ran to her and lifted her in his arms, spun her around. When he set her down again she was dizzy. "What," she began, feeling at sea more than ever with him.

"My dear, did you sleep well? I should have asked," he said. "You look so pale. Come, sit with me. Soon I will have to tell the others, but for now, I want to share it only with you." He drew her to sit on the bed beside him, his arm around her waist and her hand enveloped in his. "It's my fault you're tired. But listen to what I have to tell."

He was right about one thing—she was tired. She found herself leaning against him for support. "Tell me."

His arm around her waist tightened, as if the excitement coursing through him needed an outlet. "I woke before first light," he said. "To the morning star. It was as if a voice called to me. A musical voice, sweet and far away. And it seemed—to command me."

Rianna straightened, no longer tired. Now with every sense alert. "What was the command?"

"I knew . . . I needed to go to the woods. So I did. I got myself dressed and went out. The rain had ceased by then. In the wake of the storm was a deep silence. I did not see a bird or animal stir. I walked on, knowing only that the voice drew me on. And then—I saw it."

He put his hands on her shoulders, looked direct into her face. "As the music reached its peak I saw a flash of white in the trees. I followed after it. And when I came to a glen it stood still, awaiting me. A white hart with mane like silver frost. With deep, black eyes you could never see the bottom of. And its crown, Rianna . . ."

Elissan shook his head in wonderment. "It was a hart of twelve tines. Not ten, as make a quarry worthy of a king. Twelve, to surpass even that."

Despite herself, she was stirred by the tale. "So what happened?"

He sighed. "I was a fool—I had not brought my crossbow. But clearly it is my destiny—to fell this hart. Something from the other world was calling me. You know what I mean, surely." His gaze, though intent on her, was gentle. "I'm not the first poet you have loved."

She looked down. "Yes," she said. "I know of the Otherworld."

"I believe it was a test," he said. "Today, when we hunt, it will be for the hart."

THAT day she kept to her room. From the window watched the men ride out, looking splendid on coursers in their hunting gear.

Once she had seen them go, Rianna crept back into the bed and slept. Perhaps it was the herbs, or a need to escape her thoughts. The dreams she fell into were confused and strange; when she awoke, she barely felt rested.

It was when the first glow of sunset lit the treetops that she heard the cries of the men and dogs returning. By then Rianna had bathed and dressed, and knew she must go down.

It was soon clear something was wrong. The king snapped at the grooms who helped him from his horse. He strode inside, his rage so palpable that even Sendara backed from him. Rianna wondered if she had ever seen her father like this.

It was clear what Rianna was to do. She took a step to intercept his headlong path. Took his arm. And as if she possessed some manner of enchantments herself, Elissan froze. He closed his eyes.

"So it did not go well," Rianna said softly. "Come." She led him to a chair. Kneeling on the floor like a maidservant, she untied and pulled off his boots for him. Then took one foot into her hands and began to rub it gently. Elissan let out a sigh that was nearly a sob, and leaned back with closed eyes. She worked that way for a while. It felt degrading, and therefore in keeping with the role she had taken. When she heard the other two men come in, she didn't look up. She didn't want to see Marlen's face.

She saw Etherell first, as he threw himself onto a couch nearby. "Such a day. I hope the cooks have prepared a good dinner."

"What happened?" said Rianna.

"We quested after the hart," said Marlen, striding into her line of sight. "Which turned out to be more a tease than a Hannish courtesan. You know," he added, when he saw the incomprehension in Rianna's eyes. "Oh. All right then. Well the point is, it never showed itself. We didn't find so much as a trail or tracks."

"That is a shame," she said, keeping her voice neutral as she kneaded the king's foot. "Did you come across other game?"

"The king desired this target alone," said Marlen in just as neutral a tone. Rianna wondered what he knew of the king's mind. If he knew what this hunt meant to him.

"The call was intended for me," said Elissan. "I am sure of it." He straightened in his chair to plant his feet on the floor. Rianna ceased her ministrations and rose.

The king went on. "But today . . . today was silence. Nothing. As if I'd dreamed it all."

"No dream." It was Syme Oleir. Rianna had forgotten all about him.

He shuffled from the kitchen bareheaded, his feet bare on the carpets. Formalities had been relaxed here, as they never would have been in Tamryllin. "No dream. The white queen calls."

"*Yes,*" said Elissan Diar. "Yes. Come here, Syme. Tell me what you know."

With his usual dazed expression, the Fool crossed to the king. "Father," he said.

"Yes, yes," said Elissan impatiently. "Come here."

The Fool sat on the rug, cross-legged at the king's feet. Dark eyes shadow-rimmed and large in his pale face. He looked up beseechingly, as if he sought approval from the golden figure in the chair. "It is you she calls," he said. "No one else. Her voice is for you alone."

"Myself alone," Elissan repeated.

"The branch has turned to autumn, and she comes," said Syme Oleir. "She comes. The white queen comes."

"There he goes again," said Etherell Lyr with a yawn. "Isn't anyone else hungry?"

THAT night, the king brooded. This time he invited her to his room, and she felt she could only accede. She had begun down this road and now was no return.

The room of the king, adorned with gold silks, was soothing in its comfort. Almost she could forget there was a world outside, where there were tasks to be done. People she had betrayed.

Elissan was deep in thought that night. Rianna had an instinct that tonight was not the time to relapse to her usual role, to making light of his rank. In the past he'd found that refreshing, a lure, but she doubted he would find it so now. His sense of himself, of his destiny, was uncertain for the first time since she had known him. Perhaps the first time in his life.

They sat upright in the bed and read, each from a separate book. Rianna could hardly see the lines of poetry before her eyes; so focused was her attention on him, on the mood he cast on the room.

"What are you reading?" she asked at last. Looking over, she saw it was not so much a book as an old manuscript that had been sewn together. The pages looked near to falling apart.

He looked up, looking young as long locks fell forward into his eyes. "It is a text of the Otherworld," he said. "One of the few we have. I've been scouring it for mentions of this white queen."

Rianna infused her tone with some of her old mockery. "All right. That's enough. Lie down."

"What . . ." But he was starting to grin as she tugged the manuscript from his hands. Aware of his eyes, she placed it carefully on the bedside table. Then she rested her arms on his chest, her chin on her hands. Her eyes turned seriously to his.

"You are a poet," she said.

"Yes."

"What you need," she said, "is inspiration. Don't you think?"

She had flung her leg across him and begun to work at the fastenings of his collar. This time it wasn't dark. When his shirt parted she saw the scar: black, gold-edged, writhing the length of his left side. It was nothing ordinary. She could imagine it opening to unleash his life.

Elissan stroked her hair as she moved down, and down. Tonight she wouldn't risk pregnancy. His hands in her hair were urgent, tender, and more than once he cried her name.

SOON afterward he slipped into sleep. After some restless turns so did she. Later she awoke when it was still dark to see him seated in a chair, lit in a bar of moonlight. He was lacing his boots. He spoke gently when he saw her. "Hush now." His mark of the Seer like a risen star; his features looked sensitive in its light, and wise. "I think I know . . . what I must do. The call was for me. I must go alone. Sleep."

And so she did. She'd been having unquiet dreams, and slept no more soundly when she returned to them. When she awoke to the bright and empty chamber, she felt sunk in the layered deliciousness of the bed. She wanted to stay in here awhile. Watch the gold light on gold brocade. Just stay with the calm and beauty of this place that seemed detached from all her cares and accorded no judgments.

Moments or an hour may have passed. She began to hear a commotion downstairs. She listened, thinking perhaps there was some trouble in the kitchen—a dropped tray, a broken decanter. But it didn't stop.

She began to hear voices raised. Men shouting. The most dangerous sound she knew.

Rianna slid into her robe. It was not appropriate to appear as she did, leaving the king's room. But the dread that gripped her in that moment overrode all such concerns. She grabbed her knife from its hiding place in her pile of clothes. By the time she left the room she was running.

When she reached the top of the stairs, looking down, she saw all she needed.

Elissan Diar stood there, his teeth bared like an animal. In one fist he gripped a handful of a man's hair, his other arm flung around the man's neck. The man's head tipped back, and Rianna saw it was Marlen. His eyes were glazed; blood trickled from his mouth.

"He ambushed me," the king spat. There was a cut in his cheek, blood in his hair. "I was questing for the hart. And then a masked man jumped from the trees. But his sword—ah. I recognized *that*."

Etherell Lyr appeared behind the king, holding what looked like a bloodstained rag up for Rianna's inspection. "He thought himself clever," he said, sounding amused. "To mask himself. That he'd be taken for a thief as he fled the scene."

She remembered: Marlen, their last evening beside the fountain. *You're the first they'd suspect.*

Marlen had never meant to try for a bit of blood. He'd planned to kill Elissan Diar right there, and end it. And it should have worked. He had the advantage of surprise, was the younger of the two, and a renowned swordsman. All elements in his favor. And yet.

She saw Marlen's wrists and ankles were tied. When Elissan dropped him, he collapsed.

"Take him downstairs," Elissan commanded the manservants who had materialized around them. "We leave for Tamryllin on the morrow. For now . . . we'll question the traitor. He'll tell us everything." With a booted toe he kicked Marlen in the ribs. "You'll wish for death," he said. "Many times over."

"He'll kill you." She had come down to the cellar. In an aisle between rows of wine casks he'd been tied to a chair. He was conscious now.

"Get out of here, Rianna," he said. "They'll be down any moment."

"You planned this." Her voice sounded dead to her. "You always meant to kill him."

"Otherwise you would have," he said. "You think I don't know? And there would be no escape for you. It's different for me." His laugh was hollow. "Or was meant to be. I did hope to escape. Get Marilla, flee over the border if need be."

"What happened?"

"I . . . couldn't do it." For the first time, Marlen's guard wavered; he sounded anguished. "He was so *strong*, Rianna."

Rianna covered her eyes. She thought his face would haunt her all her life. "I can't bear this."

"Rianna." He regained himself and became stern. "I betrayed Darien. Remember? I'm the reason he's dead. This is what's coming to me. And you're a cold bitch who can bear anything. I've seen it for myself."

She couldn't smile. "Darien wouldn't want this."

"It's a shame," he said, as if he didn't hear. "I'd ask you to kill me, but we can't afford the risk. They'd know it was you."

"I could . . ." she began. The idea made her gorge rise.

"No. I will have to endure questioning," he said. "It's up to you to complete our task. I pray it won't cost your life. I can do nothing more."

A new voice. "Rianna."

Etherell Lyr stepped from behind the casks. "This seems an odd place for you."

She felt carved of ice. All but her stomach, which roiled with acid. There was no way to know what he'd heard.

"I should be here," she said. "To witness the questioning."

He tilted his head in that mock-interested way he had, that she had come to hate. She hated that he frightened her. As usual, he sounded cool and unbothered. "And why is that?"

"Because," Rianna said, her voice strengthening as Elissan Diar emerged from behind the casks as well, "I will soon be queen. A partner in the king's justice. I should see that justice carried out."

The king stood there, watching her. Blood still marked his cheek. His eyes like blue ice. He seemed to weigh her words, his gaze passing between her and Marlen.

"You are a cold one," he said at last to her. "Yet like fire in my arms. I may never know all there is to you." He extended his arm, a king's gesture. "You may watch. If you swear to say nothing of what you see tonight."

"I swear."

"Come out, Syme," said Elissan Diar then, in a different tone. Now he sounded impatient. "Stop hiding. Or I'll have Etherell drag you, and you won't like it."

The Fool scurried into view. He looked ill. "I'm here," he said. "Please don't hurt me, Father."

"You know your duty," Elissan Diar said curtly. "We have questions for this man. You know what to do."

Marlen had lifted his head to stare at the Fool. "Let me guess," he said. "He's going to sing. Cruel, Elissan. Beneath even you."

Etherell Lyr cuffed him on the temple. Rianna kept herself from wincing. She felt as if she had taken root in the flagstones of the cellar floor; that she was stone.

"Syme," said Elissan.

The Fool dragged himself forward. With each step he whimpered.

"Stop that noise," said the king. "Now."

Syme Oleir came up beside Marlen. Trembling, set his hands to each side of Marlen's head, as if to confer a blessing. "I'm sorry," he said. With sudden clarity.

And then he changed. A green luminescence filled Syme's body. He lit up the cellar. As if his flesh were transparent, and some creature of light was contained within. He threw back his head, face contorting. He wept. The light grew brighter. The tears of Syme Oleir against the green were like black blood.

So these were enchantments, Rianna thought, feeling disassociated from it all as if she floated. The thing men killed and died for. Who knew it would be so ugly?

She made herself be present, look at Marlen. *To witness.* Saw his eyes grow wide before the first scream.

THAT night he took her fiercely and without a word. Rianna endured it until it was done. The king fell asleep immediately, leaving her staring into the night. They were in her room. After watching Marlen's torture she had retreated here to be alone. He'd followed, hellbent and silent, not waiting for her to disrobe. Just skirts hiked up in the dark, more silence, until it was done.

Marlen had revealed nothing. Not about her, nor even about Lin or his mission. The torture went on until Syme Oleir collapsed. The green light died and he looked no more than himself again; once more diminished. Etherell Lyr had slung the slight figure over his shoulders to take him upstairs.

Marlen was slumped in the chair, but the king pronounced him alive.

As she lay in the dark Rianna thought of going down to him. If there was anything she could do for enchanted wounds. There was nothing she could do, but she could still be there. He should not be alone in the dark.

She couldn't do that if she was to survive; and she was their last line of defense. She, and Lin Amaristoth—wherever the Court Poet was now.

Rianna thought of stabbing the king where he lay. His throat looked tender, unprotected. But if he should wake . . . *He is so* strong, *Rianna.*

From Marlen's voice, more than his words, she understood. He had meant: Like nothing human.

The forest quiet, once a wonder, now seemed to tighten around her like a silk trap.

Rianna hadn't known Elissan Diar was to be feared more than an ordinary man. She hadn't planned for that contingency.

IN the morning when she went downstairs she could not help crying out. What swam in a pool of blood on the table in the front hall, dripping on the rug, the first thing she saw.

"You don't like it?" Elissan was grinning. She tried not to look at him with loathing. Made herself look at the table instead. There, its blood seeping into the fine-grained wood, was a decapitated head. The white hart. Eyes that looked sad to her in death. Its crown as Elissan had said: twelve tines.

"I was surprised," she said at last. "And someone will have to wash the carpet."

"I went out again," he said. "This time with no one to hinder me." His grin turned fierce. "The white queen's promise is kept."

Sendara had come in. She looked fragile and pretty this morning in her lace dress. She halted in awe at first sight of the head. Then leaped to her father with a joyful light in her eyes. "All this time, we've lacked a sigil," she said. "Will this be it?"

Elissan took his daughter's hands. Both radiant in the morning. "Your destiny and mine, my love," he said. "It comes."

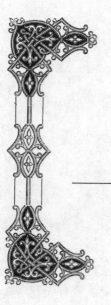

PART II

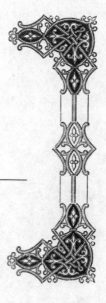

THE water was calm and it was near evening. Silver-grey lapped at black coastal rock. The color of these waters might shift a thousand times in a day as the sun wove in and out of clouds. Deep blue when it was high and bright, green when occluded, and just before sunrise or at dusk, that silver. And there were variations between: blue-grey and green-grey and silver-grey. All these variations, to him, signified one thing. All the days, from his thirteenth year until now, had added up to it. A feeling beyond thought.

Home was more than a place.

Dorn Arrin bent to the ground, picked up a round, smooth stone, and threw. The stone skipped six times on the water before it plunged.

The sound of light applause. Dorn looked to its source. "I didn't ask for your approval."

"Not in so many words," said Etherell Lyr. "Not exactly."

"Why are you here?"

"I thought I'd have a go." Etherell picked up a stone from the bank, and threw. His arm was careless; the stone sank without skipping.

"You didn't try," said Dorn.

"True." The other man looked thoughtful. Winds whipped his hair in a gold tangle. "I suppose I didn't care enough. That often happens."

Dorn looked away from him to the water. Grey and silver predominated now that the sun was gone. "I've been journeying a long time," he said. "It's felt like years. Sometimes I think I'll never see you again."

Etherell was now standing near to him. Without having moved. He reached out to touch Dorn's cheek. "If I see you again, I'll have to kill you," said Etherell. "Part of the job, I'm afraid. I'm quite getting into the role of Crown Prince. There are annoyances, but the prospect of power is . . . well, it's new to me."

Dorn didn't want to move. "Why would anyone want me dead?"

Etherell backed away. His arm fell to his side. "So you don't see," he said. "You don't know." He smiled then. "Soon you will."

WHEN Dorn woke, he had to remind himself where he was. That had become standard. As if his mind failed to grasp the changes. Each day was a new remembering.

In one way little had changed. He was in his old room at the Academy. Etherell's bed across the room was neat, as if he might return anytime.

It took a moment, then, to recall the current situation. That there were no lessons downstairs. No morning meal in the dining hall. The castle, once crawling with students, was empty. Or nearly—on another floor, Julien Imara might still be sleeping. At ground level were the living quarters of the cook and the groundskeeper, the only ones who had stayed. When Dorn and Julien had returned—finding themselves on the rock coast of his dream—it was autumn and the Seers and students were gone.

They had learned that soon upon arriving, once Owayn the groundskeeper and his wife, Larantha, the cook, had gotten over the shock of seeing them. Not that much could shock those two anymore, after all that had happened. Only one break in their composure—when Julien told them Valanir Ocune had made her Seer. At that point Larantha had begun to cry. She had known Valanir since he was a boy. The corpse dragged from the Hall of Harps had hardly resembled the man.

This was a memory Dorn Arrin shuddered away from himself.

He peeled off his blankets reluctantly—the room was cold. Luckily his clothes, including a cloak lined with vair and velvet that had been a gift from his parents one year, remained in the chest at the foot of his bed. He stoked the fire in the grate. Hardly a need to conserve firewood with a storehouse full and everyone gone.

Most important, of course, was that his harp remained on the bed-side table where he'd left it. Made of willow-wood and tin, it would not have presented as a temptation. Nothing he owned, other than the cloak, cost very much. But he wondered if his possessions had been left untouched from guilt, or superstition.

As he did each morning, he went to the window. As if in that view of water and mainland trees he might see some sign. Some indication of the enchantments that had driven even the Archmasters away. Birds remained, gulls and hawks and ospreys, calling to one another and the sky.

The Archmasters and students had fled to Vassilian, the stronghold given the poets by Lin Amaristoth. Though not the Chosen, nor Elissan Diar. Nor Etherell Lyr. Those last—that group—had done something rather different. The idea of which was a part of what Dorn Arrin strove to remember each morning. It was too vast and strange.

A Poet King ruled in Tamryllin.

As he splashed cold water on his face at the basin, Dorn's mind went back to the night they had arrived, two days ago. Julien Imara had brought them back. The journey had passed like a dream and taken months, which they knew as soon as they came to in the forest and felt the chill. When they saw red berries on the hawthorn trees.

Winter was around the corner, Owayn said dryly as they warmed themselves that night in the kitchen. Now one of the only rooms in use. The old man, who had served as groundskeeper of the Academy since before they were born, sat on a bench near the stove with his pipe and watched as Dorn and Julien dug ferociously into a loaf, meats, and fish. These were made more palatable with a vegetable paste flavored with herbs. Larantha still cooked, thank the gods.

The groundskeeper told them much that night in laconic statements of fact. More boys had disappeared. One of the Seers had died suddenly. One boy had, subsequent to disappearing, washed up dead on the eastern shore.

This was to say nothing of the strangeness that had the Isle in its grip, but of this, Owayn did not care to elaborate. He told them only that he and Larantha did not venture into the woods—no more than was needed to gather kindling. He went to the fishnets every so often to bring in cod and ling, and only in daylight.

"Ling?" Julien had asked then.

Finally, some levity. Dorn had said, with a straight countenance, "It goes well with sloe berry jam."

Of course that wasn't true, but she had understood at once, and sighed. Cuisine was not among the benefits of the Academy. At least Larantha made good bread, and the stews were not half bad thanks to Archmaster Hendin, who had lovingly tended an herb garden.

Where was Archmaster Hendin?

"Gone," Owayn had said around a mouthful of smoke.

Not dead?

Not as far as he knew, the groundskeeper averred. Apparently Archmaster Hendin had got the jump on the rest, and departed soon after Manaia. "He thought you were dead," Owayn added then, looking thoughtful. "The two of you. We all did. I believe it broke him to think such things could happen here."

Later that night when the fire had become embers Dorn had asked the obvious: Why didn't they leave?

At first they had stayed because it was home. Then, because they could not think of anywhere else to go. They had no children nor other family on the mainland. Larantha's only baby had died, stillborn, when she was nineteen.

The cook was clearing plates as this was discussed. There was a studied calm to her movements; Dorn thought he could sense emotion thrumming at her core like a plucked string. She was worried for the two of them, whom she saw as children; but she was happy. Happy they were alive; happy to have fresh faces to see and feed.

Owayn was either not aware of his wife's mood, or impervious to it. He went on. They had thought of leaving, he said. Seeking their fortune in the town of Eirne, or asking refuge in Vassilian. For now, the choice was deferred, because they could not leave.

This time of year, the waters around the Isle were choppy. It was unsafe to take a boat out. Only the ferryman had known the invisible paths to avoid riptides, shoals, and other dangers. Only he had possessed the skills to navigate these waters in poor conditions.

Dorn said, "Why do you speak of the ferryman in the past tense?"

"He's gone," said Owayn. "Got in his boat and never heard from again." He leaned back, wreathed in smoke like a dragon. His craggy features, crinkled around his blue eyes, were distant. "But people claim to have seen him," he said. "Larantha has had her dreams. Perhaps he isn't truly gone."

Dorn saw Julien shiver. He ventured, "What have they seen?"

The blue eyes fixed on him. "I can tell you what they believe . . . what is whispered in the taverns," said the groundskeeper. "That he is a ferryman, still, on waters more vast than these."

DORN knew he would find Julien in the Hall of Harps. At times she'd be examining the carvings in the walls; other times, gazing at the Silver Branch. It had changed. Clustered among the leaves, instead of flowers, three red-gold spheres in the shape of apples.

He and Julien had, the first day, risked picking up the changed Branch. When waved back and forth, the apples swayed, made a sound like chimes. A song of sweet melancholy that brought to mind long-gone summer days. But otherwise nothing happened.

Now as Dorn passed between the two statues of the goddess Kiara in the entryway, Julien looked up. The Seer's mark, often invisible, had gathered light from the Branch to her eye. Its glow, once pure silver, had warmed to the hue of a winter sun.

Shortly after the conversation with Owayn, he had asked Julien point-blank, "Are we trapped here?"

She had brought them to the Isle. She had said nothing of a way out.

Her answer was not reassuring. "The enchantments of this place and Valanir's ties to it brought us here," she said. "I don't know how to transport us out again. I can think about it."

"Or we wait for spring."

"Yes."

Where they would go remained unspecified. Julien seemed detached, wrapped in her own thoughts. Perhaps it was that she no longer knew her purpose—if she had one, still. She had completed the mission Valanir Ocune had left to her—she had carried a message of importance to the Court Poet, in Kahishi far away. What remained? She could go to Vassilian, Dorn supposed, and try to learn from the

Archmasters there. An idea with scant appeal. They had never shown an inclination to teach her.

He wasn't sure where he fit in this new order of things. According to Owayn and Larantha, the Archmasters were horrified when they awoke to what they'd done—when they thought they'd killed him. It was amusing to picture himself turning up at Vassilian, shocking them all . . . but farcical, too. He didn't belong at Vassilian, with the people who had cast him to the fires. He had studied all he needed, had been about to graduate. He could perhaps go to them, demand his Academy ring, and be on his way. That was a goal of sorts, he supposed; for spring.

That left months of winter on this island. Alone with the enchantments that had scared everyone else away.

When Julien Imara spotted him in the entryway, she called him over. "Look what I found," she said. The enchanted light that suffused her, from brow and Branch, gave her an air of command. She didn't know it, he decided. She was not the commanding kind.

Dorn went to her. She pointed to a carving in the wall. "This wasn't here," she said. "I'd have seen it. We all would have."

The rectangular tile she indicated was large, dominating the rest in size. Yes; there was no doubt Julien, and others, would have seen if it had been there before. Especially given its detail, more extensive than the rest.

The center of the carving showed a king on his throne. To one side of him, a bird with a long tail, embellished with shapes like eyes.

Encircling the throne was some design. Dorn looked more closely and felt a chill. What constituted the design, a series of spirals, were skulls.

Each corner of the tile had its engraved image. A castle on a clifftop. A woman with a harp, hand outstretched to what appeared a gate. A man with a harp in a boat, the wavy line beneath indicating water. And in the bottom left corner, a jester with cap and bells. He wore a mask that wept.

Julien traced the king's head with a finger. "Look at his crown," she said. "Does it look to you like the antlers of a stag?"

"It does. And see what he holds." A harp.

"It must be Elissan Diar—the Poet King," she said. "His reign will bring death. Don't you think it must mean something like that? When he is crowned, perhaps?"

"Surely that's happened already?"

Julien shook her head. "There is to be a ceremony at solstice time. Larantha told me. Dignitaries were invited. Word came of it shortly before . . . before people started leaving."

"I wonder why he'd brook such delay." Dorn thought a moment. "This carving," he said at last. The symbols, each one, tugged at him with an emotion he could not define. Neither dread nor fear, but with elements of each. "It is . . . a lot to decipher."

Julien did not seem to share what he was feeling. If anything, she looked revived. "Dorn, I don't think it's a coincidence we are here. Valanir would have wanted us to work this out."

"If the enchantments don't do for us first."

She looked up at him worriedly but did not reply.

HE didn't tell her of his dreams. Of twin fires opening to black. The certainty that this place of nothingness was intended for him. Strains of music, strange and wrong as on that night, would pursue him from the dream into wakefulness and daylight in his eyes. He would try to remind himself that it was over. The danger past.

Three nights, the dream repeated. On the fourth night it changed. Dorn found himself in the Tower of the Winds. It was the middle of the night, the time of song-making he knew well.

A figure at the window, wrapped in a dark cloak, turned toward him. Even before, he knew who it was. Though could not have said how. The Court Poet's face was tired. Her mark of the Seer a web of silver strands. She said, "I hope you don't mind that I called you here. We haven't met. I've heard good word of you, Dorn Arrin."

He inclined his head. "Thank you." Then looked around. "I hadn't been back here yet—in the flesh. It is the same."

"It is." She smiled. "It would have been easier to send for Julien Imara because of our shared connection, but . . . last I saw her, her mark emitted a powerful sense of its former owner. I wished to spare myself that pain. Perhaps you understand." She reached out a hand, and he saw how the back of it was veined with gold, and the dark stone in her ring. "I wanted to get a message to the two of you. Get where you can conceal yourselves."

"Why?"

Her lips thinned. "Within the fortnight Elissan Diar will gain for himself a new power. Unless we can stop him. If we fail . . . he will come for the two of you. Perhaps not right away. But you'll be targets—especially Julien, with her gift from Valanir Ocune. Do what Archmaster Hendin has wisely done. Find a place of safety."

He had a moment to take that in—her dark hair and cloak; the white, tired face with a glimmer at her eye. Behind her, a window that faced onto water and a night sky.

And then he was awakening to a new day. The persistent cries of seabirds confirmed what he had suspected last night, from the scent and speed of the wind. A storm was coming.

CHAPTER
9

THE city awaits its king.

Nameir stared at the parchment in her hand. One line, written slant and firm across the page. No signature.

Since the summer, in the course of the border wars, it had been Nameir's job to stand at King Eldakar's side, to protect and advise. The king had escaped the destruction of his home, of the Zahra—a destruction that some saw as an opportunity to wrest the kingdom from him. Since that time he'd been at war. He and Nameir had faced assembled bands, armed and mounted; archers from the palisades that lined the river.

Yet this slip of parchment, with its one line, seemed to her a greater threat than all of these.

The king glanced at it with no change of expression. "The city," he said. He stood in a casual pose, hands at his belt. A silver-haired ermine cloak draped his shoulders. He could have been the subject of one of those portraits that had graced the halls of the Zahra. It was only because Nameir Hazan had been beside him these many weeks that she saw that he still favored his right side.

He had taken the message from the woman who brought it, then with barely a glance at the paper passed it to Nameir. The messenger remained in the tent doorway. The hood of her red cloak had dropped to reveal pale, silver-fair hair. A face without expression, of indeterminate age. Gold chains encircled her neck, fell to a corded leather belt that wound around her waist multiple times. She gave a nod. "Her words."

"She doesn't say *she* awaits me," said Eldakar Evrayad with an ironic twist to his mouth.

The woman who had introduced herself as Aleira Suzehn cocked her head. Eyeing the king, as if considering whether he was stupid. With a note of forced patience, "She holds the city for you."

"Yes, I understand that is the crux of it," said Eldakar. "Loyalty." Now it seemed he might laugh. But reined himself in to attend to business. "How am I to know this is not some trick? This is the first I've heard from Rihab since . . . since Nitzan."

The Feast of Nitzan was when the queen had abandoned the king, to his humiliation before the world.

"You know it's her," said Aleira. "She said you'd know her writing."

"It's true." Eldakar looked thoughtful. As he advanced toward the woman in the red cloak, the stiffness of his posture was more pronounced. In late summer he had taken an arrow to the shoulder. One of numerous battles fought on the banks of the Iberra. Eldakar's men had succeeded in turning those of Vizier Muiwiyah back—they had retreated across the river, to their lands in the east. But only for a time. Muiwiyah Akaber was determined to take advantage of Eldakar's exile and defeat to assume the throne. To unite the provinces once more— this time under his rule.

"I don't understand," said Eldakar. "Rihab knows I can't come to Majdara. Muiwiyah's men guard all routes to the city. And my only advantage, at present, is that I'm not trapped in a siege."

"You have several advantages," Aleira countered. "One that the queen holds the capital against the traitor Muiwiyah. He tried to capture it. Her forces beat him back. Myrine wants you to know the city remains in safekeeping against your return."

"Myrine."

"Her name."

"I know," he said. "Her father told me. Each time I hear it, it brings to mind that I married a stranger."

This did not divert Aleira from her point. "There is another gift she sends."

"And what is that?"

"Word reached the queen that you were visited by Ramadian Magicians. That there are threats beyond this war—beyond Muiwiyah. A Poet King arises in the west. The enchantments he may unleash—these would make Almyria only the start, not an ending."

Smoke still rose from the ruins of Almyria. On clear days, from the hill of their camp, they could see it.

"So the Ramadians said," said Eldakar. Subtle lines around his mouth told Nameir that the wound gave him pain. "Before they fled to prepare their armies. They expect the threat will reach them even there."

"So it might," said Aleira Suzehn. "And to meet this threat you will need a Magician. Those left alive from the Tower of Glass are too young and green. Myrine sent me," she went on, proud eyes belying her words, "to be of service to you."

"Do you trust her?" Eldakar was pouring wine for the two of them into goblets of iridescent glass. Nameir was supposed to serve him, but there was no use expecting typical behavior of Eldakar. This cup of wine before bed had become a ritual. They would talk over the day's events, or the plans for tomorrow, before she went to her tent for the night.

A fire crackled in a brazier near the tent flap, left slightly ajar. This place was hardly akin to the luxury of Eldakar's former life. Maybe that was why he kept Nameir close—she was, in a way, his guide. This life was the only one she knew.

"I don't think . . . the queen . . . sent her to betray you," she said. "Lin Amaristoth spoke of this woman. How she helped her in the past. She owns a bookshop in the city, it would seem. But also knows something of magic."

"Yes." He handed her a goblet, and sipped from his. "I will have her watched. But you are likely right. I believe Lin would know a traitor. Though who among us is immune?" He smiled and Nameir could only guess what was in his mind. This was a man who had been betrayed by those nearest him not once, but twice.

First had been the queen. Then had been Zahir Alcavar, his closest friend. The first had been a public betrayal, making the king a laughingstock; the second known only to a handful. From snatches of talk she'd overheard between Eldakar and Lin, Nameir understood that Zahir Alcavar had been in league with the powers that had brought down the Zahra. Yet nonetheless they mourned him. A thing she, who recalled the horror of that night too well, could hardly understand. But knew it was not her place to question.

Aleira Suzehn—this bookshop owner turned Magician—claimed the ability to aid communication between the king and his brother, Mansur, who was stationed some leagues away by the Iberra. Her capabilities were limited without the resources of the Tower of Glass, but—if she was to be believed—there were ways she could assist them in this war.

Eldakar had settled himself in his chair. "I don't know why Rihab would choose to send a message now. She knows I'd wonder about it, though, which means I ought not think about it at all." He drank. "I can't shake the feeling that we are wasting time," he said. "Nothing has changed. We are still fighting each other instead of unifying against the larger threat."

He had returned to what had long been his preoccupation, since the Magicians of Ramadus had come with their warnings. The power that had destroyed the Zahra came from the west; and there was worse, they said, to come. They spoke of a wave of armies that would wash across the world.

There was no doubt they believed their own words. Nameir had seen fear too often not to recognize it in the faces of those Magicians. And in the way they scurried home.

"Lin moves against the Poet King," she said.

"Alone." He drank again. "I hated sending her."

"She would not have it any other way." Nameir didn't like to recall that time. After the Magicians had come with their prophecy, and Lin Amaristoth had gotten the idea to leave. Saying she was needed in the west, if it was from there the danger came. Until then she had been a participant in the war, and one who kept Eldakar's spirits up. Once she'd gone it was as if she'd taken something with her. Some element of luck.

That arrow had found Eldakar soon after.

The city awaits its king.

Nameir Hazan thought—with resentment rare for her—that, as usual, the queen maneuvered people to her advantage.

THERE was more to discuss before she left him. Food was about to become scarce unless they could secure another means of supply. This was further complicated with the onset of winter. Especially this far north. While the foothills rarely saw snow, heavy rains would muddy the roads. Disease would strike.

And more: Word had reached Nameir through one of their spies that the traitor Muiwiyah had sent a delegation to the king of Meroz, requesting an infusion of troops. No doubt he had made promises of what he'd do for Meroz, once he became king of Kahishi.

At this Eldakar laughed. "He treats with Mad King Krendak," he said. "Does Muiwiyah not know why my father all the years avoided dealings with him? The last general to think he'd achieved a truce with the Mad King ended up face-first in a bathhouse latrine. I'm afraid the Akaber dynasty will be short-lived."

Nameir could not respond in kind. In his eyes, beneath the laughter, she read defeat. The odds were piling up. If Eldakar had believed victory was likely he, himself, would have deserved the epithet of Mad King.

When she left his tent he was scowling over maps by light of a lamp, his upper body wrapped in furs. He had switched from wine to a porcelain cup with an infusion to soothe his pain.

Eldakar's brother, Mansur Evrayad, had rarely spent time looking at maps. He had left that sort of work to her. The prince trusted his instincts, which thus far had never failed.

She saw Mansur rarely now. A change in her life, after eight years in his service. It had been the wish of the prince himself—he'd asked her to serve as Eldakar's second-in-command. Her first time serving apart from the prince in years. "I can't bear for anything to happen to my brother," he had said to her. It had been soon after the destruction of the Zahra, when the grief was fresh. When each morning they'd awaken to the incalculable loss.

"If I could, I'd split myself in two," Mansur had said that day. "Half of me would be my brother's shadow. Never to leave his side. The other half would command his armies on the border. Nameir, you are the one who is nearest to being my other half. Will you do this?"

There was no way to refuse. Even when she knew—knowing him as she did—that he'd fashioned the request deliberately, with the aid of his poetic gifts, so as to make refusal impossible.

She was not really that cynical. In truth, she thought Mansur believed every word of his poetic phrases. Even when they contradicted each other.

She knew him better than most; in some ways, felt lost without him.

At night she had time for remembering. When it was quiet in the camp. She'd remember the years with Mansur, years that had shaped her. That had taught her not only of war, but of command.

As she did each night, Nameir checked on the sentries posted to the king's tent. Unlike other nights, she did not head to her own tent afterward.

Aleira Suzehn was not prepared for visitors. Nameir found the king's new Magician clad in a shift, though she wrapped herself in a red silk robe. Details that struck Nameir as incongruous in their surroundings.

"I see thoughts spinning in your head, Commander Hazan," said Aleira Suzehn. "You seem already to be somewhere else. What did you wish of me?"

"I was thinking I had better post a guard on you," said Nameir. "People I trust. This place . . . our fighters . . . they're not used to women in the camp."

"Even with you in charge?" Aleira smiled. She had strange eyes, yellow like those of a crow or cat. As she smiled, her hair fell forward around her shoulders. "Or is that a secret?"

"I am never sure who knows about me, and who doesn't," said Nameir. Eldakar most likely knew. But no need to tell this woman that.

"There are no guards posted on you," said Aleira.

Nameir shrugged. "I'm not like you." Even as she said it, noticed a scent like flowers. Though as sharp as it was sweet.

"Why don't you sit down, then, and tell me why you're here?" There was one chair in the tent. Aleira gestured to it before she sat cross-legged on her pallet. She was not so young, but slid nimbly into the pose. The Magician had painted toenails, dark red. These had been hidden before in battered boots. Nameir could not decide if she liked the effect, or if it was too much like claws.

She refocused her gaze on the woman's face. Had a moment to wonder if it was deliberate on Aleira's part to distract with such details—and then considered that men had similar thoughts of women's deviousness all the time.

Now that she was in this tent, her reasons for being here were no longer as clear as they had been. A combination of scent and allure, or something more? This woman was, after all, supposedly skilled in magic.

"I came to warn you," Nameir said slowly. As she spoke, gathered strength. "If you betray my king, the penalty will be swift."

"You care for him."

"This family is mine," Nameir said. "Beyond that, I've sworn an oath."

"What of your real family?" Aleira leaned forward, pulling the robe closer around herself.

"Dead."

The yellow eyes were fixed on her. "There is more to it."

"They were killed. A raid." Nameir shook her head. Whether because of the befuddling scent or the late hour she felt compelled to go on. "No, *killed* is the wrong word. It sounds accidental. They were murdered." She shook her head again. "Why am I telling you this?"

"And your family name is Hazan," said Aleira to herself. "A name nearly extinguished in this part of the world. Nameir . . . that would not be the name you were given. You took the name of a mountain cat when you became a warrior. Is that right?"

Nameir saw no reason to deny it. "You can see that?"

Aleira's face had softened. "I can see that you and I . . . we might have been neighbors. In a different life. Maybe our brothers would have played together. Our parents prayed at the same temple. Who knows?"

Several moments passed that Nameir felt she could see dance slowly before her eyes. She grasped for the woman's meaning. "You are Galician, then?"

A flicker in Aleira's eyes. The softness gone. "You can't trust anyone of the Evrayad line," she said. "Do you know nothing of our story, dear one? Don't you know what they did?"

"The father." Nameir shook herself as if out of a trance. "Yusuf led those massacres. Not his sons. And times are different. Mansur knows what I am. I believe so does Eldakar. They don't care."

"Not now. Not yet. Until one of us becomes too powerful. Or perhaps it won't be them, but their descendants. And then mark my words, dear one, there will be another massacre in Kahishi. As there has been time and again, everywhere Galicians live since our land was drowned. Perhaps until we are all gone, nothing but a word to scare children. Our books burned, shrines melted down." Aleira changed position, to lie on her side. She looked past Nameir toward the opposite wall. "I have done what I can in this uncertain world," she said. "I've cast my lot with the people who sheltered me. King Sicaro took me in when I would have died. He protected me. None molested me in his fortress even though I was a young girl, and considered beautiful. I won't forget. Where Myrine asks me to go, I will. Whatever I might think of her husband."

Nameir supposed this was as near an admission of loyalty as she would ever obtain. It seemed tenuous but there was little to be done but watch and wait. They could use a Magician.

She wondered, too, if the friendship with King Sicaro might be of use. Eldakar had met with the Fire Dancers' king. Sicaro had been resigned, rather than delighted, to meet his son-in-law. Eldakar was cordial and correct with the man who had sent his daughter to spy on him. In the end they'd agreed to a truce, which mainly benefited Eldakar—it spared him a war on multiple fronts. But if Aleira Suzehn could, perhaps, convince Sicaro to *help* Eldakar in this war . .

She betrayed us both, Sicaro had told Eldakar in the course of a long summer night of drinking by the Fire Dancers' tents. The only sign of emotion he showed. *My candleflame, my bright one. She was to spy on the prince of Kahishi. Not* marry *him!*

At this, Eldakar had looked stricken a moment. And then the two of them, both kings, had laughed and laughed.

"Your thoughts are spinning again," said Aleira, sounding amused more than irritated. "You must have many responsibilities, Commander Hazan."

"You can call me Nameir," she said wearily. "And—you are still beautiful." She rose.

The Magician watched her. "You are all alone, aren't you?"

Nameir spread her arms, relinquishing any attempt to hide. "I love the lords I serve more than my own life," she said. "Sometimes I don't know which I love the more. But to them, I am no more than a soldier. They have their own lives."

Aleira's expression didn't change as she stretched full length on her side. "I might be able to offer solace. For a time." Then she grinned, eyes turning up at the corners. "A temporary respite from all the spinning."

Nameir inclined her head. She felt as if in a dream. "You are kind to offer," she said. "I have—I have no experience with that. And my lady, I am afraid it would complicate things."

Aleira laughed. "You're right . . . more than you know. Such things do, even when one thinks they shouldn't." She rose too, now, and went to the tent flap. She pushed it open. As clear a signal as any. But her eyes showed no rancor—possibly even a tenderness. "You, Nameir Hazan, are a good soldier."

Nameir ducked out of the tent. Outside, the air was clear and cold. The moonlit grass pillowy soft beneath her boots; she noticed for the first time. She wasn't sure what she felt, but thought it was mostly relief.

As Nameir climbed the hill, she passed the king's tent. His guards were positioned as she liked. Moving on, she saw a seam of light beneath his tent. The king's lamp burning as he reviewed the maps. The borders, rivers, and bridges that might hold an answer. Some way of turning the tide.

CHAPTER

10

A HUNDRED times Julien Imara had envisioned coming back. A hundred variations depending on her mood. Sometimes she imagined striding through the Academy doors, head high, moonlight strategically slanting through the apertures to display her Seer's mark for all to see. In those moods, she could allow herself to forget that she hadn't earned the mark with years of study and preparation. She would tell herself it was merited for the work she had done in aiding the Court Poet of Eivar. And everyone who had ignored her, dismissed her, thought her no more than a flyspeck beside Sendara Diar . . . well.

Even this version of events, the most triumphant, had a discomfiting underside. She knew when Sendara saw her, saw the mark . . . there would be contempt. *You are nothing,* she could hear the other girl saying—or sending the message as clearly with her eyes.

Julien tried to glide past this, to the idea that even if Sendara sent that message, she would have to know that she had done nothing to stop an evil; that it was Julien, not Sendara, who had stood up to it.

Naturally when Julien Imara was feeling keenly that she knew nothing of the enchantments that had been forced upon her—she had accepted them, true, but that had been practically a reflex—her envisioning of events would dwell on the contempt radiating from Sendara. In those moods, Julien urged herself to prepare for that inevitability;

to get into the habit, before she and Dorn arrived at Academy Isle, of making herself impervious to contempt.

She did not think too hard about how Dorn could return to the place that had nearly killed him. She knew it was important but thought they would sort it all out when they reached the Isle. Dorn Arrin was older, after all, and knew how to handle things. A world of knowledge lay between sixteen and twenty. Through the eyes of Valanir Ocune she had learned some things, but even so.

All these thoughts she'd had in the cave on the north side of the Isle, where she had transported them. Later, when they reached the Academy and discovered what had happened, she felt shame. Of course events much larger than her were at work. She'd been worrying about herself, her pride, as the kingdom was falling.

Her role was clear. Especially after Dorn Arrin told her of his dream of the Court Poet. She possessed the mark of Valanir Ocune and they had the Academy library at their disposal. And there was no one to bother them. No hostile Archmasters like Lian or Kerwin. No students. No Sendara Diar, now a princess (but of course!). Julien would use her newfound powers as she was meant. With the aid of the library she would discover what she was meant to do.

IT was their first night on the Isle when the dreams began. She was on a horse racing down a mountain. Both things that would have been inconceivable in the waking world—Julien did not like to ride. But in the world of the dream it was natural. When she reached the base of the slope she looked behind her and saw another rider. A man, his white hair luminous in the sun. His horse just as white.

Involuntarily Julien laughed; it bubbled in her, joy at the race and the green mountain.

The man pulled up beside her. His eyes were blue as the sky, and he carried a harp. Gold, of course, with golden strings. His cloak sky-blue as well. "We will be there by sunset if we go fast," he said. "Can you do that, little one?"

"I can do more than that," Julien Imara heard herself say. "Right now I can fly."

He laughed. "One task at a time."

Julien had a moment to take in that she carried a harp as well. It matched the horse she rode upon: a bronze-like gold. She could have wept.

"We ride," said the man, and urged his horse to a gallop. She rode alongside but felt no jostle. The horse was hued like the sun. The sensation of flying beside this man, that they shared a mission.

In one dream, when they had ceased their ride they built a fire. When the moon rose, its light revealed the mark of the Seer on his brow. And then in the dark he told her tales. Heroes, kings, and queens lit Julien's imagination with colors bright as the fire, leaping and changeable as flames. She saw a pattern in these tales; felt their rhythms like familiar music. It made her wonder. She thought perhaps she had been shaped by these patterns all her life; that what she felt was not new, but a remembering.

SHE brought the glow of the dream with her to the breakfast table. Last night she and her companion had ridden on a slender escarpment. On one side, a wall of rock; on the other, a view down the mountain of waterfalls, and green, and mist tendrils drifting. No speech between them; but she felt as if they were in some deeper way communicating.

Each time she awoke she would hear a rise of music from that world, falling, and then gone.

That morning it was just she and Dorn in the kitchen, sharing a loaf between them. Both so hungry they'd torn it apart with their hands. But used knives, at least, to spread the jam. "What are you so happy about?" Dorn said between mouthfuls. At her answering grin, rolled his eyes to the skies. He thought she was a silly girl, probably.

It was their fourth day back. They'd found the strange tile in the Hall of Harps and decided on their course. They had spent hours in the library sifting through manuscripts and scrolls. Down there, where it had always been quiet and near-deserted—most students had no interest in books—felt most like the Academy of old. One could easily imagine, in the dense quiet, Archmaster Hendin appearing from behind the stacks to check on them.

As a student Julien had spent a great deal of time there. It was her only escape. As it turned out, Dorn Arrin had as well. As an advanced student he was allowed there at night. That, he said, had been a good time for such things. Quiet.

Julien did not say what she was thinking. *You were alone. Like me.*

What might have been different if they'd encountered each other then, in the depths of the library? Would they have found a kind of friendship, even before Manaia?

But no—Julien had been like a ghost to the other students. A girl, and soundless, and not much to look at. And Dorn had other things on his mind.

She never mentioned Etherell Lyr. She knew better than to do that. Not because she feared Dorn's bursts of anger, though she did, a little. But because she remembered how he sounded during the conversation she had overheard between the two men. She thought pain was the last thing in the world Dorn Arrin deserved.

Silly, silly girl.

Today they had decided to devote their research to Poet Kings. She wished Archmaster Hendin were there to guide them. His gentle, watchful presence in the library, though near-invisible, had been more essential than she had known, she realized they tried their hand at this task alone.

"They say," Dorn murmured, pushing the hair from his eyes, "that Darien Aldemoor and the Court Poet used this library. Something they found helped them to the Path."

He had told her of his dream of Lin Amaristoth. How she'd warned them away. He hadn't had a chance, in the dream, to tell the Court Poet that they couldn't leave. Today the waves danced so tall and white as to make a shifting wall of water. All the day it had rained, even as the sun broke through at intervals. Sheets of water from the sky above turbulent waves and a wind that could knock you down.

"It was Valanir Ocune who guided them, that time," said Julien. She knew the story, in a more profound way now than she had before Valanir Ocune had given her his mark. She could see it in her mind's eye—that box buried in the roots of the oak—as if she had hidden it there herself.

They sat across from one another in one of the carrels. Before them an array of scrolls, age-crisped and faded. So far they had found only one reference to a real Poet King—a man who had lived, not a myth. Or so it appeared, anyway. A reference tucked within another, to an occurrence so far in the past that little beyond its existence was known.

"If only we had the manuscript Elissan Diar had," said Julien. Well she recalled the way he and Sendara had pored over that page, shining with a near-identical radiance. She pulled back from reliving it—that sensation of viewing a dance of light on a far, inaccessible shore.

"I searched his room," said Dorn. "It was cleared so thoroughly you'd think he'd never been here."

"Sendara's too?"

She thought he looked at her curiously before he said, "Yes. Nothing there."

THEIR candles sank to stubs as the day went by. Words and words and words, crabbed and inconsequential. Dorn put his head in his hands and gave a loud, exasperated yawn that made her laugh.

They went to the kitchen for cold meat sandwiches and cheese. Owayn was there, about to go check his nets now that the wind had calmed. Dorn volunteered to join him.

"You'll be careful," Julien said anxiously.

His look was withering.

She understood. They were living so well because of the elderly couple's work. The least they could do was help.

"Take a knife, maybe?" she said.

"Aye," said Owayn. "I'll lend him one of mine."

FROM the kitchen door she watched them go. She knew Dorn was right, but she hated it. After all the stories. And why did they need fresh fish? There was enough smoked fish, flour, and preserves to last a good while. To say nothing of the vegetables and herbs in the garden.

But to let the day's catch rot in the nets was unheard of, at least to Owayn's thinking, so they went off. Julien sat at the kitchen hearth awhile, chin in hands.

She thought of Dorn's dream, how the Court Poet had come to him. To warn them. Yet it felt right that they were here. What would she do back home with her parents—await a marriage? She felt a stab at the thought; she missed her sister. There was no simple way to look at anything, she supposed.

The flames were hypnotic; for a while she watched them without thinking much at all.

Flames.

Julien was crouched beside a fire in the woods at night. How she knew where she was, and felt no fear, she could only wonder. She knew it was a dream.

Across from her, on the other side of the fire, sat a man. It was not the man who had accompanied her until now—though she could see her horse, tethered to a tree. Golden and awaiting her. This man, too, was golden: of hair and eye, even the tint of his skin. Maybe Dorn Arrin's age, or a bit older. She was so taken aback, and shy, she could hardly look at him.

But her harp was there, by the fire. This harp that existed only in her dreams, pure gold. She spoke to it and the ground. "I wasn't expecting *you*."

It was all she could say. She didn't know the name of the man who had accompanied her until now, on the journey that made her nights a marvel.

The newcomer's voice was as unsettling to her as his appearance. It had the quality of simmering coals. "I was told you had questions," he said. "It was decided we move to this phase. You can ask me anything."

This phase.

She shook her head. "How did you find me?"

"Not quite that sort of question." She could hear the smile in his voice. "Nonetheless, perhaps it's as well you should ask. The mark of the Seer summons guides to you in dreams. How else to complete your learning? Your first guide—he is always first, for everyone. He helps to recover what you've lost. What we all have, in the beginning. Until the wear and toll of our lives take from us that enchantment."

She dared look up. "Then why are you here?" *I liked him,* she thought, of the old man who had brought her this far. He had reminded her of her grandfather, a little. If her grandfather had been a happy man. Her looks had not mattered, nor that she was a girl. She had felt safe.

The man said, "You seek answers. About a great conflict in the world. Don't you?"

"A conflict here in Eivar, certainly," she said. "A Poet King with a mind to do us harm."

"No," he said flatly. "That is but a part of the story. But I see you don't know more." He stood. His shadow stretched across the circle of firelight, over stones, toward the trees. "Riddle me this, young Seer. Why return our enchantments at all? Why is what Davyd Dream-weaver did considered, in the pillared halls, a sin?"

In the firelight that reached across his chin and beneath his eyes, the man looked older now, and stern. She ventured up at him, "The world needs the enchantments."

"Why?"

She looked down again. "I don't know."

His arresting voice softened. "Because there are things at work be-yond what we see," he said. "With enchantments, once, we kept the perils of the Otherworld at bay. The world depended on us for that, though how many knew? Perhaps some magicians of other lands, some wizards. In service of that task, we worshiped Kiara; we prayed the White Queen to accept our songs and spare us harm."

"Kiara is one of the Three."

"Not to poets," said the man with a secret smile. "Never."

SHE awoke to something crawling across her field of vision. Her head rested in her arms on the table. Dorn was standing across the table, looking pleased. "We're back," he said.

Julien blinked. Saw the black shell and claws of the creature he'd set on the table. This had come from a bucket Owayn set down for Larantha to inspect. She had gotten out a round-bellied pot. The two warbled a tune together as they worked. The music of habit, days ac-cumulated like a long string of beads, tight-knotted. *Love, too,* Julien thought. Quiet, habitual, and strong.

Dorn patted Julien's shoulder. "Come along, sleepybones, let's get to it. It's to be crab stew."

EVENINGS were her favorite time. After dinner, Dorn was tasked to entertain them as they washed up. He'd taken up Owayn's fiddle and played a ridiculous song about a farmer and an assortment of animals; and it was the rhythm of the thing that mattered, the way it could make drying a pot or scrubbing down the table feel like dancing. And then Owayn took a turn with a song about a maid who had the hearts of all the townsmen on a string, so great was the beauty of her face. And as he sang he began to follow Larantha around the kitchen, as she reddened and shooed him off.

Later still, the two men smoked pipes, and Julien asked if she could try it. That didn't last—she thought tabak fumes were nasty, and screwed up her face. The men laughed. She and Larantha played a game of Hide-the-Badger near the fire, an easy flipping of cards that allowed them to take part in the conversation. Owayn told stories of Archmasters who had made fools of themselves, such as one who got himself stuck in a puddle of glue he'd spilled and had to stand there all night until Larantha found him in the storeroom the next morning. "Standing like a statue," she said, "if any statue could look as angry as that."

"And you'll never guess who it was," said Owayn with a grin.

Larantha rounded on him. "Don't you dare!"

"Let's just say," said Owayn, "that it wasn't someone with a sense of humor."

"But that could be almost any of them," Julien said, and they had to agree it was true.

When it grew later yet, Larantha spoke of the poets whose memories she enshrined. Darien Aldemoor had been a favorite, with his merry ways. She had known he was flattering her to get extra food, but he had a way of doing it that made it all right.

"That boy could break every rule and do it in such a way that you wanted to help him at it," she said, shaking her head.

"Marlen Humbreleigh was another matter," said Owayn. "We knew he was a bad apple."

"Don't say that," his wife remonstrated. "He was one of my boys. I knew his heart. He was only bad if you thought that of him."

In moments like that Dorn and Julien would exchange a look. Both amazed to be speaking, in ordinary terms, of people who had become legends in their lifetime. Darien Aldemoor, Marlen Humbreleigh, all the rest, eating meals from this kitchen as they were now.

THAT night she went up to her room, warm and content. But then the memory of her dream in the kitchen arose. The strangeness of it.

She put on a nightgown—her favorite of the ones Alisse had made, with mother-of-pearl buttons. The night sky caught her eye. She went to look at the stars, cloudless now, and knew she was awake. Before she had time to think, she was slipping into shoes and going downstairs. When she reached the main level she was tempted by the Hall of Harps. But knew her purpose lay farther beneath. She kept descending until she reached the library. Lighting the taper at its entryway she entered, then lit a lamp.

Perhaps what they needed wasn't hidden. Not obscure, but in plain sight.

Hours later Dorn Arrin found her. He looked pale, perhaps worried to see her there in her white gown like an apparition. "What are you doing here?" he demanded. "Did you sleep at all?"

She leaned on her elbows at the table. "Come here."

He did, and sat. Sometimes she could do that.

She ran her hand across one of the books spread before her, the smooth vellum. Finding the page she sought, slid it across to him. "Read this."

"*A History of the Academy, Volume IV*," he said, checking the binding. "Not what I expected, seeing as you're still awake."

She smiled, but otherwise didn't react. She watched him read. She was not tired yet, though knew she soon would be. Meanwhile she liked to observe his bent head to the page; the angles of his face she knew well. When he lifted his head, there was a crease of puzzlement in his forehead. "All right. It says the Academy was established in order to—to guard against forces from the Otherworld."

"In a time past remembering," she said. "But see what else it says."

"I did. That the boundary to the Otherworld is here, in the seas about this Isle. It's why they put the Academy here, I suppose."

Julien gestured further down the page. "Look," she said. "It speaks of a battle in the Otherworld. One that never ends. Between a White Queen and a Shadow King."

"This king—do you think it's Elissan Diar?"

"That, I don't know," she said. "But look at this." On the next page was drawn a shape, two spirals that twined together, made a circle.

"That's the shape from the carving in the Hall of Harps." Their eyes met. Dorn shook his head. "I feel no nearer to understanding this."

"The battle—I found more about it in this book," said Julien, holding up *Tales of Academy Isle*. "It repeats and repeats, in different forms, from the beginning of time and forever. The first poets were dedicated to keeping it contained in the Otherworld. Otherwise, it could overwhelm the mortal plane and destroy us all."

"Then how to stop it?"

"Something about their true names," said Julien. "The king and queen. It's not clear. We won't find everything in these books." She thought of telling him about her dreams since they'd come to the Isle; of the Seers who had come to her as guides. The words stuck in her throat. She felt that to speak of it, that secret, would shatter it. She wanted it safe.

"TODAY Owayn and I are checking the nets on the western shore," said Dorn over breakfast. "Want to come out this time? If the catch is good, we could use another pair of hands."

Julien mumbled, her chin perilously near the jam on her plate.

Dorn laughed. "I didn't think so. You'll sleep all day, most likely, then repeat the same folly tonight. I may start calling you Owl."

She pouted. It was too much to hope that he'd think of a delicate, perhaps more flattering name for her. But she was too tired for indignation. By the time Julien crawled into bed she thought she'd sleep for a year.

A FLURRY of whispers, of voices. Julien felt as if she were trying to wake, that something required her attention, but the weight of sleep pinned her down. *What is it*, she murmured. *What, what do you want.*

She thought she glimpsed the fire of earlier. Heard the sensuous voice of the golden man. But all from beneath her eyelids; she couldn't wake. Couldn't make out words, though from his tone knew it was urgent.

Danger, she heard him say, and she felt fear. And guilt. It was her fault; if there was danger, she was the only one who could stop it. Being what she was. And instead lay sleeping, useless.

The flames came into focus. So, too, did the man standing over her. "*The boy*," he hissed. "Why did you not tell me? She'll want him back."

"She?"

"He belongs to her." A note of sadness amid anger. "The rite of Manaia cannot be unmade."

She gritted her teeth. "Wake me," she said. "*Help me.*"

SHE was standing in her room, already dressed to go out. It was like Manaia—how well she remembered that.

The western shore. He belongs to her.

This time she couldn't find a way to transport herself as she had that night. Perhaps because she could not calm herself enough to breathe. Perhaps for reasons beyond that. She didn't know, and there wasn't time. She ran downstairs and out the door before Larantha saw her. The last thing she wanted was to worry the kindly woman.

Owayn and Dorn were together. That meant Owayn was in danger, too.

Julien ran out the front doors of the castle. She ran into the forest and made for the western shore. Desperation was an ice rod up her back. In her mind she reached out to the golden man. To the older man, too—her first guide.

Help me. Her breath scraped her lungs like a blunt knife. *Help. Me.*

Now in the distance she could hear it. Howling. Their screams?

No, she thought, running toward the sound. No. Those were not human sounds.

Tears blurred her eyes. *Help,* she begged. If the older Seer could hear her, he would have compassion. He would, she was sure. And that was her only hope.

First thing she saw, through the trees, was water. Blue now that the sun was high, sparkling.

Then a glimpse of white—two faces. Dorn and Owayn stood back-to-back. Their knives upraised. Surrounding them were large white shapes. Shapes that lifted their heads to howl: white wolves, as if answering a call. They circled. Julien saw Dorn say something to Owayn. He wouldn't know, of course. That he was the target.

Julien shrieked. With excruciating slowness, calculation, the wolves turned their heads toward her.

She lifted her arms wide, an uncharacteristic motion, as if something moved through her. Her lips parted before she knew what she would say. The words that came were in a voice she didn't know, nor a language. Something else spoke through her. She heard herself, and it was as if her voice joined a host of others: the old Seer, the golden Seer, and more. More and more. Back and back through the years.

A time past remembering.

And then she was collapsing to earth, her head striking the root of a tree. She lay winded, gasping. Closed her eyes.

When she opened them, Dorn was kneeling beside her. "Again," he said, and sounded anguished. "Again you saved me."

"They're gone," said Owayn, behind him. "Whatever you did, girl—we've been lucky."

She let herself go limp. Now that the voices had done speaking through her she had no voice of her own. Dorn took her hand. "I'm sorry," he said. He looked up at Owayn. "I should have told you. They—whoever *they* are—mean to have me. I've put you all in danger."

"Hush," she said. Finding she could speak. "I don't care about that. I won't let anything happen to you."

His eyes were as sad as she'd ever seen them.

Owayn said, "It's about time we went back." Determined to be stoic. "Larantha will be worried."

"I'll say," said Dorn. "The two of you—I can't thank you enough. Nor expect your forgiveness."

"Enough," said Owayn. "You're a good lad. Don't talk that way. None of us reckoned with the consequences of Manaia. How could we? The Seers who might have helped who know more than we can . . . they all ran away." He sounded resigned, maybe even contemptuous. "But you are a Seer, Julien Imara. You should have this. It was in the nets today."

He drew something from his cloak. A flash of gold. He held it out to her in cupped hands. A torc, such as had been worn centuries before, but not since. When she took it she saw it was indeed gold, fashioned of two entwined spirals. Fingers of black-green seaweed clung to it yet. It smelled of ocean.

She hefted the torc gingerly. It had a cold weight in her hands.

"I can't accept this," she said, extending it back. "Your nets, your catch. Trade it for a plot of land far from here, green and safe, and start again."

A birdcall broke the unnatural silence of the wood. Owayn said, "You are a good-hearted girl. But no." His eyes were thoughtful. "Through the years, the sea has brought us gifts. But never like this. I believe . . . it isn't meant for us."

THAT night the old Seer, her original guide, came to her. He looked solemn in a way that twisted her heart. Until now, it was only with him that she could be without a care. The world's sorrows had caught up to them, even here.

They were on the side of a mountain, on the path they'd taken through all the dreams. Those journeys had been conducted in sunshine; this time it was night. The trees outlined black against a starry sky. "You know what I have to do," she said. "We can't stay on the Isle."

He nodded. "Your gift today should tell us something," he said. "Let me see it."

Julien had the torc in her hands. She handed it over. Even in the night its color flared, yellow gold.

After a moment he said, "As I thought. It comes from the west." He looked downcast. "That is where you must go."

"The sea from which none returns," she recalled from her reading. "That seems . . . unwise."

"You're in danger either way," he said. "I am sorry. I was hoping there would be time to tutor you." Moonlight picked out the lines of his Seer's mark. "You know why the Academy was built where it is. That place is the boundary. To the west . . . It is said that past the border are hidden islands. I have never seen them. This torc—"

"You believe it's a sign," she said.

He bent to meet her eyes. "Take care, now, child. If you and the boy take a boat out alone, you'll be killed."

She looked at him questioningly, hoping he could advise her further. As if in response, he said, "You have everything you need, Julien

Imara. All but the wisdom of years, and no one can give you that. For that, you'll need to live long enough. I hope you do."

Julien Imara awoke with the torc in her hands, though it had been in the chest at the foot of her bed when she went to sleep.

RIANNA was shining. She gazed at the result of her preparations in the mirror as a maid laced the back of her dress. She heard a stir outside. Carriages bearing guests had begun to arrive at dusk. She could picture it: lords and ladies, perhaps some merchants, arrayed in their best finery, wrapped in fur against the cold. The last of the red and yellow leaves had fallen to be muddied in the streets. Winter was here.

There had not been time to make a gown specially for the winter ball, but the wardrobe of the prior queen remained. Under Rianna's direction, the tailor had altered a dress of silver jacquard, its embroidery like ice veins in graphite. This matched the jewels given her by Elissan Diar, a diamond collar of three tiers. It was the most valuable piece the queen had owned. To make sure it was displayed tonight, Rianna had ordered the maids to dress her hair in coils at the top of her head. Diamond earrings like raindrops, a gift that soon followed the collar, were shown to advantage too.

A queen had worn these things—the gown, the jewels. And, it seemed, a queen would wear them again. Elissan would announce their betrothal tonight.

"Leave me," she told the maid with a peremptory nod, as if for practice. Never too soon to begin one's reign.

Once alone, she continued to study herself in the mirror. She shone like silver and ice, but for the gold of her hair. It would do.

Her mirror now was long, silver-backed, with a gilded frame; the room reflected in it no longer the cell she had inhabited as one of Sendara's ladies-in-waiting. This was a vast chamber with red velvet hangings, carpeted, with a great canopied bed. The ceilings were gilded, adorned with art. It was the grandest room she'd ever slept in.

There was a blemish on her left cheek, she noticed. She had a powder, mixed with an ointment, that might conceal it. Her box of paint pots was close at hand—there were layers of powder on her face already, to make her flawless.

As she mixed the ointment and powder with a stick, she recalled the night they had returned from the hunting lodge. It had been a long, horrible journey back; Marlen, unconscious, tied to the back of a horse. The bloody head of the hart slung in a bag beside him. In all that time—the hours of travel—Rianna hadn't dared let emotion cross her face, lest Sendara notice. The princess was in a better mood since the death of the hart, as if it had renewed her sense of self. Her destiny was tied to her father; and he was destined for greatness.

Upon their return to Tamryllin, Elissan Diar had come to Rianna's small room before she had even unpacked. She had backed from him. And she remembered how he looked in that moment, trembling, almost as pale as the Chosen.

"I did a terrible thing," he said. "Can you forgive me?"

She could have laughed—there were so many things he could have been talking about. But of course, in his mind, the torture and imprisonment of Marlen Humbreleigh was not terrible—it was justice for an assassin. Likewise beheading the lords he considered traitors. The taking of her city, which he saw as his due.

No, he appeared to mean something else. But she needed to be sure.

She had stood there, her arms around herself. "I don't know what you mean."

"I think you do." He didn't try to touch her or come near. "That night . . . I felt that I was losing myself. Like the enchantments in me had overcome the man. I turned to you to feel right again, when I should have let you be. All I could think was—that I needed you."

Now he was kneeling on the floor, the cold floor of her bare room. She felt she had to step forward and cradle his head. He was crying.

"I won't let it happen again," he said.

"I know," she said. "I know."

"Marry me," he said.

When he left her room shortly after, she was wearing the diamond collar around her neck. It was decided.

The temple to the Three in Tamryllin, the Eldest Sanctuary, was empowered to annul marriages. Rianna's alliance with a traitor could be wiped clean from her life and soul as if it had never occurred.

Such annulments were usually frowned upon, and costly. The rules were different for a king.

Rianna turned away from the mirror. Her reflection was only the most apparent aspect of her days of preparation. The facade.

A knock. Rianna hastened to the door. It was one of the downstairs maids—Carille. After the door had closed behind her, the maid said, "My lady, I've had word."

"Yes? Make it quick."

Carille was very young, but clever. "It's not good news," she said. "He isn't in the dungeons. Chances are he's being held somewhere else, but Erec doesn't know where."

Rianna narrowed her eyes. "Well then. If you can persuade him to find out, I'll increase your payment. A pair of sapphire earrings to match the bracelet." They heard footsteps in the hall. Carille immediately knelt at Rianna's feet and began to fuss with the hem of her skirts. Looking up at Rianna—her blue eyes a good match for sapphires—she said, "I'll try."

"Good," said Rianna. She liked Carille, and the maid's relationship with a Ladybird was a stroke of luck. For days Rianna had watched, spying from hidden passageways, until that detail came to light. It was the only way she could think of to discover where Marlen was imprisoned. Once she knew, she still had no idea how to free him . . . but one step at a time.

"Thank you," she added, loudly, just as there was a knock. "You may go."

When Carille had gone, Etherell Lyr came to stand before Rianna. He was attired handsomely in black and silver, as became an Academy poet. On his lips a sardonic smile. "The king sent me to escort his lady."

"That was kind of him," said Rianna. It had, in fact, been her idea. Her words, as she recalled, had been along the lines of, *Make the wastrel earn his keep.* The king had laughed.

"Well," he said. "Let's go."

Always with the courtesies, this one.

She bit her lip and looked down. Trailed her foot so her silver skirts swished. "I know we must. But—" She made a helpless motion with her hands.

He laughed. "Lady, if you're trying to entrance me as you have the king, you'll have to do better than that."

She looked up at him with what she hoped were limpid eyes. She had bitten back a retort so violently she felt it go down her throat. "You are quite wrong," she said sweetly. "I was going to ask—a favor."

She saw only cold detachment in his eyes. Dealing with Etherell Lyr was interesting. Rianna was used to her beauty having an effect on men. Sometimes it made them want to mistreat her—there was that, certainly. In a man who preferred other men there might be admiration, or jealousy. Always *some* effect.

With him she felt she met the eyes of a snake.

Once he had frightened her. Now it was as if, after seeing Marlen tortured, she'd been wrung of fear. Or else numbed to it.

"What does my lady desire?" he said. Drawing out the last word suggestively. He imagined she desired him, she supposed. Well, that could be useful.

She affected a self-deprecating laugh. "Would you believe I haven't danced since before I was married? My father used to give a Midsummer Ball. Before . . . well, it was long ago. And you know how it is—I am the king's intended. Everyone will be watching."

"You're afraid you'll make a mess of the dancing," he said. Still with the cool look to indicate that he might believe her, but also might not.

"Will you do a few steps with me?"

"If this is an excuse to touch me, I suppose I can be generous," said Etherell. "Let's to it, then." He advanced to her with an exaggerated bow. She curtsied, hoping she appeared sweet and vulnerable, not like she wanted to spit him on a nail.

Then they danced. At first she was confused—she put her arm around his waist; he disengaged and reminded her that this was, in fact, the man's position. He placed her hand on his shoulder, his arm around her waist. He guided her through some steps. They revolved around the grand chamber, past the fireplace, past a landscape painting (undulant hills, a shepherd's cottage). Past the mirror, where for a moment Rianna glimpsed herself, pale and triumphant.

He said, "That'll do. Anyone watching will be satisfied that you can handle the role of king's consort." He smirked as if to indicate what he thought of that role, and withdrew. As ever, his motions were elegant. Almost elegant enough to obscure the odious words, that smirk.

"Now let's go," he said. "Elissan will think you've seduced me and have my head. And I don't mean that metaphorically."

To reach the Great Hall they took the main staircase: wide, marble stairs in full view of everyone. A sea of guests filled the hall. Rianna was aware of stares as she descended, at a stately pace, on Etherell's arm. She knew the sort of couple they made. Royal consorts-to-be, the two of them, both shining.

Elissan Diar's idea to hold a winter ball had surprised her. Until she saw the sense in leading to the coronation with a display of splendor. Word would spread of the magnificence of the king and his future queen, to every corner of Eivar and across the mountains. This was no mere upstart, would be the message.

And everyone knew who Rianna's husband was: right-hand man to the Court Poet. Here was a potent symbol of the old regime's end, crushed beneath the heel of a new king.

Rianna's smile, as she descended, masked these thoughts. It occurred to her that perhaps this moment, more than the intimate ones, was her most significant betrayal.

She hoped Ned's father wasn't here.

As they reached the final stairs, Etherell turned to her. Leaned towards her to make himself heard above the chatter. "I'm not convinced by this sudden attack of shyness," he said. "I know what you are. Like calls to like."

She widened her eyes at him. "What an odd thing to say."

His cordial smile was put on for onlookers as he backed from her, and bowed. He said, almost cheerfully, "I'll be watching."

No doubt, she thought as he left her side. But there was little time for more thoughts about it. Elissan Diar was before her. The gold brocade jacket became him. He extended his hand to her, said, "I can scarce breathe to look at you."

A space had cleared around them. Rianna was aware that people watched. She met his eyes with a fierceness, as if they were alone. Murmured, "Have you missed me?"

Since their betrothal—since the hunting lodge—she had not invited him to her room, and he hadn't initiated. He'd wanted her to know his promise held; from now on, she would be the one to decide.

He didn't answer right away. His hand encompassed hers. He said, "Dance with me."

That was when she noticed the music. Oh, this drew her to another time, even if this palace was nothing like her father's house. Her father did not have such a vast space as this, stairs ascending to multiple pillared galleries. But the fashionable music, played on lute and pipe, brought back to her being young, unspoiled, unbelievably carefree. When the most daring thing she could imagine was sneaking out at night to the back garden to meet her paramour, a poet. And never to do more than kiss. Darien had handled her carefully, reverently, as if she were made of glass. He had thought her delicate, breakable, and so had she. They had been right and wrong, at the same time, in ways she was still learning.

She went through the movements of the dance while her mind was, just then, in another place and time.

"What are you thinking?" said Elissan Diar. He sounded teasing, but possibly concerned beneath that. Would he worry that she was having second thoughts? Sometimes she couldn't read him.

But she knew how he would respond if she met his eyes again, so she did. "I was considering," she said, as they spun a turn, "that I may go to bed tonight still wearing this collar. And nothing else. What is your opinion?"

He trailed his hand down her bare back. "That depends," he said. "I'd have to see for myself."

She held his gaze the rest of the dance.

When they neared Etherell and Sendara dancing together, Rianna sensed it at once. The princess looked enraptured. Her partially braided hair flowed around her. Etherell seemed, as usual, distracted. Once in a while he glanced Rianna's way. No doubt about it—she had aroused his suspicions.

She tried not to think about it. To focus instead on her response to the music, and the gaze of the man she was to marry. She saw him struggling to hide infatuation. She thought she understood why. He had his pride—vanity, really; that trail of great beauties littered in his past. Somehow this time was different. That had become clear to her the night he gave her the necklace. A development she had not foreseen. Nor, it seemed, had he.

It had to do with timing, she thought. He had met her at a time of life when all things seemed significant. It had given their meeting, in his mind, a significance. Something it would not have had if he had encountered her when he was still on his journey to the throne. She would have then been a part of that journey, not the destination. So she believed.

She would have liked to ask her mother to what extent luck, as well as foresight, played into these matters. Though her mother had met a singularly unlucky end.

Near the musicians she caught sight of Syme Oleir, sitting alone, looking dejected. Dark hair stood up from his pale forehead as if it needed a comb. He wore a lime green jacket, she noted. With any luck, he wouldn't wander from that spot. But if her luck didn't hold, the distinctive jacket would be a sign. Few wore that color. It was not in fashion. It had most likely been dug up by the tailor something old no one wanted.

As she danced with the king, Rianna thought she could guess what was being whispered by the guests. *Traitor. Whore.*

I know what you are, Etherell Lyr had said. But he'd meant something else.

"When I first saw you on the stairs you looked pale," said Elissan. "Do you need wine?"

She smiled. "I was nervous before so many people," she said. "I'm all right now. Though wine . . . I would like that very much. Later on."

"Later," he said, and stroked the inside of her wrist. She shivered a little. A reminder: Not every response was in her control.

He grinned, pleased to see he could gain the upper hand. He was about to speak, but there was no telling what he would have said next. In that moment there was a shriek. Unmistakably a girl.

A shocked silence punctuated with gasps. People feared the worst. But Sendara Diar was not in the least injured. Her face was red, and she was screaming at Etherell.

He had backed from her, his face like stone. Nothing roused Etherell Lyr's contempt, Rianna thought, like outbursts of emotion. That was true of many men, and especially of him. What he said was low, unintelligible at this distance.

Sendara continued to scream. *"What is this?"* She brandished something in his face. Rianna could not see it properly from here, but knew full well what it was. A white satin handkerchief, edged with lace. Saturated with a musk scent. For good measure, with a smudge of lip color on it.

"Who is she?"

What made it amusing, if you thought about it, was that Etherell Lyr took no interest in other women. She had found nothing to indicate any inclinations that way. Nor towards any men. He was a model of fidelity, in his indifferent way.

Elissan Diar had broken from Rianna to make his way to the couple. No doubt to stop them making a scene. The king cared very much for the appearance of things.

Sendara was crying. She looked every bit her age in that moment, not a day older. "I'll *kill* her!"

Etherell was making a half-hearted attempt to raise her to her feet, but she pummeled him with her fists. He didn't look concerned, however, or sorry. He was calm. He was likely thinking back, to the exact instant when someone might have slipped a woman's handkerchief in his jacket pocket. The edge protruding just a bit, so it would show. There was even a chance it might drift to the floor as he was dancing.

Rianna had very little time. She glanced around for it and there—yes, there by one of the buffet tables was the lime green jacket. She moved slowly, trying to be unobtrusive. A problem: She'd had to make herself spectacular for tonight, but also needed to blend with the crowd when necessary. There was no such thing, she thought irritably, as a perfect plan.

The king had called to the musicians to resume their playing. Sendara had resorted to quiet sobbing, and allowed only her father to come near. Etherell Lyr lingered there—at the moment, his life depended on it. On convincing them of his innocence.

There was still time.

When Rianna reached Syme Oleir, who seemed not even to notice the commotion, she bent over him. "Syme."

He looked up. Dulled eyes looked past her, as if into a nightmare.

She gripped his shoulder. "You're coming with me."

A KIND of madness had driven her since their return from the hunting lodge. It seemed that everything that had come before, all she'd done, had been a game. Now it was time, past time, to stop playing.

Better yet: to make others dance to her tune.

Somewhere in the tunnels beneath the castle—carved in its limestone bedrock, older than any remembered king—was Elissan Diar's weapon. And this was somehow connected to Syme Oleir. She did not understand how this could be so, but she put it together. Working backward. Syme's magic, used to torture Marlen. The Fool's ring on the stairs. And there was the king's strange attachment to his Fool, which only made sense if Syme Oleir was more than he appeared.

An old tale had given her an idea. She took a satin purse, stabbed it with a pin. Then filled it with flour, the coarsest she could find—too fine, and it would spew like smoke and be useless.

These tunnels, extensive and complex, had intimidated her. She had feared getting lost. The flour would mark her trail.

In the homespun dress of a servant she explored through the night, candle in hand. Night after night. The flour sufficed only a few times, for by the next day it would be eaten away by ants and mice. Rianna wanted permanence. A system. She found another way to mark the tunnels. With a brush and a small pot of malachite eye powder she drew a small, glittering green "X" on the limestone at various turns, just below eye level. Signs to herself: *I was here*. Or she would draw an arrow, to indicate the way back to the stairs.

More than once, she wondered if her mother had ever ventured down here in her work as the king's spy, and if so, what she had done to find her way.

Her earliest explorations led to storerooms. Jars of oil and wine filled more than a few of these. That was only the start to what she found. One room was devoted to sacks of imported rice. Another to spices, rare and precious as gold—the scent of that room made her mouth water. And another, yet, to bales of fabric: wool, muslin, jacquard, velvet, satin, and more, of every imaginable shade.

Last and most interesting to her were the storerooms for weapons. There were several but she only took the time to explore one. A rack of spears against one wall; swords against another. An assemblage of daggers. She examined these and found one she liked; it was small, well-balanced, with a leather-covered grip that made it comfortable to hold. The blade nearly black and whorled with cobalt blue. It was filmed with dust; she used rapeseed oil from another storage room to clean it. Near the hilt was emblazoned a gold sigil: a hawk, its talons dug into a hare. It was unknown to her. Whatever dynasty it might have signified was past.

The deeper tunnels had a strong smell of chalk and dust, like a cave burrowed in the earth. As the nights went by, as she dared go deeper, she found other things. There was the room that contained nothing but complete suits of armor. They stood like warriors at a vigil. One hundred stood there, at the least. This room unnerved her, silly as she knew that was, and she did not care to explore it.

That was the last of the storerooms. Afterward saw her passing other chambers. Most were bare cells. Others, farther in, were furnished. There was a room with a long table and chairs. The chair at the head large and grand, intricately carved, inlaid with gold. Spread on the table before it, a parchment; upon inspection, a map. But she could not make sense of the lands it showed; it had no territories or landmarks she recognized, nor could she seem to read the place names. The letters shifted, evaded comprehension.

Beside the map was an inkwell and pen, a gold chalice and decanter. Everything was thick with dust, the wine in the cup like powdered cinnamon. It occurred to her that insects ought to have been attracted to it, but there were none.

She came to a room with rich furnishings of blue velvet and silver thread, all centered around a great canopied, curtained bed. The curtains were drawn. At the foot of the bed was a chest. On the wall, a landscape painting that showed a series of islands on a misted sea. Upon one island, the nearest one, was a castle.

Rianna had stepped inside, curious. But as she neared the curtained bed, a sickness welled in her stomach. She knew a warning when she felt one—whether it came of instinct, or something else. She had a sense of something old and watchful, and shut that door behind her when she left. Marking the door with two "X" symbols: *Stay away*.

On the night she went deepest yet into the tunnels, as she was marking a new turn, she heard something. She froze. Each night she came down here, she was risking discovery. And though she had tried to think of a clever excuse if she was discovered, there was very little that could explain her being here.

What she was hearing, she realized, was music. Her heart thudded. It was a harp, but was all wrong. No way to explain it other than that: it sounded wrong to her. Was like a fine knife gliding through the sinews of her body, delicately, twisting under her skin.

She followed the sound. Quietly, staying close against the wall. It took some time, but she had a feeling this was what she had been seeking all along. No matter how the strains of the harp made her want to turn and run the other way.

She came at last to a door. The harp was loudest here.

In the same moment, she heard footsteps. Someone coming up behind her.

She blew out her candle and sped her pace, passed the closed door, turned a corner. Flattened herself against the wall. When she heard Etherell's voice, she started shuddering, and hardly breathed. Her hand went to her knife, though she had few illusions. Etherell Lyr was practiced at killing.

"Open the door," said Etherell. A banging sound. "Syme. Come. That's enough."

The music halted.

After a moment she heard the squeal of hinges. Syme muttered something. Etherell said, "I can't understand what you think you're doing there alone. The king won't like it."

Syme spoke tonelessly. "Down here, none sees a monster."

"You're not a monster," said Etherell. "You're a servant. Believe I know the difference." Rianna could hear the grin in his voice. Knew, somehow, what lay unspoken. Those who looked at Etherell Lyr saw his beauty. He saw something else.

Almost she pitied him then—the first and only time.

"None but you can open this door," said Etherell. He sounded like he was reasoning with a child. "You're not supposed to come in here alone. What if something happened, and we couldn't get to you?"

They moved away, and down the corridor, before Rianna could hear if there was a response from the Fool.

When they'd gone, Rianna tiptoed to the door. It was locked. But there was no keyhole, no sign of a bolt. How, then, was it locked?

Under the door, shining out in the hall, the glow of green. A light she'd seen before.

No need to mark the place. She would remember.

In the days that followed, she had set plans in motion. These plans had led to this moment. A moment that saw her holding her shimmering skirts in one hand, while with the other she kept hold of Syme Olcir. He didn't protest. Didn't even seem aware of what they were doing.

She kept to the edge of the room. Dodged behind guests who were craning to see Sendara, her father, and her lover. No doubt they'd rarely seen such a good show.

You're welcome, she thought with a curled lip. She thought, then, of Darien; how he'd loved a good performance. She thought he'd have approved this plan—which did not necessarily mean it was a good one.

The problem had been, all along, that the Fool was precious to the king. If he was not near the king, he was under the eye of Etherell Lyr. Rianna had had to think of a means to distract them both. And long enough for her purpose.

They passed the musicians, who bravely played on. Past the great hearth with its crackling fire. For the first time she saw how Elissan Diar had chosen to display the hart's skull and antlers: above the mantel, for all to see. Bleached pale as ivory. Those sad eyes she remembered— that she could not forget—were gone.

"Come on, Syme," she urged, the one time he hesitated. They stood at the door that opened onto the steep staircase to the tunnels. "You first." She had to prod him forward. "Go on."

Her candle and tinder were there on a shelf where she'd concealed them. For a time, they descended without speaking. The music of the ball, the roar of voices, were all they heard awhile. Likewise the clamor of the kitchens. With time and as the dark increased, so did the silence. By the time they reached the bottom of the stairs, all they could hear was the highest pitch of a woodwind as if it played alone.

"Now," she said. "You're going to take me to the door only you can open. You know the one."

"As my lady commands," he said, and she startled. Every time Syme Oleir spoke as a man would, it came as a surprise.

In silence he led the way. By now the last remaining sounds from above had faded.

Elissan Diar might be looking for her. For both of them. Once he noticed the Fool was missing, he might raise all the castle to a search.

Her heart sped at the thought. They had reached the door. Syme touched his hand to the door handle. His palm glowed green, to match the light beneath the door, and it opened.

Rianna had had no idea what to expect. But just as she was attempting to grasp what she saw, she remembered: only Syme could open the door. She shut it quickly behind her. There. Now she had time to look, and consider.

Before her, at the center of the room, was an iron cage. The height of a man, barely three widths of one. For a wild moment she thought it was Marlen Humbreleigh but no—the figure in the cage was not tall enough for that. What paced within was a creature, glowing green, in the shape of a man. He looked familiar; when he turned to her, Rianna gasped.

"Come home," the man pleaded. He gripped the bars.

"*Avan,*" she murmured.

No, no, that was impossible. Her father was in the south. And indeed, the next minute, the figure shifted again. This time, a woman. Lin Amaristoth, looking pensive. Her eyes met Rianna's eyes. In the soft, melodic voice Rianna remembered, said, "I should never have taken him with me. I'm so sorry."

And then it began to change again. Rianna knew what must be next, and turned away. Determined to ignore the creature, at least until she had answers. "Syme," she said, trying to keep her voice level. In this light, the Fool's face was green. "What is that thing?"

Behind her, the voice she'd been expecting.

"I know what you did. But I left you. I can't expect that you'd wait."

She would not look. The thing was testing her. And if she saw Ned it might break her, even though it wasn't him. She could break later, in the privacy of her room, when this was over. Assuming she lived through it. Not now.

The Fool was looking at her with a glazed expression. He took her hands. He seemed desperate for her to understand. "It's a monster. But as long as I live it's mine. *My* monster. I am it, and it is me."

"No more riddles," she said. "Tell me clearly. What is your relationship to this creature?"

His grip on her hands tightened, his gaze into her eyes intensified as if to convey all he could. He looked exhausted. "To keep it prisoner . . . costs life," he said. He spoke haltingly, and she could see he struggled. For Syme Oleir, the business of forming words, clear thoughts, was not what it was for other people. "Slowly, slowly, with time, I feel them leaving me. The years I won't have. No songs, no love, no life for Syme."

"You keep it prisoner," she said, as it dawned on her. "And at such a cost. But why?"

"It is a spell," he said. "If I break the spell—if I let the monster free—Father showed me what would happen. Pain and more pain." He began to shiver. "Pain and more pain." His face crumpled. Rianna stared. Then let go his hands, to wrap her arms around his thin frame. He was a child, and alone, and she had not known with what suffering until now.

From behind her, Ned's voice. "We are divided by more than mountains now."

Remarkable how it knew.

"What *is* it, Syme?" she whispered. "This horrible thing. What's it called?"

He wept into her shoulder. "Father says . . . it is a weapon he captured. He calls it an Ifreet."

WHEN they surfaced, she kept hold of his hand. She'd half expected to encounter a search underway for the two of them. She had a story prepared: that she had found Syme Oleir crying in a corner and tried to help. That she had followed him downstairs, to his favorite spot, to coax him back to the party.

But no one was looking for them. The dancing went on as before. She let Syme go. As he slipped away, she saw him making for the tray of meat pies as if nothing had happened. Perhaps he'd already forgotten.

She stood in the entryway to the hall, watching the arcs of dancers: the nimble steps of the men, whirling skirts of the women. The music seemed to have more energy, a quicker tempo.

In the corner of her eye, a flash. She turned towards it. Down the corridor, out of sight of the dancers, was the peacock from the garden. Its tail like ice and silver. She met its black, depthless eye. Only a moment. And then it moved on, quick and silent, to the next room.

Rianna might have followed, but something told her she would not find that bird if she went searching for it. She felt a chill.

Skirts in hand, standing tall, she went looking for Elissan Diar. The hairs at the back of her neck were prickling. Almost she would have preferred to deal with a search party, with interrogation, than this. Whatever *this* was. A sense of something being—not quite right.

She went back the way she'd left, past the hearth. Above the mantel, saw the hart's skull. But not as she'd seen it before. Rianna stopped short to stare. Someone had laid on the skull—as a joke?—a crown of woven ivy leaves. And . . . now this was strange. Icicles hung from the antlers, from each branch. They caught the lamplight.

She saw the hearth was dark. The fire had gone out.

Rianna turned to survey the room. The dancers. Faster and faster they whirled.

Her eyes seemed to play tricks. One man who passed her, a lord she recognized, danced with a woman in a fashionable purple dress. The next moment, he held a woman in a glacier-white gown. Her skin white too, seeming to shine. She cradled his head in long-fingered hands and he was drawn forward, as if they would kiss.

And then she changed, back to the woman in purple. The man caught her up as the dance required; by the time he set her down, he seemed unaware there had been a change.

Elsewhere Rianna saw something similar. A young woman dancing with a stout courtier was suddenly paired with a different man; slender and in black, a silver-bound sword at his side. A mask made of black feathers framed his eyes, which were bright red.

When he vanished to be replaced by the courtier again, the girl looked momentarily dazed. Then resumed as before.

Rianna pushed through the crowd. She was determined to find Elissan Diar, to demand an explanation.

As she looked around, she kept meeting the gaze of one of the Chosen: they were positioned at all corners of the room. Still as stone. She thought their eyes burned with a strange intensity, a contrast to their pallor; but maybe she imagined that.

At last she found Elissan. He danced with a woman in green. The woman's lips were red, redder than any lip color Rianna had ever seen, as if she had been devouring rare meat. A thicket of reddish hair streamed past her waist. About her eyes, a mask of ivy leaves.

When Rianna approached, the woman changed. Now she was a pretty young lord's wife, of about Rianna's age. Rianna had seen her before, could even recall her name if she bothered to. Rianna tapped her shoulder. With an apprehensive, guilty look, the woman backed away.

Rianna confronted the king. "What's going on?"

He blinked. His lips stretched in an uncertain smile. "Rianna."

She took his hand, nudged him to continue the dance. Nothing to be gained in making a scene. In a low voice she urged, "Tell me. What enchantments are at work?"

He stared.

She leaned closer so none would hear. "Elissan. *What's going on?*"

Still he looked confused. At last, with some hesitation, "Sendara was crying. But she'll be all right. Come here, I missed you."

Seething, she let him draw her close. He held her tightly. He smelled of forest, she thought; of pine needles and winter.

His head pressed to hers, he said again, "I missed you." He stroked her back. Differently now than earlier. This time as if he tried to confirm she was real. His hand moved up to the nape of her neck, to her coiled hair. To the cleft of her jaw. Feeling his way like a blind man. "Everything's better now that you're here," he said. "You seemed so long away."

She circled the room with him, faster and faster, to a melody she had never heard. The musicians labored hard: they sweated in the lamplight. Even though the hall was cold.

No way to gather her thoughts. Elissan was no help; at the moment he looked like a handsome, vacant doll. A mannequin king. She had hardly had time to register what she had learned far beneath where they danced, in the heart of the tunnels. The creature that consumed the Fool.

Each time their dance took them to the edge of the room, there stood one of the Chosen, motionless, with that intent stare into the distance. Certainly not looking at her. Nor at any of the dancers. And yet—she thought, whirling around again in Elissan's embrace—she saw a difference, in the customarily blank expressions. When she looked closely.

As if they waited for something.

CHAPTER
12

"ARE you ready?"

Julien sounded as if she asked herself as much as him. They stood on a stone outcropping on the western shore. It was not yet daybreak; grey sky met grey, tossing waves. The winds were biting. Julien's hair tangled and flew, but she was composed. Awaited his reply.

Dorn hefted the Silver Branch in his arms. "As I'll ever be." She had told him he must be the one to carry it. "Do you think . . . Is there too much fog? To be doing this?"

Beyond what they could see of the water, the mist was white and solid as a curtain.

"We'll let him be the judge of that," she said, cool and distant. Unlike herself.

Dorn shivered a little. *Him.*

"All right," he said. "So it's to be now, then."

"Yes. Now."

Dorn inhaled some of the chill air and sighed it out. *Now.* He began to wave the Branch in his arms, slowly, back and forth. A strange motion; it brought to mind a ritual. The red-gold apples, which until now had not stirred, shimmered with movement: released their song. It was low, yet not drowned out by the winds and water; seemed instead to join with these. Once more Dorn found himself filled with a yearning for things bright and gone. As he waved the Branch, felt he released this feeling to the wind and inflicted it on himself with the same act. It pierced him like a kind of grief for nothing he could name.

Julien kept her eyes on the water. The torc from the groundskeeper's nets was clasped at her neck.

When she placed her hand on Dorn's arm, he took it as a signal. He ceased the motion of the Branch. The apples trembled once more, then fell still. And quiet. Now there was no sound but wind and the crash of waves. Yet the music had left its imprint on him; he felt an inward tug, that longing.

A gasp beside him. Julien was pointing into the mist. He saw the outline of a shape. A shape that soon resolved itself: A boat that rose and dipped with the waves; a man who paddled it. As the two watched, the boat pulled toward the rocks where they stood. Came to a stop.

Dorn released his breath, slowly. Now he could admit it to himself: He had not expected this to work. Was disturbed beyond words that it had.

Julien led the way. As she had led throughout, ever since the day of the white wolves' attack. The ferryman, standing in the boat, watched her approach. A face white as the mist, eyes dead blue. "Payment for passage," he said.

Julien unfastened the gold torc from her cloak and held it out. "Will this do?"

The ferryman paused, as if in thought. Or more—as if he listened for something. Then said, "It is acceptable." He took it from her. "You may enter."

Julien turned to Dorn, then, with a tremulous smile more like herself. "So we're for it, then."

He forced a shrug. "We always seem to get into one scrape or another." Together they climbed the rocks to where the quayside gave way to pebbles. The boat waited, unnaturally still; impervious to currents and waves. The ferryman waited too. He looked straight ahead.

As Dorn climbed aboard, he thought of how this was the same boat that had brought him to the Academy all those years ago. That boy of thirteen who'd turned every intent in childhood to reaching this place, to the treasures of knowledge and art that lay within.

And now . . . ?

"What do you seek?" The ferryman, toneless.

Julien had seated herself across from Dorn. She said, "Take us to the lost Isles."

Without another word they were pulling away from shore, gliding toward the mist. When it enveloped their boat Dorn could see nothing but white, not even his own hand, but they slid steadily on and through.

SHE had told him of the plan the morning after the white wolves' attack. She'd had a dream, she said. She'd had several. She didn't want to go into detail—it had something to do with Seers coming to her. To teach her things.

"I think it's supposed to be secret," Julien had said. Looking regretful. "Something every poet goes through, once they become a Seer. For a while I didn't have to talk about it, I thought. But one—the eldest, and wisest, I think . . . he helped me see what to do. How to get out of here."

They had to get out, of course. Dorn couldn't imperil the couple on the Isle with his presence any longer. It made him sick to think he had done so at all.

Whatever was coming for him, it should have *him*. No one else.

There was still Julien's safety to consider, but for now it seemed he must rely on her—she was a Seer. As for the rest of what she told him . . .

"Hidden islands?" he'd murmured. "Gods."

They were in the herb garden that morning. The plants in their great pots slick with dew. The light was grey, as it was so often on this isle. So often that it had become a part of his life. He had not noticed, not really, until their journey to a white-lit desert far away.

He recalled her face upturned to him, oddly canny. She had asked, "Are you really surprised?"

"You're not?"

She thought a moment. Then, "It's not that I knew. Of course not. But . . . there are things I have felt at times. I can't explain it, but you've been here longer than I have. You may understand what I mean."

He thought it over. "I didn't know right away, not when I was very young, that I was in a place of strangeness," he said. "Later, I blamed it all on Elissan Diar. Perhaps I became too much *of* this place to see it clearly."

"And I was always outside." This sounding shy, and downcast.

"Not quite," said Dorn. "Outside and in, is what you were. No one saw you. But you saw things. You still do."

She looked grateful, with a hint of tears. Dorn felt, alarmingly, that the girl's need was strong, and he could do nothing about it. What she needed, he was not even sure. Certainly he could not assure her of her value. He didn't believe anyone could do that for another. They all knocked about the world, he thought, trying to find their place, to feel as if they belonged.

That the Branch would summon a boat to them—the boat, the lost ferryman—seemed too bizarre to credit; and yet. So many strange things had happened—what was one more?

They'd told Owayn and Larantha of their plan. The two had accepted it without question.

Larantha had set to work preparing packages of food for them. Bread, oat cakes, dried fish, a jar of sloe preserves—things that would keep. And she worried. What would happen when they ran out? "Here's some money, too," she said to Dorn, pressing a pouch into his hands. A provision if they reached a place where there were people . . . where life was ordinary.

"I can never repay you," he had said to her, and it was clear he wasn't referring to the coin she'd thrust into his hands.

"Just stay safe," she said. Late that night she baked special biscuits for them. The smell, of cinnamon mainly, crept into Dorn's sleep and made him hungry even in his dreams. A biscuit with butter was the first thing he ate that morning. The morning they set out to the western shore, loaded with their packages, and the Branch.

Owayn saw them off at the front gate. "If it goes as planned—if the ferryman comes for you—tell him he owes me a card game." Then grinned crookedly, as if he knew very well neither of them would say that, in the unlikely event that the ferryman, lost to sea, answered their call.

* * *

THE night before they were to leave Academy Isle, Julien visited the Hall of Harps.

It had been an evening like the rest, with music and stories, no one speaking of their departure. As if there were an unspoken pact to make this last night count against all the rest to come. Julien knew that short as the time had been, she'd miss them both. She and Dorn had been privileged to get to know them, beyond the limited interactions of the past. Beyond what students usually got to know.

There were more stories of Archmasters. But there were others, too, that Owayn shared through pipe smoke. Of spirits of the sea—Singers, he called them—who resided in the wilder currents. They were blue and green, like the water. The Singers would catch a boat in their watery grip, and sing a verse: The sailor would only be allowed to live if he could supply a verse to match. So the game went on, back and forth. A sailor who succeeded would be borne safe to his destination with the Singers' voices surrounding them; those who failed were drowned.

"It would be simple for you," said Owayn to the two of them with a fond expression. "The two of you living and breathing verses as you do. But you won't encounter such things if you're with the ferryman. He knows all the secret routes. Ways to avoid the Singers."

So despite their plans for the morning they went to bed late, stretching out their last night on the Isle as far as they could. By the time Julien went to the Hall of Harps it was the middle of the night. She wanted to be alone there once more. *For the last time?* A thought that was either reasonable or self-indulgent in its drama; she wasn't sure which. They *were* going into danger. But wasn't there a presumption that to worry—to envision the worst outcome—was self-indulgent? Perhaps that was simply how she'd been raised.

The room was changed now that the Silver Branch was gone. That was one thing she had wanted to see—the difference. With its enduring source of light removed, the Hall was dark; even the gold harps dull by light of the moon. The wall carvings left in shadow.

Julien Imara lifted her flame to the new carving, the one with the king enthroned. The skull spirals. And in one corner, a poet on a boat.

A thrill went through her. Were she and Dorn Arrin already part of something foreordained—a story?

She wanted to turn inward, to ask that white-haired Seer she'd come to love. She wanted to reproach him. *You abandoned me. And I don't even know your name.*

Tonight Dorn slept with the Branch by his side . . . in case. If there was any chance at all that, for a time, it might afford protection.

The carving reinforced for her their other purpose. It was not only to remove Dorn Arrin from the Isle. She'd had to piece it together alone, with the aid of books and hints such as this carving; the Seers in her dreams had been oblique. The central image of the carving was surely a sign of the Poet King. The skulls . . . those were as dire a sign as she could imagine. That they made the shape of the spiral seemed even worse.

The coronation was to take place any day. *The turn of the year.* A time of significance for poets. Julien knew that, without knowing how she knew, or anything more.

It was perhaps too much to hope that they might stop a ceremony in Tamryllin from here—the edge of everything.

She thought of Valanir Ocune giving her his mark of the Seer. Perhaps there was a purpose to everything, and what seemed impossible could by ingenious means be overcome.

FOR a long time they saw nothing but the white of fog. The movements of the ferryman at the oars were steady. He neither faltered nor spoke. Once or twice, Dorn tried to engage him. He did not answer.

It was cold, bone-deep, on the water. Winter had come. Julien huddled in her cloak. Across from her, Dorn seemed not to feel it, so lost in thought was he, though the winds battered at him, too.

When the sighting of land was upon them, Dorn called out to her. Julien looked over her shoulder and saw a vastness: black cliffs rising from the mist. She felt frozen, and not from cold. This boat had signified a between-time where she could do nothing, make no decisions. That was about to end.

"There are a number of lost Isles," she said to the ferryman's back. "Which is this?"

He did not turn. "The first." The deadened quality to his voice unchanged. "That which is nearest the border."

The border. She shivered uncontrollably now.

"And its name?" Dorn Arrin, sounding stern. Perhaps a cover for unease.

The ferryman turned. His face still lifeless. "This is Labyrinth Isle."

It would be a long night, people liked to say. The solstice, the turn of the year. It was rung in with songs, as if these were weaponry against frost and dark.

This year there would be songs for yet another reason: to celebrate the crowning of a king. A man who shone like the sun. It would take place in the hour before twilight. Eve of the longest night.

Rianna paced in her room. No one was allowed in—no maids, no servants to attend to her. The carved-oak double doors of her chamber barred against intruders. She had to think.

She had failed. A thought implacable as a boulder.

Soon she would have to descend. It would be a day of festivities, of display. All of Tamryllin would turn out in the streets to watch the king's procession. Their new king.

It was a day remarkable for other reasons. It had snowed the night before in Tamryllin. Not heavy snow—no more than the width of four fingers coated the sill of her casement. Still, it was unusual. Rianna had seen snow only a handful of times in her life.

Elissan Diar would likely regard it as an omen. A benediction on his reign. Silver-white like the hart he'd shot, like the queen that visited his dreams.

Rianna knew the path of his mind. She had been as intimate with him as with anyone in her life. Yet she had not killed him when she'd had the chance.

The night of the winter ball she had thought to take her courage into her hands, despite that she very much wanted to live. She had planned to lure him to her room and investigate the wound in his abdomen as he slept—his weakness. It was likely she would be killed, but what did that matter? Or so she told herself, knowing it mattered to her very much; would matter to her father, her daughter, to Ned. If she'd been willing to die, truly willing, she could have put an end to this long ago.

She had finally gone against her desires, her nature, the day of the ball. She had arrayed herself in finery and planned to die. But that night, after she had returned from the tunnels with Syme, the king had turned strange. He'd retired to his room with a close guard of Chosen all around him. Rianna had tried to follow, even to use her wiles on those men. They'd blocked her path. Elissan Diar had not even seemed to notice the interchange, appearing lost in thought. There had not been another chance to get near him since. Always, the Chosen clustered around him. They even surrounded his bed at night, a measure Elissan would have scoffed at weeks ago. A living wall, chill and silent, between the king and the world.

Protecting the king, once their assignment, had become their obsession.

She had hoped uncovering that weapon in the underground tunnels would lead to something. But all it did was recall the cruelty of the man who loved her. To safeguard a magical weapon for his use, he had sacrificed a living boy. And it was through the Ifreet, and Syme Oleir, that he had tortured Marlen in that cellar.

And so this day had come, the one that would doom them, and Rianna had not even managed to give her life to kill the king. She was ashamed, relieved, and furious.

A rap at her door. Rianna knew she could not afford to ignore it. She slid the bolt, nearly fell backward, when Etherell Lyr charged inside. "The king wants you." His voice clipped and cool. "And you, my lady, are not dressed."

"Is that your business?" she shot back. She was done being sweet to this snake. "Why are you here?"

"He sent me." No need to say who. "He trusts you, even though he shouldn't. I told him, you know. That you aren't to be trusted. But the king has made himself more a fool than Syme Oleir when it comes to you." Etherell looked as if he smelled something distasteful. It made his appearance all the more elevated; a highborn lord in the presence of rabble. "You are to dress and come down."

"I take orders from you?" said Rianna. "I think not."

"From him, you do," said Etherell. "Be grateful it's me here, not one of the Chosen. You won't be so lucky next time." He turned away.

"Why? What do you think one of those boys could do?" she called after him, mocking. Her face and neck were hot. He strode on. She added, "How did you win Sendara back? I'll bet you had to work for that, more than you liked."

He turned. The fury that crossed his face a match for her own. Only a moment, before his features relaxed. He grinned. "I always, always get my way, Rianna. Best remember that." He turned once more and went off down the hall.

She stood there fuming. A useless spat, that was. Her pent-up rage expended, impetuously. But she didn't see how it mattered anymore. Perhaps all she could do was see how things went, and try to save herself. If Elissan Diar attained a sort of enchanted power today, that might be the most she could expect to achieve: escape, retrieve her family, and seek a place where enchantments would never find them.

And another, awful thought: What if it wasn't love of her family that drove her to think that way? What if love was the cloak to conceal a coward?

This thought as she stripped to her underclothes and began to dress. The gown for the coronation had been picked well in advance. Three gowns she had, for the three occasions that mattered most in her life at the palace: Silver for the winter ball; for the coronation, gold brocade. And a third dress, red velvet, belted with intertwining fillets of gold and crystal. The one for her wedding to the king.

Rianna was grateful that she didn't need a maid's help with the fastenings of this gown. And she knew how to dress her own hair. For today, she made a braided coronet of some, allowing the rest to flow unhindered. *A crown,* she realized belatedly; but decided the symbolism, however unintended, would serve.

Then there were the knives she strapped to her thigh and between her breasts. The latter knife viciously slender so it would not disturb the shape of the bodice; a silver-hilted dirk.

There may yet be a chance, and if so, she would take it. And hope her father would have the sense to take himself and Dari far, far away.

Music had begun to flow upstairs. Musicians, tuning up for the day's events. The procession would wind through the major thoroughfares of the city. Elissan and Sendara Diar would scatter largesse to the crowds, loaves of bread, and coin. Then would come the ceremony in the Great Hall, with the doors to the courtyard left open so the adoring public might catch a glimpse.

And after that, festivities, spilling out in the streets; wine and music provided for all the people. Elissan knew how to win their hearts. The city was fickle, Rianna thought disgustedly; they cared not that the throne had been seized by magic, that good men had been executed. They imagined a sun-haired king could rescue them from grief.

She had fastened the diamond collar at her neck and begun to choose out rings.

Another knock at the door. Rianna's lips tightened. Whoever had come to fetch her would get the rough side of her tongue, Chosen or not. She was not a servant, to be bidden and threatened. She put away the jewel box and went to the door.

It was Carille. "My lady." She was white. "I have news. It's what you wanted, but—but not. I am sorry."

Rianna felt sick. She pulled Carille into the room and closed the door. "Quick," she said. "Tell me."

"It's him," said Carille. "Marlen Humbreleigh." She swallowed. "I'm so sorry, my lady. He is alive, in one of the cells below. One of the most remote, and heavily guarded. That's why we had such trouble finding him."

"You found him," said Rianna tightly. "Then why are you sorry?"

The girl avoided her eyes. "He is unconscious. And"—these words tumbled out—"they say he's not like to ever wake again."

More music from below, a gathering of strings and flutes. Rianna closed her eyes. Then: "Tell me where," she said, hearing herself as if from a distance. In flat tones Carille told her the exact location of the room.

Rianna nodded. Then patted Carille's hand. "You have done well." She took the jewel box out from its drawer, fished the sapphire earrings from their compartment. "These are for you. For your wedding day. May it be a happy one."

"My lady," Carille said as her hand closed over the jewels. "What will you do?"

Rianna shook herself, as if from sleep. She'd thought she hadn't had hope, but it seemed . . . it seemed she had. Now that was done.

"Don't you worry about that, girl," she said. "Go on now. You shouldn't see me again. It is going to be dangerous after today." She reached out, on impulse, to smooth a curl that had come loose from Carille's cap. "Forget all this," she said, "and go back to your life."

THE ferryman let them ashore in a cove. It was carpeted with sand, strewn with seaweed. The rest of the coast was stony. As they clambered from the boat, Julien asked, "Will you wait for us?"

"I have other tasks," said the ferryman. "But you paid the fare. I'll return when you call."

They watched him go. The boat slipped away into the mists and from sight.

"Well, he's talkative," said Dorn. "Now what?"

"Now I go on," said Julien, "and you wait here."

What he next uttered was recognizably, and inventively, a string of curses. He glared from beneath his sodden hair. "I'll be damned if I wait here. What do you take me for?"

"A fine poet," said Julien, straight-faced. "Well-versed in the art of cursing."

"I'm serious. Do you think I'll send you into danger alone? You think that of me?"

She crossed her arms before her chest. "Look. It's not my idea. What I'm . . . what I'm feeling is that I must go on alone. You know, from the Seer's mark. What's more, I don't think you'll be able to come with me. The mark is what allows me to go farther." She looked up at him earnestly. "Dorn, I don't want to be alone. I'd so much rather you were with me."

"Then I'm coming with you," he said. "I'm certainly not waiting around in this cove." Adjusting the Branch, which must have been awkward to carry, he moved to stand beside her.

"All right," she said, resigned. And perhaps relieved. "Come, then."

They strode forward together. Julien began to pick her way over the sharp stones. Delicate white seashells with thin purple stripes were scattered in profusion, crunched underfoot.

She was alone.

"What . . ." Julien looked back. Saw Dorn standing in the cove, staring after her. "Aren't you coming?"

He looked dazed. Then deeply annoyed. "I can't."

"What do you mean you—"

"I mean I can't! All right?" Dorn kicked at the sand. "You'll have what you asked. I can't seem to take a step out of this cove. It's like walking into a wall."

"Oh," she said. "Sorry."

"Go on," he said. "Get—whatever it is you're supposed to get done, done. And then come back so I can get out of here. And tell the enchanted powers, while you're at it, that they are a massive bother."

"I will," she said, "but—Dorn . . ."

"What?" His look of annoyance increased. As if he knew already what she would say.

She drew a breath. "If, for any reason . . . I don't come back . . . You have the means to get out of here. Please don't wait too long for me."

He cursed again. "I refuse to be a pawn in this game," he said. "I will not be a fucking coward. I will stay here, in this cove, until I rot. This place will have my bones before I leave you behind. So you'd best come back. You hear me?"

"I love you," she said. Then turned quickly away. And didn't turn back again as she made her way across the pebbles. She felt the heat of embarrassment in her ears and her hands shook, but her tread was steady. She hoped it showed resolve. Rather than what she felt, which was too complex to sort out. Where the pebbles ended was a hill, steep-sloped and green. She began to climb.

The hill turned out to be of an odd shape, though she could only tell once she reached the top. She stood awhile to catch her breath. The wind was stronger here at the summit. It smelled of grass. She looked down she saw water, silver-blue.

The hill was perfectly round, and flat at the top. At its center was a hedge that flowed with the shape of the hilltop, in circular fashion. *Labyrinth Isle.* She approached. The hedge was tall as a stand of poplar trees, and dense. She could see nothing at all through the leaves.

She began to traverse the circle of the hedge. Below crashed the waves; above, a flock of geese flew crying past.

It took time, though she never knew how long, before she arrived at the door. It was oak, and nearly overgrown with ivy. She felt a touch of wind at her neck, featherlike. A murmur: *Enter, Seer.*

Julien opened the door to the hedge maze.

THE king's procession had returned from its rounds. It was afternoon. Rianna had absented herself, pleading a chill. Instead she had stood in the Great Hall, in her gold gown, drinking wine from a jeweled chalice.

First to enter the palace was a row of the Chosen. Their pace like a grim march. Behind them, the king. Elissan Diar was resplendent in white. All but his cloak, a rich crimson, lined with ermine.

Behind the king, another row of Chosen, and musicians to announce his passage. And then Sendara Diar and Etherell Lyr, looking to Rianna's jaundiced eye like siblings.

When the king saw her, Rianna raised her cup. "To the king of Eivar," she said. "His reign be everlasting."

At once, she felt cold. *Everlasting?* What had made her say that?

"Let my beauty come to me," said the king to the guards who surrounded him. Then laughed when they remained steadfast in place. "We must forgive my boys. They are zealous on my behalf. After, my love, we will celebrate this day. And this night, the start to all our nights together."

She nodded. Her fingers around the cup had grown numb.

After. Her eyes followed a group of Chosen who bore the crown on its red cushion. Her first time seeing it. It was not what she expected.

The crown was delicate, tall, and fashioned of what appeared to be white crystal. It was translucent, absorbing and containing all the light.

"Where did that come from?" she murmured.

Suddenly Etherell Lyr was at her side. "No one knows," he said. "It was in the king's room one night. He said it came to him in a dream. We are going to be an odd family, aren't we, Mother?" He laughed into her eyes.

"I pity your mother," she said coolly. Was unprepared for the sudden surge of hatred in his eyes.

Syme Oleir danced before them. He was dressed in red and gold motley for the occasion. "All is ready, ready at last," he chanted. He spun on gold pointed shoes. "Ready for the White Queen."

"Perfect," Rianna said, refilled her cup, and drank too fast.

AT the entrance to the maze was a stone bench. There was clothing folded on it. As Julien approached to examine it, the door to the maze swung shut behind her. And clicked, as if locked.

Dress yourself. That murmur again.

With only a moment's hesitation Julien stripped. First her cloak, then the dress her sister had made, dark blue wool, with lace at the collar and cuffs. In her underclothes and boots she shivered and inspected the clothes from the bench. The dress was black with silver trim. It slid easily over her head. And fit as if tailored for her. Though black, it was smooth and shining. There was a cloak, also black, lined with silver fur.

She'd left her bag behind in the cove. Unless she planned on carrying her blue dress and old cloak throughout the maze, she'd have to leave them here. She folded them neatly, not knowing quite what she felt. There was a good chance she'd never see these things again.

She knew the meaning of the black and silver. Had never thought to wear it herself. She was too new a Seer, and made wrong. So she'd thought.

There was no more guidance from the maze. Julien had a choice now—right or left. She took a right. It was vital to keep on, to hope there was a reason for all this. Ahead and around her were hedges, nothing else. The maze confronted her with a new choice at every turn. The hedge was so high as to block the sun; she felt cut off from the world, more than this Isle already was.

The sun was high when she reached a clearing in the maze: a space like a courtyard, paths leading from it in all directions. At its center a stone fountain green with moss. Rising from the fountain was a small, raised platform of stone. Sunlight glanced from the water, from the platform, and Julien saw what looked like a spark. She drew nearer.

There, resting at the center of the fountain was a ring.

The wind a gentle tease of sound. *Take it.*

Julien reached out carefully, mindful that she could easily drop the ring in the depths of the fountain. Inlaid in the ring was a single, large pearl.

She tried to recall the lore of gemstones. What was the pearl?

She couldn't remember. She put it on the second-to-last finger of her right hand, as she had seen poets wear their rings. The pearl seemed to grow luminous for a moment, but that may have been the sunlight. The day had turned clear and bright, warm for winter in the north.

Now she noticed that around the rim of the platform where the ring had been were carved symbols. She remembered these from her reading—runes. But the meaning of the runes was lost.

As she watched, the symbols wavered, shifted. Became letters she could read. One phrase, rounding the rim of the platform.

I have worn many faces.

It sounded familiar, as if she'd heard it spoken in a dream. She ran her fingers along the engraving. The wind was quiet.

Which way now? she asked the wind. Three possibilities branched from this courtyard, unless one counted the way she'd come.

There was no answer. Julien was left to trust to her impulse. Or was it the mark that guided her? So she went on, choosing at random the path directly ahead. Was again plunged into the confusion of the maze. Her pace was stately, by necessity, for the black and silver raiment was heavy. With time, Julien fell into a rhythm. She walked at a slow pace, chose new pathways, and listened for the wind.

She didn't know how long she wandered in this way until she reached another clearing. Here she halted a moment to stare. Surrounded by birch and willow trees was a gazebo of intricate shape. It seemed carved of ivory. And everywhere were flowers. Hollyhocks waved like tall dancers in the breeze; roses crept around its pillars and amid the latticework. Wisteria dripped from the archways, scattering petals on the ground.

It is winter, she reminded herself. But there was no arguing with what she saw.

She approached the gazebo. Of course she must go inside. She mounted the steps.

Then gasped with more amazement. Her hands went to her face. In that moment she knew two things: That there on the round stone table of the gazebo was the most magnificent harp she had ever seen. And that it was for her.

Julien felt tears prick her eyes. She hardly dared to step forward, for this dream to disappear.

Claim your right, said the wind.

She stepped forward. Tested the strings. Perfectly tuned, their tone was crystalline. Each note evoking in her a similar emotion to the chime of the Silver Branch.

This can't be mine, she thought.

The wind again. *It is.*

It was attached to a baldric of silver chain. When Julien lifted the harp, it seemed to have no weight; likewise when she slung it across her shoulder.

It is enchantment, she thought. *It will dissolve when I leave this place. Be a dream.*

It will not, said the wind. *It belongs to you. Now go to the final place. It is straight, to the right, and right again.*

Julien left the gazebo. The sun she stepped into seemed to cut into her, so raw was she feeling then. And happy. It was all she could do not to cradle the harp in her arms, to weep over it. She knew now was not the time.

Straight, to the right, and right again.

A short distance and she'd reached it: another door in the hedge. This one made of polished silver. She saw herself in it, and for a moment stood there mesmerized. The person looking back at Julien Imara, arrayed in black and silver, with a gold harp—with a mark that blazed even in sunlight—was without doubt a Seer.

The wind was wordless now, but she sensed a message on its current. The latch was encrusted with green gems, the same shade as the hedges. She turned it and stepped in, unless that was out—from one maze to the next.

At first it was dark. Too dark to see, yet Julien felt no fear. The wind was with her.

Time to wield your power.

The darkness lit suddenly. Julien found herself looking into a grand chamber hung with tapestries. A fireplace at one end, above which hung—oddly—the skull of an animal. Its antlers caught the light from silver candelabras that lined the walls.

Antlers.

A nagging thought, but this dissipated as she saw the people at the center of the room. How could her eye not be drawn there, to Sendara Diar, looking lovelier than ever. Kneeling before her was Etherell Lyr, bestowing to her some gift. Julien couldn't see the offering; whatever it was, the girl looked delighted. And he—well, he looked beautiful, too, as she remembered. She could not imagine a man who looked like him, looking at her that way. Any man, really. Not in this or in any life.

Did you want to know what has been happening across the sea, in Tamryllin?

The wind again.

"Not really," Julien said aloud.

Now Julien saw what Etherell Lyr held out to Sendara. A gold coronet, finely wrought and studded with gems. She bent her head so he could set it on her brow. "My queen," he said. "So you will be, one day."

She is princess, said the wind to Julien. *Someday the queen. Married to Etherell Lyr. And a Seer.*

"So?"

You can change it.

The image rippled strangely before Julien's eyes, as if she saw it in a pool, and something had disturbed the water. *There are myriad paths from each moment. The smallest thing can make a change.*

The image froze. Sendara and Etherell stood before the mantel with joined hands. Gazing into each other's eyes. Julien hated the feeling the sight of it made in her stomach—knew it for something ugly. She wanted to look away. But also wanted to keep looking, as if that ugliness were a beast that demanded to be fed.

It would be easy to make a change. The voice, creeping into her thoughts. *With the power of a Seer, you might reach in . . . influence events. Etherell Lyr might meet someone else before the wedding. Or his love could wane. Men are fickle.*

"What I want," Julien said, in as firm a tone as she could, "is to stop the coronation. That's why I'm here."

This is the power offered you. To act on your desire.

"It is a test." Julien felt a rush of anger. "You're testing me, to see if I'll do something horrible with this power. I won't. You can't tempt me this way."

A silence. She waited, hearing nothing but the sound of her breathing. And seeing before her that image, of the couple framed in candlelight. *You watch it all like some sort of shadow,* Sendara Diar had said the last time they spoke.

The agony of that night returned. Julien had felt discarded, worthless. She had revealed all she was, all she dreamed of, to Sendara Diar in long talks at night, long walks through the woods. And in an instant learned what it was worth. In revealing herself she had earned disdain. Nothing could eliminate the shame or how it hurt. Not her mission with Valanir Ocune, not Dorn's kindness . . . nor even becoming a Seer.

This is no test. The wind had returned. *There will be no consequence for you. No one will know. Your power in this is absolute.*

"You think I'm a monster," said Julien. "That this is my desire."

Reach out. See what you can do.

Just to see, Julien reached out. Immediately as she did, the image wavered. This time with more violence than before.

She had made so many choices, moment by moment in the maze, to reach this place. Turn, and turn, and turn again. Only to discover that those had never been the real choice at all.

Say what you want. And it will be.

"I want a guide," said Julien. She was trembling. "This is the Path, isn't it? Or near enough. I should have a guide, then. I need help. Please." The image had grown still again. The two figures, golden-headed and richly appareled, bent towards each other. They looked like the subjects of a painting.

The beast inside her frightened her. She didn't feel strong enough to confront it. Perhaps if there were someone else here—someone who might see how disgusting she was, how foul—she would have no choice but to mask her temptation. To do right.

There will be no consequence for you.

Power without consequence. Her most base desires, without consequence. How could such things be?

"You asked for me?" A man's voice. And then he was there, at her side. He was tall, and wore the black and silver, and a sword. Julien caught her breath, for he was handsome too, despite the faint scar down one side of his face.

"So you see that." He sounded amused. "Most people don't notice it. This place brings out what we are, I suppose. What we've done, and what was done to us."

"Who are you?"

"That seems beside the point. You asked for a guide." He tilted his head as if to get a better look at her. "Goodness, are you even sixteen?"

"Last month," she said defensively. "You seem young, yourself. For a guide. Oh . . ." She realized what she had said, and cursed herself.

"Young to be dead, you mean," he said. "I agree. Often we have no say in the matter."

"I'm sorry," she said. "That was awful of me."

He laughed. He looked savage when he laughed, with white teeth and dark hair that went flying. "I know something of being awful. More than a little. Now what have we here?" He looked at the frozen image of Sendara Diar and Etherell Lyr with joined hands. "Oh gods. Those two."

"You know them?"

He shrugged. "It is a contest, which of them is a worse nuisance."

"I have the power to undo Sendara's happiness," said Julien. "I must be a monster. Why would such a temptation fall to me?"

"You've answered your own question," he said. "But take heart. We each have a monster within us. Some manage to keep it in check, is all."

"That doesn't help," she told him. "And I don't believe it anyway." There were good people in the world, she was sure, who would not have thought twice about something like this. Something made Julien different, flawed at the core. She kept thinking what it had been like to touch that image, to make it ripple under her hands. She thought of Sendara Diar's contemptuous look, her smirk; the easy confidence with which she contemplated the world. Of the way everyone lined up to praise her, to tell her she was special, destined for greatness.

And what did Julien have? She had only become a Seer through disaster. By default. In her time at the Academy, she'd been invisible. Useful to Valanir Ocune, but that was all. Useful because no one saw her, or ever would.

The man watched her. He said, "I think I see why I was chosen as your guide, Julien Imara."

At the sound of her own name, Julien twitched as if struck. "Why is that? Who are you?"

He had dark eyes, she saw, that grew intent when he was serious. "I was . . . I am Marlen Humbreleigh," he said. Then smiled, though gently, at her gasp. For of course she knew who he was. "This I can tell you, Julien Imara. It may be true that you won't suffer consequences if you turn your hand to this—to undoing the happiness of Sendara Diar. But one thing I know." His voice dropped deeper. The voice of a singer, albeit one who would never sing again. "It is a tricky thing, to be someone's rival. When you join your fate to that of another—when you become the shadow to their light . . ."

"Yes?"

He smiled. "Why then, you are never free."

THE king sat on the throne. So far this ceremony had not gone the way Rianna had expected. She knew it was usually the high priest of the Eldest Sanctuary who performed the rituals, with prayers to the Three.

The priests had been invited, but watched from the crowd, in their gold-belted robes of purple. It would have been an insult too great not to have them here. But nonetheless, Rianna wondered if it was much better to have invited them, if they were to have no part in the ceremony. It was a break with centuries of tradition, a surprising one. She'd have thought Elissan Diar would want the support of the priests of the Eldest Sanctuary. Every king did.

Instead, Elissan Diar followed quite another rite, one that involved only the Chosen. Before the crowded hall he had stripped off his shirt, his impressively muscled torso and its scar showing to effect. The gentle light of sunset caught the droplets that one of the Chosen sprinkled on Elissan's naked shoulders from a golden bowl.

"Kiara," Elissan called, "see me cleansed. The last rite of purification is performed."

An uneasy stir in the crowd. It comprised nobles, mostly, and landed gentry, and the wealthier merchants and artisans. Just outside the doors rank dissolved, and anyone who managed to elbow their way through could bear witness to the rite.

To invoke Kiara alone of the Three was forbidden. A heresy. Though one that throughout the centuries poets, without fanfare, had practiced. Elissan Diar now made the heresy public, legitimized it as king.

After the sprinkling of the water, Elissan was given a white towel to dry himself. And then a white tunic, belted with gold, which he put on.

Rianna wondered if the city had ever seen a display quite like this.

"Kiara," said Elissan Diar. "I clothe myself in pure garments, to honor thee." That was when he sat upon the throne. On the dais, to either side, three Chosen stood. Others took various positions on the steps. They seemed not to notice the ceremony, yet were perfectly attuned to Elissan's movements, as if he was their center. Rianna imagined that if someone were to, for example, fling a knife at the king right now, these men would throw themselves in its path. There was no misreading their intensity by this time; they were, one and all, prepared to die.

One of the Chosen held the red cushion where reposed the crystal crown. "Kiara." Elissan's voice. "See my coronation dedicated to your worship, now and for always. Everlasting."

Everlasting. Rianna swallowed hard. She was far from the dais, from everything. Her failure a knot in her throat.

The crown was set on Elissan Diar's head. He looked down at those assembled. His expression one of beatific solemnity. As if at last he was at peace. The crown with its intricate design seemed to writhe, its points to grow and twist as if it were alive. Its pale glow settled upon him.

In its light, the mark of the Seer blazed for all to see.

Etherell Lyr spoke then, from the last step of the dais. "Behold, the Poet King."

Clearly this had been rehearsed. The people responded, with hesitation, "Behold, the King."

"Long may he reign."

They were more comfortable with such terms. "Long may he reign!"

Elissan Diar lifted his arms. In the glow of the crown he was magnificent. "And now, rejoice!"

The musicians in the upper balcony began to play a triumphant air.

But there was a disturbance in the crowd. Rianna craned her neck to see. And had only a moment to wonder before people started running in all directions, and she saw.

At the center of the room, in a space cleared by fleeing spectators, was a woman. But that was not an apt way to describe her. She was taller than most men, her skin whiter than alabaster, her gown white. The hair that flowed to her waist was reddened gold. Around and about her was light, pale as the glow of the crystal crown.

The woman's mouth was blood-red, her teeth very white as she smiled at Elissan Diar.

He regarded her open-mouthed. Then said, "The White Queen." He rose from his throne, and bowed. "You honor me with your presence."

She laughed, a tinkle like broken glass. "You have summoned me," she said. "And for that I shall honor you." Her hands reached out, long-fingered, and made a motion of twisting together.

Elissan's head was gone. A mess of blood exploded from his shoulders. Shrieks filled the hall.

"A painless death is, it is said, the greatest boon a mortal might receive," said the woman. "So I have given thee, little poet. How kind of you to summon me to your realm. It will offer much amusement."

Rianna was cold and reeling. Her wits returned enough for her to recall one thing. Sendara. The girl was screaming nearby. Rianna grabbed her shoulder. "Gods, girl," she said, hoarsely. Sendara couldn't see her, couldn't seem to see anything. Her eyes stared and she was shaking. Rianna spotted one of the priests hiding behind a chair. "You," she hissed. "Take the princess to the Sanctuary. *Now*." Then turned back to the chaos of the room. She wasn't sure what to do, but that was one less thing to worry about. She crouched behind a pillar.

So she saw the Chosen gather before the woman in white. More were coming, from other parts of the castle, to join their comrades. At first she expected them to attack. They'd been so committed to protecting Elissan.

They assembled before the dais. The woman watched them come. Their movements were ponderous as ever, their faces blank. Slowly they gathered before her like ants to honey. And then, to a man, they knelt. Their prostration so deep that their foreheads touched the floor.

"Arise, my deathless ones," said the woman. She surveyed them with what might have passed, with her, for affection. A delicate smile on her lips. "How long I have trained you to my service. Over many nights claimed you for my own. And now there is much to do." The young men stood at attention. None looked back at the corpse on the throne, nor at the blood that coursed in great gouts down the steps.

Smiling still, she said, "It is time we went to war."

14

It was dusk when Aleira Suzehn climbed from the watchtower. When she reached the ground she staggered and nearly fell. Nameir, who was keeping watch below, went to her. "Are you all right, Magician?"

The face that turned to hers was drained white. "It's happened. As the omens portended. But to feel it, and *see* it . . ." Aleira stumbled again. Nameir caught her arm. The Magician forced a smile. "You'll think I'm drunk," she said. "But no, I was watching the stars as always. But this time . . . I must see Eldakar at once."

Julien Imara had closed her eyes so she would not see the bright image before her anymore. "You. Powers. Whatever you are." She realized she had no idea whom to address. She had thought of it as a wind, but of course it was more than that. "I will not do it. You hear me? Let fate take its course."

I will be free, she told herself, a wild hope; a prayer.

There was no response. She opened her eyes, turned to Marlen Humbreleigh. "I hope that did it."

"It does." He motioned with his hand. The image of Sendara Diar and Etherell Lyr was dispelled. Now she and Marlen were alone in what appeared a corridor of stone.

"So these . . . powers, whatever they are," Julien said. "They must be

good, ultimately. Sending a guide who would convince me to do right."
The idea was comforting.

Marlen shrugged. "I didn't convince you of anything," he said. "Had
you been bent on the other choice . . . My presence would have helped
there, too. I could not have judged you—not when I myself have done
the same."

That was less encouraging. "I hadn't thought of that."

"All the Otherworld is double-edged," he said. "Who we are, what
we decide, plays into whether it ends up good or bad. So it seems to me.
Though I haven't been dead very long."

"I'm sorry you're dead," she said, and he laughed. She blushed; it had
been a silly thing to say.

"Me too," he said. "There are things I would have liked to have done.
And at least one person I leave behind who cares for me. That used to
seem like not enough. Until I learned that some don't have even that.
And I had done nothing to deserve it. It was a gift."

Julien clutched the harp close to her. Thinking of unexpected gifts.
Even if she was alone for the rest of her life, she was a Seer. And with a
harp like this. Surely that meant something? Even if there was no one
who looked out for her; even if there never would be.

"What now?" she said. "I need to stop the coronation."

Marlen shook his head. "That was never a possibility. Nothing could
have stopped it."

Julien looked at him with dismay. "You mean to say *it's happened*."

"Oh yes," he said. "And if you feel out of sorts about that, think how
I feel. I gave my life to do the impossible. To stop a thing that was foreordained. Marilla would be furious."

He shook his head with new ruefulness. Then turned his attention
back to Julien. "But you are a Seer, at the center of Labyrinth Isle.
There is power in that. And I must leave you."

"Wait," she said. "Is there anything . . . anything at all you can tell
me? That might be of use?"

He laughed. "The world has come to a sorry pass when its youth
ask me for advice. No, Julien. I am not wise. I am only a rake who was
granted a second chance." He looked her over, then, in a way that made
her blush. "That is a lovely dress, you know. Quite becoming. Well.
Good luck."

He was gone before she could say goodbye, or thank him. He *had* helped, she thought, whatever he said about it. He had shown her that to be someone's shadow was not fated. It was a choice.

It was too late to tell him so.

Marlen Humbreleigh, gone. The last of the three of that ballad, lost with the rest. The fox, the hound, the snake. That story had reached an ending.

Double-edged, to have gained his help through death.

And she was alone in a stone corridor at the heart of Labyrinth Isle. Julien Imara, who was accustomed to being alone more often than not, had never felt so alone in her life. But a mark of the Seer lit her way in the corridor, and there was the harp. That was hers. Despite everything.

That, and an end to choices, helped her move forward into the unknown dark.

RIANNA crawled on her knees. The White Queen was saying things to the Chosen in a low, musical voice, but Rianna could not concentrate on that; her attention was on staying out of sight. She crawled to a pillar and waited until the Queen's gaze was diverted the opposite way. Then crawled to another. She did not even know if the woman would care if she *did* see her—perhaps she'd dismiss her as inconsequential, a flea. On the other hand, she might decide to make Rianna's head explode regardless. For the amusement of it.

That image would never leave her mind. Not as long as she lived.

When Rianna reached the last pillar—the one right before the exit to the hallway—she took a moment to catch her breath. Her heartbeat impossibly loud in her ears. Rush, rush, rush.

Blood so red.

She heard the woman speak. "We depart at midnight," she said. "I know you dear mortals like to rule from buildings like this, but I will not confine myself. Certainly not in this hovel. We take to the road and gather folk to us. Whoever can be—persuaded." She laughed; again a sound that brought to mind, for Rianna, things broken and destroyed. But also a strange beauty.

Rianna crawled out, into the hallway. With effort she stood—all that time on her knees had made her legs seize up. Her skirts were slathered in blood and dirt. But there was no time to waste. She had one idea. And not a great distance to go in order to test the theory.

The alternative—if she was wrong—was to run, run, run as far as she could before the midnight bell.

Or she could look for Marlen, see how far she got doing that. Hold his hand one more time, to see him off. She didn't know if that made sense, if she wanted to preserve herself for her family. There had never been anyone to guide her in these matters; even the imagined guiding hand of her mother had been a fantasy. Something she had told herself, a story.

The truth was she had never had a guide. No assurance that she did right. She'd had her rage, that was all. The only constant.

It turned out her theory was correct. Syme Oleir was where she'd hoped he'd be, munching pastries in the abandoned pantry. But of course Syme had not had the sense to run away like the rest of the palace staff. And of course he'd come for food. Thank goodness, thank all the gods, that he was so predictable. She crept up to him. "Syme," she whispered.

He looked up at her. "My lady."

"You were right," she said. "The White Queen has come."

"Yes," he said, though it wasn't clear if he understood. "Father got his reward. And I was hungry."

"His . . ." She shook her head. There was no seeing inside the darkened mind of this boy. "Syme, we need to go downstairs. Please."

He held up the biscuit he was eating. "When I'm finished."

She snatched it from him and dashed it to the floor. He looked at her as if she'd killed someone, with shocked horror.

She made a noise of impatience. "Take me downstairs, and I'll give you three more biscuits like that. With jam."

His horror turned instantly to contemplation. "Jam." He looked at her earnestly. "I want the blackberry."

"Fine." She took his arm. "The White Queen will kill us if she finds us here. Do you want that? I don't think so. There's no jam for dead people. Come on." With each prompting she urged him with a tug of the arm toward the stairs. At last he went of his own accord, though not without a longing glance back at the pantry.

It seemed an eternity in the tunnels. By the time they reached the door to the room with the Ifreet, she thought she'd jump out of her skin. And now it seemed Syme had had a chance to think about what they were doing. He looked at her with new apprehension.

"Open it," she commanded, as if she were queen after all, and he did. The Ifreet paced the cage. The only source of light in that room a poisoned green. It barely seemed to notice them come in. Its shape was like a man, but featureless and green. It muttered to itself, taking no notice of them. A small mercy.

"You control this creature, Syme," she said. "And we have to leave. Can it come with you?"

He looked fearful. "It is always with me," he said. A sad, serious tone unlike himself. "The cage is . . . the cage is for studying. Father wanted to study it. *To observe its behavior*, he said."

"Well, that's over with," she said. "We must take it away. Before the White Queen finds us."

"Quite a plan."

Rianna spun around. A figure stood in the doorway. By light of the Ifreet gleamed teeth, a grin. But she knew who it was even before he stepped into the room.

His sword was drawn. "I don't need to harm anyone," said Etherell Lyr. "Syme, take the Ifreet as Father showed us. And then let's be off. You and me—we're family." He turned his grin on Rianna. "So kind of you to open the door."

"You followed us." She had drawn the knife from her bodice. Was stalling for time, trying to think.

She was no match for that sword.

Etherell took another step into the light. "I knew I could count on you to put your nose where it didn't belong. And Syme has taken a shine to you, poor Fool. That was helpful."

"I followed you, too." A new voice in the room. There was someone beside Rianna.

Lin. She had slithered, eel-like, behind Etherell and into the room.

"The Court Poet, I presume," said Etherell. "I'd hoped to make your aquaintance."

"I doubt that," said Lin. She was, if possible, thinner and paler than when Rianna had seen her last. She looked like a ghost in black. She held a sword as well.

The women stood shoulder to shoulder now, with Syme behind them.

Without taking her eyes off Etherell, Rianna said, "You're a bit late. Missed quite a party."

"I saw it all," said Lin. "A woman in black, and veiled, escapes notice during a coronation. I'm sorry I couldn't stop it."

"You know—"

"About Marlen? Yes."

"Sorry to interrupt," said Etherell, "but I believe you were about to turn the jester over to me." He advanced another step with the sword extended.

Lin said, "*Ready.*"

And Rianna knew it wasn't addressed to him.

Together the women moved to strike. Side by side they advanced, Rianna with both knives out now.

Etherell dodged their blades, then launched his own attack. He was laughing. "A merry dance," he said, even as Lin's blade slid into his guard.

He parried it handily, his cloak wrapped around his arm to act as a kind of shield; but it was a near thing. He backed away.

"I'd forgotten," he said, "how little I care for this dance, when not driven by hatred." He sounded fascinated, as if at a discovery. "I . . . *don't care.*" He shook his head. "Now, Elissan . . . he cared so much for power. He *wanted* it so much. I suppose that was his undoing."

"You wanted it enough when it meant killing me," said Rianna. Her heart still beating fast. "It's only now that there are two of us that you don't dare." She knew she was baiting him, and it was stupid, but she was angry.

But whatever hatred she had roused in him once seemed to have dissipated. He looked at her almost with affection. "You would have been queen, Rianna," he said. "And yet. Don't you feel the slightest bit . . . relieved? To be free of him? All that intensity. All that desire."

She didn't know what to say.

Lin Amaristoth spoke. "Why don't you join us?" Rianna glared in her direction, but Lin didn't seem to notice. "We could use another sword-arm."

He laughed. "I don't think so. That would be more intensity, it seems to me. I feel it coming off you even from here."

Lin smiled thinly. "You'll find that, with poets."

"Yes!" he agreed. "It's exhausting. I'm ready to be done with the whole business."

Rianna felt compelled to speak. "We can stand around talking," she said, "or we can do what we came here to do."

Etherell grinned at her. "We had some good times, didn't we, Rianna," he said. "It was interesting to think what I might do with some magic. But it might be just as interesting to see what you two do with it. My ladies." He bowed. "I will look forward to seeing what happens now that this Queen is here. And now you, Lin Amaristoth. Should be quite a show."

"A show?" Rianna bristled. "That Queen is a monster."

"Perhaps," he said. There was a private light in his eyes, not quite a smile. "I'm not one to judge." He went to the door. "I suggest you move fast, if you mean to escape." And with that, and without a backward glance, he slipped out. They heard his departing steps in the passageway.

Rianna let out a long breath and relaxed her stance.

"He's right," said Lin. "We had best move quickly."

"If you knew him," said Rianna, "you'd never want to say he was right about anything. And they called *Marlen* a snake. Ha." Their eyes met. Lin looked drained, but real, entirely herself. Now that she was here, Rianna couldn't believe she'd ever thought the Ifreet could look like her. She said, "I have never been so glad to see anyone."

Lin held out her hands, palms upward; a helpless gesture. "You can say that—after I've failed you."

Rianna knew what she meant. It was not about the coronation of Elissan Diar.

Rianna shook her head. "Ned is his own man. Besides—he betrayed you, too." She stepped forward and put her arms around the other woman's shoulders. Lin was trembling.

The Court Poet said, "I'm so sorry."

For a moment they stood there. Then broke apart. "Syme," said Rianna. The Fool had, throughout all this, been uncharacteristically silent, and looked downcast. He came to life at her address of him. "Do what we came for, and let's be on our way."

JULIEN could see nothing ahead but the blaze cast by the mark on her eye. A trail of light, nothing more. To each side, the stone walls were cut into the shape of archways. But there was otherwise no ornamentation in the walls, no change as she went on. Julien found herself increasingly grateful for the cloak. It was getting colder. She wondered if she was going deeper into the earth.

She came at last to a chamber. It was bare, but for brass candlesticks set in the wall in each corner. Their light flickering and serene.

Before her was a pair of doors. They were of wood and plain, save for the symbol of the double spiral carved into each. Shapes that seemed to shift and twist before her eyes.

Now is your choice, Julien Imara.

The wind again. Julien had wondered if it would ever return. "*Now is my choice?*" she said. "I thought we did that already."

There was an arch carved into the wall between the doors. Julien noticed because it began to gather light, as if the candles fed into it. Soon the wall within the arch glowed and it was like a window: and it looked out on a landscape. She saw green hills, and cliffs, and the great open sea. The view shifted, to focus on a castle that hung from a sheer cliff. Its towers were like spikes, tall and sharp.

The view changed again, and she saw—as if she were a bird—two armies massing in a field. And then she was nearer, and saw that leading one of those armies was a woman in white, with white skin. Her lips like blood.

And then all this faded and the room was candlelit again. The wind said, *The White Queen and the Shadow King are here. They will destroy everything to destroy each other.*

Julien swallowed. "Why? What do they want?"

A sound like a chuckle in her ear. *Little mortal, you could never hope to know. They will never cease their battle. Not until the seas devour this world and every other. Perhaps even beyond that. Beyond time.*

"Elissan Diar unleashed this," Julien said. She remembered now. The carving. The antlers. She had mistaken the spiraling skulls for what his reign would bring. When in fact . . . "He's dead, isn't he," she said.

There is little to be done. The doom of your world nearly certain. But there is one thing you might try.

"What is it?" A knob of terror was forming in her stomach. This quiet place, this maze, was so detached from everything. Had lured her into feeling safe. She heard her own voice, breathless. "What must I do?"

We offer you the Queen's true name, said the wind. *It can be used once. That is the rule. And will only weaken her for a time.*

"I'll take it."

The sound of the wind turned silky. *There is a price.*

"Name it."

The wind played with her hair. Seemed almost to sing. *Julien Imara, little Seer. You have only one thing of value.*

"My harp?" Julien swallowed. "Of course I'll give that up." Though her stomach dropped at the words.

Yes, said the wind. *The harp. The ring. Everything that goes with them.*

It took a moment for her to understand. "You mean . . ."

Choose the door on your right, and you emerge as you are. A Seer. With all the gifts of the maze. Choose the left—you will have the Queen's name. The Seer's mark of Valanir Ocune will be accounted a fair exchange.

The voice was still close to her ear. *Nothing is freely given or gained. The deeper you go in the Labyrinth, the more you stand to lose.*

Julien stood there. This room pressed in on her senses with sudden clarity, as if every detail mattered. The doors, the candlelight, the silence. It all stood still when she did.

Standing still was a delay. Not an escape. She spoke. Her voice thick with effort. "This is the true test. Before . . . that was a game for you. Wasn't it? To see if I'd harm one of my own, a mortal, for your amusement. When this—taking the one thing I treasure . . . that is what you were after all along."

The wind was silent. Julien remembered riding with the white-haired Seer on the golden horse, and the green mountains. The harp she'd owned in those dreams. It was alike, she realized, to the harp she now carried. The one chosen for her, by whoever decided such things.

She remembered the night Valanir Ocune had given her the mark.

His dreadful pallor when he knew he was dying. He had channeled what remained of his life into that act. All his hopes, all he knew, given into her care. And since that night she had gone forward with that, the terrible responsibility.

And pride. Oh, the pride and the delight. The music of the green mountains welcoming her to a world where she would never have conceived of belonging.

"So I must go back, then," she said aloud. "I will be no more than Julien Imara. Invisible girl on the stairs."

Or remain a Seer for the battles to come, murmured the wind to her. *Will you sacrifice all for a small, temporary weapon?*

Julien lifted the harp to eye level. Even by candlelight it shone with a fierce fire. She knew she would never see its like again. And had an intuition, in that moment, of the music that might have emerged from it at her hands.

All the might-have-beens in the world would never change what had to be.

She let the harp drop on its strap, to rest again at her side. Looked down at the smooth folds of the black and silver dress. And went forward, step by slow step, towards her chosen door.

AFTER a long while, as the sun moved behind the clouds of afternoon and the gulls called, he let himself lie on the sand and listen to them, and the waves. It had seemed a point of pride to stand there at attention with the Branch, to maintain the rigid stance of indignation, but as time wore on that seemed ever more pointless. At last Dorn Arrin set down the Branch on the sand, lay himself beside it. He meant only to rest a moment. He ended up falling asleep. His dreams were full of strangeness, and music; at one point, he himself was singing, that elegy from the night of mourning for Archmaster Myre. Mourning, mourning, as night bled away to dawn.

When he awoke it was dark and Julien Imara lay beside him. She was curled in on herself and crying. Dorn was made instantly aware that he was cold, that he had done the unforgivable by falling asleep, and that something must be wrong.

"What happened?" He sat up. "Are you hurt?"

She looked up. And he saw it immediately, as moonlight fell there on the beach. Her young face, unmarked by time and now, unmarked by enchantment. She looked younger still in that dress, with its lace collar and cuffs, though he'd never tell her that.

"I lost everything," she said. "And I don't even know if I did right."

He took her hands.

She looked at him with renewed tears. "Please don't let's talk about what I said before."

His heart ached. "Of course." He had planned on saying something about being young, and being thrown together with someone, and the future she might have—a future so clear and bright to him he wished he could make her see it. But now was not the time for any of that—and perhaps it would have been presumptuous, anyway. As if he were one to talk. There was always that distance, vast as a country, between knowing a thing and believing it.

"Something terrible is about to happen, Dorn," she said. "There's to be a war."

"Of course there is," he said with a sigh. "Come, sit a minute, and tell me everything when you're ready."

She kept ahold of his hand, and they sat on the sands as the moon rose. The full solstice moon, its twin reflected beneath in the dark and churning waters.

THE golden-haired man knelt in the throne room on the tile. The room had been tidied; the Chosen had meticulously removed all evidence of the corpse. The air smelled of lye. Outside, a cold and silent winter night; unnaturally silent in the streets of Tamryllin.

When the man arose he hardly appeared humbled; his lips wanted to stretch in a grin. "I'd be honored to serve you," he said. "Especially if it means leaving this castle. It's grown too small for me, as it is for you. I admire that about you."

The White Queen reached out to stroke his hair. "You have your own ideas, mortal," she said. "I see that in you. There was a time when you trained with my deathless ones. But not for a long while. You are not of their number anymore."

Etherell Lyr had stiffened at the touch. Then shrugged. "I hope your grace will accept me as I am," he said. "A mortal with ideas. I see the appeal in being deathless . . . but there seems little joy in it."

She surveyed him with a changeless expression. There was not a line in her face, as if it was ever changeless. "I can give you great power," she said. "But first you must prove yourself. You are a hunter, are you not?"

"Indeed, your grace," he said with a lazy smile. "And rather a good one."

"Look here, then." She motioned to a gold-framed mirror on the wall. A haze filled it, then cleared to show a face. The Queen looked to Etherell Lyr. "This mortal is mine. Find him for me."

He raised an eyebrow. "He's alive?"

She smiled, a look at once brilliant and alarming. "He passed through fire and many doorways and has at last returned. And he belongs to me. I've tried to retrieve him—even sent my hounds—to no avail." She looked down with what might have been amusement. She stood a full head and shoulders taller than him. "Perhaps what I was missing all along was *you*, little mortal. With your connection to Dorn Arrin, and your skill at hunting."

"Like as not," said Etherell Lyr. "Of course. I'll find him for you."

PART III

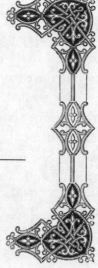

CHAPTER
15

IT was the first day of winter when Muiwiyah Akaber returned home from the battlefield. He came with an entourage of men-at-arms and immediately demanded a bath be drawn. It had been a grueling month on the front lines, not so much because of combat—Muiwiyah seldom engaged in the fighting. That was what sons were for—his three heirs, who fell over themselves to prove their worth as heirs apparent. Especially now, when Muiwiyah was poised to become king over all Kahishi. It was useful, to have them at loggerheads and dependent on their father's approval. So it had been all their lives—he'd made sure they hated each other. It meant Muiwiyah could trust that they would not band together against him; that each would strive to excel in battle.

The best will inherit, he had told them since they were children. Now the stakes were higher than they had ever been. The best would inherit a throne.

Despite that he had not participated in much of the fighting Muiwiyah despised the front lines, where the food was hardly up to standard and comforts few. The chill and rains of winter made the arrangement all the more intolerable. The vizier-turned-king had decided the battle was in capable—not to mention highly motivated—hands, with his sons at the helm. He would return to the comforts of his castle in Zirtan. Though Muiwiyah Akaber had only recently declared himself king, he had lived in imperial splendor all the years, ever since Yusuf Evrayad had bestowed on him the title of Vizier of the East Province.

It was an honor that chafed. It had come to Muiwiyah only after he'd surrendered his claim to the throne. There was simply no standing against Yusuf Evrayad. But the emasculated elder son, Eldakar—that was another matter. And the attacks from the north, culminating in the destruction of the Zahra, had presented the perfect opportunity.

Muiwiyah's castle was decorated with the banners of East Province, the silver gazelle on a field of green. The sight of them gave Muiwiyah stirrings of discontent: as king of all Kahishi, his banner should incorporate elements of all the provinces. He'd give orders to the seneschal to procure cloth for the tailors, and to have them come up with new designs. Whoever created the design he most liked would receive some sort of favor. As Muiwiyah rode across the drawbridge he reflected on this with a newly satisfied smile. There would no longer be provinces at all, when he was done with Eldakar. That had been Yusuf Evrayad's grand mistake—imagining unity could exist in Kahishi so long as it was divided.

Yusuf's other mistake had been allowing his eldest son to marry that whore. But it all worked to Muiwiyah's benefit now. The whore who ruled in Majdara—who would soon be dealt with—had made Eldakar Evrayad deeply unpopular, distrusted.

Muiwiyah smiled a little as he thought about Eldakar's whore. She was very toothsome. She had turned out to be capable in battle, as well—but that would only make his conquest the sweeter. A wildcat that would not be tamed might still be brought to her knees. Muiwiyah had ideas of what she might do for him, on her knees.

With attendants at his heels, he made his way to his chambers. He felt a vast relief when he arrived here, at his personal sanctuary. After weeks of living in a tent, it was a balm to his heart to be back—to be home. Each piece of armor his attendants removed, each weight, was like removing a weight from his spirit. He had been under so many pressures, between the battle to the west and the siege of Majdara. He felt these lift away with his armor, then his clothing, and he gave a great sigh as he settled into his bath.

It was pleasant, then, to recline in the water, as servants poured ewers of scented water over his shoulders and back, and imagine the things he would do to Rihab Bet-Sorr. The servants were discreet, making no comment on whatever acts Muiwiyah felt compelled to as a result of these imaginings. They simply continued to bring the ewers, massage his shoulders and head, and wash his hair. The sensations, coupled with a more intense pleasure, were delightful.

He was a proud man who didn't care what his servants thought. He was handsome, still, despite being past middle age. And active among his concubines. The aura of power he projected, his skill in battle, had carried him far—until he'd hit a wall. That damnable wall of Yusuf Evrayad's victories. So he had accepted the appointment of Vizier of the East Provence, and awaited his moment.

That moment was fast approaching, Muiwiyah thought as the attendants toweled him dry. He gave an involuntary groan of contentment when they slipped on his silken robe, at the feel of it against his skin. How good it was to have grown sons now, who would endure the privations of war instead of him. He was done, at least until it was time to bring the full weight of their forces against Majdara and the whore. He wanted to be the one to crush the capital, to lead the march into the city. To look Rihab Bet-Sorr full in the face as she knelt in the dirt, her eyes a mixture of pride and fear. He could see it already. If he had been younger, the thought would have made him hard all over again.

It was said that Rihab consorted with Fire Dancers and thieves. That she'd taken over the criminal element of the city and trained them in battle. A strategy that could only last as long as Muiwiyah's forces were preoccupied with Eldakar on their western flank. Once Eldakar was dealt with and Muiwiyah brought the full weight of his forces to bear on the city . . . he predicted it wouldn't last a week.

Now it was time for his meal, which he had looked forward to as much as the bath. Though he had been given the best of what was on offer on the battle lines, it was pitiful fare. The covered dishes that the servants brought forth now, the birds and goats' flesh slathered in spiced sauces prepared specifically to Muiwiyah's tastes, made him close his eyes in anticipation. Perhaps it was worthwhile to go away, to experience hardship for a time, as a means of savoring common pleasures once more.

A profound thought, he decided, and considered calling a minstrel to note it down. But the repast beckoned, and wine. These were more pressing than posterity.

"You have another message from Ramadus, your excellency," said one of the servants, from a kneeling position, his forehead to the floor.

It was irritating. He was trying to enjoy his dinner. "I know what it says. Leave it and go."

The servant deposited the scroll, sealed in a leather case with the insignia of the court of Ramadus, on a silver tray beside Muiwiyah's couch. He did so with his eyes lowered, and without raising his eyes backed from the couch until he reached the threshold, and only then turned to go.

Muiwiyah was chewing morosely now. He'd been so looking forward to his dinner. Ever since departing the camp, in all the hours of riding through cold and rain. But if he didn't read the message now, it would prey on his mind, even though he knew what it said. They were all the same these days.

He tapped the scroll from its case into his palm. Unrolled it. Sure enough, the same song as ever. The Magicians of Ramadus saw a great darkness approaching from the west, so on and so forth. It was essential for Kahishi to cease its battles and unite.

Whatever their game, it was a pathetic one. If they were allied with Eldakar Evrayad, some tale spun of a prophecy was hardly going to work on Muiwiyah. And if not—well, the country would be united once he crushed Eldakar, wouldn't it? The South Province waited, deliberately neutral, to see who would win. They would join Muiwiyah once he demonstrated his superior strength. Kahishi would find new inspiration behind a leader like Muiwiyah. It had been weakened from its core by a sapling coward like Eldakar.

Either way, Muiwiyah was doing the best possible thing for the country. And once he was king, the Ramadians would have no choice but to treat with as him. They put on a show of strength, but trade with Kahishi was as important to them as it had ever been. Some of the world's finest olive oil came from groves near Majdara. Ramadian princes were eager to wrap themselves in crimson, a rare dye produced from beetles that lived in particular trees south of the River Gadlan. For all the noises the Ramadians made about war, war was expensive. Muiwiyah was not convinced that Ramadus wanted war, not if there were other ways to access the riches of Kahishi for themselves.

Alliances were key. When Muiwiyah won the throne, he'd marry

one of his sons to a Ramadian princess. That same marriage Eldakar
Evrayad had spurned—a diplomatic disaster. Muiwiyah was his country's savior—that was clear. His one regret was that Yusuf Evrayad
would never see it.

That night he had a girl brought to him—a new slave from the east,
luscious and golden-haired. She looked nothing like Rihab Bet-Sorr
but Muiwiyah was a man of diverse tastes. He appreciated life's finer
pleasures—in food, women, and wine. This particular girl was more
subdued than he usually liked, but in some ways that was ideal after the
rigors of the road. She did what was expected of her and he didn't have
to think. In that way it was similar to his bath, an uncomplicated indulgence. Before he slipped into sleep he allowed her to stay—the girls
brought to him were searched thoroughly, and there was the chance he
might awaken with new appetite in the night. Especially after a long
time away.

Muiwiyah did awaken in the night. It was very late. The moon was
high, light angling through the windows. The girl lay still beside him.

That was when he saw she lay atop the covers and that her wrists
and ankles were tied. Her mouth bound with a gag.

When he tried to scream he realized two things: He was gagged,
and someone held him from behind. The knife flashed as it sank into
his throat, screaming pain. Shock of red, of his own blood. His life.

A man stood before him now. A man in simple clothing, pale by
moonlight. *An Eivarian,* said Muiwiyah's fevered thoughts. The man
said, "Pleased to make your acquaintance, my lord. My name is Ned
Alterra. That was for Myrine, daughter of Sicaro, queen of Majdara."

Muiwiyah tried to speak. Nothing came. His body canted sideways
on the bed.

The man went to the window as he cleaned his knife, a motion deft
and fastidious. He seemed to have forgotten the vizier whose life bubbled away on the bed. He spoke to himself or the moonlight. "After
all," he said, "I hate traitors."

MIDNIGHT of the winter solstice a procession was seen passing through the streets of Tamryllin. Seen, rather than heard; it was nearly silent. Those who observed the procession, and could tell of it afterward, watched through the slits of drawn shutters. Or rather, caught a glimpse; anyone who watched longer than a moment would not tell of it, for those people—men, women, even children—would stumble out in the night, stumble in silence after the silent procession of armed men. These in turn guided, at their head, by a majestic figure in white. It was as if the moon itself passed for a moment before each window, if moonlight could leave a lingering chill behind.

The people who glimpsed this, and did not look for more than a moment, shivered in their blankets and prayed.

Everyone had shut themselves indoors directly after what had happened at the palace. There had been a single, unifying compulsion, stronger than panic, to seek shelter. Forgotten were the planned reveleries of solstice night; the rejoicings for a new king. Everyone in the city, from the wealthiest aristocrat to the lowest pauper, was gripped by the same terror. The poor, if they had no homes, took refuge in temples, where priests wandered with eyes like the damned.

Those who took refuge lay on benches, gazing upward in supplication at the marble or painted eyes of gods.

The taverns that had meant to be open all night for the celebrations closed immediately, opening doors only to entreaties from those who sought shelter—often people from the castle. No one could imagine staying in that castle tonight, perhaps ever. Those who had not seen what happened to Elissan Diar still knew, without the doubt or distortion associated with rumor. As if the knowledge had been passed without need for speech. As if they themselves had been witness. And now would never forget.

Those left in the streets would end up joining the procession, which was increasingly ragged at its edge, as it wound through Tamryllin from the castle, through streets, and at last to the gate. They were soon lost to the night, but the residents of Tamryllin nonetheless kept to their homes, temples, and taverns afterward and huddled there past daybreak, sleepless.

The next morning the people of Tamryllin found that, overnight, the fine blanketing of snow from the day before had frozen into a coating like glass on the paving stones. That roofs and windowsills dripped shards of ice. Frost made glittering spirals on the windowpanes.

That morning everyone would know of someone who had gone missing. These were permanent losses. Those who followed the White Queen on solstice night were never seen again.

AFTER the tolling of the midnight bell, after the castle fell silent, Rianna directed them to an underground chamber. But when they reached the doorway she found she could not go in, as if something pressed against her and held her in place.

"Rianna." Lin Amaristoth, coming up beside her.

Rianna turned to her. It was all a haze, suddenly. For so long she'd been expecting to break; was this what it felt like? "I can't do this," she said. "It's my fault."

"No," Lin said coldly. "It's mine." She advanced to the cot where Marlen Humbreleigh lay outstretched. His boots dangled over its edge. He'd been so tall.

Rianna could not bear to look. His words came back to her. *You're a cold bitch who can bear anything.* He'd said it to make her strong, she knew that, but she also thought he believed it. And he was wrong. She couldn't bear that he'd been near for so long while she ate and slept and danced upstairs. That he'd died alone in the dark.

"We have to bury him," she said.

"We must do something," said Lin. She had knelt beside the bed. She bowed her head. "It must have happened . . . he must have gone . . . not long ago."

Rianna couldn't bring herself to look directly at the man on the cot. Didn't want to see his face. There were already so many images that haunted her, awake and in dreams. Nonetheless, she knew she must be present here, not a coward. She watched the proceedings from the corner of her eye.

Lin Amaristoth bent and put her lips to his forehead. Then stood. As Rianna watched from the doorway, Lin removed her black cloak from her shoulders and laid it over the body. Then the Court Poet raised her arms. Very softly, she began to sing.

Rianna found herself shivering. She wanted to ask what the point was of covering him, of singing, but could not speak. She saw as Lin's sleeves fell back to reveal her arms that they were veined with gold.

Syme Oleir, looking timid, crept past Rianna to stand near the strange tableau at the cot. Rianna had forgotten about him. The gold light from Lin limned his features as he looked up at her.

When Lin lowered her arms and fell silent, Syme spoke. "No songs, no love, no life."

The Court Poet put her hand on his shoulder. "It feels that way." She turned her gaze to Rianna. Her eyes seemed darker, like caves, with a spark of life within. "On my travels something happened to me," she said. "I am still not sure what it is. One thing I know is that I feel . . . a kind of affinity . . . with the dead. I think I can stop his body corrupting. Until we honor him with a resting place. We'll come back for him, Rianna. When this is over."

Rianna raised her head, defiant. And angry. "If we can."

Lin spread her hands. It seemed an eastern gesture to Rianna, and evasive. "Yes."

This reminder of Kahishi sparked Rianna's anger even more. But she recognized that for what it was. She knew it was a defense against breaking. That she was angry because for all the Court Poet's enchantments, she could not revive the dead.

Rianna said nothing more, only took Syme's arm so he'd move again.

They departed the cell. For a time they were silent in the corridor that would take them to the stairs.

In all her nights in this place, Rianna had never known it to be so quiet. Not even the call of a bird outside, nor wind in the chimneys.

As they neared the stairs, Syme spoke up. His voice scaled to a whine. "You promised blackberry jam."

Lin looked to Rianna with a raised eyebrow. Rianna shrugged. "It's true, I did."

"Then let's go."

THE kitchen was dark, and cold; the hearthfire had gone out. Rianna set about rekindling it as Lin lit tallow candles. Soon there was a blaze going at which the women warmed their hands. They didn't speak. Rianna's hair fell forward, made a curtain between her and the Court Poet. She felt distant from everything, too deep in a black melancholy to speak.

"Jam," said Syme plaintively.

"Right." Rianna turned from the fire, began opening cupboards. She found the jam jars on one shelf, and another where the biscuits were kept. She brought these, and plates, to the table.

With a whoop Syme seized a biscuit and applied himself to the jars of jam, opening each one to peer inside, and sniff—presumably to discover which was blackberry. The women sat across from one another at the table and watched. It was something to look at for a while. The hiss of the fire like a crone whispering. Its light dancing on the floor and Lin's face. Rianna looked away, to the window. Nothing there but black, pale points of reflected candles, and frost forming on the panes.

"You should probably eat something," said Lin.

Rianna raised a shoulder. "Perhaps."

"You're angry with me." When Rianna opened her mouth to protest, Lin raised her hand. "You're right to be. I sent him into danger. And you. I can't imagine what you've been through."

Rianna couldn't stand it. She was afraid she would cry. "I made my choice," she said harshly. "Not for you. I wanted . . ." She stopped. What had she wanted? She cast her mind back to midsummer, to autumn . . . a different time. To brushing out a sulky princess's bright hair; to the view of red and yellow trees from the window. She had imagined she was dealing with a corrupt king, with some access to magic. Something she could stand against in her own way. "I thought I might be of use."

"And you were," said Lin. "You found Syme. What he is."

The boy—for so he looked right now—had jam all over his face. All his attention fixed on the biscuit, as if it were the center of the world. He looked happy.

Rianna said, "You know what was done to him?"

Lin looked away. "I feel it. Such a cruel enchantment. The last person who held the Ifreet . . . I knew him. He took its burdens on himself. What Elissan has done to this boy . . . it's unthinkable."

"I thought it might go away when Elissan was killed."

"But it hasn't. And I can't lift the spell. I don't know who can. The man who once held the Ifreet . . . he is dead. And we lost Valanir." Lin looked back again to Rianna, her expression hardening. "There is no one to turn to anymore. I've become the person I must turn to. And the one to blame when things go wrong."

"We didn't know the risks," said Rianna. Her mind shied away from that night: of Marlen's torture, of the king gliding silently into her room. Marlen's words: *He is so* strong, *Rianna.* "No one knew. Even Elissan didn't know what he was dealing with. He thought he was to be king, when all along he was being fattened up as prey."

"More than that," said Lin. "The enchantments he reveled in, that he used to make war, to take Tamryllin . . . He never gave thought to the cost. Nor to the boundaries between our world, and the Other, that he weakened through his actions."

"Allowing in this White Queen," Rianna said. "Do you know anything about her?"

"All I know is that each time I tried to reach out in my thoughts, I encountered her," said Lin. "I knew if she sensed me, it would be nothing to her to snuff me out. The way you'd pinch a gnat. So I stayed in shadow, looking for some way in. For all the good it did either of you."

"You're here now," said Rianna. "What do you mean to do?"

Lin shook her head. "I don't know yet. But when I was saved from death . . . a long story . . . I was told it was to turn back a shadow." She turned back one of her sleeves, to observe the gold veins in her arm. "I can only assume I'm here, alive, to fulfill that purpose. Or to try."

The fire whispered at them.

"I think I envy you," said Rianna. "That you have a purpose."

"There's nothing I could have done without you," said Lin. "Or Marlen."

She shook her head, as if to dispel the cloud. Then unexpectedly smiled. "I was so angry with Valanir at times," she said. "I understand him now. If only I could tell him so."

THEY'D gone to Rianna's room and bolted themselves in. The fire had gone out in there, too, and it took some time for a room that vast to warm. Rianna made up a bed for Syme, a featherbed she dragged from another room and laid out on the floor. He doffed his ridiculous jester's gear and curled up in the bed almost at once, still sucking jam from his fingers. Rianna lowered herself to the floor to gather the covers around him. He grabbed them up and shut his eyes. Was asleep within moments, his mouth hanging open. His breath came out in long sighs.

Rianna looked up at Lin, who was watching. "It's been a long time," Rianna said, "since I've thought about being a mother. Sometimes it feels like a dream I had."

"It's a long time since you've seen her," said Lin. She sounded wistful. "I missed you, you know. When I was . . . caught up in my work. And you in yours."

Rianna narrowed her eyes. She was sitting on the carpeted floor, still, beside the featherbed. But had changed from the bloodstained gold dress to her grey one. That gold gown, she thought, was ruined in a way that went deeper than stains. It could as soon be burned. "Is that what it was?" she said. "Your *work*?"

Lin looked at her lap. She sat in a high-backed chair by the fire. "There's something I kept secret. Even from Ned. I found out I was dying."

Rianna started upright. *"What?"*

"But not anymore," said Lin. "The same magic that brought me near death and left me marked—it saved me, too."

"That ring." Rianna had noticed it several times—the black opal on Lin's right hand. She'd never seen a gem of so many colors. "Does that have something to do with it?" At the other woman's nod, Rianna pursed her lips. She said, with an edge now, "Do you know what I've been doing? Why I have this grand chamber and a diamond collar?"

If she had thought to discomfit the Court Poet, it didn't seem to work. Lin's gaze was steady. "You went through a rite of fire, as I did," she said. "And brought out something whose value we can only begin to guess." Her gaze slid to the sleeping form of Syme Oleir.

The sudden hostility that had surged in Rianna just as suddenly died. She looked at the sleeping boy, too. Marveling at what the pitiful form concealed. "There's something you should know," said Rianna. "The White Queen—she said she trained the Chosen for battle. But more than that. She called them her 'deathless ones.'"

Lin's expression didn't change. "Sounds like we'd better operate on the obvious assumption, then," she said. "Until proven otherwise."

Rianna hugged her arms to her chest, to warm herself. "I know what it *sounds* like."

"Yes," Lin said. Cool in her high-backed chair. "They can't be killed."

CHAPTER
17

FOR various reasons, Nameir Hazan would always remember the evening she was summoned to King Eldakar's tent at the beginning of winter. It was urgent, the young guard had told her, his boy's voice catching; and Nameir thought she heard fear in it. Maybe she had not been thinking clearly. She always had fears, inchoate, with regard to Eldakar. He looked fragile to her, with his stooped posture as he bent over maps. The pain he carried.

She was in her tent, darning a torn shirt by the glow of the brazier. Her thoughts carried away by the rhythms of the task, and the day.

When she received the summons, she ran.

The night was warm for winter. A pine scent carried from the cypress trees. Nameir ran across the grasses to the king's tent. The guards at its entrance parted immediately to make way for her.

She ducked inside, emerged to light. It took her several moments to take in what she was seeing. Eldakar sat in his usual chair. Aleira Suzehn was there too, standing alongside. And then—

"My prince," she said.

"Nameir," said Mansur.

She hadn't seen him in months. He was a little browner than she remembered, a little more weathered around the eyes. Right now he was smiling at her. A real smile. "We won."

* * *

IT had happened fast. Muiwiyah Akaber was dead, assassinated in his own palace. Probably someone who held a grudge, was Mansur's guess. Muiwiyah had ruled his province with a will of iron. And wartime always induced a degree of chaos. Someone had evidently seen that chaos as an opportunity.

"I suppose," said Eldakar.

Disregarding the skepticism in his brother's tone, Mansur went on. From there the tides of war had shifted within days. Muiwiyah's three sons—Nikram, Rajir, and Miralfin—had turned against each other. A three-way civil war erupted on the border. Mansur had seen his own opportunity then.

"We crushed them," he told Nameir. "Oh! You should have been there. We will sing of that day for years to come. When all seemed lost . . . the enemy came tumbling down. Undone by hatred for each other." He reclined amid cushions with a cup of wine, his color high; that cup had likely not been his first.

Eldakar addressed her dryly. "You should sit."

Nameir took it as a command, allowed herself to sit in her usual chair. Except nothing was as usual about tonight. Her mind caught on the grand words of the prince. "All seemed lost," she said. "So you thought—"

"I expected to die," said Mansur with a shrug. "Mostly I was worried for Eldakar. Once we fell, this camp would have been overrun."

"King Sicaro would have sheltered you," said Aleira. She spoke from where she sat cross-legged on the tent floor, eyes hooded in the half-light.

"I would not have run," said Eldakar. For nearly the first time since Nameir knew him, he spoke sharply. "More would have been killed, if I'd done that, than if I'd surrendered. I will allow people to give their lives for Majdara, and the Zahra as it was. Not for me."

"This is grim talk when we should be celebrating," said Mansur. "Eldakar, I suspect you've never even been drunk. That's the trouble with your poems. Too much sobriety."

It was true that Eldakar's wine cup was untouched on his desk. He looked at it ruefully. "I reject this charge against my honor," he said. "I have abdicated sobriety at various times. I was probably drunk when I met my wife. You know how that went."

"Not your fault," said Mansur. "I couldn't tell she was a piranha when I was sober, let alone drunk." He lifted his wine cup for a toast. "To being eaten alive . . . by beautiful women!"

Eldakar started to laugh despite himself. They both drank. "I can't believe you would have died for me, you idiot," said the king.

Mansur grinned. "It's what brothers do." He reached out and patted Nameir's shoulder. "And you," he said. "You'll have that land you've been promised all this time. Can even retire, if you like. You've earned it."

He sounded jovial, and it made Nameir feel odd; that he'd been thinking of her retirement. Though of course he meant well. "Thank you, my lord," she said.

"Oh come," said Mansur. "None of that, Nameir. Drink. You're too wound up."

"Mansur is right," said Eldakar. "You have served us like none other, Nameir. When the battles ahead are done—you will have whatever you ask."

Thankfully they moved from that topic, then, to that of battles yet to come. Aleira spoke of what she had seen in the stars. Of a wave of destruction destined to come east over the mountains. Mansur listened soberly to this. For a while after she spoke there was silence.

Mansur was watching Aleira Suzehn with fascination. Her pale hair was loose around her shoulders. The shadows of the tent hollowed her cheekbones to knife points; her gold chains caught the light. And there were those strange eyes that could arrest one's attention at any time.

To Nameir, the Magician had become a familiar presence in the camp. After her descents from the watchtower, each night, the Magician would solicit Nameir's help, as if whatever she'd seen in the heavens left her unsteady on her feet.

Nameir would offer liquor in a flask, and wait for the Magician to regain herself. They'd stand in silence, breaths smoking in the winter air. Once Aleira had said, with a small smile, "They don't deserve you. This terrible family."

Nameir had said, with a twinge of discomfort, "The sons are not the father."

"No," Aleira had agreed. "No, indeed. But what the father did . . .

his obscene bargain . . . it twists my readings of the stars. As if even the heavens cry against it."

"What do you mean?" Nameir had asked, despite misgivings. She wasn't sure she wanted to know. "What bargain?"

"All that he built, he bought with the souls of a city," said Aleira. "Souls that are still trapped beneath the earth—neither alive, nor dead." She looked at Nameir. "These men you cherish so much—I don't know if they will ever find peace. With something like this on their heads. It's not their fault. It was the father. But that is no concern of the heavens, where these things are written."

"If they fall, then so will I," Nameir flung back, with vehemence surprising even her. Without awaiting a response, set off down the hill. But the next night had joined the Magician on the hilltop again, again offering the flask. They had not spoken of it since. They spoke of other things, like Aleira's life in the fortress of the Fire Dancers; the studies that had led to magic. Subjects of interest to Nameir, that did not touch on anything that was painful, or confusing.

In the course of time Nameir came to forget her initial impression of Aleira Suzehn, seductive in her tent. She recalled it now, seeing how Mansur looked at her.

He asked Aleira, "I hear tell that you lived among the Fire Dancers. What was that like?"

The Magician lowered her eyes momentarily. Then smiled. "From them I learned not to hate all men," she said. "Only most of them."

"That sounds like a challenge," said the prince with his easy grin. The Magician held her smile but did not respond.

Then Aleira turned to Eldakar. An abrupt shift in tone. "You should know, my king," she said. "The assassination was no accident. It was a gift."

"She told you?"

"She didn't have to. I told you before—she looks after your interests."

Eldakar didn't answer. Nameir thought she saw a tightening in his jaw. He looked at her then, as if he felt her watching. Said, "Nameir, my herbs—will you steep them for me?"

She rose at once. He took her hand as she passed, and she understood. At once felt grateful to Mansur for sending her here, to this king who let her know with every gesture—even without words—that her presence mattered.

LATER, she and Mansur bade the king good night and went out into the moonlight. "I want to talk to you," he murmured to her. She followed him to his tent. For the first time it was beginning to sink in . . . the war with the East Province was done. Those nights of poring over maps, of watching Eldakar with that sinking, helpless feeling . . . done. At least for now.

When they entered the tent Mansur said, "I wanted to thank you." His color was high from the drink, and his eyes looked larger, as they did sometimes when he'd indulged. "I didn't want to say this in front of Eldakar—I worry for him. The wound, and all he's lost—I don't know what I would do if you weren't looking after him. I see that you have."

"I came to know him . . . when you were ill," said Nameir. Veering away in her mind from that time. "I understand why you love him."

"Yes," he said. "I only wish I knew how to protect him."

Nameir looked down. "I think it's too late."

"A heart may heal. Women have broken mine often enough, and here I am," he said, smiling. He went to his pallet. He motioned for her to sit beside him. "How have you been?" he asked. He moved nearer. Though she had not seen him since the summer, she knew his scent; she could not have described it, only that it belonged to him, and made the hairs stir on the back of her neck. "I'm worried about you, too," he said.

She stared at him. "Me?"

"You take care of everyone except yourself."

She stared some more. "You're drunk," she said.

He seemed to think about it. Then: "Maybe," he said. "It's good to see you, you know." He had begun to stroke her lower back.

She stiffened. A hundred thoughts washed through her. Impossible to distinguish one from another just now.

He had never touched her this way.

She moved the hand that was touching her so it lay quiescent in her lap. Still an intimate gesture, still strange. He had always treated her like a comrade in arms. Certainly not as he did women. What was different? She searched his face.

"You expected to die," she said.

He nodded. Reached out with his other hand for her cheek. "Yes," he said. "And when I saw you, I knew . . . I'd come home."

The next moments would always be strange in her mind. She released his hand so he could stroke her back again, and then join his mouth with hers, and she didn't know what to do—she had never done this with anyone—but she surrendered to it. She had wanted this for longer than she could remember . . . but was it *this* exactly? And then he was easing her back on his pallet, and before she knew what was happening he was naked. That was the part that would stick in her mind later, that seemed discordant. That it happened so quickly. That she didn't have a chance to register what was happening, or what she was feeling. His quick eagerness sped everything forward.

She helped him undress her, and he spent a little time teasing her body, and she began to feel like perhaps this was what she wanted after all. The intensity of his focus on her made her think of rain on parched earth.

Still she wished he would speak again, or meet her eyes. *You wanted this*, she reminded herself, and gasped, and tried to lose herself.

It was when he had begun to ride her—his dark eyes sleepy and pleased and gazing in the distance—that she located the source of her disquiet. She wanted to say the words. To tell Mansur what he meant to her—what he had meant since the beginning. But his faraway gaze could have been seeing anything. He had not in all this time said her name.

She had gotten as close to him now as anyone could. And it turned out even then—even this close—he could still be far away.

When he was done he said, "Thank you," and kissed her mouth. They lay still awhile. He stroked her arm. She clasped his hand. She could feel the words trapped in her throat, still, as if they were pebbles.

He had his own words, she knew. She had heard his poems often enough. Elegies for unrequited love, paeans to its attainment. Heartfelt and sensuous in either case. If he was not using such words now, she had to think it was because there weren't any.

Words like that were not for her.

Thoughts that passed within moments as she lay beside him. Feeling exposed and at the same time, somehow, unseen.

Finally he said, "You had better not stay—people would talk. Thank you for a delightful evening." He smiled at her, pure gratitude. She returned his smile as best she could, and began to dress. By the time she left he was asleep.

THAT night she washed herself before bed. She had never given thought to the logistics of how a man and woman came together. It turned out, the result for a woman could be messy. At least there had been no pain. And she didn't think she had to worry about a child. It was something she had given thought to, and consulted with a village doctor about once, years ago. A woman doctor, and Galician. Such a person, Nameir had thought she could trust with her secret. The doctor had told her that since Nameir had never bled—a result, the doctor said, of relentless exercise—there was little risk of pregnancy. It was a relief. Until then, Nameir had been aware of the possibility as if it were a flaw in her armor; a fatal weakness.

Although she couldn't imagine trusting anyone enough for intimacy, she had thought—optimistic at nineteen—that someday it might happen. That maybe she wouldn't always be alone.

At that time she had been fighting in numerous campaigns, never serving one commander for very long. She went where the demand was. Never forming a bond with warriors of her rank, and certainly not with her commanders. In the border wars that had plagued Kahishi when Nameir Hazan was young, there was no sense in growing attached to one side, when you might find yourself fighting against them the following spring. So it had been since she was thirteen, tall and strong for her age, until she was twenty-four. At which time she had come under the command of the king's son. And everything changed.

Those years of being alone, before Mansur, had been hard. But Nameir wondered if there hadn't been a certain freedom in it. In the years since, she had orbited Mansur Evrayad as the spheres were said to do around the sun. Yearning for light and warmth. Never getting close. And like a sphere in orbit, trapped.

Naked again, but clean, Nameir crawled onto her pallet. Only then did she realize that she was trembling. Which was strange. She'd thought she was feeling calm enough.

It took her a long time to fall asleep.

IN the morning she headed straight to the king's tent. She found him sitting at his desk in nearly the same position she had left him the night before. He was writing. She looked to the cups beside him. The wine goblet was barely touched. Only the herb infusion in its blue porcelain cup had been drained.

"My king," she said. "Did you sleep at all?"

He looked up from his papers. She read the answer in his face, drawn and shadow-eyed. He said, "I had to think."

There was a mood in the tent this morning she could not identify. "Think about what? We won."

Eldakar grimaced, then tried to turn it into a smile. "Yes," he said. "Are you here to escort me? Let's go." Before they left, he donned a cloak. He took up his sword from its resting place against the wall. It had lain there ever since the wound to his shoulder. Keeping company beside his lute, which was also untouched. He glanced at the instrument as he fastened the sword to his waist. He said, "I wonder, Nameir. Who could sing?"

And she was worried all over again, without knowing why.

They met Mansur in an open field. Their men-at-arms had gathered, but left a cleared space for their prince. Beside Mansur stood the three sons of Muiwiyah, chained at the wrists and ankles.

The atmosphere was boisterous; the men were aware at this time that the battalions on the east border had won the day. Their relief was palpable. Nameir wasn't sure if the men knew how close they had been to losing. She thought not.

When Eldakar and Nameir broke through the crowd to where the three prisoners stood, the men looked up. They were handsome, all; broad, tall, with the rugged features of their father. It was as if Muiwiyah Akaber stood there in the flesh, three times repeated. With a difference: the father was hardened by age and a life of tyranny. His sons had hardly begun.

"Eldakar!" The one who called out thus looked to be the youngest. "You know me. You remember."

Eldakar stood at the edge of the clearing. He said, "I remember well. Your family's visits to the Zahra. Clambering in the gardens while our fathers were in council. I recall now, too, how you always wanted to play at war." He winced, hastily added, "I don't judge you for that, Miralfin. I know your father let you think of nothing else."

The other man replied, quick and urgent, "I made a mistake. I should never have joined against you. Tell me how to repent."

One of the other sons spoke up. "Of course you seek to curry favor with Eldakar. Always a coward, as Father said."

"And he said you were a fool," said Miralfin.

At last the third son spoke. "You are both fools," he said. "Only one of us has a chance of surviving this. Don't you see? One to rule in the East Province." He fixed his gaze, attractive and sullen, on Eldakar. "Our father was wrong to rebel against you. I was wrong not to break away from him and join with you. I beg your forgiveness, Eldakar Evrayad. If you grant my life, all East Province shall serve you and what's more, shall send tribute. Our father's wealth was vast."

For a moment was a silence. There were stirrings among the men who watched, but these were muted by the sigh of a wind that flowed steadily across the hill.

Eldakar said, "I have no grudge against any of you. But I won't prolong this. It would be cruel. And I don't see another way."

The prisoners understood him before Nameir did, from the way their eyes widened.

So did Mansur. "Brother," he said uneasily, "perhaps—"

"I am your king," Eldakar reminded him. "You had time to offer me your thoughts last night. I have thought this through."

"I see no headsman," said Miralfin, panicking. He knelt down in the dirt in his chains. "You don't mean this. You wouldn't be so cruel."

Eldakar's sorrow reached Nameir where she stood. "I am the headsman," he said.

THE bodies of the three sons of Muiwiyah were to be sent home. Along with them went a message from Eldakar Evrayad—a command to the East Province to pay homage to their king.

Eldakar had insisted on performing the executions himself. The men had grovelled in the dirt, screaming for mercy. Nameir had had to hold each still when his time came. The worst had been the execution of the last brother, the oldest; Eldakar had begun with the youngest who had been his friend. At that point, with the two bodies swimming in blood around his knees, the scene had taken on a quality of the worst moments Nameir Hazan had experienced in battle. His horror came through in every scream. And through it all was Eldakar, expressionless, sword dripping blood.

When it was done, the crowd had gone completely silent. There was a play of small, fleet shadows in the grass. Carrion birds circling beneath the sun.

"The ravens shall not have them," said Eldakar calmly. He spoke from a face that was stained with blood down one side, where the artery of his former friend had sprayed. "They shall be buried with honor among their people." He looked to Mansur. "See it done."

He began to make his way out. The crowd parted, still silent, to let him pass.

Nameir followed. Her shirt was spattered red. They'd been butchers today, not warriors. A thought she saw mirrored in Mansur's eyes before she turned away.

Eldakar walked with what she thought was unnatural uprightness as they made their way to his tent. The activity of the day had almost certainly taxed his wound. But he walked without signs of distress until they were in his tent. Then he allowed his shoulders to slump and reached for her arm. "If you wouldn't mind, dear," he said. "I am not sure I can stand on my own much longer. Will you help me?"

"Always," she said. She helped him undress. There was water at the washstand already. Though she thought it might take several washings, certainly several changes of water, for him to be completely cleansed of blood.

"You understand it, Nameir?" he said. She held on to him as he slowly dipped the rag in water and applied it. He wasn't looking at her. "I won't ask if I was right," he said. "No one else should have this stain on them. And the idea of rightness . . . that seems impossible." He looked at his hands, gloved in fast-congealing red.

"I can't presume to know," she said.

He spoke in the same hollow tone, turned away from her, as he scrubbed his hands. "The tale of the weak king Eldakar . . . it has harmed more than myself. It can't go on. Not if the land is to unite and survive. This victory will be temporary if the narrative of a weak king is kept aloft, like a banner summoning the provinces to war among themselves. So it seems to me. I thought about it all through the night. I wanted to be wrong. Yet I couldn't see another way."

His hands were clean now, or near enough. He let her help him into a robe. Then she helped him to lie on his pallet, and set more herbs to steep for his infusion. "You should sleep," she said. Then felt it was not enough, and took his hand. "Eldakar," she said. "I am honored to call you my king."

He squeezed her hand. "You have always been kind to me."

WHEN she left his tent she allowed her legs to carry her where they would. It was hard to think clearly. Until she came to a tent—not her own—and pushed her way in.

The tent of Aleira Suzehn was unchanged. There was a scent of spices from the brazier. There was the flickering light. The Magician sat in a chair, oddly still. She said, "I was expecting you, Nameir. Or perhaps it would be correct to say—Melila. That was your name. I found it in the stars. Melila Hazan, torn from home, her language gone. Remade into a weapon so she might live." In that moment Aleira looked all of her age, and sad. "It's all right," she said. "It's a tale I know."

Nameir found herself unable to speak.

"I wish I could have saved you," said Aleira. "For so long, I thought only of saving myself. I'm sorry."

Nameir knelt beside Aleira's chair. Up close, the Magician smelled of hearthfires and another, familiar scent. Not alluring, or exotic. Something that drew her to another time. A kitchen, a bright home, a place that was safe. Something that made it all right to rest her head in this woman's lap, just now, and stay like that awhile.

THE dreams were gone. It had only been two nights but Julien knew. Two nights submerged in ordinary dreaming. The usual pitiful swamp of yearnings and fears.

Loathing was a metallic taste in her mouth when she awoke. Little comfort in the place she woke to: a frigid room, a hard bed, not a hint of daylight peering through the shutter slats.

She dressed, made her way down the sagging staircase—boards weak from seawater as well as age—passed the brooding hiss of embers in the fireplace of the common room, and left the inn. The day was grey and the wind hit her in a smooth blast. She huddled in her cloak and kept on. Black rock lined the coastline, and beside it a strip of amber sand. A path like an invitation, wherever it happened to lead. Especially if it led nowhere.

She didn't think that loathing—of herself, more than anything—could be shed through walking; but perhaps forgotten for a time.

They had arrived the day before. It would be too much to call it a hamlet—it was a cluster of fishing cottages, no more. But there was a small inn, or what passed for one, perched windswept on the brink of the coast.

Their destination had been more or less decided for them. The morning they'd summoned the ferryman to retrieve them from Labyrinth Isle.

"Are there other islands we might visit?" she had asked the ferryman. Though in her heart, already knew what he would say.

"They are barred to you." He did not even look her way.

He didn't need to tell her that it was the mark of the Seer that had allowed her to go as near the boundary as she had. And that was gone.

Dorn tried to make light of it. "Might be just as well," he said. "We're running out of things to give away."

"Take us to the mainland," she had told the ferryman, steadily as she could. "Someplace where we might get our bearings."

So he had brought them here, to this place with its creaky inn and cottages. In the boat she and Dorn Arrin had made a plan: they would say they were brother and sister on the road. They had not yet discussed where they would go from there. To his home? Hers? Neither seemed safe just now. Not if this White Queen was looking for Dorn.

I won't let anything happen to you, she'd said the day she saved him and Owayn from the wolves. And just a handful of days since she'd become, at best, a hindrance. She had one thing of value, that might or might not be useful. A name that could only be uttered once.

A bad bargain, her thoughts sneered, and she didn't know. She didn't at all. Perhaps someone with more wit than she would have made another choice. She had blundered into becoming a Seer, for no reason that did her credit; she had, perhaps, deserved to lose it after all.

She was striding along the path by the coastline. Sunless, the water was the color of iron. It flung against the rocks, cast streamers of foam all along the cracks and crannies in their sides. A rush of sound—water and winds combined. Along the shoreline as she passed, a bird unfurled its wide black wings to dance. A cormorant.

She kept on. The sand was tight-packed and wet. Bleached carapaces of sea creatures protruded, polished by tides. Hidden treasures. She thought of kneeling to dig one up. A token—some tangible thing to take from this part of her life.

She remembered being very young—four? five?—gathering seashells on a warmer shore down south. Such simple joy. No ambition, no awareness of her smallness in the wider world. No awareness of herself at all, in truth. Just happiness, simple and all-encompassing, in the act of unearthing the shore's gifts with her hands.

The sun had begun to rise. Here in the west what showed was a band of brighter grey above the water.

As the light grew, she saw that ahead, among the rocks, there was movement. A figure grey as the day. She kept advancing. Saw that the figure was a man. He was coming towards her.

She didn't have time to feel afraid. He let down his cowl, no doubt so she'd know him. So she would see that it was Archmaster Hendin.

He lifted his voice to be heard above the surf. "There you are." Before she knew what was happening he'd engulfed her in a hug, damp with sea spray and scratchy with his beard. Then, "Dorn. Is he—"

"He's with me," she said, coming out of her shock.

He uttered a fervent prayer skyward, to Kiara and the gods.

"How did you find us?" Julien asked. She had a moment of doubt. How could this be him? But it was; she knew that kind face. The only Archmaster who'd been kind.

He pointed to his eye. "The Court Poet sent me a message. She had a sense that you'd left the Isle and it worried her. I was able to trace you, mark to mark, until the coast. Then it went dark." His face creased. "I feared the worst."

"We're alive," she said. "But there is much to tell."

He studied her. "You were a child when last I saw you," he said. "I'd have had you remain one still."

"It didn't protect me," she said. Not knowing where the words came from. "Being a child. It's better this way."

THEY huddled together in a corner of the common room, as near the fire as they could. The room was empty. Their morning meal had been gruel, thick and tasteless, the bowls long since pushed aside.

Julien thought that despite everything, Archmaster Hendin looked happy. He had seemed to catch alight when he saw Dorn, though did not embrace him as he had Julien. Instead he'd hung back, awkward, as if ashamed. It was only when the younger man reached out that the elder stepped forward to an embrace, and then, Julien saw, with effort held back his tears.

"I will never stop blaming myself," said Hendin at last, when they faced each other again.

Dorn shook his head. Was even smiling. "I've seen things that I'd only thought to hear about in songs," he said. "Things I would never have once believed. I wouldn't trade that away. And I wasn't harmed, thanks to Julien."

"Yes," said Hendin, turning his glistening eyes to her then. "I am in your debt, young woman, though I can't think how to repay it."

"Let's not speak of debts," said Julien. "There's too much else to discuss."

Dorn Arrin cast her a look of concern at this. She knew she ought to be grateful that someone cared enough to have concern. Instead she felt more bitter yet, that he would never see her the way she wanted. It was a morning for feeling raw, it seemed.

As they ate they exchanged their tales. The innkeeper ignored them, with a disinterest that seemed genuine rather than studied; he truly didn't care. A sallow, reedy man who smelled of tabak, he made himself scarce. Archmaster Hendin had been staying in this inn for some days, watching for them, trying to figure out what to do next if they did not come.

More had passed since they'd left Academy Isle than just two days, if the Court Poet had sent word of it a week before. It seemed that time moved differently on the western sea. Just as it had folded in on itself, collapsed, in their first journey home.

Still it came as a shock to the Archmaster, she saw, to hear that Elissan Diar was dead. The death of the king, what that could mean. Nor what had happened since. The Court Poet, who had communicated to Archmaster Hendin when she feared for the two of them, had not done so again.

It took hours to tell the Archmaster everything. At last, Julien Imara told of the bargain she'd made within the maze.

"Tell me this," she said, looking up to meet his eyes. "What is the meaning of the pearl ring?"

He appeared to hesitate. Only a moment. "*The moon that comes out from a cloud, a shine that never fades,*" he said, quoting from the lore of gemstones that every poet learned by heart. "The pearl represents the emergence of art, usefulness, kindness from pain. It is meant to say something about the Seer you were. And the one you may be again, years from now. Don't forget that possibility."

"Someday," she said. "Maybe." In many years, if she studied enough, and was invited. And even then, the harp fashioned for her in the Otherworld was gone.

The part of the tale that affected him most, though, was that Dorn was in danger. It was Dorn's turn when it came time to narrate this: he told of the dreams he had of being swallowed in some darkness—dreams that evoked his experience of Manaia.

"He belongs to her," said Julien. "That's what I was told. But who is *she*?"

"I think you know," said Archmaster Hendin. "After all you've heard and seen."

"The White Queen."

"Elissan Diar let her through the portal to this world," he said. "And now you have her name."

"But it will only weaken her for a time," said Julien. "I don't see how that's much use."

"It means we need a strategy. But I will think on this more. Meantime, based on your tale, Dorn is being hunted. And so we three will be, until we find a way to safety."

"But where is that?" she asked.

He fell silent.

"Let the White Queen have me," said Dorn. "I won't see anyone harmed for my sake." He was making an effort to sound brave.

"There is to be no talk of that sort," Archmaster Hendin said sternly, for the first time sounding like the one in authority. "Don't forget, you two—I am a Seer, and the enchantments are back. That has for the most part brought nothing but trouble, but there are *some* uses. I've discovered ways to keep us hidden on our journey."

Dorn was staring at his hands that lay flat on the table. "Our journey? Where are we going?"

"To Lin Amaristoth, wherever she may be," said Archmaster Hendin. "I don't know if she can keep you safe. But she may know what to do."

THAT night she and the Archmaster sat at the table alone. Dorn had gone up to bed. Lulled by firelight and ale, Julien raised what she had wanted to ask about all this time. "The man from my dreams," she said to Archmaster Hendin. He was reclining with his feet on a stool, smoking his pipe. She almost felt guilty disturbing his evening ritual, but need drove her on. "The Seer, I mean," she went on. "Do you know anything about him?"

He went still. For a moment could have been a statue, but for the wisp of smoke that curled toward the ceiling. Then looked at her with an expression she could not read. All she knew was that she was accustomed to seeing Archmaster Hendin as *kind,* as if that were all of him, his defining trait. Now she saw other things. "Do you know, Julien Imara," he began, and stopped. Then went on, his voice made rough by some emotion. "Do you have the least idea how lucky you are?"

Her response was to stare.

"You don't, then." He tilted his head toward the ceiling, as if to contemplate something in the dark of the rafters. When he returned his gaze to her she felt relief; here again was the man she knew, his first thought to soothe and assuage the feelings of others. Not someone she had to fear.

"Of course you don't," he said, and laughed a little. "It's like everything that comes to us when we are young. We don't know the value of the gift until it's gone. What you had . . . as far as I know, you are the first Seer to have done so since Darien Aldemoor returned the enchantments. I don't think the Court Poet has had these dreams. There were things that went wrong for her, things we'll never fully know. But you . . ."

"Maybe you don't understand," said Julien, feeling defensive. "They were just dreams."

"Just dreams." He shook his head. "You saw the first Seer. Don't you understand? You went through what was meant to happen for all of us. I have read of it—the Seers who come in the dreams of new initiates. The first of these—his purpose is to restore you. The idea is that for art we need, more than anything, to see the world as we did when we were just beginning. With wonder and surprise."

"Until the wear and toll of our lives take from us that enchantment." Julien recalled the words of the second Seer from her dreams.

"Yes." This spoken heavily, with a glance down at his knotted hands.

"And then, after, come other guides. With lessons to offer. A chain from down the years, giving what they have learned. Making a new place for you."

A chain. It was true—in that time she had felt connected to something in a way she never had before. For a brief time she had not been alone. She'd been part of a tradition that went back to the earliest song, to the first poet. She looked at him with new eyes. "And you never had that."

"No. It was taken from us when Davyd Dreamweaver prayed away our powers." He put aside his pipe and leaned forward. "I know you are dealing with loss," he said. "It may be hard to understand what I'm trying to say. But someday—someday when you are reaching for a melody or the right word, that well of enchantment will be there for you to draw upon. And I believe when that happens, you will understand."

She struggled with it. But never again, she thought. Never again, that race down the mountain. On the other hand: Archmaster Hendin's face. She said, "You think—you *really* believe—it is better to have had something like that, and to lose it, than to have never had it in the first place?"

Now he smiled. "Every time."

MOONLIGHT was spilling into Dorn Arrin's room when he went upstairs. He noticed that first. He distinctly remembered leaving the shutters closed against the chill. Now wind swept into the room along with faint light. Enough light for Dorn to see, a moment later, that he was not alone.

"Not a sound." Etherell Lyr had come out from behind the door. Held up a hand in a warning. He closed the door and slid home the bolt.

Dorn felt his knees buckling, but managed to stay upright. "So. Are you here to kill me?"

"Not you, no. But if you call for help, I'll kill the girl in a trice. And the old man, and anyone else you think to summon."

"You'd do that."

"You know I would."

Dorn took a step forward. "I saw you kill Maric," he said. "But Julien and Archmaster Hendin are innocents."

"Not like me." Etherell was smiling. "Or you, I suppose." He leaned close to murmur silkily in his ear. "Are *you* innocent, Dorn Arrin?"

Dorn's fists clenched. "You enjoy your power over me, don't you?" He kept his voice down. No one else should be harmed. "Well, go ahead. Is this some service to your master? He's dead, you know."

Etherell's smile bared to a snarl. "He was never my master. And yes, I know he's dead. I saw him die. This Queen—you should see her, Dorn. She is going to turn the world upside down and sidewise in ways that will be fascinating to watch. And for some reason she wants you."

"I know," said Dorn. "She's wanted me since the fires of Manaia. And you'd feed me to her."

"I don't think she means to kill you," said Etherell. "Not right away. If she didn't have a use for you, she'd have wanted me to kill you here. Save a lot of trouble."

"Yes. Trouble." Dorn's arms went limp at his sides. He could not have said, just then, what he was feeling. He was remembering a dream of Academy Isle at twilight. A stone skipping on the water. Blue-grey and green-grey and silver-grey. He said at last, "We're a long way from home."

Etherell clapped his shoulder. "You are, perhaps," he said cheerfully. "I'm spared all that. I have no home."

CHAPTER

19

THERE were warnings before the procession came. Each time. Word of them spread, mouth to mouth, in whispers. A fire snuffed out suddenly in a grate. A stove gone cold, its pipe sprouting dagger icicles in moments. A film of ice on a basin that had been warm enough before. Windowpane that for decades of winter had endured would, one day, freeze and crack.

There were subtler warnings too, and these came earlier. A child who woke screaming from dark dreams night after night. A man and wife, once tranquil, taken to throwing crockery at each other's heads. Cows dried up, horses restive, dogs slunk flat to the ground, whimpering. A raven that would perch on the windowsill, fix its blood-red stare and not be shooed away.

Following the warnings—subtle or strange—came the procession. It was led by laughter. Mirth gone wrong, a chilling sound. When its leader appeared, an impossibly tall woman who shone, she was surrounded and trailed by followers. Some looked as if they had painted their faces with a substance like powdered diamonds, luminous to match their lady's skin, scarlet-lipped like her, too. All carried weapons—some swords, but otherwise there were axes, picks, clubs, slingshots. Torches, intended both to light the way and to destroy.

The impulse was to look at her and to look away, to run from her and draw near. Her hair was alternately like flame or blood, depending on the light. Her eyes shifted from ice-blue to cat's green but were always cold.

In one village there were warnings in the days since Tamryllin. Its people had prepared, armed themselves, organized. A group of brave men rushed the procession with torches and blades. They yelled with the old pride of the Eivarian hills, of tribes that had ruled here. For after all, their king was killed and they were abandoned now to this strange frost and fire. They had prepared for war.

But the warnings had not told them all. The White Queen's men—hardly more than boys—who met the charge did not look much like fighting men. They were not especially well-muscled, and there was a blankness in their eyes. At first they seemed to fall easily to attack—one took a hatchet square in the chest. Blood erupted and he went down. The villagers felt a rush of hope. They renewed the attack, burying their blades in the bodies of these boys.

The woman who led them laughed like music. That was when the boys were stirred awake. They reached to pluck the blades from deep in their chests or abdomens or skulls, and as the terrified villagers watched, the wounds closed and the boys rose to their feet.

That was when the villagers began to run. Some escaped; others were brought down by the blades of the White Queen's men, or, more horribly, torn limb from limb by those less skilled in weaponry. By people who had come lurching in pursuit of the White Queen from Tamryllin, from the towns and villages, and now had only one purpose in mind: to make others like themselves, or make them die.

And as the White Queen laughed and went on through the roads, people from all around began to find themselves drawn to her. Some painted their lips with the blood of the slain, and soon their faces glittered white as well, and there was no mistaking them, then, for anything but members of this procession, that went dancing and laughing through the villages and shattered windows, broke down doors, dragged people screaming from their homes.

There was the choice: To join these tormenting hordes, or be torn apart by them.

For most, the choice was clear.

* * *

A NIGHT of spinning snowflakes, melding with the white that clung everywhere—rooftops, sills, and streets. The tavern fire was built up against the cold, lamps lit against the dark. And other things. The snow offered a temporary solace; for as long as it fell thick and silent over all, the village was safe from attack. Or so they hoped. The White Queen's procession was seen moving east and away from here, towards the border mountains that led on to the desert; but even so. No one would feel safe until the madness of this winter reached an end. Night watches had been appointed in every village, at sundown everyone retreated behind bolted doors.

In the corner, a poet cloaked in black, a dark stone on his hand. He strummed a gold harp near the fire. The tavern patrons had cleared a space; despite the castastrophe brought upon them all by the Poet King, poets would always be revered in Eivar. Especially here, in the west, where the art of poets had been born in ages past. Their origin an isle out to sea, now lost in mists. If any tales were true.

All the tales were true. The events of the winter were proof of that.

Anyone who could leave their homes had gathered here to hear the poet's songs. There was naught else to do on a winter evening, but more than that, it offered comfort. Ballads old and new spilling forth, and to the old ones—the ones most familiar—people sang along, hopeful, mournful, as snowflakes fell beyond the panes of glass.

The poet's strange companion, a thin boy who didn't speak, stood with his nose pressed against a windowpane. As if he had never seen snow before. He was simple, the villagers thought, probably a servant, though they'd never heard of poets having servants before. Sometimes he'd turn from the window, arrested by a particular song, and begin to warble it himself, or do a dance. Once in a while, the poet held out his hand to the simple boy, or lay it on his thin shoulder. And kept on singing. His voice clear and strong. He could not have been more than a boy himself, with that voice.

So Lin Amaristoth imagined were the thoughts that passed through the minds of these folk that evening at the fire. These people wouldn't know that as she sang, she was doing several things. One was to weave a barrier that might conceal this village for a time, at least while she was here. The snow was a lucky chance, but no way to know if that alone would halt the White Queen's march.

Another thing she did was reach out with her mind to see beyond the boundaries of this village. To discover what moved in the night, and where enchantments might be awakening in answer to the White Queen's call. The answer to this last was hard to read, but was disquieting: it seemed to be, simply, *everywhere*.

The third thing she did, in lulls between the songs, was listen. With a drink in hand, or a bowl of mutton stew, she listened more than she spoke. For one thing, she did not want to be discovered as a woman—there would be questions, or worse. For another, she had much to learn. And so she did. She learned that the White Queen—for so everyone was calling her—appeared to be moving east. Leaving a trail of murder and destruction in her wake, accumulating followers. But heading toward the border mountains.

That was the prophecy the Ramadian Magicians had seen. Rather than be content to rule in Eivar, this White Queen would circumnavigate the world.

But there was more. And this was stranger yet, for being unexpected. Some counted it a nonsense story, not to be believed; but those who told it guaranteed they'd seen its truth with their own eyes.

It was this: A castle had sprung up, from nowhere, on shores not far from here. Where once had been nothing but ragged cliff now hung a pile of twisted spires against the sky. Stranger still, no one had found an entrance. A light might show in upper windows, late some nights; and yet, no door. Some intrepid children, and later, a band of duty-driven men, had gone looking. They had circled the walls and seen nary an opening, nor even a foothold to climb to the upper stories.

Some nights there could be heard the sound of revels from the upper windows, as of feasting and song, but surely this was some wives' tale. Not a true one.

Lin had hid a smile at this; for of course, a story told by women must be fabulation. Women who sat by the window and spun or carded, for hours on end, seeing all that passed in the street; women who, on market day, purchased tales of far-flung events from merchants along with their spices, cloth, and cheese.

"If I were to see this castle," she asked one of the men who told the tale, "how would I get there?" And so he told her of the path she'd take, were she to be so foolish as to seek out this enchantment—for so it surely was. Two days hence, westward, through pine forest to the sea. North, from that point, to where the cliffs were most sheer and treacherous. There it was.

She chose a more traditional ballad to sing, after asking that. To divert from the strangeness of what she'd asked. A song of a northern tarn, flat as a mirror, and how it got its name. A king's daughter so beautiful her reflection in the water had stayed a thousand days, and so the place was named for her—Lake Sinon. The song was old as the name, but this version, grown popular in recent decades, was from Valanir Ocune. Most wouldn't know that; they'd think there was only one version of the song—the one they'd known all their lives.

But Lin Amaristoth knew. As the wind howled in the eaves and thundered against the windowpanes she reached out, with this tribute to her companion of what seemed long ago. Once in a while she averted her eyes from those in the room to look instead into the flames, but it was all right. She didn't cry.

Ned had said she was hard, but she didn't think so. She thought that to appear so, and to be it, were two different things. He couldn't know she felt ground inside to powder. That she didn't know from day to day how she went on.

The difference now—between now and earlier, the time before the Fire Dance—was that the evidence that she *must* go on was etched into her skin. The gold that made a tracery on every part of her was, in its way, a command. She had something left to do. Even if she didn't know yet what it was.

A child was at her knee. A little girl with dark curls—old enough to speak, but not much more. Lin smiled down at her as the song was done.

The child was staring at the gem on Lin's right hand. "What is that?"

"A black opal," said Lin. "I think."

Another sort of command, the gem was; though she liked to think of it as a gift. One poet to another.

One Seer to another.

Syme had wandered over. He noticed the little girl and knelt beside her. "It's filled with fire," he said. "That stone. It's full of wonders."

He might have sounded lucid. She couldn't tell for sure.

"It has secrets," said Lin, looking from the awed child to Syme Oleir. "Like some people." Then to the child, who had narrowly missed a spark that hissed onto the hearth, "Don't sit too near the fire."

Syme's face went slack. She knew that look. In the time they'd been on the road together, she had learned his faces. He said, "Not all who enter flame can rise again. Not all come out unharmed and with gifts."

"That's right," Lin said, in a tone to end it. "I think it's time for another song."

"Not all can gain the keys to death." He looked past her as he spoke. But she thought he was speaking to her still. He touched the gem on her ring with a fingertip. She saw green light in his eyes where before there had been none; felt a shiver all through the veined gold markings on her skin. She didn't know what it could mean.

"Be careful," she said. Spoke lightly. "Or I may take you hunting with me for a castle without a door."

THAT night she tucked him into bed as if he were her child, as she had done all their nights on the road—five in all, so far. It seemed a comforting ritual for him. Lin wondered about his parents sometimes, where they were. Maybe they thought their son was dead. Telling them he'd died was the sort of thing Elissan Diar would have done.

She had tried asking him questions about his time with the king, about himself. It had not gone well. In one instance they had been in the forest and he had sat down suddenly on the ground and begun to scream. Which obviously would not do at all. It was sheer luck that she'd had pastries, purloined from the castle, to quiet him. She had stopped asking Syme anything about himself, or his past, after that. She observed him, as Elissan Diar apparently had done; though she didn't relish the comparison.

There were times he made himself useful. On a few occasions he danced when she played to entertain the crowds, or sang a song himself. In those instances Lin could close her eyes and imagine she was living the traditional life of a poet on the road, traveling with a companion as many young ones did. As she had done, once, with Leander Keyen. As she'd dreamed of doing with Valanir Ocune—among her various dreams involving him.

But that would last briefly, never more than two songs together. Syme would revert to his volatile self, and her task would be to distract attention from him as much as anything.

Before bed, before she went upstairs, she watched the men play at dice and listened. Snatches of conversation came to her at random.

If luck favors me, I'm heading south. First chance I get.

They say there was nothing left of him. Just bones. Though it's just a rumor . . .

There's that castle, no one knows what's in it. Or who.

My wife's cousin heard that someone saw a woman at the window, a woman in a red gown. And behind her—a man as huge as a giant.

Maybe he was a giant.

This was the oddest journey Lin had ever undertaken. As yet she didn't have a destination in mind. Since Tamryllin she'd borne west, where she sensed the enchantments were strongest, veering away from the bustle of river towns and toward the coast. Stopping in every tavern she could along the way. Her purpose was the gathering of knowledge. What she had learned tonight was the strangest thing so far, raising more questions than it answered.

A castle without a door. But the White Queen had no castle. She took pleasure in pillaging at random, in open air. She had become synonymous with the dark and winter frosts.

Lin knew she should undress and sleep, but was transfixed by the snow. From her window, one floor up, she watched as like glittering dust the flakes whirled on the winds, and down, by lantern light. This was one of the better places they'd stayed; the room had its own fireplace. It was wonderful to be warm. In the next bed Syme murmured in his sleep, tossed, sometimes whimpered.

She had escorted Rianna part of the way from Tamryllin, though the girl had insisted it was unnecessary. As if Lin could have done otherwise. In her man's clothes she had offered some protection for Rianna, whose loveliness could not be disguised. She had watched as with a straight back the girl had ridden away to the south, where her father and daughter awaited. She hoped they would be safe.

Safe was a relative term. Lin had had word from Kahishi, from Aleira Suzehn, that Eldakar was wounded. He was alive, he was safe. But the thought of him hurt was like a wound to her heart; she would have taken that arrow for him. She was better equipped to bear it, she thought, and deserved it anyway, for one thing or another.

These were common thoughts for her to have; she knew that, too. Once Ned Alterra might have helped stave them off with his careful reasoning and insights. But through his folly and her own, they'd lost each other.

Her experience of Kahishi lived within her like a warmth to which she kept returning. Despite that there was pain in it. In this room was her most vital link to the magic she'd found there. To the dance that had marked her with a command. *Turn back the shadow.*

Syme was also a link to Zahir Alcavar—an idea of insurmountable complexity for her. There was no simple way to think of the Magician, and perhaps for that reason she had sought the company of Eldakar so often. They'd loved and been betrayed by the same man.

But what mattered most now, about Syme, was the creature he contained. The weapon he'd become.

She looked across the room to the sleeping figure in the bed. "I know I need you," she said, softly so as not to wake him. "I wish I knew why."

20

HIS wrists were tied. Etherell had bundled him out the window of the inn, down the rope he'd used to get inside. Reminding him of the danger to the lives within if Dorn should resist. "I'll burn the place down if you try to get away," said Etherell before he made his own descent. He spoke casually, as if the words weren't horrible. "And anyone trying to escape would face me before they got far. You don't want that."

That was true—he didn't. He descended the rope into Etherell's waiting arms without protest. Allowed the other man to bind his wrists. And while this moment, in truth, called for a quip, he held his tongue. Julien would know his voice, if no one else; and the idea of her blood on his hands was . . . well, it was unthinkable. From here he could see lamplight through the ground floor window where she and Archmaster Hendin were. This was a wretched farewell to them both.

He'd been allowed his cloak, nothing else. Not his harp. Not the Silver Branch, inconspicuous in its wrapping, which Dorn suspected Etherell's White Queen would have wanted. He hoped Julien Imara would keep and care for those things. He trusted she would.

The ocean hungered for the shore tonight, to judge from its roaring. They turned from it toward the trees. Around and about for an endless stretch were pine woods, growing more mountainous to the north.

At last Dorn thought it safe for mockery. He looked down at his hands. "So. How long had you been waiting to tie me up?"

Etherell threw back his head to laugh. "You haven't changed."

Dorn glanced around. "I don't see a horse." He'd envisioned a bumpy ride tied to a horse, into the night and the gods knew where.

Etherell grinned at him. "Remember those enchantments you so despise? They're very useful. The White Queen sped my journey so I'd reach you in time. And she gave me a way to find her, wherever she happens to be." He took from his pocket what looked to be a stone. It was milky white in his palm and smooth as glass. "All I need do is hold on to you—like so," said Etherell, his hand on Dorn's shoulder. "And now to think of her—which isn't hard. You'll see."

The stone in his palm came alive with a rose-colored light. There was a flash, temporarily blinding.

When he could see again, Dorn saw they were on a hilltop. By light of a bonfire he saw a cluster of figures—those were men. He saw also that down the slope were camped many people, these swallowed in darkness. His gaze was drawn to the figure that blazed most visibly on that hill. A woman in white.

He knew her immediately. Of course he did.

He turned to Etherell. "How did you say she killed Elissan Diar?"

"I didn't," said Etherell. "You don't want to know."

She reclined in what looked like a bower constructed of branches, cushions, and silk hangings. Behind her, a pavilion had been set up. It was green and tasseled all around with gold. The men surrounding her—he knew them. Academy poets, Elissan's Chosen. One held a chalice within her reach. What was in it was anyone's guess.

She caught sight of the new arrivals, rose. To Dorn it seemed she towered over them even from a distance. Then, like a girl, clapped her hands with clear delight. "My offering! You found him. Well done, Etherell Lyr. You shall be rewarded."

"Not the way you rewarded Elissan Diar, I trust," said Etherell with a bow.

She laughed. "Did that unsettle you, mortal sapling? No, I hold to my bargains. Power I promised you, and so you shall have, when we cross the mountains together into battle. I will give you a kingdom or two, as many castles as you like, since you dear creatures enjoy that sort of thing."

She clapped her hands again. "Dorn Arrin! Long have we been parted from one another, against the laws of all that is sacred. You know as well as I do that you're mine."

He felt fear twist in his stomach. But he had always known that someday he would have to stop running. Ever since the night of Manaia, the fires had been destined for him. Better to face it now than to keep running. Better to stop putting others in harm's way like a coward.

He bowed, though it was awkward with his hands tied. "It seems so," he said. "Regardless of my thoughts on the subject."

She came forward to him. Took his face in her hands. Her fingers were so cold. Her eyes, up close, glittered like the frost. Her lips like blood. Now he felt fear, in truth. "You are like your friend," she said. "Well-spoken, charming. How I enjoy poets. In various ways, I always have. Some have adorned my bed when I felt the need; though it has been long since I have cared for the pastime. Especially since it tends to drive mortals mad, rendering them quite useless." She teased him with a glance. "Is that the fate you'd choose? The delights of my bower, in exchange for madness?"

"If my choice has anything to do with it," said Dorn, "I'll thank you, no."

She laughed again. Released his jaw and stepped back for a look at him. "You have no choices here at all, Dorn Arrin," she said. "You were given to me, soul and body, to do with as I please. The contract of Manaia is sealed in blood—it cannot by any means be broken. It was wrong, very wrong, of that girl to take you from me. If I see her again—well, she and I will have a talk."

He froze. Wondered what he could say, if anything, to distract her from thoughts of Julien Imara. He cleared his throat. "If I may ask," he said, "what is your purpose in our land? You left the castle. And the crown."

"Oh . . . castles. Crowns." She waved a hand. "It is my opponent, whom you may know as the Shadow King, who hides himself in castles. My way is to roam free. To sample pleasures—new, or expected. Whatever falls like ripe fruits in my lap, in this delicious world." She smiled wide, and for the first time he wondered if the redness of her mouth was somehow, against all reason, real blood. But that was preposterous, surely.

Her gaze delved into him. "I see you know a little. Of the war between myself and the Shadow King."

"Yes," he said. "What is the reason for it?"

She was suddenly close to him, her hand encircling his neck. Like a ring of ice around his skin. Her breath on his face smelled like flowers, the poisonous kind. He thought to breathe it in might kill him. "Don't ask questions you're not ready for," she murmured. "This form you see—this shape, this voice—is the one your mind can handle." Her breath cold in his ear. "For us, it is a game. For you, the axle-tree of everything you know."

"If you don't want me for your bed," said Dorn, "why did you summon me?"

She stepped back. Cocked her head, as if to consider him.

Etherell said, "As you can see, my friend has a way of getting down to business."

She smiled again, and stroked the back of Dorn's neck. The chill traveled through him, yet somehow was not unpleasant. He could understand, almost, how some accepted the offer of her company in return for madness.

"It's simple," she said. "I need you to steal something."

THE next day they stood on a hill, gazing across to the castle. Its towers were sharp, pointed; it looked to have been carved from the stones of the cliff itself. Below crashed the waves; surrounding were the green hills of the west, cloaked in ivy-clad trees and dotted with sheep. Dorn Arrin wondered what people here had thought, to awake one day to this castle appearing above them.

He wondered other things, too, like how his friends were faring without him; how they'd felt to find him gone.

"What are you thinking?" Etherell Lyr, sounding playful.

"That you made a fool of yourself last night." It wasn't what he'd been thinking, but why miss an opportunity to insult him? In any case Etherell had spent the last night drinking and dancing like a fool. Even dancing with the Queen, leaning close to her, as if she were some village girl he was wooing. He'd invited Dorn to join their dance, as well. Like he'd forgotten his own treachery. Dorn had turned himself around, deliberately, to watch the stars instead. And drink alone.

"I know you're sore with me," said Etherell. "Look, all you have to do is steal this—whatever it is—for the Queen, and she won't kill you. And meanwhile you get to see what's inside that enchanted castle. I'd go myself, if it didn't have to be you."

"That's easy to say," said Dorn. "For all your professed eagerness for adventure, you seem very attached to your own neck. Going along with one conqueror, then another. You seek power, that's all."

"That's all?" Etherell was studying his nails. "What else is there? Anyway, we should keep on, if we're to be there before sundown. Those were her orders."

"I should make you drag me the whole way. What do I care?"

"You want me to carry you, perhaps." Etherell sounded sarcastic. "Look, there's no time for a tussle in the grass. And I'm sorry for that—it would do you good."

Dorn spat at him. "Go to hell."

Etherell put his hands on his hips. "I don't think you understand. She'll kill you if you fail. She'll kill me, too, if I fail to get you there; but never mind that. Wouldn't that be a stupid reason to die—because you're angry with me?"

"She'll kill you, too?" Dorn sneered at him. "Really? Do you *promise?*"

"Probably." Etherell shrugged. "Make my head explode, perhaps, as she did to Elissan Diar. Or twist my limbs off, one by one, leaving the head for last. One thing I can say for our Queen—she's creative. And she gets her way."

Dorn found himself moving forward, down the hill. He felt too tired to fight, though he didn't want the other man to see that. But it was true—he didn't want to die.

Ahead, the cliff rose higher, a wall above the sea. It cast a shadow all across the downs.

"I suppose you know why I had to wear these absurd clothes?" That morning, folded in his tent—for he'd been given his own pavilion, a place of honor—was a suit of green and gold brocade. Emblazoned on his chest in gold, the symbol he'd come to know too well: the double spiral. There was also a sword, though that was next to useless—he wouldn't know what to do with it. But he knew it was a treasure—the scabbard studded with green gems, the hilt chased with gold. The metalwork showed an eagle with a rabbit in its claws.

And then there was the gold harp, gold-strung, standing alongside the green clothes. He'd half expected it to vanish at his touch, it was so fine. That would be his disguise—a wandering poet. A disguise that was also truth.

"I don't know why you'd complain," said Etherell. "You look remarkably well."

"I feel like a trimmed goose marching to the feast."

"No." This the other man said with sudden seriousness. "You're not a sacrifice. This is a mission. A quest, if you will. And she has given you her word that she will only kill you if you fail."

"You take her word?"

"I do. Lies come of weakness, if you think about it," Etherell said. He sounded as if this were a thought he worked out as he spoke. "In a true position of power there is nothing to conceal."

"Interesting, given that you've been lying all your life."

"Exactly." Etherell smiled at him. "Look, we're here. This is where you go on alone."

They were a short distance from the cliff face. The sky was stained red with the setting sun. So was the sea.

Dorn turned in his tracks. He had to put aside his rage and hurt, just now. Other things mattered more. "Etherell," he said, "if I fail—"

"Yes?"

"Please don't let her kill Julien. I know if you want to, you can protect her. You have more power than you think."

The winds picked up Etherell's hair. He was looking up thoughtfully at the sky. He said at last, "I'll do what I can. I like the girl."

"Swear it."

Etherell gave a laugh at this. "I don't make promises," he said. "Not ones I mean to keep. I'd rather not lie to you, after everything."

"So that's the best I'll get from you," said Dorn. "Well." He turned away. Began to walk through the grass to the cliff face. His face was stiff and stinging, with fear or something more. Fear made sense, right now. The abode of the Shadow King was just ahead. *He might kill you,* the White Queen had said, when instructing him last night. *But I think not. He loves poets' songs almost as much as I.*

The cliff face was smooth, apparently unmarked; but he knew what to look for. *When the sun is just above the horizon, the light will catch upon it.* Her voice in his head again.

Soon he found it, engraved lines flashing back the remainder of the sun. A small carved symbol—the double-spiral within a circle. It was about the size of his palm. Dorn touched his hand to it, fingers spread. Again as instructed. He heard a rumbling, quickly stepped back. A scrape, a creak of stone against stone, and then a door was opening. Had heaved itself ajar, leaving a doorway just tall and wide enough for him to walk through.

He looked back. Etherell Lyr was already gone. That stung, too—that he had not even thought to see him off.

It's time to get used to pain, he told himself. And to strangeness. Go on. He stepped inside. The door swung shut behind him, a creak and a click. He turned instinctively—an animal's aversion to a trap—but there was no sign of the door from this side. No seam in the wall, no symbol. He pushed experimentally, since the door had opened outward, and—nothing. No way back.

A spiral stair led upward. Torches bracketed in the wall were burning. He set his feet on the first step and rehearsed in his mind what he'd been told to say.

When he arrived at the top of the stair, a man was waiting for him. He wore the livery of a servant. "You're expected," he said. "Come this way."

Dorn hefted the harp as he went. Followed the servant down a corridor where here and there were various doors, all shut. It seemed ordinary enough so far.

At last they came to a hall with a great fireplace. The room was huge and bedecked with holly. Near the fire sat two people. As Dorn approached, he saw that it was a man and a woman. The man was reading from a book propped on a desk. The woman, young and ravishing in red velvet, was seated on the carpet with the dogs, two hounds with coats like bronze. She threw a holly branch for them to fetch.

They both looked up. The man, Dorn saw, was entirely unprepossessing. A face and figure he'd have been hard-pressed to recall, of perhaps middle age. He was neither tall nor short, neither large nor thin. His neat, greying beard made Dorn think of a town banker. His clothes were simple; his rank denoted only by a length of chain with a jeweled pendant. "A good morrow," he said courteously. His accent was, perhaps, a touch unfamiliar. "We don't often have visitors." He looked Dorn full in the eye. Here was one thing that caught Dorn's attention: the man's eyes, green, gold-flecked, hard to read.

Dorn came forward. He'd been instructed what to say. "I am a poet, come to entertain your majesty this New Year's Day."

"How did you enter here?"

"The lore of poets is nearly lost, but not forgotten."

The man stood. By some trick of the light seemed taller. "And do you know me?"

At this, Dorn bowed low. "You are the King who is new to this land, yet older than its mountains," he said. Grateful that he'd been schooled to recite from memory. "You are the one who hunts prey, even to the ends of the earth, and brings it down."

From the hearthrug the woman clapped her hands. A gesture unsettlingly like the White Queen, but this woman did not arouse fear. She was not of a great height, nor luminous. Only her hair shone, alternately like gold thread and honey in the firelight. "Something new, my lord," she said. "Let's have this poet to sing in the New Year."

The grey-bearded man issued a small bow in her direction. "Very well, my lady," he said. "I know how you love your entertainments." Then turned back to look Dorn in the eye. "So, Dorn Arrin. It seems you can stay."

Dorn hadn't told this man his name. He stood staring a moment.

But the other man was already sitting at the desk again, the book tipped up before him. It was leather-bound in black with gilt embossing. The cost of binding that book would have made Dorn's father swoon. Yet there was no title on the cover or spine.

Without looking up, the King waved a hand. "Go. Get settled in your chambers. Supper will be served shortly, and then you'll sing."

SUPPER was a ludicrous affair from Dorn's point of view; he hadn't seen such a spread in all his life. The long table was covered in its entirety with dishes of gold and silver, and each of these displayed some fowl, or fish, or in one instance, a piglet. That was to say nothing of all the sauces and soups, the wines and ales in jewel-encrusted decanters. The aromas recalled to him that he hadn't eaten properly in days—not since being cosseted by Larantha on Academy Isle. Given his situation, it was difficult to summon an appetite.

At one end of the table sat the King, though Dorn had trouble thinking of him as such. He'd expected the so-called Shadow King, opponent of the White Queen for eternity, to be more imposing. At the other end sat his lady. Dorn had never learned her name. Either of their names, come to that.

A servant had led him to the hall, the same one they'd been in earlier, but now with a trestle table set out and laid for dinner.

The holly branches decorating the hall recalled to Dorn his ostensible reason for being here: the feast of New Year's Eve was in two days. On the third day—dawn of the New Year—if he had not fulfilled his mission, the White Queen had promised Dorn would perish on the spot. Wherever he happened to be. She had laid this enchantment upon him, her hands first on his forehead, then her lips. And then, of course, had smiled.

She'd given him next to no guidance about what she wanted. It was a keepsake, she said, something she needed back. The implication being that the Shadow King had stolen it, though Dorn was not sure he believed that. If that were the case, she could have just said so straight out. Instead she hedged, and would only say that it could take several forms, and Dorn would have to be aware enough to recognize it when he saw it.

His life hinged upon this. To identify what she wanted, and steal it for her.

It seemed impossible. He probably didn't have long, so why not face that, and take what he could? So he thought as the servant seated him at the exact center of the table, between the Shadow King and his lady. He tried every dish, every ale and wine. All of it excellent, even better than it smelled. His last days would be sweet ones, he had suddenly decided. As last meals went . . . these would do.

As he ate, the couple engaged in polite conversation. The King planned to go hunting on the morrow. She reminded him that it would rain at midday, so he should go early. They didn't seem to notice the stranger at their table, until the end. It was only when they'd all eaten their fill that the King asked Dorn to sing.

As Dorn Arrin rose and took up the harp he had a thought that almost made him laugh: He had dreamed of performing before kings. Now here he was.

The White Queen hadn't advised him what to play, so Dorn followed his instincts. He sang of the turn of the year, green turned to snow, the chariot of Thalion circling the earth. It was a tradition, this song, and seemed appropriate for this hall.

When he was finished, there was a silence. Dorn kept his eyes down, not daring to look at either the Shadow King or his lady.

At last the lady spoke. "I am satisfied, my love," she said. "Are you?"

"It is pleasing enough," said the King. "Sometimes the oldest airs are the ones we most enjoy, especially at a time of celebration. It's settled, then: the poet will stay with us until the New Year as our honored guest."

Dorn dared a glance at them. They were smiling at him, all courtesy. So he bowed low as he could and said, "An honor indeed."

Then it was time for dessert, as if there had not been enough to eat already. The servants brought out cakes of almond and honey, a cherry pie, a strawberry sorbet that the lady remarked was in the fashion of the east. By the time they were done Dorn thought he'd never eat again. This was a far cry from the small bites of smoked fish and dry biscuit he'd been living on since leaving the Academy. Surprisingly he did not feel ill from the indulgence. Just mildly stirred by wine, content. Thoughts of death seemed a worry for another time.

His chambers were another ludicrous indulgence. Dorn had marveled at them before, and now did so anew, especially when he saw that the enormous bed had been turned down for the night, and a scented bath drawn. He wanted to collapse into bed, but it seemed a shame to waste a bath. He doffed his green clothes and luxuriated in the warm water for a time. He emerged, smelling of lavender, and collapsed into the soft bed. Its coverlet was cloth of gold.

That night was the most restful he'd had in longer than he could remember. He didn't dream.

He was startled awake the next morning. Someone was sitting at the foot of his bed. It took a moment for his eyes to come into focus, after the wine he'd drunk the night before. He was not accustomed to drink. Another moment, and he saw it was the lady. She was smiling, and positioned in such a way as to accentuate her breasts, which her low-cut dress displayed to effect.

Dorn became aware, quite suddenly, that he was naked under the coverlet. He drew it farther up to his chin.

"You slept a good while," she said. Aside from being cut low at the neckline, her gown was splendid, a concoction of silver and gold, fitted to her like a second skin. Her hair was pulled up in a net and sparkled with gems. Dorn wondered if he'd ever seen a woman so beautiful, and doubted it. The terrifying White Queen hardly counted.

"I was tired," he said, aware of the absurdity of the situation. He spoke casually, as if he were not petrified. He could only guess what would happen to him if the lord were to discover her here. "It was—it is kind of you to visit and wish me a good morning."

"You could return my kindness by any means you like," she said. "My husband is out hunting."

"Right," he said. "If you turn your back, I will dress, and sing for you. Would you like that?"

She appraised him. "What if I don't turn?"

"I really would prefer you did."

She laughed. "You are a strange one, Dorn Arrin. I'd heard tell that poets have lusty appetites—and a way with the ladies."

"I'm sorry to disappoint you," he said. "Really. But I will sing myself hoarse for your pleasure."

She pouted. Then turned her back. It was bare, white as alabaster, with a single dewdrop diamond from her necklace dangling at the nape. He could imagine how most men would feel, and react, in this situation.

He drew the coverlet about himself when he stood, not trusting her. Then retreated behind a screen to dress himself. A new set of clothes had been provided—these crimson, lined with ermine. He was astonished to find they fit him perfectly.

When he came out from behind the screen, he jumped. A different woman sat there now. This with coils of black hair that reached her waist, scarlet lips, and dark eyes, where before they had been blue. But the dress and necklace were the same.

"Perhaps now?" she said. This time in a voice that was lower, more throaty. She lifted a bare shoulder. "I know men have their preferences."

For a moment he could do nothing but stammer. "You are lovely," he said at last. "But how would it repay my lord's hospitality if I took liberties with his wife?"

She laughed, low and musical. "He'll never know."

"But I would." He grasped for the first thought that came to mind. "It's a matter of honor."

She sighed. "Suit yourself, then. Sing for me. Then come to breakfast."

THEIR breakfast was lavish, with various types of bread, cheeses, and cold meats. There seemed jam from every fruit for him to try, as well as fresh fruits. On a silver dish was served a honeycomb.

The lady insisted he eat, in a teasing manner; she spooned various kinds of jam for him to taste, even fed them to him. Urged him, leaning close, to lick the spoon. He kept up a polite manner as best he could. Earlier in his chambers, he had sung to her; a ballad of a king on the hunt. He hoped it would send a clear message, but afterward at breakfast she seemed by no means deterred.

Meanwhile he had to recall that there was a more pressing matter to be concerned with than the virtue of the Shadow King's wife. There was the matter of his own impending demise. So while he deflected her flirtation, he was careful to be courteous about it. He needed her goodwill. She might be an ally, given her willingness to betray the King.

When she urged him to tell of himself, he saw an opening. "I wander throughout Eivar collecting tales," he said. "I hoped, in these enchanted halls, to find marvels to recount. So far there is my lady's unearthly beauty—not to mention your ability to change shape. A marvel I will sing of, to be sure."

She laughed. "That is nothing. I get bored and change all the time." She was currently back to being honey-haired, having changed at some point in their climb down the stairwell. Dorn had not seen it happen; perhaps it was between one shaft of sunlight and the next.

"To you, it's nothing," he said. "To me, a wonder of the world. But so far this castle seems a bit . . . ordinary? I'd have thought a King of the lands beyond would have a palace full of marvelous things."

"You mean enchanted objects, perhaps," she said, leaning forward over the table in a manner that he suspected was an intended lure. The diamond necklace sparkled between her breasts.

"Yes," he said. "Exactly that."

She smiled. "Come with me." She took his hand. He thought better of protesting, and followed, hoping it was not some trick.

She led him to a door, and he noticed it was lovely; carved mahogany, with a finish like glass. She looked back at him over her shoulder and set a finger to her lips. "We must be quiet here," she said. "Or the servants will get us into trouble. Especially you."

That got his pulse going. He followed after her. She closed the door behind them and locked it. He surveyed the room.

It looked like a library. The walls were lined with leatherbound books. Dorn tried to read the titles, but the letters shifted and blurred before his eyes.

Sunlight streamed from tall windows that looked out on a garden. The trees seemed to give the lie to its being winter; their boughs loaded with white and pink cherry blossoms, swaying slow and serene in a breeze.

There was no way a garden like that existed atop a wind-torn cliff. Not in any season of the year.

Dorn turned his attention to the room. Everywhere were objects on display—how to single out one or another? He saw swords mounted on the wall. Nearby, a hand mirror turned facedown on a table; its back looked carved of ivory. When Dorn picked it up, instead of seeing his reflection, he found himself looking into another room, where a man with his back to him was rummaging through some papers. Dorn put the mirror down hastily.

There were other things: An hourglass filled with what looked like powdered gems in place of sand. A great gold globe encircled with rings, engraved in silver with the constellations. A crystal sphere mounted in brass, that changed color depending on where one was standing. And from one angle seemed filled with smoke.

In one instance he turned and suppressed a yelp. But the warrior he'd spotted in the corner turned out to be an empty suit of armor. It was tremendous, taller and broader than a man had any right to be. The plates so black they seemed to absorb the light. The helmet was huge, with the antlers of a hart. Clasped in one gauntlet was an axe handle thick as a young tree with a massive black blade. Dorn stepped aside in case the axe should fall. What an idiotic manner of death that would be.

But who fit into this suit of armor? Was it for show?

The lady watched him but said nothing to guide him or explain.

At last he asked, "What did you want me to see?"

She looked mischievous. "Oh, do you know what would happen if we were found in here? Down below, there are no dungeons. My lord doesn't care for those. Instead he has a trapdoor that opens to the ocean. Isn't that marvelously clever? You should have heard the screams of the last people he had thrown down there."

"You sound oddly calm at the idea of being drowned," he said testily.

"It would just be you," she said with a sweet smile. "Now, then, you wanted to know what is in here. As you can see, this room is filled with fascinating things. The books, in particular. But there is one thing . . . ah yes." She had a wooden box in her hands suddenly, though Dorn didn't see where she'd gotten it. "Look."

Within nestled an amulet on a chain. The pendant took the shape of a sphere and was paper-thin—hammered gold. And engraved at its center . . . Dorn's heart sped up again.

"Perhaps I thought of this because of the symbol on your clothing when you arrived," she said, resting a delicate hand on his chest. "It's the same, isn't it?"

Dorn stared at the double-spiral engraved in the amulet. "It's the same." He darted a glare at her. "Is this a trick?"

"You want this?" She lifted the amulet by its chain to the light. "It *is* lovely."

In that moment he found himself making a decision. Not knowing what else to do. He met her gaze. "My life depends on it," he said.

THE lady wasn't smiling anymore. She looked almost sad. "That is a great shame," she said. "For I don't see how you can have it. My husband checks on all his treasures every night at bedtime. If this were to go missing he'd notice right away, and have you drowned."

Dorn found that he was kneeling before her. "Lady, I am putting my life in your hands by telling you this," he said. "I'm trusting you don't want me thrown down the trapdoor."

"Go on," she said.

"There is an enchantment on me," he said to her. Saw that her expression didn't change. Well, why would someone like her be surprised by enchantments? He went on. "If I don't recover that amulet by dawn of New Year's Day I will die."

"Let me see," said the lady, and laid her hands on his head as he knelt. She looked down at him, and her eyes shone, blue gleam like a cat. He did not think it was a trick of the light. "Yes," she said. "There is enchantment here. A strong one." And then he saw her expression shift, and whatever glimpse of power or strangeness in it had gone. Now she was all gentleness. "Rise, Dorn Arrin."

He obeyed. Her hands, which had been in his hair, had moved to his shoulders. "I will help you," she said. "There is a simple way to go about it. My husband only checks on his treasures before bed. On your last night here—on New Year's Eve—I will obtain the amulet and bring it to you after he has gone to sleep. That way you shall have it on New Year's Day."

"But . . ." He looked down at her. "That is more generous than I could ever dream, my lady." He swallowed hard. A thought had just occurred to him. "But I can't ask that of you. To risk your life."

She stared at him a moment. For the first time since they'd met, the lady of this strange castle seemed truly startled. Then she gave a laugh, light and thrilling. "Dorn Arrin, son of a bookbinder," she said. "That is a noble thing. That you'd give a thought for me, at your peril."

"No one should die for me," he said.

She leaned forward and, before he could draw back, kissed him glancingly on the mouth. "I will be safe," she said. "You have my word." She tasted of something sweet, like berries.

"You mean—"

She was radiant in the summer light. "Yes," she said. "I will perform the task for you."

A new thought occurred to him. "In tales there is always an exchange," he said. "If there is something I can do . . ." He had visions of doing her bidding in the bedchamber, and steeled himself. He supposed it was better than dying.

She put her hand to his lips. "No," she said. "This I'll do as a friend. And I've already gotten my kiss." She smiled with new mischief, and took his hand. "Come walking with me," she said. "Come to the garden."

THAT evening just as the sun set, the belling of hounds and cry of horns told of the Shadow King's return. He arrived on a black horse, servants riding behind with the game he had killed. Dogs coursing at their heels. Dorn Arrin saw it all from the window where he and the lady sat, playing cards and whiling away the hours with conversation. They had spoken all that day, yet if Dorn tried to cast back his memory to catch hold of what they'd discussed, it eluded him. He certainly knew no more than before of who or what she was. Even though it seemed they had walked a great while after their exchange in the lord's library, conversing in the shade of the cherry trees.

The lady greeted her lord with an embrace and a kiss. "You have had a successful venture out, it would seem," she said as she stepped back.

"Twenty deer," he said. "And now, we feast."

The air was soon filled with the smell of venison from the kitchen as the cooks prepared the meal. Supper was an even greater affair than it had been the previous night. Once again, the lord and lady chatted politely; the King announcing his intent to ride out again on the morrow.

So it was startling when the King turned suddenly to Dorn, whom he'd ignored until then, and said, "So how did you find my castle today, Dorn Arrin? Did my lady make you welcome?"

With effort, Dorn kept his face impassive. He felt like a stone was lodged in his throat. "Quite," he said. "You are both more than generous."

"The duty to honor poets is sacred," said the King. "Traditions must be observed."

Dorn thought of what the lady had meant to do for him that morning in the bedchamber, and thought *honor* was one way of putting it. He hoped nothing of his thoughts showed in his face. It was hard to believe this ordinary fellow was an immortal King, but it would be deadly to forget.

After dinner he sang for them again. When it was time for sleep, the same bath awaited in his chamber, scented, steaming as if it had just been drawn. The bed turned down invitingly for the night. This time when he slept he dreamed, a confusion of images from the day. Last he saw was the pendant with the double spiral swinging on its chain.

He awoke to the sun in his eyes and the lady standing at the window. She had drawn back the drapes to let in the daylight. It shone directly in his face so he had to squint to see her. She wore a dress that seemed studded in its entirety with diamonds, low-cut and revealing every curve. Dorn came awake quickly, alert at once.

"Good morning," he said with desperate cheeriness. "I suppose it's time for breakfast?"

"It will be a fine day." She dimpled at him. "And later, a fine night for thievery, don't you think?"

"Of course," he said. "Though perhaps you shouldn't say that so loudly."

"My husband left at dawn for the hunt," she said. She came away from the window to sit on the bed. "We may plot, and scheme, and do as we like. As loudly as we like."

"I'll sing for you again," he said. "If you just let me to my clothes."

She slid nearer on the bed. "You are a puzzle."

"Look," he said. "I don't want to die. Is this . . . is this something you require, for my life?"

She looked hurt. "We have a bargain. I wouldn't break my word."

"Thank you," he said. "I'm truly grateful. So please, let me to my clothes and I will sing. We'll have breakfast. We can play games or walk in the garden. Whatever else you like."

"But what about what you would like, Dorn Arrin?" She was looking at him clear-eyed, with earnestness. "There must be something you want. And you know, I can be anything."

She had changed in the moment she spoke. Now Etherell Lyr sat at the foot of the bed.

Dorn could hardly breathe. He pulled the covers to himself. "Stop it," he choked. "Get out of my mind."

The man at the foot of the bed spoke in the voice Dorn knew. "But isn't this what you want? And why shouldn't you have it?" He edged nearer, until he was sitting beside Dorn on the bed. He lay a hand on his chest. A move reminiscent of the lady, but this was not her, not in any tangible way. The voice was right. Even the familiar scent. He was dressed finely, like a prince, but not too fine. He looked himself in every way.

"I shouldn't have it," said Dorn, with effort, "because it's not real."

The man raised a hand to play with Dorn's hair. "Real enough. Trust me," he said, and flashed the grin that was all too familiar. "You'll know it well enough, before I'm done with you."

He was almost on top of Dorn now, though the covers were between them. "And why should Sendara have all I have to give, and not the person who loves me truly—who has loved me for years?"

Dorn turned his head away. He was trying not to cry. "I don't know how you know these things," he said. "But it's wrong to use your power this way, lady."

And now she was herself again, if there was a self that could be said to be her; she was a woman again, at any rate. Sitting beside him on the bed in her shimmering dress. She reached to touch the corner of his eye, with a look of wonder tasted his tear. She said, "You are so strange. Why would your heart's desire cause you grief?"

"Please," he said, flinching from her. "This is too much."

She squeezed his shoulder. "Dress, then," she said. "Though it pains me to let you go on, so unhappy, without giving you what you wish."

Now he could only laugh, albeit shakily. "So you are trying to be kind. That's unexpected."

When he was dressed—this time in white and silver, which again fit perfectly, she said, "Sing to me of love. I know poets have a thousand different ways to describe it. I would hear how it sounds from you."

So he chose a love ballad among the many there were, and sang it to her. And then they went out to breakfast, and walked in the garden again. Before he knew it, it was evening and the hounds and horns were announcing the return of the King. Dorn Arrin felt a chill, as if they announced his fate instead. It was, after all, his last evening here, when much would be decided.

The King came in, sodden and muddy, but pleased. "My dear," he said when his wife greeted him at the door. "I have had quite a victory today. The white boar that has been about our forest is caught at last."

She clapped her hands. "How appropriate for the New Year's Eve feast. I will have the cooks set to work at once."

"Yes," he said. "And order them to set a fourth place setting. We will have a guest, in addition to our poet friend."

She smiled into his eyes, as if to share something private. "But of course," she said. "On this of all nights. She comes."

The words made Dorn's hairs prickle a warning. But surely . . . ? But no, he was right. That evening, when the table was set for four, a knock came at the door. The lady was playing with the hounds, while Dorn read a book of poetry that was, at last, in words he could read. A loan from the head of the household. The King, changed into clean apparel, was reading from his black book at the desk. In all, the scene was very like the one Dorn had arrived to days before.

When the servant opened the door a cold wind blew in, a pale winter light shone inside. A rich voice Dorn Arrin knew too well said, "What a delightful place."

And then she was there, the White Queen.

The King had risen from his seat. "Be welcome," he said with a bow. "Now let's to our dinner."

Dorn's thoughts were racing. What was she doing here? She did not acknowledge him; she swept by to the dining table. He had forgotten how tall she was, and how she terrified him. It seemed absurd that she was the opponent of this unassuming man who hosted them. But by now he knew appearances were deceiving.

The boar was enormous, nearly half the size of the long table and served on a gargantuan silver plate. To accompany it there was, as usual, a seemingly endless parade of dishes.

For the White Queen was brought a special dish on a gold platter, which the servant proffered with a bow. A slab of red meat, raw on the plate. She ate it with her hands, blood dripping from her jaws, eyes agleam. It ought to have been disgusting, but instead seemed to heighten her beauty. Dorn thought of a song he might compose, "Ode to the Huntress," to capture what he felt as he watched the White Queen feasting, dripping blood.

Once the plates were set aside and the Queen had cleansed herself with a basin of rosewater, she said, "Now to business. Though first I wish to compliment you on your household. The food is excellent, and the hall quite pleasant. Though I prefer the woods."

"Someday perhaps we will dine in your woodland halls together," said the King, impeccably polite. "Meanwhile. The appointed place and time. It is your turn, this time, to choose."

"You know these choices are not arbitrary," said the Queen. "The stars align in ways that make some places, some times, auspicious. At any rate: the appointed time is the same as ever. Ten days hence. The place—there is a field between the mountains and desert to the east."

"I know the place."

"Within sight of the tallest mountain is where we'll meet," she said. "Your armies and mine."

"Done, then," said the King. "For a beginning."

"Yes," she said. "The start of our campaign. I hope for a bracing one this time. I crave a challenge. Last time we laid waste to the world too soon, it seemed to me, before I'd fully sampled its delights."

"There is value to efficiency," said the King. "We have our differing priorities as ever."

She laughed.

"Shall we have more wine?" said the King. "And then a song, before the final toast. Our drink to the New Year."

For the first time the Queen seemed to notice Dorn was there. "A song," she said. "Yes. Sing, Dorn Arrin." She rose from the table to approach him, bent to touch her lips to his forehead. He found a strange sensation filling him, like wine, but stronger, more intoxicating.

She commanded him. "Sing of the end of the world."

So on that New Year's Eve, Dorn stood before the Shadow King and White Queen and for the first time in many months, composed a song. He did so on the spot, words coming to him as the melody spilled from his hands. And as he did, he could not be sure if the words were his, or if they had been instilled in him through the White Queen's kiss. But he knew one thing. As he sang of forests laid waste, mountains tumbling down, seas washing away the palaces and cities of the world, the grief was his alone.

When he looked up—when it was over—the King and Queen looked not at him, but at each other. Both impassive. But the honey-haired lady looked his way, and it seemed to him there was compassion in her eyes, though for something distant; as if she contemplated a game animal—perhaps a deer or boar—about to die.

They remained in the hall, the four of them, seated around the fire until midnight. Dorn was exhausted and alert at once. He and the Shadow King's lady played a new game of cards. The deck depicted lords and ladies in the hunt. There were animals of the hunt—hawks, hounds, harts, foxes. The king wore black armor and carried an axe; the queen wore white, and bore a long, slender bow that reached the ground. It was hard for him to concentrate on the game; it was intricate, of the lady's devising, and she seemed to keep changing the rules.

The White Queen sat, regal in a wing-backed chair, and watched the flames.

At last the hour of midnight struck, rung by the chapel bells. On this cue, the servant appeared with goblets, four on a tray. "Mead for the New Year," said the King.

The Queen raised her cup high in both hands, looking up at it, the lines of her jaw fine-cut. She said, "To victory." And drank.

The others followed suit. Dorn tasted gingerly of his, then drank it down; it was powerful and sweet, and he felt wrung of resistance.

The White Queen made her farewells and left the hall, and the King took the hand of his lady.

And so Dorn stumbled upstairs to his room, led by the servant that had escorted him twice before. The scent of lavender from the steaming bath, as before. The candle beside the bed, its rich coverlet turned down to reveal the luxury of an eiderdown mattress and pillows.

But Dorn did not head directly for his bath. He went to the window. In the dark of the new moon he couldn't see much; he only knew, from daytime, that the landscape was a garden of blossoming trees, and a forest beyond. No sign of ocean, nor the cliff by which he'd entered. When he had walked through that hidden door he'd traveled farther than he knew, stepping into a mystery never to be solved. Perhaps that was what all enchantments were.

It was his last night here. The lady had promised to steal the amulet for him, to have it on the day. To save his life. But now that the time was nigh, he had begun to think ahead. What happened after he saved himself? He would return to the White Queen. He would never be free. And the oncoming catastrophe stretched its shadow far beyond his life.

Tonight he'd sung of the end of the world. And in doing so, believed it.

He might save himself tomorrow from the Queen's fatal enchantment. But there was worse to come.

In the end, he went into the bath because he hoped the warmth and lavender scent would soothe him for a time. After, lulled by the bath, worn out by the day, he was soon asleep.

It was still dark when she woke him. He could see right away that something was wrong. Even in the faint light she looked pale. "Wake," she said gently. "Would that I had better news."

He sat up, feeling as if someone had poured ice water on him. "What do you mean?"

She was still a moment. Then: "The amulet is gone. I went to where he keeps it and—the box was empty. And I could feel it was nowhere in the room. He must have guessed our plan and made it vanish. Or sent it to another world—it matters not. It's out of my hands."

He was shaking. "I'm to die at dawn."

She joined him at the bedside. "From what I know of such things . . . it will be quick."

"How does it work?"

She shook her head. "To ask that of enchantments is like pouring water onto wind. And the White Queen's enchantments are of the strongest kind. Only my husband is a match for her."

"And you can't—you can't plead with him on my behalf?"

He was certain she looked sad now. There was no need even for her to answer.

He wrapped himself in the coverlet and went to the window again. It was not yet dawn. He wondered how much time he had.

It will be quick.

That was something. Not enough.

How had it all happened so fast? He thought of the people he would never see again. They would never know what had happened to him. That he'd perished in an enchanted castle, on a fool's errand.

A hand on his shoulder. Somehow he knew it before he turned: Etherell's hand. For once all the mischief in his face had fled. Or so it seemed in the half-light. "This is my fault," he said. "I found you for her. I didn't think you'd be killed. I . . . I didn't think at all."

Dorn didn't know what to say. He knew this wasn't the man, and yet. And here were words he'd longed for, without knowing. "Why did you do it?"

Etherell rubbed at his eyes. "I don't know why I do anything, don't you see?" There were tears in his eyes.

"The man I know would never care," said Dorn. "Would never cry."

"You don't know me," said Etherell. "How could you? I've hidden behind walls of my own making. From myself most of all."

"This is only what I want to hear." Dorn shook his head. He felt heavy with the sadness he had not allowed himself to feel in a long while. "It's not true."

The other man's arms came around him. It was so warm there, and the scent enveloped Dorn, and he was powerfully reminded of what he'd wanted for longer than he could remember. "You are going to die," said Etherell. "Shouldn't we be together once, before that happens? Unless you hate me too much. That I'd understand."

It was hard to speak. "Never," Dorn said at last. "I couldn't hate you. I want you more than anything."

And before he knew what was happening Etherell had leaned forward for a kiss, and they were locked together, moving towards the bed. Etherell had removed his shirt, his trousers nearly undone, and Dorn found himself moaning with all the longing he had ever felt when their flesh met for the first time.

It was when they were in the bed, and Etherell was astride him, that Dorn held his face in his hands. With his fingertips caressed his face, cheek to jaw. He said, "I love you so much. I can't do this."

Etherell grinned. "You won't have to do anything, you know."

"No." Dorn gently slid the other man off him and sat up. "It isn't you. You're not the man I love. I want this so much, but it's a lie. I don't want my last act in life . . . to be that. Chasing a shadow."

The arms that came around him from behind were unmistakably those of the man he loved, as was the scent. And then in his ear, a murmur that made all of him stir. "Are you sure?"

Dorn covered his face. "Yes, I'm sure. Please, change back. My lady. Please."

She was standing at the window, now, in her diamond-studded dress. She was looking out at the landscape, as if despite the darkness there was something there that she could see.

"Dorn Arrin," she said. "You have surprised me." Then turned his way, and smiled. It was a smile unlike earlier; there was something cold in it. "I would have given you a night like no other," she said. "And it would have been your last."

The room melted away. That was how quickly it happened: one moment he was in the castle chamber, the lady at the window. The next, he was naked and crouching in a forest glade under the night sky. His bones rattling from the cold.

Etherell came out from the shadows of the trees. Shook his head. "You really did it."

Dorn tried to cover himself, to hide. "Get away," he hissed. "I already told you. What more does it take?"

"What?" And Etherell looked so confused that Dorn knew, suddenly, that it must be him after all—not the lady. As if to confirm it the White Queen emerged from the trees, her light preceding her.

Here they all were, then.

"So I didn't get the damned amulet," said Dorn. "Go ahead. Make it quick."

She laughed, loud and long with her head flung back. Then looked down at him with mirth still lingering. "You are the most entertaining mortal I've owned," she said. "I'd rather you didn't freeze."

And there was softness and warmth around him. He looked down at himself. The green and gold clothes he'd worn to enter the castle were upon him again.

"They tried every means to tempt you and they failed," said the Queen. "It was really quite well done. And now you have the Shadow King's name. A thing to weaken him when the moment is right. You shall be my weapon, Dorn Arrin."

He sank back in the greensward, stunned. Now that she had said it, he could feel it within him; a whisper of something new. Yet it was all so confusing. "But—the amulet . . ."

"That must have been a decoy," she said. "They were clever. And I couldn't reveal the nature of your task. It would have been against the rules." She seemed to study him. "But, in a pinch—when you find yourself amid enchantments—the most powerful weapon is truth. The one nearest your heart most of all. A thing poets knew from the world's beginning, until they lost their lore, and they forgot."

He stared at her. He felt emptied of words; of everything.

She reached out a hand to him. "Rise. There is still time left to the night, and you have earned your rest." She looked to Etherell Lyr. "Escort him to his pavilion."

Dorn did everything he could to avoid Etherell's eyes. Thankful that it was dark. They walked in silence, side by side, up the hill to where the Queen's encampment was.

At last they reached Dorn's pavilion. "Hang on," Etherell said. "Your shouting at me—what did you mean by it?"

"None of your fucking business," said Dorn, and dropped the tent flap in his face.

CHAPTER

22

THE city awaits its king. So had Myrine written her husband a month before. With the East Province brought to its knees, it was time for Eldakar Evrayad to march on the city of Majdara. To return home.

Not that it would feel like home. A thing everyone felt in the ride south, but did not say. With the Zahra a charred ruin on its mountain, Eldakar was heading for a palace he'd never lived in, a place in the city that had belonged to his family but meant nothing to him. The glory of the Zahra—its gardens, the myriad gilded rooms, the Tower of Glass—gone. It had been his life from childhood; the place of his greatest joy and pain, passions and betrayals. Was in itself more than all of these. Obliterated in a night.

Wherever they went in the city, Nameir thought on the long ride, they would always be reminded when they looked up and saw it. The mountain where once had shone the towers, the one of glass most of all.

Their procession was a worn one, she thought as they neared the city gates. The victory had been so close, so near defeat. And the gory murder the king had committed to cement his leadership weighed on them all. Something was gained, to be sure—no one would question his ability to make the decisions of rule again. But it seemed to her that something else, impossible to name, was by the same means lost.

They arrived on an afternoon, crossing the bridge that Myrine's troops had guarded against Muiwiyah. The Plaza of Falcons was bright in the sun. The palace where Myrine ruled was located there. The same palace where Yusuf Evrayad had once resided until the Zahra was fully built. It had that history.

After sorting out where Eldakar's troops would be housed and fed, Nameir Hazan and Prince Mansur accompanied the king into Myrine's presence. The king and queen had not seen each other since last spring; since she had abandoned and humiliated him before all Majdara.

One could draw a line, however indirect, from that act, to Eldakar's seeing the necessity of personally executing three men. A man who had been humiliated by his wife had no chance of respect. For a king, the stakes were far higher.

Or so Nameir found herself thinking. She didn't know if Eldakar would have said the same. No doubt, knowing him, he would have denied that anyone bore responsibility for his actions but himself.

He looked composed as ever as they traversed the marble halls with its vaulted ceilings and arched windows. It was a conventional palace. Beautiful, with a history that preceded the Evrayad line; but it was not the Zahra.

Before they entered the chamber where the queen was, Mansur placed his hand on his brother's good shoulder. Then they went in.

Queen Rihab—no, Myrine—was alone, without even a token guard. She wore sombre robes, not the ceremonial gems and brocade. Perhaps she'd deemed these inappropriate to times of war. There had been rumors that the queen had for a time taken to dressing like a man and wearing a sword. Not today. Her dark hair was unbound, without a jeweled comb or diadem to be seen.

The king stepped forward. It reminded Nameir of the way he'd stepped into the circle where the Akaber brothers were bound, before he'd killed them. That slow yet determined gait.

The queen watched him approach. Nameir was struck by the vulnerability in her face. There was no way to misread it. A vulnerability accentuated by the lack of face paint, which would otherwise have made a formal, exquisite mask of her face.

Nothing like the queen Nameir had seen in the past. Dissembling, charming, mocking. None of that. Not today.

Eldakar stood before her. "So I'm here," he said. "Myrine, Rihab. Whatever it is I am to call you."

"Eldakar," she said, and her voice seemed to break. "Please. Let me look at you."

He didn't move.

"I heard about your shoulder," said the queen. "Our best physicians must look at it. They've told me there is a surgery that may help."

"You are all business," he said.

"No."

Nameir felt uncomfortable, standing there; she wondered if Mansur did too.

Myrine went on, "I am keeping a distance if that is what you desire," she said. "What you desire is what matters. I'm yours. If you want me."

He winced. "Oh, my love, don't talk that way." And then they were in each other's arms. Mansur nodded meaningfully to Nameir, and they left the room like a shot. Down the hall Nameir could already hear the queen's cries, and felt desperately embarrassed. And other things. But she didn't want to sort through any of that.

"That was quick," she said to Mansur as they went out to the plaza.

His face burned red. "Yes."

She could guess some of his thoughts. His wife, who remained in the home of her parents with their daughter, had his official loyalty. But she knew that his heart, or at least some part of him, would always be claimed by the queen. It was the way of all men, perhaps. They couldn't stand against Myrine. Not Eldakar, despite what she'd done to him. Not Mansur.

IN the courtyard she ran into Aleira Suzehn. The Magician was brushing down her horse, a pretty palfrey. She looked up as Nameir stepped from the shadow of the doorway. "So the king and queen are together."

"Very much so," said Nameir.

Neither of them had spoken of the night Nameir had let her guard down with the Magician. Nameir was grateful for that. But the Magician's manner had subtly changed toward her since.

After a long ride amid hundreds of men-at-arms, this courtyard was peaceful. It was shaded by fragrant linden trees.

Aleira was looking at Nameir with unusual intensity. "Melila," she said. The name on her lips was musical. "Is this where you belong? It may be the fate of Galicians to wander . . . so the Ellenicans and Alfinians would have us believe. And they do their utmost to make it so. But with the Jitana, I found something of a place. There may be a place for you."

Nameir forced a smile. "Only you would ask such a question after two days' ride," she said. "I can't think of anything just now but of rest, perhaps a bath."

"For the king's right hand, a bath shouldn't be too much to ask," Aleira agreed. "I only suggest you give some thought to it. I will help however I can." She patted her horse's mane. "Now I am off to check on my bookshop. It has probably been looted, but the idiots who loot Galician businesses wouldn't know a valuable manuscript if it hit them between the eyes. So. Wish me luck."

And she was off, and Nameir didn't watch her go, but she felt her steps grow lighter as she made her way to her quarters. There was someone in the world who cared about her. It made no sense but it was something. And mattered more than it would have just a short time before. She knew it had something to do with the night with Mansur but that memory was like a bruise, too tender. She let it alone.

The idea that she had not yet found her place . . . that was new. It raised the possibility that someday, maybe, these people and events would not be everything to her as they were now.

A thought like heresy. Her first response to it was guilt. Then she recalled that even Eldakar, who had needed her, didn't anymore. Neither brother needed her. She'd been useful, and in the future someone else could be useful in her place. That was all.

DINNER was a celebratory affair. Only the commanders of their armies were present, which made for strange company; the queen's commanders had been thieves and cutthroats in former lives. They possibly still were. They arrayed themselves like peacocks, with plumed hats, jewels, magnificent scarves. And sported titles: they were lords now. More than once Nameir had met Mansur's gaze and saw he looked as scandalized as she was.

But what was to be done? These people had been effective in the city's defense.

Nameir watched as Aleira Suzehn and the queen were reunited; how they embraced, and the queen had whispered in the Magician's ear. She felt a pang; a reminder to herself: *Don't forget.* Aleira belonged to the queen, just like Eldakar and Mansur.

Eldakar and Myrine presided at the head of the table. They had changed their clothes, Myrine's hair sleek from bathing. Her contentment radiated down the table. Often she leaned against Eldakar's shoulder, that did not detract from her power. She seemed, rather than dependent, confidently possessive. He had returned to her.

After dinner came business: a council of war. They sat in a room with a long table, its windows looking out on the city square. It was quiet tonight. The only sound from an open window, the plash of the city fountains.

"My people stand ready," the queen was saying to Eldakar. "They are trained and now, with the infusion of your troops, we are better equipped. At the same time, we'll need to increase our supply. I've been working on that ever since Muiwiyah's siege was lifted." She looked to Aleira Suzehn. "How long before the attack?"

Aleira stood. "I've had word from Lin Amaristoth," she said. "She said there is an army on its way that is—well, she said they can't be killed."

Myrine narrowed her eyes. "Enchantments. Isn't there anything you can do?"

"I'm a Magician, but not in the way of Zahir Alcavar," said Aleira. "I'm sorry."

"This is familiar territory," said Eldakar. He sounded weary. "Little has changed."

"The Court Poet works on our behalf," said Aleira. "And we have more than doubled our forces here. This isn't over."

The council went on: Aleira saw the first attack taking place near the border, north of the Gadlan. The stars indicated it would be not a week from now. Their troops in the East Province would be commanded to assemble.

"We will move them into place—send the order," the queen told Aleira. "That will be our first step. I will consult with the Fire Dancers in the city. Magic will be key in this war, if we are dealing with forces such as this. Perhaps my father can help." She reached beside her to Eldakar, stroked his back. "There's nothing more we can do tonight. Let's to bed."

He seemed deep in thought. When she addressed him, it took time for him to surface. Then Eldakar said, "You go ahead, my lady."

Myrine was expressionless. Nonetheless, Nameir thought she saw the shaft go in. "You've been away so long." She turned his hand over to caress his palm with her fingertips. "Come."

He turned to look at her. "I'd like some time to myself," he said. "You go ahead."

She rose. Tossed her head, as if to save her pride. She was so beautiful, Nameir thought.

"I suppose you must be tired from your journey, among other things," said the queen. Her tone edged to cut. "I won't tax your stamina." She spun on her heel to depart. The meeting dispersed.

SOON after, Nameir waited by the front door. She cooled her heels there awhile, with the patience only an experienced soldier can bring to tedium. She couldn't be certain she was right. But it had been a long time in the camp up in the hills. There were things she knew.

Eldakar caught sight of her the moment he stepped into the front hall. He looked pained. "Am I that predictable?"

"Only to me," she said. "If that helps."

"So you know where I'm going."

"I think so."

"Well, come along, Nameir," he said. She followed after.

The Plaza of the Falcons was everywhere lit: at the doorways to palaces, by the fountains, by the gates. When they left all that for the dark of night outside the gates it seemed like they had crossed a great distance, from one world to the next.

Once, this path would have been lit as well. No longer. Now this mountain was a haven for jackals, their eerie calls sounding in the dark.

Nameir remembered how it had once been to mount this path. How the splendor on the mountain came into focus as you went higher. Once, the Tower of Glass would have been distinct at night, lit from within. Once a garden scent would have overtaken them. But winter had come, weeds had begun to win against untended blooms.

"It hasn't been so long," she heard Eldakar say softly. It was hard to see his face by the light of the torch. "You'd never know."

She nodded. The supernatural armies of the west had set fire to everything. Time alone was not the culprit—it had taken up where the fires left off.

She followed him to a place where grass gave way to tile. Fragments of walls, of archways. She saw pieces: whatever within the scope of a single torch. Some of the tiles were reflective, as if made of something that shone. Perhaps by daylight she would see a pattern. But she saw networks of cracks, lichen eating between the tiles. The smell of busy, devouring life. The earth was reclaiming the Zahra, stone by stone.

Above arched the starry sky that once Magicians in the Tower of Glass had observed for prophecies.

She heard something. A rattle of falling masonry.

She laid a hand on Eldakar's arm.

A figure emerged from behind a ruined wall.

"Sorry," said Mansur. "Didn't mean to startle you."

"You could have ended with an arrow in your gut," she said with mock-severity.

"Unlikely," he said. "Even you can't hit targets in the dark."

"What are you doing here?" said Eldakar.

"I saw you leave," said the prince. "I followed you."

"It's a pity we didn't bring cakes to roast over a fire," said Eldakar, amused and tired. "I hadn't planned on an expedition."

"You wanted to see it again," said Mansur. "I understand. But do you think that's wise?"

Eldakar seemed to consider. Somewhere near, an owl was calling. More distant, the chirrup of singing frogs from the abandoned fountains.

"You mean, is it wise to see it like this?" he said. "I don't know. I came to visit my old ghosts as much as anything. Do you see where we are? The throne room."

And now that he said it, Nameir saw the cracked tiles, the broken walls, cohere. Still, it was hard to picture. Never had the throne room been open to the elements and the sky.

"You hated being king," said Mansur.

"It's true. I could never fill this room as Father did." Eldakar stood with his hands in his belt, a moment. Then began to walk again. Nameir knew where they were going, and thought Mansur did too. They followed. It had been their choice to come. It was not for them to say what should be done, or to judge. Nameir had initially thought her instinct in coming along had been to guard Eldakar, but now she found in herself another motive. She had been with him in his hardest times. It made sense to accompany him here, though the enemy was harder to see. There was nothing here to defend against, nor attack with sword or spear.

It was the quiet of mourning they dealt with here in the broken ruin of the Zahra.

"You know where we are," said Eldakar. They'd come to a place of bare earth and toppled trees. Here and there, the skeletons of hedges.

"The gardens," said Mansur.

"Now a home for coyotes and jackals," said Eldakar. "To tell the truth, I always knew what we had couldn't last. Though I don't know how I knew."

"It's your melancholy nature, my dear brother," said Mansur. "You never think you deserve to be happy." He sounded as if he'd been thinking of this a long time. "We are given so little in this life," he said. "So little time. There is no sense in finding reasons to be sad."

In the torchlit dark Eldakar shook his head. "Our father built the place on blood," he said. "Nothing could last here or take root. Not for long."

He lowered himself to sit among the stones. The other two followed his lead. The chorus of singing frogs was louder here. Nameir thought against all odds, the sound was comforting.

Eldakar leaned back where he sat. And then, very softly at first, began to sing.

Winter saw you in ruin,
Your light quenched
Your finery in rags.

Winter saw me return
to hold you in my arms.
Once more.

Nameir felt, more than saw, that Mansur was uneasy; that this grief was something he didn't want to approach. She knew him well. But he loved his brother, so he stayed. She knew that too. They stayed with Eldakar as the flames of the torch dwindled and the stars grew fainter in the sky.

PART IV

CHAPTER
23

THE last night of the year Lin Amaristoth found herself in a village
south of Tamryllin, down in a green valley, a day's ride from the border. A tavern, crowded with patrons to welcome the New Year, doors
barred against the night. Against what lurked outside.

Lin sat in a shadowed corner, her hood pulled up, and watched.
Syme Oleir dozed in a chair beside her, peaceful for once. She needed
to watch, and think. Her last conversation with Aleira Suzehn, conducted by means of enchantment, had given her much to think about.
The smells of good and simple food filled the room. People tucked in
to chicken pot pies and mutton stew with root vegetables and beans.
Winter fare. This village lay accessible to the main road and various
estates; as such, the clientele included some merchants and craftsmen,
those who could pay. They were of a mind to eat and drink to turn away
the night, since they knew—in their heart of hearts—that bolted doors
and shutters did not suffice.

Lin had listened to enough talk, each place she went, to know people
understood the danger. Even if they didn't understand what it was.
The drinks tonight would be spiked with brandy, and there was milk
punch, a specialty for the New Year in these parts. Light, warmth, and
drink, to ward off terror.

She had eaten, and so had Syme—the reason for his unaccustomed
calm. He'd had two pies and what seemed a hogshead of stew, and she
didn't care, as long as he let her be for a time.

Earlier that day, she'd lain in bed, arms resting at her sides, and talked to Aleira. The Magician told her what she had seen: Two enemies colliding at an appointed time and place, within sight of Hariya Mountain. Ten days hence.

Though Lin could only see the reddened dark inside her eyelids as she listened, in her mind's eye she saw the Magician. They had not seen each other since the day, long ago, when Lin and Zahir Alcavar had found the Fire Dancer's lair. Lin could well recall the intensity of the Magician's gaze. And she recalled the first time Aleira's voice had intruded on her thoughts, reaching out, with the news of her appointment in service to Eldakar. That husky voice, with an undercurrent of wryness. With her eyes closed Lin could pretend they were in the same room.

"So," Lin had said softly. "Ten days. And you think I can do something."

"You passed through fire and are marked by it," said Aleira. "To turn back a shadow. What else could it be?"

What else, indeed. As she sat in the dining room of the tavern that evening she turned over that question in her mind.

She always came back to it—this question of her purpose. In the Tower of the Winds she had grappled with it, when she tried to expel the verses trapped under her skin. It had been like descending a dark stair in search of light, only to encounter a deeper dark the farther she went. Losses all the way down.

A burst of noise. Lin stirred from her reverie. From one of the tables there was shouting. Two men had jumped up, young and hot-headed, and begun to circle each other. Their fists upraised. And then a third man emerged as if from nowhere, and charged them. Another yet jumped onto a table and flung himself into what had become, in seconds, a melee. She heard the crack of bones.

Before she could think—all thoughts chased from her head—she was standing on a chair herself. Her harp in her hands. Lifting her voice in song.

Onlookers tumbled back to stare: first at the fight, then at the poet.

Listen! She sang.

To a tale of dark forests
And the heroes who,
With glittering swords and spears
Turn back peril and the night.

The pandemonium went on. But some were turning to listen. There was a trick to a song like this. Something that before the enchantments returned had existed only as a phantom pull within the music. But now that the mark of the Seer meant something . . . now that there were powers to draw forth . . . a song like this worked in unseen ways. Words and notes together made a rhythm; the rhythm like a beating heart. An incantation.

As Lin sang on, she felt more than saw the growing wave of quiet that began its slow progression from where she stood; now at the fringes of the brawlers, now penetrating until their shouts had died. Now all that could be heard from the crowd was the low moaning of an injured man and even that began to fade, as another man shouldered him up from the floor and began—silently—to lead him away.

As Lin tossed, with the rhythm of inevitability, a tale of grandeur to the crowd, the quiet deepened. Music filled the silence. The tale of a hero facing down the demons of night resounded from the rafters, resounded in her listeners, who had settled in their seats as if struck down. She wove the tale to hold them, its rhythm accelerating as she drew them through tragedy, sacrifice, the deep losses suffered so that when the sun rose in the morning, people like those in this tavern could return to their days, safe to work and make love and forget the shadow that had loomed above them all.

And as she wove the rhythm to enspell the people in this room, she knew she could never be one of them; that although she could produce this melody, could be a light for them, her place was with the shadow.

Not all can gain the keys to death. Syme's words.

She recalled standing over Marlen's body, singing to avert the corruption of death. She had done that more than once on the battlefield in Kahishi.

The keys to death.

She had been bound to a stake and burned. She should have burned to death.

As she stepped down, the people, men and women, young and old, seemed to wake; they begged for another song, another.

Syme Oleir had awakened. He was looking up at her with burning eyes. She couldn't tell if it was him, or the Ifreet, that looked at her.

He said, "Sing of Asterian in the realm of the dead."

She looked around. Though a hush had descended, she didn't think people could hear. He had leaned close to whisper.

"No one wants a tale of failure," she said to him, softly as well. "Not tonight."

He caught hold of her shoulder. Lin, startled by the urgency of the gesture, was drawn to look at him. In his eyes was a strange light, and again she wondered whether it meant her good or ill. "The myth of Asterian takes many shapes," he said. "In some, he fails. In others, he retrieves his love from the land of death. And in others, still, their journey goes on, after. In adventures through the many worlds."

The many worlds. She had been in that corridor, more than once, with its doors that went on.

She leaned to him. "Which of you is speaking?" she said. "Syme Oleir, or the other?"

He smiled. As ever, it looked wrong on his face; foolish and menacing together. "He wants to kill me," he said. "The other. He'd rather I die—that *he* die—than help you. That is how much he hates." He put a hand to his mouth. "He won't let me speak, except in riddles."

"Asterian," she said, and he nodded.

She was about to speak again, to dig to the heart of that riddle, when she felt a hand on her arm. A woman, very pretty, with chestnut curls and imploring blue eyes. She wore an attractive blue dress, lace-edged. With all her wiles the woman said, "Will you please sing again?" She leaned forward. "We'd be ever so grateful." She dropped her eyes. "*I* would be."

Lin recalled that to this crowd she was a young man. How they could still be fooled she didn't know, but earlier, to reinforce the disguise, she had hacked off her hair.

This woman, it seemed, desired a song and a poet in equal measure. *So this is what it's like.*

A wry thought. Though of course she knew, thanks to the memories of Edrien Letrell that for a time had flowed together with her own. The pleasures of being a famed, sought-after man were no stranger to her.

How Darien would have laughed if he were here.

Lin tried not to smile. She bowed. Then leapt up on a bench at the center of the room, cloak flowing around her. A theatrical gesture. All the faces upturned to her now. She had them.

Thoughts of Darien beguiled her yet. She imagined he stood in the corner, watching, smiling to himself. He would have given this song all his energy; and with equal alacrity, later that night, would have made love to the woman who with a deliberate, swaying walk had approached the bench.

Lin drew a breath to refocus her thoughts. Darien Aldemoor wasn't here. She spoke. "This night we turn to a New Year," she said. "A night for dancing. Clear a space."

Nothing she did tonight could dispel what was coming. But with this power she could make them forget it for a time. For a night.

Rhythm was again her tool. This time her aim was not to calm her listeners, or put them into a reflective frame of mind. This time it was to make music that would go to their arms and legs, set them to dancing. Instead of a hero, she sang of a trickster; one who set a town buzzing with his schemes, jokes, and—of course—his seductions. A song with roots that went as far back as the most ancient, though most here wouldn't know that. For Tam Rinnell, the renowned scapegrace, was what remained of Tamrir, one of the eldest of the forgotten gods of the Thracians. A god of luck, thieves, and journeys. Of boundaries, too. Now reduced to a man in tales that made people laugh.

Tapping her foot on the bench, Lin sang. The words came fast. Her nails danced on the strings. Some in the crowd, recognizing the tune, joined in; others grabbed a partner, or formed a circle, began to dance. And the rhythm she'd begun was picked up by shoes and boots, amplified until the floor shook.

She thought if Darien Aldemoor had been here, he'd have approved. There was an element of Tamrir in him.

The two of them had crossed boundaries together. Of course. For a time she had been a crossroads between life and death, this world and the Other. Darien's enchantment had done that to her. And the effects of that night reverberated, much as music now thundered from the rafters of the dining room. From Tamryllin to the Zahra, from the lair of the Fire Dancers to the Dance itself.

She could sing even as she recalled Zahir's eyes, as he told her all—or so she had thought, at the time—in his chamber overlooking the courtyard of jacaranda trees. Some part of him had been urging her, even then, to defeat him. He was tired, she thought, of what his commitment to love had led him to do. Tired, sick at heart. Some part of him wanted her to find him out. She thought that, anyhow, though she would never know.

The dead were always with her—that much, she did know.

Asterian. The keys to death.

As she recalled the words of Syme Oleir, she became aware of him watching her. When he looked up at her that way, she felt a terrible responsibility to him. He was only a boy, for all that he looked world-weary now, watching her sing.

The song was over. She ended it with a flourish and a bow. The room filled with cheers, followed inexorably by new demands. *"Another!"* was the cry. She smiled and accepted a cup of water for her parched throat. Her eyes scanned the crowd, but it all ran together; she didn't see the girl. She was looking for someone she knew, even though that was impossible. She was always looking for the people who mattered to her, long after they were gone.

Syme's voice in her head again, as he watched her. *Asterian.*

Zahir Alcavar had done all he had for love. Love of family, of a city destroyed. He'd planned to journey with her to the Underworld, for her connection to it was strong. It had been strong ever since Darien Aldemoor had done what he'd done, and now—

She handed the drained cup to someone in the crowd. Without preamble began another song. Another for them to dance to, as the night wore near to midnight. Cheers and thundering boots shook the floorboards. She would send them rejoicing into the New Year if she did nothing else in life.

Her blood coursed warm as it hadn't on any night since she could remember. Warm to every fingertip, her face and neck. She imagined elbowing her way through the crowd when the song was done and find-ing Valanir Ocune waiting at the back of the room. Finding that he'd been there, alive, watching her all that time. Watching her sing. Later he'd tell her what he'd have done differently, would critique her per-formance. But not tonight. Tonight she'd take him upstairs and they'd forget everything that had ever happened.

Her eyes met Syme's again, the only one who stood silent and still amid the dancing.

I think I understand, she thought, and meant it for him; as if it were a message.

As midnight struck, and her song was done, someone handed her a cup. She drank, and found it sweet and strong.

This was life. This room, these people, this dance. The winds that whistled against the windowpanes. Life was a place, a moment. Amid other places and moments. One crossed a boundary to get there, and to leave.

When she bowed for the last time and jumped from the bench, she was engulfed in admirers. There were those who wanted to kiss her hand, others who shook it. She detached herself with a small smile; enjoying it but also aware that she was apart, drifting from them even now.

The girl who had sought her out was there too, looking hopeful. It was like a dart in Lin, that look. Lin Amaristoth had never been a girl like that, so lovely; but she'd had similar hopes. To be as near the music as one could get; to share intimacy with a poet. That was before she'd known it didn't work that way; that such intimacy was the same as with anyone; that music existed beyond such moments. Beyond any person.

She murmured in the girl's ear. "You are lovely. I'm afraid I must be off. But I'll think of you."

The disappointment mingled with a sudden light in her blue eyes were almost more than Lin could bear. Life was there too, in those eyes. Not just in the dancing and song. Of course Darien had known that, too.

Lin had come to a new understanding as she sang in the New Year to these people on a winter night. Life was here, and she didn't belong. She had passed through and would leave a mark, as the fire had left markings on her skin. She was on her way to somewhere else.

This she thought even as she felt the warm, sweet drink all through her. She was ablaze with it, with the rhythms she'd poured forth all night.

The crowds didn't follow her to the stairs. As she left the people for the staircase she crossed a minor boundary, from celebration to silence. The sounds of revelry gently faded out. She began to ascend. The stairs were lit by candles, each sheltered in its small alcove in the wall. And as she ascended to greater silence, she saw them—the three of them—lined up on the staircase. Darien Aldemoor first, blond hair tousled, grinning to have watched her let a girl down easy. It would have amused him to no end.

Valanir Ocune was several steps up from Darien, with a smile more muted; only in his eyes. Whatever he would have said, she saw in his face; so much had passed between them on their last days together. She was grateful for that. That they hadn't held back.

At last at the top step, just before the door to her room, there was Zahir Alcavar. Eyes that blazed in any light, as she remembered.

"I'm on my way," she said. "I understand now what to do."

And she could not tell if he heard or understood; he looked pensive, and turned away. And in any case it was not him, only an imagining born of her desire to see the ones she had loved and lost.

But Syme Oleir was beside her, his shoulder under her hand as she ascended the stairs. He had been there all along. Once in their room, she closed the door. It was dark, but for a single candle on the dressing table.

"I think I know what to do, Syme," she said. "What we must do, together." It was so dark in here, after the light. "The last things."

He looked pale and drained, and nothing like she'd come to know. The man he should have become—that he'd been cheated of becoming—was in his face, in this dim light. "I've already lost everything," he said. "I'm ready."

JULIEN Imara didn't want to be in a gloomy castle when somewhere out in the world her friend was captive. But Archmaster Hendin had urged her to think strategically. To have any chance of defeating the White Queen they would need the joined power of the Seers. So here they were in Vassilian, last stronghold of poets ever since the Isle had come undone. Hendin had gathered six men, some of the last Seers alive, who had agreed to stand with them. It was not much—it was so little —but the Archmaster had a plan.

So as the old year gave way to new they hunkered in this unlovely fortress where Lin Amaristoth had been born. That had belonged to her ancestors. She had given it to the Academy for the training of po-ets. Reminders of her family were everywhere: In the hall of portraits, where proud, dark-eyed men and women posed in dark clothes. Their wealth evinced in certain touches: A sumptuous cloak, a jeweled pen-dant or ring.

Lin Amaristoth wasn't to be found on these walls, but her parents were, and her brother. Each painting had an engraved plaque to iden-tify them by name. Her mother had been a true beauty, voluptuous, her eyes challenging the artist. In appearance the brother took after her, though he stood more haughtily for the portrait, remote, as if the artist had caught him unawares. He wore a sword at his side, his posture regal. It was said he'd been killed in a duel for a woman's honor.

The hall of portraits was where the Seers and poets of Vassilian took their meals at a long table, one of the only articles of furniture not draped in cobwebs. Housekeeping was lax, assigned as chores to young poets who skimped where they could. Many spoke often, wistfully, of the groundskeeper and cook at the Academy, whom they'd failed to appreciate.

Since fuel was scarce and they could not heat many rooms, they used the hall of portraits for councils, too. It was a while before Archmaster Hendin could convince his colleagues that the information he had about the upcoming battle was reliable, much as a star-written prophecy could be. It took more time, after that, to convince the Seers to join him. Julien sat through it all and yawned. And was then ashamed, because at least she wasn't at the mercy of the White Queen.

She could imagine Dorn Arrin telling her, witheringly, how silly she was being. That didn't help at all.

Julien kept thinking back to the morning she had knocked at the door to Dorn's room in the seaside inn. The dread that formed in her chest even before it made sense, as if she already knew. They'd ended up breaking down the door. There was no mistaking what had happened. Dorn Arrin would never have gone anywhere without his harp. Not voluntarily. And then they had seen the open shutters and, looking outside, the rope.

The whole way to Vassilian she'd battled tears and shame. Shame that she was weeping like a child; and that in doing so she was making matters worse for the Archmaster, who was just as grieved.

The plan Archmaster Hendin outlined to the six other Seers was to include Julien Imara. She had a means of weakening the Queen temporarily—whatever that meant. When the time seemed right on the battlefield, Julien would release the secret name. And if that created an opening, the Seers would act. Joining together they would launch an attack on the Queen when she was weakest.

This didn't take into account the Queen's opponent, but it was the best they had. Hendin reasoned that if the danger was in the battle between the two, perhaps there was an advantage to be had in ending it with one side the victor. Though of course who knew?

Ten days from the New Year they would take a position overlooking the foretold battlefield, and await their moment. It seemed a slim chance to Julien, but she could think of nothing better.

At nights she slept in Lin Amaristoth's old room, which Hendin had opened to her with a key. "It hasn't been slept in since she lived here," he said, and Julien knew it was his way of giving her something. To stay in the Court Poet's childhood room, to see where the figure Julien admired had begun.

But the room made her sad, for it was comfortless. In that way it was like the rest of the castle, for it seemed the Amaristoths, who believed above all in wealth, did not believe in its indulgences. Everywhere weapons hung on the walls, far outnumbering paintings or tapestries. Lin's bed was narrow, the bedclothes warm but of a rough fabric. Her closet was filled with dresses, most of them dark. But some were fine, of whispering silk and smelling of scent, and if Julien shut her eyes she could picture the Court Poet in one of these, revolving in lugubrious tandem with a suitor in the hall of portraits.

The room possessed a single luxury, a silver-backed, full-length mirror on the wall. Julien avoided looking at it.

None of these objects spoke to the kind of person Lin Amaristoth was—the first woman to be Seer and Court Poet. But there was a shelf of books, and these Julien handled with reverence. It was like finding friends in a place of strangers.

Some nights she sat at the window, which looked out on the massing dark of pinewoods, and wept silent tears. She felt a fool, but at least no one could see. She tried to remember the last words she'd exchanged with Dorn Arrin, but couldn't. Probably, she thought, they had been *good night*.

Little changed in the course of their stay in Vassilian until they drew nearer the time they were to leave. The mountain roads were impassable in the snow—it was with magic that the Seers would cross to Kahishi. Near the appointed battlefield was a ring of standing stones, a site of ancient magic they could draw upon to aid the crossing. Julien didn't understand these details and didn't care. She was too preoccupied with thinking about where Dorn might be, and trying not to think about it.

At nights she and the Archmaster sat in the hall of portraits and talked of their lives. Now was their first time seeing each other, she felt; as if an equality had sprung between them. The distance of teacher and student had evaporated in recent days.

He told her about being the third son of a minor aristocrat, how he had grown up reading as much as he could and studying the harp. He'd had a tutor until it was time to send him to the Academy. A straight path it had been, without hesitation or regret.

Julien, for her part, spoke of her family. Only a little at first: It was the first time she'd tried talking about herself to anyone since Sendara Diar. With the other girl there had always been a sense of forced patience, of politeness; whenever Julien had spoken of herself, she had felt as if Sendara was trying to appear interested. The Archmaster was different, though this time she spoke with more reserve. She wanted to be understood, but had begun to realize that perhaps that wasn't possible. She didn't think anyone could know why she had felt trapped, when her life was to all appearances a good one. Nor did she think anyone could know what it had been like at the Academy, to be an outsider in the halls at night.

When Archmaster Hendin spoke of his youth, of his tutors and how he'd been encouraged to learn, she couldn't conceal her envy. It had been natural for him to have those things. One didn't spend time thinking of the air one breathed.

But he tried to understand. "There are myriad paths to learning," he said once. Julien knew this was the man who had tended his students as attentively as he did his garden, and she was grateful, if not entirely convinced.

She tried not to think of herself in that black and silver-belted gown, the image of confidence that had gazed back at her from the reflective door. Calm, sure of her powers. That was all gone. She was back to scurrying in hallways like a child.

As the grey days in Vassilian slipped by, their plans weren't real to her; she knew these days would end soon; that the topic neither of them touched was the danger ahead. But it was difficult to believe.

Until the day before their departure when she saw Archmaster Hendin in the corridor. He looked the way he had when they'd realized Dorn was captured. Worse.

She ran to him. "What is it?"

"Nothing." He avoided her eyes.

"Tell me. Is it—is it—"

"No."

Julien would never have wanted to admit how relieved she was at this, when he looked so upset. She pressed, "I know there's something."

"Well." He leaned back against the wall, suddenly. "I'll have to reveal it in council anyway. I've been trying for some days to reach Lin Amaristoth to tell her our plans. And to see if she had news."

"All right," said Julien. "What did she tell you?"

He looked past her, as if there were something of interest on the bare wall. "Nothing," he said. "When I reached for her, I felt what I have in the past with others. There's no mistaking it."

"I don't understand." Though maybe some part of her did; her hands were trembling. "What others?"

He stared straight ahead. "The ones who died."

As the White Queen's weapon, Dorn Arrin was closely guarded. Nights, he could hear her followers dancing and coupling loudly outside; but he was kept apart from all that. He went nowhere without at least two of her guard, the so-called deathless ones, as escort.

Each day Etherell Lyr tried to get him to come out of the tent—for a drink, for a meal by the fire—and each time Dorn refused. If he was going to be used in this way, he'd keep as much dignity as he could, despite the indignity of recent events. He was only glad that no one but the Shadow King's lady had seen how near he'd come to betraying himself.

He certainly wouldn't stoop to the indignity of asking the Queen what would become of him after the battle. He suspected that once hers, always hers, and that this would be his life, unless he found some way to escape.

There was one thing he held over her: Julien Imara had possession of the Queen's name. It wasn't much of a hope, but it was something. As long as the White Queen didn't know that, there was still a chance.

So his thoughts were astir with a peculiar combination of listlessness and hope.

Their last night before the battle the White Queen came to him. He saw the light of her first, the night paling to frost-white, and then she was in the tent with him. She looked satisfied as a well-fed cat.

"Tomorrow it begins," she said. "You will be of key importance. Now listen carefully."

As she instructed him for the following day Dorn found he couldn't speak, nor tear his eyes from her. She seemed to have grown taller since he saw her last; and he couldn't shake the image of her devouring raw meat at the feast of the Shadow King. The blood of the world nourished her, he was convinced, and she intended to drain it all.

He had no choice when she set this new charge upon him. It was like times before; she kissed his forehead, and he felt it go into his bones. The King's name made him a weapon, and tonight—even before the battle—her use of him had begun.

CHAPTER
25

THOUGH the remains of night cloaked the field, Julien Imara could see the armies massing. The hilltop offered a view of the field to her and Archmaster Hendin where they crouched among the standing stones. From the west, from Eivar, came what had to be the armies of the White Queen. Even from a height Julien could hear them howling, see them cavorting below. Taken together, they made a wave that continuously rose and fell without rest. The Queen's side was chaos. The only sign of order was the armed men who guarded her pavilion; these, Julien guessed, must be the Chosen.

The army of the other side was the opposite: It was how Julien had always pictured an army to look. Battalions in sombre grey formed tight formations as far as could be seen to the east. For each battalion a banner, plain black. From this side, the King's side, there was a silence, despite that his army numbered so many; they stood motionless as chess pieces on a board.

Julien did not know which was more unnerving: the silence of the King's side, or the howls from the Queen's.

As the shadows lifted, daybreak a gauze veil on the battlefield, Julien could see that between the two armies lay a space they did not cross; not even the unruly followers of the Queen. The strange formality of this battle, with its assigned time and place, perhaps extended to how it would play out.

Julien turned to Archmaster Hendin, whose grey eyes surveyed it all without changing. He looked calm. This was their only move, a desperate one; but perhaps, knowing that, he had moved beyond fear.

"How will you give the signal?" she asked. She had expected the other Seers to accompany them through the portal. They had sung through the night in the hall of portraits, Archmaster Hendin and the other six, for hours after the sun set. They'd stood in a circle. The light of each Seer's mark had grown brighter with each hour that passed, until the beams from each had met to join at the center. Julien had watched as this central point of light hung in the air, lengthened and widened, until there was no mistaking what it was. A tear in the fabric of the world.

There had been a time when with those same powers, she had created one of these. Now she could only watch.

She had felt hunger and awe, seeing this spectacle of enchantment from which she was barred. And she had thought that surely these Seers, with their immeasurable gift, would want to pass through the doorway they had themselves created. But no. At the last moment they had drawn back, leaving Archmaster Hendin and Julien Imara to go through alone. They kept their eyes averted, as if ashamed, and promised to be of help when called.

"When the time comes, we seven will act together," said Hendin to her now. "After you've made use of the name, I'll signal them. We are connected, always, even across distances." He looked tired. Perhaps such talk recalled to him other Seers to whom he'd once been connected.

In response to his look, Julien said, "I don't believe the Court Poet is dead. It's too stupid. She can't be."

He gritted his teeth, an unusually hostile-seeming gesture for him, though she read it as pained. "Stupid things happen, Julien Imara," he said. "Surely you know that. And I know what I know. When I reached for her I felt as I would if I reached for Valanir Ocune, or Seravan Myre."

"What did you feel, then?"

"Nothing," he said. "That's the point."

Meantime, the sun was rising. A band of palest rose stretched behind the mountains, layered with the pallor of the sky. And slowly brightened. As it did, the slate and grey of the mountains changed, to green with hints of gold. The tallest mountain, Hariya, flung back the sun from pale stones. *Peaks of gold*, she thought, and was struck with the desire to expand it into something. Some song.

Above the battlefield, dark, great-winged birds were circling.

Daylight illuminated the splendor of the White Queen's pavilion, green and gold. Julien's breath was sped by a sudden thought. She tugged Archmaster Hendin's sleeve. "What if Dorn is in there?"

"It's possible," he said.

"There must be a way to get him out."

From the fields below, the sounds that reached them were sharpening, as if they had earlier been muffled in the dark. The screams and laughter from the Queen's encampment were piercing even up here in the hills.

Jackals in a graveyard. As soon as Julien had that thought, she wished she could forget it.

No sound from the King's side, save one: a thin whine, like a blade at a whetstone.

"I'd give my life to get him out," said Hendin. "But we must await our chance."

She knew what he meant. There was this battle to get through first. She hated it, but couldn't think what else to do. Guards made an impenetrable thicket of spears around the pavilion. And she knew what the Chosen were like. She remembered their dead eyes when they had thrown Dorn Arrin—and her—to the flames.

There was one thing the Chosen didn't have. They didn't think for themselves. That was a weakness, Julien thought.

She knelt in the grass. It was ribbed with stone and beaded with dew. The circle of standing stones had begun to catch the sun, their shadows darkening. At Julien's feet was a cloth bundle, water-stained and ragged. The wrappings were neat, as Dorn Arrin had been the one to do it, and he was meticulous in all things. It took Julien some moments to undo the wrappings, to see the first gleam of the Silver Branch until the rags had fallen away to reveal it all.

"This was his, at least for a while," she murmured, turning it over in her hands. Each of the red-gold apples caught the light, a gentle glimmering. "And he must be out there."

YOU know what to do.

Her metallic whisper in his ear when he awoke. Dorn Arrin was alone in his pavilion, and yet. It was as if she'd whispered him awake. He had gone to sleep the night before somewhere in Eivar—he knew not where. He never had known where the Queen's encampment was. The hillside from which she wandered, at will, with her gaggle of followers in tow. Throughout the countryside she'd traveled, gathering more to her as she went, but always returned at night to the same place.

The morning was different. When he awoke he knew they had traveled in the night. He'd been warned of it, but he thought he could feel it, too.

Etherell Lyr put his head inside. "It's about to begin," he said. "Get dressed." He sounded unhurried and calm, which likely meant he felt the opposite. "You should see this," he added, and a note of excitement came through. His head vanished from the tent flap.

That got Dorn's attention. He quickly dressed in the new, clean clothes laid out for him. A ritual he had nearly ceased to notice. These were different than in the past, however. He had grown used to colors. The clothes laid out for him today were black, trimmed and belted with silver. The formal dress of Academy poets.

After he'd fastened the belt about his waist he went to the tent flap and, very carefully, glanced out. He was nearly afraid to look. The ululating screams of the Queen's followers were an indication of what he'd see, and he knew what to expect today: the battlefield.

When he peered out, he was looking over the shoulders of the Chosen. He corrected himself: her deathless ones. Elissan Diar had named them his Chosen, but the self-styled Poet King was more irrelevant than a memory. What the White Queen had made of them was what mattered. Etherell had told him of it, how they pulled axes and swords from their bodies and healed in moments. How they could not be killed.

It had been an evening when Dorn Arrin allowed himself to be dragged out from his tent, as it took more energy than to resist. But had kept himself aloof. Nonetheless, after offering Dorn wine, Etherell had insisted on talking about this and that. Two nights past, it had been.

"So those boys will live forever," said Dorn, musing. Despite himself, the wine loosened his tongue. "Pity Elissan Diar didn't choose the kind or the witty ones. It is the arrogant and the irritating who are to be immortal, to blight the world for all eternity. That figures."

He said that even as the immortal ones clustered around him, guarding him and preventing his escape. Perhaps he wanted to get in a dig. Whether they understood or not. They never made a sound, nor changed expression. If what they had was eternal life, it was like death.

At this, Etherell lifted his cup. "It could be worse," he said, eyes alight. "She could have made me immortal. To annoy you for eternity."

To this, what seemed a goad, Dorn had not replied. He didn't want to give the other man his attention; he'd given more than enough. When Dorn considered the years he'd endured, when all along the person he pined for was not even someone he knew . . . he couldn't imagine a greater fool than he'd made of himself.

The morning of the battle he saw, beyond the Queen's half-naked followers with their swords and spears, a sombre, organized massing of grey-clad figures to the east. The armies of the Shadow King. They obliterated the green of the meadow like ants, were still and silent. Dorn thought of the fog that hung on the seas around Academy Isle.

To the north he saw the foothills and looming above these, the mountains, and he wondered. There were places to hide in those hills. And Julien Imara would do everything she could to use her weapon on the day, if he knew the girl at all.

And then the Queen was before him, shining white, but for the points of red above each cheekbone. Her hair more gold this day than red, falling to her knees and partly braided. Her eyes had a violet light. She said, "When the time comes you must be ready, Dorn Arrin. Not that you have any choice."

She set her hands on his head. Like some parody of benediction.

"My opponent and I will duel this day," she said. "That is the time."

And he knew it was as she said, that he had no choice at all.

She considered him. "You're hiding something." She glanced behind her, to the hills. "You have friends waiting up there to help you, perhaps," she said, and he tried not to gasp at this. Her slow smile was dazzling. "No one can take you from me, Dorn Arrin," she said. "However they may attempt it. You are mine."

She strode away. He saw that she held a long sword, a blade fashioned of cut crystal, containing and bending the sunlight, splitting it into colors that swept the grass.

Dorn looked up to the hills again, murmured a prayer. He hoped Julien would keep far away from him.

Etherell had wandered over. "You see?" he said. "Isn't this all a marvel?" Never had his features looked so finely chiseled, his eyes bright.

Dorn spoke, in part, as a deflection from what he felt. "I'm not sure which aspect appeals to you."

"All of it," said Etherell Lyr. "I had grown so tired of things as they were. So dour and ordinary."

Dorn looked away from him. "There's nothing ordinary about you."

Just then a shrill call sounded. Or so it began, until it rose to a higher pitch; where it became a thread of melody. It fell gentle on the ear even though it had risen high, to be heard throughout that battlefield.

Under the influence of that sound, even the Queen's followers fell still. They froze mid-motion like flies caught in glue. Dorn's gaze traveled to the space of wildflowers and grass that lay between the armies. Into that space a horseman was approaching.

As the rider drew near Dorn could see he was fully-armored, immense, in black plate. He was huge and carried an enormous double-bladed battleaxe. His stallion was black as soot, with bright red eyes.

The Queen came forward to meet the rider, sword in hand. Though she did not ride, she appeared fully as tall. It had to be an illusion. The notes of the horn rose higher yet, sounding from hill to hill before at last they died away.

The horseman raised the visor of his helmet. Within all Dorn could see were a pair of blazing red eyes. "It is the appointed time," he said. His voice like a rumble of thunder. "In the appointed place."

"Then let's begin," said the Queen, and flung up her sword. Their blades met, crystal and black. A flurry of sparks went up. Dorn thought of sunlight flashing from the surface of winter ice.

In that moment Dorn heard her voice as he had upon waking, private in his ear.

You know what to do.

And so as the White Queen and Shadow King battled on the grass. Dorn did what she compelled of him. From the back of his mind he drew it, as if it were a wrapped treasure he had kept in wait. Though he spoke it softly, almost to himself, he heard it echo in the air around him. And farther, as it traveled across the battlefield. The King's true name, or one of them.

One was enough.

The first thing he saw was the way the White Queen, who already shone, became in that instant like a white torch; and her laugh brought to mind bloodshed. "You're mine," she cried.

The black rider was changing. He began to shrink, to alter in shape. In moments he was the man Dorn had known in the castle, nondescript and greying, riding a grey gelding. His axe had become a plain, serviceable broadsword of a size appropriate to the man. His face impassive. "Not just yet," he said. His voice now of a man, no more. But calm "I do not yield."

She laughed again. "You will."

Then Dorn heard something else: a voice he knew, calling out. From such a distance he should not have heard it. But it was not an ordinary cry. It came of enchantments, he knew, just as his own had done.

The White Queen hissed. She began to change. For a moment Dorn Arrin thought he saw a bird, a white peacock, in place of her; but soon she had changed again, back to a woman. But greatly reduced in height. Though she still shone, it was faint, no longer the blaze of before.

"So," she said. "So, so, so."

The Shadow King inclined his head. "You may not care for honor," he said. "But it seems we now have a fair fight."

"I care only for blood," said the Queen. Her sword, transformed to steel, still extended. "I'll take yours either way."

* * *

THOUGH it was hard to see what was happening in the field, it was clear something had changed when Julien Imara released the Queen's name to the wind. From a distance she could see both figures diminished in height.

Why both?

Archmaster Hendin wasted no time wondering. He stood at the highest point of the hill. A murmur came from him that as Julien listened, became a tune. He closed his eyes. His hair and cloak stirred as from a gale. Over his right eye the mark of the Seer showed complete. Sparks chased each other along its strands as the Seer continued to chant.

Below, the duel went on. Its sights and sounds less fearsome now that both parties were diminished. They could have been any man and woman fighting, if not for the strangeness of a mounted warrior fighting a woman on foot. But Julien could see little of it. They were small enough now to look, from here, like insects.

And in their weakened state, the Seers worked against them.

Julien began to feel her spirits lighten. She looked to the green pavilion and thought she could make out one of the figures, tall, in black. But knew she wanted it to be him, and couldn't be sure.

That was when she heard a sound behind her. Like choking. Archmaster Hendin was clutching his neck. He looked like someone was strangling him from behind, though there was—of course—no one there. They were alone on the hill.

Julien ran to him. She tore his hands from his throat but it was no use; his face was turning blue. With horrible clarity she understood: the magic had put him in harm's way. Now that she wasn't a Seer, there was nothing she could do.

The Seer's eyes opened, but only the whites showed. His knees buckled and he fell, as she tried to catch him. She ended up on the ground beside him, on her knees. He lay on his back in the grass, convulsing. And then went still.

Julien held his head. She had begun to sob, and now felt she could do nothing else, bent double over the Archmaster in the grass. She had no powers. She had given them up in return for one thing, the tiny thing she had used. Used up.

Down the hill the duel went on, a ringing of blade on blade. It seemed irrelevant. But soon would sweep them all away. This thin plan of theirs—the name, the gathering of Seers—had been their arrow-shot. The only one.

So steeped was she in grief that it took several moments—moments that might have been hours—before she noticed a change. The sound of the blades had paused. No, stopped altogether. A rising wind came toward her that smelled of earth and wet. The live, sweet smell of a storm. A tingle in the air that precedes lightning. The winds strengthened to a gust, powerful as the breath of a giant. The grasses bent flat, smooth as green water. Julien held to Archmaster Hendin, afraid he'd be torn from her by the wind and lost more fully, forever.

A roaring had begun, low and ponderous in the distance. Through the curls that flew around her face Julien could just make out the battle-field, where people had begun to run in all directions. Both sides were chaos. As the wind swept the grasses the Queen's pavilion tipped over onto its side. It lay waving like a great green banner.

That was the moment Julien saw, on the horizon, what looked like a pillar of black smoke. It was opaque, edged with gold light. Like a patch of night on the horizon. There was beauty to it, yet it looked like something from nightmares. From it came the roaring, which had swelled like multiple thunder strikes. And grew louder. A cacophony—hundreds, perhaps thousands of cries. All different, yet united.

What came through in every voice from the widening night was rage.

So she was almost not surprised, then, when from the pillar of darkness they came, figures of black. They were hard for the eye to fix upon, as if made of smoke. But real enough to carry swords and spears. Their roaring rose higher, and Julien heard something else that ran together with their fury. It made her shudder. A chamber of torture would sound like this, if its victims numbered in the thousands. As if they shrilled out death agonies on the battlefield. And still they came.

CHAPTER

26

THREE days before the battle, Lin Amaristoth arrived in Majdara. Though enchantments had aided her in reaching the capital along with Syme Oleir, the two were profoundly weary. But there was no time to lose.

It was worth it all to see Eldakar's face when she was brought before him. They clasped hands. She saw he was altered. Lin knew he'd taken an arrow to the shoulder, but now, seeing Eldakar's face, thought there was a wound that went deeper.

"It's been too long," she said.

"I agree," he said. "And you've picked quite a time. I would never have asked your help, but here you are. And Aleira keeps prophesying doom for us all." He kept his tone light.

Lin chose her words carefully. "I am here about that," she said. "I mean to be of help, if I can. But I can't promise it will work. It is something dark and shadowed, that still eludes me. This man—Syme Oleir—he is necessary to the mission." She motioned Syme to step forward. "Syme, this is the king of Kahishi. Show respect for his grace, King Eldakar, son of Yusuf Evrayad."

Syme stood staring. Lin prodded him, but it did no good. He had retreated into himself.

She sighed. "I'm sorry," she said to Eldakar.

"We don't need formalities," he said. "Not you and I. Your companion is welcome." The gaze he turned on Syme, for an instant, was of piercing curiosity. There was something strange about the young man, and Eldakar was unlikely to miss that. But was too polite to question Lin, or try to draw him out.

The room was full of light. They were in a solar of tall windows, opening to balconies strung with green vines. In summer these would be dancing with bees and hummingbirds in the blooms. Even in winter Majdara was far enough south that the day was mild, the sun's beams playful on the mosaic tiles.

It was not the Zahra, but it was a place that brought to mind her time there. The time had been short yet sprawled in her memory as if to take it over, a glistening chain of days.

The Zahra was the reason she was here.

She could have bypassed this place, and seeing Eldakar again, in pursuit of her mission. It would not have occurred to her. Though she hated farewells, always had, and the thought crept up that this might well be one.

They had taken their places on a couch. Syme had thrown himself with a child's abandon to a pile of cushions on the floor. At any moment he might start to whine. She had biscuits ready.

"There's something I feel, when I look at you," said Eldakar. The sun and silence of the room seemed to enfold them both. "As if you're not really here."

Perhaps she was saying goodbye within herself, without knowing it. And this king who knew people so well, even as he hadn't known the hearts of those closest to him—he could feel it.

"I have a job to do," she said. "One that I hope will help us both. But it's a risk."

"The dark and shadowed thing," he said, and smiled. "No surprise that it's a risk. Lin, sometimes I wonder why you have not been allowed to live in the world as you were meant. Always you are bent to a mission for others."

She was startled. Though with Eldakar, perhaps she shouldn't have been. She thought of Zahir Alcavar giving her the Tower of the Winds, a space of her own, away from her responsibilities. She thought of Ned's loyalty. There had been some solace, some kindnesses along the way.

She said, "A lot of things are not as I'd want. But there are other things for which I'm grateful. This friendship is one."

He smiled. "I know you mean that," he said. "But I'm not sure I can compete. You have other friends here, as it happens." And before she knew what he was about, he rose and opened the door. Standing in the doorway a man, hovering with lank awkwardness on the threshold. Beside him, a woman with golden hair.

Lin felt as if her breath had been knocked from her. She looked from one to the other.

Head high, Rianna Alterra strolled into the room. She was resplendent in the light. "We thought you'd come," she said. "We heard that bitch was on her way east."

At last Lin found her tongue. "So you came here."

Ned came forward too. "We couldn't let you face her alone."

THE night Ned came home, Rianna had lain wakeful for hours. She'd been home only a handful of days herself. She knew it was cause for joy to be reunited with her child, with her father. But there was the White Queen in her mind's eye. The abattoir the throne room in Tamryllin had become.

And it all was more vivid, in a way more real, than being home.

She went through the days holding Dariana and reading to her. And of course disciplining the child. Her grandfather had spoiled her with sweets and late bedtimes. It was not necessarily a happy occasion when her mother returned. But that night she'd fallen asleep with her head in Rianna's lap, after shrieking for hours, as if deep beneath the thwarted rage she *was* glad.

Rianna sensed a steely quality in herself, and knew it was not what her child needed or deserved. She tried to stifle it, along with the memories that reared up. She remembered Elissan Diar's face just before he had ceased to have a face.

No surprise, then, that she couldn't sleep.

So she was awake when there was a sound on the stair. An urgent footfall, too quick to be her father. The stairs in this house, a country home, were made of wood plank; the sound from every footfall carried.

When Rianna met her husband at the doorway to her bedroom it was with a knife. She held it poised in hand and watched him come. He saw it, his drawn face turned to her in lamplight, before she lowered the blade to her side. The shadows beneath his cheekbones were more pronounced, and he nearly had a beard. That wouldn't do, she thought.

His eyes had followed the knife as it was lowered. When he spoke, he sounded hoarse. "I saw you make a decision, just now. Dare I have cause to hope?"

"Not a decision," she said. "A pause to consider." A long moment she stood there, looking him over. "It would help your case if you shaved."

"At once, my lady," he said gravely.

It meant standing aside for him to enter, bringing with him the smell of wet winter roads. She watched as he lit a lamp beside the basin. His neat, economical motions as he drew the shaving kit from his pack. She knew its contents well: Soap like a smooth pebble in its wad of paper, bottles of soothing ointments, and a blade. He went to the basin, and the mirror there. Light glanced from the blade's edge.

She stood at a distance behind, in the shadows beyond the lamplight. Watched as he caressed his left cheek with the blade. Stubble scraped away to reveal pale skin, uncomfortably sharp bone. He cupped water in his hands to rinse.

For as long as he worked, he couldn't speak. Nothing unnatural, then, in a silence.

When he was done he looked thinner yet, and exhausted. He didn't cross the shadows to her. He stood at the basin and looked at her where she stood at the foot of the bed. They watched each other. Rianna caught a wariness in his eyes.

She realized she still held the knife. She put it away. Now was not the time for theatrics. And in truth, she didn't know which emotion she would choose to display even if theatricality had been her inclination. She didn't know if she felt anything.

At last Ned spoke. "I'll go first," he said. "I know about Elissan Diar. Of the golden-haired mistress who would have been his queen. It is not the talk of the village taverns as much as what came after, but it is a part of the tale that traveled."

"Yes," said Rianna. "What you heard is true." She still didn't know what she felt, only that his words had planted in her a coldness. She could only stand there and look back at him, and say those insufficient words. *What you heard is true.*

Ned moved forward. Rianna stiffened, but he didn't come near. Instead he sat down on the bed with a groan. "That's better," he said. "I hope you'll pardon me. It was a long ride. I came as fast as I could, after I'd done my last job for the queen. The worst of them. I think she knew I'd be done with it all after that. But I didn't tell her. I slit a man's throat and that was the end of it. I came home."

"I would not have been his queen," said Rianna. "I would have killed him. Should have, when I had the chance. I failed." The words came slowly, with a flat inflection, but what she felt was the old bitterness.

"You'd have been killed if you'd done that," he said. "I'm glad you didn't. I'd die if you did, don't you know that?"

She shivered a little.

He lay back on the bed and stared at the ceiling. He said, "I've been thinking of the time we freed your father from imprisonment. When we came against Nickon Gerrard. You and I, we had just pledged ourselves to one another, but we'd had no time. Until then I'd been running at death . . . I courted it like a fool. And suddenly here was fear. Knowing what I could lose."

He stopped, and lay gazing upward into nothing.

She said, "I remember."

"But then I came back," he said. "And we were joined, and happy as we were—that fear soon dwindled to memory, and I wonder what else we forgot."

Rianna joined him on the bed. Swinging her legs up to lie beside him and look up at the ceiling too. There was nothing to see. It was too dark.

She reached for his hand. It closed around hers, and she felt, all at once, the coldness within her rush away like melted ice.

LATER that night he said to her, "I heard other things on the road. This Queen is on her way east, though none know why."

She lay curved into him. "If you go after her, I'm coming with you."

"You want to put the fear of the gods into me again," he said. "Is that it?"

"I'll do other things to you first," she promised, and changed position on the bed. When she cupped Ned's head in her hands he said, "I've learned something from all this."

"What?"

"To shave more often."

Later still, they held each other and drifted into sleep. Rianna dreamed of a road, of horses and a long ride. As if her mind traveled where soon the rest of her would, through the roads that led to the mountains, by whatever route was unhindered by the snows, and farther yet. She had looked at maps, had an idea of the course they would take. Through desert, then through fields, across the River Gadlan to Majdara.

RIANNA insisted on meeting with Queen Myrine the day they arrived. Ned looked green at the suggestion but that only strengthened her resolve. She knew she was a sight, haggard after days of hard riding. They'd changed horses several times, drawing upon her father's connections at various inns. Nights they collapsed, so tired they hurt. By the time they reached Majdara, Rianna felt as if her bones had been taken apart and reassembled by a mad toymaker.

She did not intend to let that get in the way of confronting the woman who had lured away her husband.

She ended up having to wait. Suave servants led her to rooms where she might bathe and dress in a velvet robe of crimson. Not a color she would choose, but the velvet felt ravishing on her skin. Her wet hair she braided and wound around her head. She kept her knife under the robe, though she knew it was next to useless here.

The familiar resentment had flared in her when they first arrived at the gate to the palace and Ned had said something hurriedly in Kahishian to the guards. Sounding at ease with them, and they wellacquainted with him.

She thought she understood what his reasons had been for staying. Before he'd become a hero of Majdara there'd been a price on his head. In tricking him into helping her escape to the city, Myrine had laid the trap to keep him there. He'd had little choice but to do what he'd done—organize and command her force of thieves in the city's defense. A clever trap. Rianna mulled it—that particular stratagem of the queen's—as she strapped the knife beneath her skirts. Clever, clever.

When at last Rianna was ushered into the queen's presence, she was pleased that her request had been granted: They were alone.

Myrine sat in a throne. She wore a purple gown embroidered with gold peacocks. But what Rianna saw right away were the flawless features, the sleek coil of black hair.

Rianna came to stand before the queen. Her lip curled. "I don't know what I expected," she said. "Perhaps that you'd be taller."

The queen sat looking at her with impassive dark blue eyes. Then said, "Now why would I need to be tall to achieve what I have? You know the world, Rianna Alterra. We have other weapons at our disposal, you and I."

"We?"

The queen didn't answer. She was staring at Rianna. Looking her over in a way that, from Rianna's point of view, could be considered rude. And then the blankness of her expression fell away, like a curtain drawn from a light: she was smiling. "I see now why Ned was immune to my advances."

Rianna swallowed. Then raised her chin. "I didn't know whether to believe him."

The queen's gaze was steady. "You know he doesn't lie."

Rianna sank into a chair. She wouldn't cry, but felt the same release she felt, sometimes, with tears. "So that's settled."

Myrine inclined her head. "I am glad," she said. "You and your husband are most welcome, though I'm afraid we'll soon be preoccupied with a siege. I don't suppose . . . once you've eaten and rested . . . that I could interest you in a game of chess?"

AFTERNOON turned to evening as the three of them talked. A loaf of bread with poppy seeds and date paste had been reduced to sticky crumbs on the plate. At some point Eldakar had left the room. He had taken Syme with him, promising him pastries of candied almonds and burnt sugar, confections of violet cream and rosewater set in neat little puffs. The Fool was lured away. Eldakar indicated he would soon return. But as the shadows lengthened, light altering from white to gold to dusk rose, it remained the three of them.

Ned lounged on the couch, legs stretched in front of him. Rianna sprawled on the carpet with her head against Lin's skirts. Lin stroked her hair, the endless soft gold of it. Seeing them together, after everything, lifted Lin's heart like nothing else in many months. Last time she'd seen Rianna, she'd felt she couldn't reach her. Now she felt as if a sister had been returned to her from that long journey; that the frozen Rianna of Tamryllin had entered through an enchanted portal, and emerged from it the woman she knew.

And Ned. She had forgiven him long ago.

"How did you know I'd come here?" Lin asked.

Rianna looked up at her. She had been drinking *khave* flavored with cinnamon; it made her eyes bright. "We couldn't be sure," she said. "It stood to reason you'd put yourself where the danger was. It's what you've always done."

"You can't help me."

"Nonsense. A good sword arm or two will be of help."

Lin's throat tightened. "It's dangerous. You saw what this Queen could do, and her opponent is likely much the same."

"We're all in danger if this goes the wrong way," said Ned. "Let us do something about it."

A dream and a nightmare, both, to have them back like this. She had seen battle not long ago. She didn't want either of them in the hellscape she recalled. Especially not when the enemy could kill the way Elissan Diar had been killed.

Lin searched for something to say. It was not her place to make decisions for them. Either of them. She was no longer in a position to give commands, to render prohibitions. Being Court Poet didn't mean much in these times. It meant nothing. The palace back in Tamryllin lay empty. Lin's service there was done.

Whatever she decided to do now, she did for herself. She couldn't attribute it to the weight of the Crown, not this time.

The outlines of the two of them, her beloveds, were blurred in the dark of evening. And then light, from the open door—Eldakar stood there. "You are all invited to dinner," he said, smiling

On their way to the dining hall, Ned Alterra pulled Lin into an alcove. "We haven't talked," he said. "I told you I was sorry by letter. That is not enough. I don't know how to make amends for what I did."

"There is no need," she said. "For apologies, amends. If you are going to battle to fall on your sword for me, please don't. Your happiness is what I want more than anything."

"I don't deserve that," he said. "But no, I won't put myself needlessly in harm's way. It would be irresponsible."

She laughed. "You are the same, after everything," she said. "*Irresponsible*. Oh, Ned."

He looked sheepish. "It's just . . . I was such a fool."

"I don't know how many would have done differently," she said. "Her power is lost on me, but I think I understand it."

"She is teaching Rianna to play chess," he said with a wince, and now Lin could not help giggling helplessly like a girl as they made their way down the hall towards dinner.

THE evening passed in a whirl of food, drink, and laughter. Just the five of them, banqueting in a fire-warmed chamber.

Rianna and the queen had, against all reason, taken to one another; they leaned together talking. Lin kept company with the men; the three shared tales of the campaign. These were mostly jokes. There was little to say about the battles; none of them gloried in acts of war. Ned went into a story of brokering peace between two factions of the Brotherhood of Thieves that had emerged despite Myrine's best efforts. It was clear she would have simply hanged the perpetrators if Ned had not intervened.

"You'll never guess what did it, in the end," said Ned. His long, awkward body loosened, made graceful by wine. His hesitant manner turned urbane. "We discovered that one of the leaders, a fellow calling himself the Brotherhood Fiend—no, really—was worried about marriage prospects for his daughter. You should have seen him—forearms the size of another man's waist, tattooed skulls all over him. Very like the men I encountered at sea. But when talk of his daughter came up, he was like any concerned father. She is shy, apparently. And so we cut a deal. A husband for the daughter from the other side, if both sides worked together."

"I suppose even the most skilled thief can't *steal* a husband," said Lin.

A shouted laugh from across the table. The women had overheard. "This one did her best," said Rianna, inclining her head towards

Myrine. The queen looked amused, dignified, while Ned turned bright red.

After the dessert courses had been savored, along with pots of tea, Lin excused herself. As she was leaving, glanced behind her. The couples had found each other: the king and queen leaning together, Ned and Rianna. The four involved in animated talk. She heard their voices as if through water, sounds that echoed. Amid the lamps and candles that surrounded the table, the four of them glowed. They were drenched in light. She watched for what seemed a long time, but was likely only a moment.

Then turned, and when she saw Syme, felt a sense of being pulled along in a current. It was that feeling of having dreamed all this once, of knowing before she began what was to happen. It was all arranged.

"You're ready," she said. It was not a question.

The Fool's eyes in the candlelight were like pools of ink. In his lime green jacket, was absurd and dapper as he bowed. "My lady," he said. "Time to go."

CHAPTER
27

THE dark outside the city walls was a live thing. It was tangled with hedges of stinging nettles, with thistles that snagged in her sleeves. Other invisible growing things, roots and tendrils, reached out to trip her. With one hand she held a lantern; with the other, reached to feel her way. Syme a silent shape, a half-shadow, at her side.

What had been a manicured path up the mountainside was over-grown. She imagined there were already vines breaking up the stair-way paving stones, though she couldn't see them in the dark. She only knew she had to watch her footing, had once or twice nearly pitched from the steep incline. An unceremonious and pathetic end that would be. So she made her way with care, keeping an eye on the circle of light cast by the lantern. The moon and stars were obscured tonight.

As they strove through the reaching growth of the path she thought of where they were headed. His words to her at New Year's Eve.

The myth of Asterian takes many shapes.

How he knew that was anyone's guess. The Syme Oleir who attended the Academy—a stolid, rotund boy, well-liked by other students—was unlikely to have known the sinuous transmutations of a myth. He'd have known, like everyone, the one recorded in writing. In popular songs.

Now he claimed to know versions in which the poet Asterian did not fail. In which he reclaimed his love, Stylleia, from the dead.

To begin the tale: The lovers were on a riverbank, and Asterian sang to her. And then, catastrophe: she stepped on a viper in the grass. Her limbs would have seized, skin turned blue. Dead in an instant as the heart-wrung poet held her by the waist and screamed his lament.

Stylleia would have seen the world slip away like the shore from view of a boat going out to sea. Finding herself in eddies of nothing. Until she reached the farther shore and disembarked. The start to her journey, the one each soul by one turn or another must take.

There would be more to the journey on the farther shore, Lin thought as she tramped the black and broken path on the mountainside. Still no moon to be seen. The dark of hedges that loomed each side of the path was ragged and rife with thorns to block her way. She recalled when these were flowers that had drifted in a breeze to fill the air with scent. Roses, lilacs, falls of wisteria.

That shore had vanished utterly.

At the first landing she began to see traces of the ruin. The sphere of lanternlight fell on leaning piles and scatterings of rubble. Cornerstones exposed like a giant's broken teeth.

Lin raised her lantern. She felt a tug of helplessness. How to search through all this? Each level of the palace was huge, and there were three in all.

"You know this," said Syme. "Remember why we're here."

Zahir.

She recalled a boy with Zahir's eyes, rooting in the wreckage of a city. Grief turning to desperation as he realized this was no ordinary wreckage. That while death was bad enough, there were things worse. In his eyes she'd seen the beginning to the plot that would shape all he did thereafter. Not knowing then, as a boy, the doors he'd walk through on the way. Doors that once opened could not be closed again.

"So, the Tower," she murmured.

Her light caught a flash in the corner of her eye: Syme's teeth. He had smiled.

She went on climbing.

The destruction of the Zahra was the first piece. The first paving stone on the path Zahir Alcavar had sought all his life. As long as the palace stood, the souls of Vesperia were trapped. So he'd turned all his ingenuity to creating this, the rubble she picked through now.

But that destruction was only a start—the first step. Zahir had imagined them—himself and her—harrowing the Underworld together. The two of them, harnessing the powers of the Ifreet to enter that realm. He had not planned on being dead. Unless she was right that in some corner of his soul he had not meant to live. Aware there was too much death on his hands.

One might have desires that are opposed, blades crossed in the heart.

Hope for the souls of Vesperia had not died with Zahir Alcavar. Not when Lin Amaristoth had in her possession the Ifreet, and what Syme had called the keys to death.

There were many versions of the myth of Asterian. What was one more?

"We're close," said Syme. "There." He pointed. Before them was an arch that stood, unsupported, in the midst of rubble. In the lantern light the stones shone. Marble, she thought. An arch of marble that had been in the Tower of Glass. Around them the stillness of the night, punctuated with cricket calls and the occasional cry of the jackal.

Lin stood there, thinking. She had an idea. "Hold this." She handed the lantern to Syme.

He took it. Then aimed it a blow to her face.

"*What* . . ." Lin ducked. The lantern fell to the ground. Its light winked out.

But even in the dark she could see him. She knew his outline better than she did her own.

It wasn't Syme standing there anymore, but Rayen, loose-limbed and smiling. "Hail, my dear." The voice was his as well.

She drew a breath. She knew what this was. Even as she watched, saw the green glow that outlined him as he advanced to her. He looked the same as he had the day he'd tied her to the ground.

"Come no closer," she said, drawing blade.

"You'll kill me?" His hair flung back. "Oh, I hope so."

"I know." She felt cold all over. Syme's voice, New Year's Eve: *He'd rather die than help you. That is how much he hates.*

When Rayen came at her with his blade, she parried and dodged and tried not to attack. Until his blade whistled past her ear and she met the blow with a vicious slash of her own. It missed him narrowly.

He was laughing. "Your hatred is useful," he said. "But I think there is someone—one person in the world—you hate even more."

He changed again before her eyes. Shrank, narrowed. Became a slight woman. Large, dark eyes. A plaintive voice. "Won't you kill me?"

Lin gritted her teeth, backed away. She'd never heard that voice, high-pitched and grating in her ears. Yet knew it for her own.

"You can't think this will work," she said. "I know you want me to kill you. These are child's games."

The other Lin, green-wreathed, drew her sword. Lunged forward. Lin, the true one, dodged the blow.

The other Lin said, in that grating, destestable voice, "Darien died for you. So did Valanir Ocune. So did Zahir Alcavar." They stood inches apart. The other Lin hissed, "Look at me. For *this* did such men give their lives?"

Lin sprang back. "I agree." Her lungs were bursting from the long climb up the stairs. "And if I were to die now, it would be even worse. After what they gave."

The other Lin looked genuinely outraged, her plain face twisting. "That great men gave their lives for *this*." She gestured downward. "An obscenity."

"I know you mean it," said Lin. "I know even though you are mirroring my thoughts, you mean them. But you will have to work harder than that to make me throw away this chance to do right. One thing, at the end."

There was no use speaking to the creature, she knew. She did it to stall. She couldn't kill it, nor did she know what else to do.

The other Lin flashed a smug, ugly grin. "I have many tricks." Then looked astonished, eyes widening. *"No."* Its cry was not in Lin's voice. It was a multitude, emerging from the perfect circle her mouth had become. A cataclysm of voices, a murder, a swarm. Its eyes were orbs of green.

When the light died the shrunken figure slumped to the ground. It lay curled there.

"Syme," she said, running to him.

He sat up with a groan. "I turned it back," he said. "For now. That is all I could do. And it fights me."

"You'd do this to help me," she said. "Syme." She found she could not speak. Then met his ingenuous gaze, and knew she could not be silent. "When I use the Ifreet for . . . for this next thing . . . I don't know what will become of you. If you'll survive."

At last, she'd said it. She could not bring herself to lie to him. Not even by omission.

A commander was supposed to lead men blindly into death. She couldn't do it. A commander was not what she had ever wanted to be. She thought of Darien, wandering carefree, paying his way with songs. She'd wanted that for herself. But even Darien hadn't had it for long. The world had caught up to him and the poet's life he'd been meant for.

She waited for Syme Oleir to speak. He had gone still. They crouched in the mounded dirt and grass among the stones.

At last he said, "I know." He looked at her calmly. "I've always known that, Lin." Reaching out, he caught hold of her hand. Used it to lever himself upright. He stood beside her. "Everyone needs a purpose. Something to make their lives matter at the end." He looked down at his hands. "Even, perhaps, a Fool."

SHE had built a fire beside the arch. It was small, striving in its cage of twigs; she had not built it to burn for long. She didn't have much time. At any moment the Ifreet would take possession of Syme again.

She wanted light to see by. Syme sat near the fire to warm himself.

It was deep night. She thought of the people she'd left in the city. One way or another, she couldn't keep them from the fight. But they were incapable of following where she went now.

Asterian had gone to the Underworld alone and so would she. Or near enough. She wasn't sure how far Syme would accompany her.

He watched her. She stood at the base of the arch.

"A song of lament opened the way," she recalled.

"How will you find things to lament, my lady?" he asked ironically, and she smiled.

As her hands stirred the strings, she reached for something. For a song. She thought of nights in the Tower of the Winds, reaching for melodies within. She had sent her mind down the well of her past as if it were a bucket, been forced to gaze at the things, exposed and squirming, that it drew forth. She'd felt revulsion, shame at the sight of them, but they were hers. Her shadow. Therefore her song.

Again she thought back to the boy Zahir Alcavar had been. Rooting through a ruined city for his dead. In a blink the young boy who had desired to be a singer had changed the course of his life; had gone on to do harm like a deep scar in the earth.

As she played she could see his eyes, that had stayed the same from his childhood until the day he died. She remembered the hopeless chill of his gaze that night, when he knew—when he took in—that she could not be party to his plan.

She sang to him as if he were there.

Syme said, "Look."

A light around them was growing. The gold of her skin glowed, spilled between the seams of her clothing. And grew brighter.

"Keep on," Syme urged in a whisper.

She sang on, leaning to the harp as if for ballast.

Valanir Ocune had carried her to the bed that night as if she were a bird. She never forgot. Nor did she forget the still, quiet box of light that had been her room, when she found what she had not thought to find. With him or anyone.

She opened herself to the lament. Followed the melody where it led.

And before her, in the space encompassed by the arch, a spiral of brightness was beginning. She saw a vista of green, daylight on the hills north of Tamryllin. She was with her friends again, hand in hand, looking ahead to a tale yet to be unwound. One that she had thought, then, could not be so bad, as long as they faced it together. Darien's grin, Hassen's stoic endurance of his friend's wit; there they were. She had thought to join with them must mean that even if the shadow still fell on her there would be light from them, their songs and laughter. And that it would last.

It was all right to be a fool when you were young, she thought. Especially for love.

Asterian had gone to the realm of the dead for love, and in some renditions of the tale—a tale that history had rendered into as many fragments as a shattered jar—he failed.

His love was no less real for that.

Syme was beside her now, and he made a frantic call like a bird. "*Go go go,*" he shouted, his arms raised as if to fly. Reminding her of a gull. He flared green, then the gold that radiated from her skin, then green again. She realized he was fighting it again, fighting hard. "Sing!" he screamed to her. "I am gone, I am lost, you go."

So here was the final lament, she thought, tears coming for the first time. She would find words for the sacrifice of Syme Oleir if it took the rest of her life. Or—lacking that time—she'd find them now. He screamed and she sang at a pitch almost a scream, and the gate that had begun as a vision of daylight turned black. Unfurled for her like a banner.

There were many avenues to death, but few entered in the flesh.

Syme screamed to her above the stormcrack of the opening gate. Winds and thunder poured forth as if it opened to a stormy sea, but she knew . . . she could feel in its clammy smell . . . that the storm was somewhere deep beneath the earth.

She didn't know how to help him, other than to close this gate and let it go. Lin mourned him as they gazed at each other across the widening abyss. She sang on the edge of death.

At last the gate was wide as the arch, and Lin knew she could no longer delay. She stood before the storm a moment. Looked at Syme screaming to her. And then she jumped.

DORN Arrin hunkered down in the grass. Otherwise the wind would have knocked him over. The oncoming storm had blocked the sun. An artificial night had fallen.

Etherell caught his arm. "Steady."

"You know what this is?" He had to shout.

"No idea."

It was hard to see what was happening. The black wave of a new army was sweeping toward them. He had a vague impression of people running, the Queen's army fleeing before the wave. Wind and flashes of lightning came with it. A collective shriek arose, and Dorn felt, tugging at him, a current of emotion like sorrow.

"Oh gods," he said. "It is the dead."

Etherell didn't hear him. He looked out at the advancing army—for such it had to be—a wall of spears made of night—and seemed puzzled.

It was bearing down fast.

"They're about to attack us," said Etherell. "Well." He drew his sword.

That was when the first wave of dark spearmen swept into the ranks of the King's army. Into it, and through. The King's grey warriors crumpled like paper thrown in a grate.

Next the dark army came for the Queen's front ranks. The young men who had been Academy students, Elissan Diar's Chosen, made immortal through magic. They stood and faced the onslaught as it came. And to a man they fell. Not for the first time. And then lay still, which was new.

In later days when the bodies of the Chosen were heaped on a pyre, no one believed they'd burn. People expected that the men would rise, dead-eyed and intent to kill. No one stayed to watch the pyre burn itself out. It took days for the flames to die away. In the northern villages, which were near Almyria, they saw the smoke and were reminded of things they'd been attempting to forget.

What remained was a hill of ashes. A month later, following the winter rains, a rose garden sprang from the burned patch of grass. In time the field became famous for its profusion of white roses, delicate blooms that didn't belong in the mountain climate but would nonetheless endure, year after year.

MOMENTS before she led the attack, Lin Amaristoth had turned to the army behind her. Their cries rang in her bones. Men, women, and children wore the same face, masks of suffering.

The wind from the portal whipped at her, at all of them. But she was the one who felt it. She was still alive.

"When you fall here today," she said, addressing the ranks of tortured eyes, "your pain will end. You will gain a true death."

The souls of Vesperia cried assent. At her command, they charged.

* * *

JULIEN'S mind had narrowed to a single point: to shield Archmaster Hendin from the storm winds. The noise of battle blended with that of the storm, and she looked away from it all, wrapping them both in his cloak.

Dorn was out there, she thought. But she had no idea what to do about it. She had no powers. She had nothing left.

She clung to the Seer's body as wave after wave of battle crashed beneath her. Julien trembled, and didn't know if it was fear or from the force of the noise. The clangor and screams.

After whatever form of time it was that passed, after however many assaults took place in the darkened fields below, the noises ebbed. Then faded to the sound of wind, and then were altogether gone.

It might have been quiet a long time, the winds gone away, when an instinct made Julien Imara look down at the field. She saw someone climbing the hill. Heading towards her.

And what could she do? She had a knife, but didn't know what to do with it. But would anyone want Archmaster Hendin's body? Why would they? A sob rose in her throat.

The storm was lifting, and with it, the inky dark. Sunlight was breaking through the clouds. The purplish-blue of the hills was brightening again to green. Now she could see who was coming. A slight figure, moving with purpose through the grass. Bringing her own light as she came.

"Julien," said Lin Amaristoth. "What's happened?"

Julien stared at her. The Court Poet shone as if she had been dipped in gold paint.

"Oh I see," Lin murmured. She knelt beside Archmaster Hendin in the grass.

"I lost him," said Julien.

Lin's expression was tender. "Perhaps not," she said. "The gate is still open."

"The gate?" Julien looked down the hill. Saw the patch of dark that hovered in the field like a departing storm.

Lin didn't answer. She was murmuring over the Archmaster. She put a hand to his closed eyelids. Then smiled, fell back, as his eyes opened. She was still shining. "Welcome back."

* * *

THE Queen stood like a lone white pillar in the field. Two other figures, smaller and dimmer, alongside her. Everything in her presence
was dimmed. As they approached, Julien tried not to look at the bodies
that lay scattered on the field. Academy students, most of them. The
only ones who had not vanished or fled. They had been trained to obey,
to fight to the death, and they'd done so.

"Your grace," Lin Amaristoth called across the field.

The White Queen's hair danced in the wind. "You."

Julien hung back with Archmaster Hendin, a few steps behind
Lin. But gave a cry when she recognized Dorn Arrin with the White
Queen. He was dressed in the formal black and silver of a poet. She
stared. Something about seeing him fitted out that way made her uneasy.

Etherell Lyr was there, too. That was strange. She wondered if he,
too, had been captured.

Coming forward, Lin sketched a bow. "It is my understanding," she
said, "that your opponent has gone. That it's over."

The White Queen curled her lip. "He was always skilled at saving
himself, and little else." She looked at Lin, up and down, undisguised
contempt. "So you're the one who ruined it."

Lin spread her hands. "We act on our own interests, your grace. It is
the way of battle. But there is something I can offer you." She pointed.
"Over there is a gate that will take you wherever you wish to go. Any
world at all. I don't have that sort of power, but you do. You can use it
how you like."

"It would save trouble." The Queen's eyes grew thoughtful. "You are
fortunate that my strength is diminished. My name was used against
me. No use destroying you, when I must restore my strength."

"The fortunes of war undo us all," Lin said delicately. "How may I
speed you on your way?"

"You need do nothing," said the White Queen. "I will use your portal."
She closed a hand like ivory pincers around Dorn's wrist. "This one
comes with me."

Nearby, the croak of carrion birds as they hovered and fought among
themselves. Picking at the bodies.

Lin said, "What would you take instead?"

The White Queen laughed. "Nothing. He is mine. If he doesn't come, that portal will stay open, and I will return for him when I've regained my strength. Nothing that belongs to me can stay. These are laws beyond even you, Seer."

Julien sprang forward. Everything blurred around her: Dorn's face, the grass, the luminous pillar that was the Queen. When she spoke, and the Queen's gaze fixed on her, she quailed. But stayed the course. "I read . . . I have read something about . . . exchanges. One mortal for another."

"That is true," said the Queen with a dismissive gesture. "You're all interchangeable."

"Good," said Julien Imara. "Take me."

Now Dorn spoke up. "Don't you dare."

She turned to him. Her gaze caught on his like cloth on a nail; she couldn't look away. And thought she would never forget how he looked then: pale and lost, but resolute. Behind him, she could see crows capering a shadow dance on the field among the dead.

A memory: *Nothing is freely given or gained.*

In her innocence, or stupidity, or both, Julien had imagined she'd lost everything. But it was only power she'd lost. Only that.

Lin Amaristoth said, "I will not see my poets give away their lives. Either of them."

Julien felt Archmaster Hendin stir beside her. He'd been hardly able to speak since Lin Amaristoth revived him. Now he was coming to himself.

"I'll go." Etherell Lyr, coming forward.

A breeze stirred in the grass. After the events of the morning, its murmur passing through was peaceful. Even if they could see, several paces off, the darkness that hung in the distance. The gate.

Dorn was white as paper. "What are you doing?"

"I betrayed you." Etherell stood at ease, stating a fact. "This makes it right."

"You can't stand to be in debt."

"Besides." The other man grinned. "Have you considered the adventure?"

"There must be another way."

"No." It was hard to read Etherell's serene blue eyes; no way to know what he thought or felt. "You know there isn't." He turned to the Queen; with a mocking gesture extended his arm to her.

Dorn said, "Wait."

The serenity of Etherell's expression wavered. "It is better," he said. "I don't really belong here. I hurt people." He fixed Dorn in his gaze. "I hurt you."

Time seemed to move differently here, as it had on Labyrinth Isle and the western sea. It seemed only moments later the White Queen and Etherell Lyr were a distance away, heading for the patch of blackness on the field. Julien blinked; she had not seen that happen. The two moved steadily. Until the Queen set her hand on the back of Etherell's neck. He vanished into the dark. She followed close behind, through the gate.

The light of afternoon folded over them as it closed.

THEY were back on the hill of standing stones, away from the stench of the field, by the time the sun began its descent. The shadows on Hariya Mountain deepening. Its surface reflected every change of the sun, much like the sea. Soon an entourage from King Eldakar would come—his Magician had sent word. Until then, there was nothing to do but rest and wait among the stones. Julien Imara lay back on the grass, her cloak wrapped around her. She wanted shelter from her thoughts. It had felt like the longest day of her life. Archmaster Hendin had fallen asleep where he lay.

Nearby, Dorn Arrin sat picking a blade of grass to pieces.

"So, Julien," Lin Amaristoth said. She was the only one who appeared at ease, seated cross-legged in the grass. She looked different than when Julien had seen her last—she wore trousers, and had cut off her hair. "You had the Queen's name. How did that happen?"

Julien curled deeper into the cloak. "It was a . . . a bargain. I went to the Lost Isles."

"The what?"

Archmaster Hendin stirred. "Wait until you hear, my lady," he said. "What this girl has seen and done. I'm afraid it'll make you jealous."

Lin smiled. "Poets thrive on petty jealousies. I should like to hear." Her glance at Julien was kind. "When you're ready."

"There's one thing I don't understand," said Julien. "When the Queen was weakened . . . so was the King. But I didn't have his name."

Dorn spoke, the first time in a while. "I did."

Julien gaped. "How?"

"Never mind." Though it was dusk, he had visibly reddened.

"You can't be like that!"

"Oh yes I can."

"A story like that would be invaluable for our archives," Archmaster Hendin began, then stopped when Dorn Arrin looked at him with a face like thunder.

Lin Amaristoth spoke. "Perhaps we ought to put this interrogation to rest," she said. "And simply say thank you."

Dorn covered his face with his hands.

Julien knew better than to go to him. She ached. They remained silent after that, and watched the last red bands of daylight disappear.

WHEN the king came, he and his entourage went to work to build a pyre for the slain. It took the better part of the day.

The next day they spent traveling to put a distance between themselves and the smoke. They plunged into the forest, rock-strewn pinewoods that reminded Lin Amaristoth of northern Eivar. But she was far from home. At least the winter here was gentler.

"Does Rianna want to kill me?" she asked Eldakar as they rode.

He grinned. "Best put your affairs in order."

"I thought so."

That night they pitched tents in a glade. Eldakar invited Lin to dine with him alone. There was an air about him she had never seen, excitable and melancholy at once. When they were alone she asked after his health.

"My surgeon predicts my shoulder will be better by spring," said Eldakar. "I think it is getting better. Though I always know when a storm is coming."

"That's useful."

"I hope so," said Eldakar. "In years to come I'll need every skill I possess."

"What do you mean?"

For some moments he was silent. The brazier threw an orange glow on his features, still fine, despite all he'd weathered in the last year and more. He had many good years ahead of him, Lin thought. And now the threat of war, at least a war of the enchanted sort, had been put to rest.

When at last Eldakar spoke, his mouth had a sardonic tilt. "I'm not going back to Majdara."

She blinked. "I know it's not the Zahra," she began.

"It's not that," he said. "I'm not returning to rule. I'm leaving this land. Probably not forever, but we'll see."

"You . . . you are king."

"I was," he said. "And I hoped, when I went back, that I could put behind me what I've done. That the graceful rooms of a palace, the love of the most beautiful woman in the world, would help me forget. But it follows me. Into every corner and cranny of every chamber, no matter how gilded. Underneath it all is blood."

"You mean—"

"My father bought his throne with the blood of a city. And the only way to hold that throne is to keep feeding it—more and more blood."

"Does the queen know?"

"I told her," he said. "I told her she could come with me, if she likes. Mansur would make a good king. After all the upheaval, the people would accept him, I believe. But I think I already knew her answer."

She didn't want to ask. The hiss of the brazier filled the silence for a time. At last Eldakar spoke again. "She wept," he said. "More than I've ever seen. But she stayed. She is made for the throne in a way I never was."

"Does anyone else know this?"

"Not yet. Mansur would try to stop me."

"Eldakar," she said. "The things we've done—we can't leave them behind. Our shadows accompany us where we go."

"Yes," he said. "And it does. It will. But my throne stands on innocent blood. I refuse it."

These three words he said with an expression only a king could wear. She wondered if he knew. The cold nobility in the way he held himself; that certainty. *I refuse it.*

He went on. "As long as my people needed me, I had an obligation to them. But they don't anymore. The people cheer her name in the streets. Majdara has its queen."

Lin swallowed the lump in her throat. She had counted on Eldakar to be there, across the border, for years to come; a friend she might visit and reminisce with until they both were old. But he didn't need to hear that. "I hope we meet again someday, Eldakar."

"I, too," he said. "What are your plans?"

"Well," she said. "The king of Eivar is dead. The former king and queen were exiled, and I'm pleased to hear they are safe—but they will not be restored. No one wants that. Likely there will be a ruling council for a while. Bids for succession . . ." She trailed off. She'd been trying not to think about these political concerns. They had seemed trifling after the past few days. After the Underworld.

Now they rushed to the surface: the messy, tangled problems of the living.

Eldakar looked sympathetic. "Here," he said. "Have some wine."

At dawn Nameir Hazan was saddling her horse. Checking and re-checking each saddlebag again. The stench of the pyre clung to her nostrils, but nonetheless she felt the beginnings of something inside her. Something light and free.

She had done her part for the king. For the last time. She had come with him to help put to rest the slain, and now she was done. She'd bidden farewell to everyone. To Aleira Suzehn, who had hugged her and given her a blessing. In Galician, of course, words Nameir didn't know but that had the chime of home.

Home was nowhere, but that didn't have to be a bad thing. And it might be waiting beyond the horizon. She was taking a chance to find it, or at the very least, to be free.

Predictably, Mansur Evrayad was aggrieved when she told him. It had been late at night, but she had not joined him in his tent; she feared what he might try if they were alone there. Not that she feared him, but her own capacity for resistance.

Even when she knew there was pain behind that door, she didn't trust herself.

In the shadows of the trees they'd argued. He was impassioned, pleading. Then threatening. Then pleading once again. At last in a fit of characteristic generosity, he'd given her a gift: a silver-hilted dagger that was in his family. "Come back," he said. "You have to."

She had allowed herself then, once more, to touch the curve of his cheek. Then knew she had to escape, and said nothing else, not even a good night.

Maybe she would return someday. She didn't know. The world was large, and she had seen only a corner of it. Someone with her skills might see much more. At the dawn of the next day she wanted to think only of the road ahead, not what lay behind. She was hardly immune to sadness; she only knew she might find something more if she went in search of it for the first time in her life.

What she didn't expect was an approach from the king himself, just before she was to ride off. She was checking her horse once more. When she saw Eldakar Evrayad emerge from the trees, she braced herself. He had taken the news of her departure quietly the night before. He had given her a gift, too, a ring with a single ruby. In gratitude for her service.

He had not tried to convince her to stay, but she could imagine it easily enough. The offer of a title, of more land.

"I'm leaving," she said.

"I know," said Eldakar. "I was wondering if I might come with you."

She stared at him. "That depends," she said. "I'm done with kings and princes."

Eldakar's laugh rippled through the glade. "So am I."

AFTER the talk with Eldakar Evrayad, Lin couldn't sleep. Her mind was like a courser in the hunt. Racing, racing ahead.

So much work to do when she returned. It was staggering to contemplate. No way to know, as yet, what had happened to the palace. The work it would take to make it habitable again . . . and for whom? All the lords of Eivar would try to assert themselves. Some would claim royal ties. There would be battles.

And where would she be, in all this?

There was the Academy. Now that she knew about the Lost Isles, the proximity to the Otherworld, it explained so much. And made it imperative to strengthen that fortress for the years to come. The Academy must be again what it was long ago: a sentinel against things like the White Queen and the Shadow King, from countless other threats that might engulf their world from the one beyond.

There was the body of Marlen Humbreleigh to put to rest. Her enchantment would conceal him until she returned. And she already knew what she would do. Marilla, years ago, had confided to her that Marlen wished more than anything to be buried beside his friend. Beside Darien Aldemoor. And so he would be. Lin would see to it.

The Underworld would have more mischief in it now, she thought. Between those two.

That realm of the dead was like a dream to her, hazy and undefined. She remembered only one thing clearly: calling the souls of Vesperia to her, and her disappointment when she did not see Zahir Alcavar in the crowd. Disappointment, followed by relief. His death had been true at the end; there was that.

She didn't know what had become of Syme Oleir. For his sake she hoped his soul had departed cleanly. She would issue a formal request to the queen of Kahishi, Lin thought. To find the body of Syme Oleir in the ruins of the Zahra, and send him home. And to erect a stone or cairn to mark the spot where he'd fallen, for Lin would explain: this was the man who had saved Kahishi at the end. Who'd saved them all.

When her eyes had met those of Archmaster Hendin in recent days, she thought she saw a reflection of what she felt. A sadness and relief that permeated every thought.

She shifted on the hard pallet, suspecting sleep would never come. And tomorrow, the start to the long ride home.

Her eye caught a sliver of lantern light at the tent flap. Someone was there. Lin sat up.

A woman's voice, a murmur. "Am I welcome?"

Instead of answering, Lin rose. Went to the tent flap to show Aleira Suzehn inside. They had only spoken briefly since Aleira had arrived with the king's entourage. Only of business. Never mind that they had spoken nearly constantly across the distance of many miles, ever since Aleira had mastered that skill. Lin sometimes forgot it had been a year since they had really spoken face to face. In her mind that time was hazed in its own strange light, for it had been in a crypt beneath the earth, the lair of the Fire Dancers. When she and Zahir had knelt at their sacred pool and heard the prophecy. A forecast of death.

Aleira had watched them leave the crypt fully expecting Lin would die. Lin had seen it in her face. The Magician—then only known to her as the bookseller—had looked hopeless, lost in mourning.

Entering the tent with her lantern, the other woman didn't seem much changed. She still favored the color red. Her hair was still a shining glory past her shoulders. The lantern light softened her, for Lin knew well that in other times, by other lights, she was pitiless as marble.

"How did you know I was awake?" Lin asked, leading her inside. She sat on her pallet. Motioned to the tent's only chair.

Aleira didn't sit down. "I guessed. I know you take responsibility for everything that happens, like Eldakar. Worse than him. How could such a one ever sleep?"

Lin smiled. "It has been a problem."

"I'll be riding back tomorrow to my queen," said Aleira.

"In a few hours."

"Yes." Aleira paused. "I have thought of you since our last meeting," she said. "What I would have felt if you'd been killed in the Fire Dance. And I've thought of how it must be for you, must have been. It all makes me angry."

She was standing nearer now, and even in the dimness Lin could see the color rise in her face and throat.

Aleira Suzehn said, "My lady, if you would let me ease your cares just this night, I'd consider it an honor."

She reached out a hand; their fingertips brushed. Lin was taken aback. Yet a part of her recognized this as one of the paths she had foreseen, somewhere deep within her all along. Still she said, "I don't—I don't know if I can."

Aleira stroked a strand of hair back from Lin's forehead. "What if you didn't have to do anything? Just this once."

Lin choked a laugh. "I suppose I can try."

She let the other woman take her hand. Then, before anything else, Aleira blew out the light.

* * *

THAT same night in a dimlit room in the same country, two women faced each other across a table: one dark-haired, the other fair. On the table was a board of checkered squares. The pieces arrayed upon the board were locked in a still, silent combat.

The space around the table was candlelit; great tapers in brass sconces with clawed feet. They were massive, made to burn through the night. Myrine was known for keeping odd hours; for seldom sleeping much at all.

Behind Myrine—also known betimes as Rihab Bet-Sorr—the window began to show the first signs of daybreak. Before her were her pieces, carved of onyx. The queen always took the side of black.

"You'll be leaving me soon," she said to the woman across the table.

Rianna selected an ivory piece from her side, at last, and played it. Knowing as she did so that the other woman, far advanced in skill, with a mind that made Rianna think of the moving parts of a clock, would use it to advantage.

No matter. They passed the time this way.

"I'll be going back to my life," said Rianna. "As will you. Queen of Kahishi."

With a quick movement, half-absent, the queen knocked one of Rianna's pawns from the board with her priest. Too easy. Her mind elsewhere.

Her eyes, turned to Rianna, were nearly wistful. "You and I know what it is to find ourselves at a crossroads," she said. "To make a choice that alters everything. And not know how in later years we will be judged . . . or come to judge ourselves."

"Everyone alive has some experience of that," said Rianna. She motioned to the board. "It's what we do here. I thought that was why you liked it."

"No," said the queen. "I like this game because it makes *sense*. Because when I construct a perfect strategy, bringing all the parts together, the results can be foreseen."

Rianna recalled a castle of underground passageways twisted around a secret. Of the way she'd become bound up in its web, despite her plans. "People aren't pieces," she said at last, but gently.

The queen considered. Turned to the window, which had brightened further. Now could be seen a white illumination; the sun pressing through a density of fog. When she turned back again, to the warmer glow of candlelight, she smiled. Almost tremulously. "I feel as if I've known you all my life," she said. "Promise you'll visit." She reached across the table for Rianna's hand. "Promise you'll write."

EPILOGUE

SPRING had come to Academy Isle. Soon it would be a year. When Manaia came, after the students had gone out to gather wood and build the need-fires, that would make it a year to the day. The colors the island wore in spring—the bright blue of the water, bright green, the snowy white of the rowan trees—met Dorn Arrin's eye when he turned to the window. The same view, every year.

He'd come back to graduate. Student life had resumed, once word had got about that it was safe to return. Soon he'd have his ring and be on his way. He'd be sad to leave; but also knew he couldn't stay longer. There was too much of the past here, and nothing else.

Some evenings he sat in the kitchen with Owayn and Larantha and Julien after everyone else had gone to bed. No one asked him questions. Sometimes they sang. Sometimes Julien told of the battle between the White Queen and Shadow King. Other times she told of Labyrinth Isle; how Marlen Humbreleigh had come to her as her guide. That made Larantha cry, but there was happiness mixed with her grief. She'd always said there was good in him. He'd proven her right at the end.

At nights Dorn would crawl into bed. Once he slept in Etherell's bed, as if that might lead to dreams of him. Some clue where he was. But there was nothing. There was not even a scent on the bedcovers. Etherell Lyr, the man who came from nowhere and had gone the gods-knew-where, had left nothing behind.

Archmaster Hendin had promised to move along the procedure for choosing a gem for Dorn Arrin's ring. Then Dorn would be on his way. He knew now that there was a purpose to the enchantments beyond power and aggrandizement; he understood that. But he still wanted none of it. And he thought, perhaps it could be allowed that he'd done his part. That he'd earned some time to wander and understand who he was outside these halls.

There was a part of him that refused to believe Etherell Lyr would not one day walk into the room humming, beginning to change his shirt or shave or idle away the time. A part of him that wouldn't accept it, not as long as he was here.

Once, in the kitchen, Julien Imara had regarded him solemnly. As solemn as anyone could look while gnawing bread and cheese. She had said, "I know you don't want to talk about it. But perhaps, someday, a song?"

Dorn had smiled at her. "If I do that," he said, "I'll make sure you're first to know."

It was an idea that had been spinning in his mind for quite awhile. Since New Year's Eve. The night he'd sung in an enchanted hall, to an audience of beings from another world, of the devastation of his own.

Not yet, as it turned out. Spring had come again.

THE first thing Julien Imara had done, upon returning to Academy Isle, was go to the Hall of Harps. She felt as if she prepared the way for those soon to arrive. With reverence and some regret she'd set the Silver Branch on its dais. Once more, the Hall of Harps was illumined in its soft light.

Next she checked the carvings. And saw that the great tile that had shown an antlered king on a throne surrounded by skulls in a double spiral—it was blank now. Not a mark remained.

As the last days of winter rolled by, students and Archmasters began to arrive. There were those in Eirne who, for a fee, would make the run in their fishing boats when the waters were calm. Soon the Academy halls were ringing with voices again. Julien was still the only girl, but now she had private lessons with Archmaster Hendin. More girls would enroll eventually, he predicted; but until then, he wanted to make sure she was caught up.

Cai Hendin was appointed High Master following a vote; it was hardly a surprise. No one was sure what his actions in the battle had been; but he was the only Archmaster who had taken action. He began to steer the Academy to a new mission. The enchantments were a necessity, he taught; a responsibility. Poets stood guard at the edge of the world.

No one had ever viewed the work of the Academy in that light—not in centuries, anyhow. Some might feel it as a loss, removing the focus from their art. Julien Imara did. Dorn had taught her to see it that way, and she could not help but see it, in part, through his eyes. But it also gave her a sense of purpose that was exhilarating in its own way. Archmaster Hendin had told her that if she stayed the course she could become a Seer again. This time with a mark of her own.

There were nights she dreamed of their sea journey and Labyrinth Isle; some days she felt an essential part of her was gone. She didn't know if a new mark could make that right. Someday she'd see.

One day she ran into High Master Hendin's chambers. She had not made an appointment and was breathing fast from running up the stairs.

He sat at his writing table. Julien knew he was in regular communication with Lin Amaristoth about affairs of government in Tamryllin. Lin was attempting to mediate talks among the nobles, but tempers ran short. A war of succession was inevitable. Fortunately Lin could expect aid, whatever she required, from the queen of Kahishi.

A particular scroll on the desk, Julien recognized: the work Archmaster Hendin returned to whenever he could. He had questioned her again about Labyrinth Isle, for the purpose of noting down every detail she could recall. He was writing a chronicle; an account of all that had happened within that year. Though it was not yet finished, he had titled it already, letters flourishing across the page: *The Poet King*.

Looking up now, he fixed her with a stern look. "This had best be important."

Julien stood on the threshold of High Master Hendin's study, suddenly feeling awkward. She remembered standing in this same spot when this had been Elissan Diar's chamber. The man who for a brief space had been the Poet King. In her mind's eye she saw him and Sendara in the shaft of light.

As far as she knew, Sendara Diar was with her mother's people, no doubt learning the airs that befit a Haveren of Deere.

"It's important," she said. "The carvings in the Hall of Harps—they've changed again."

He looked amused, resigned. "I thought that might happen," he said. "I will come down to see. You know it's the reason I stayed. Knowing I might be needed, still." He smiled. "Otherwise, Julien Imara, I would have taken the Silver Branch, used it to summon the ferry to me, and gone out to the Lost Isles. I've been ready for some time."

"But not yet," she said hopefully.

"Not yet." He stood. "Let's see what's to come."